"That Artery Is Ripped to Shreds," Jefferies Said. "You're Losing Him."

Scott felt a pain run from his chest down to his left hand. A moment of dizziness overtook him as suspicion became hard reality: the patient was as good as dead.

"Help me, Dr. Jefferies," he said, struggling to control his voice. "I can't do this alone. I don't have the training."

"You know I can't do that, Dr. Goldman. This *is* your training. Any interference on my part will destroy the integrity of your evaluation."

The heart monitor rang out with a sustained high-pitched tone, indicating a flatline. Blood spurted from the artery irregularly now, and with less force.

"You're on your own, Dr. Goldman. This one is your responsibility."

This was grotesque: crucial minutes had passed in which something could have been done. In Jefferies's voice was the suggestion that the older surgeon was enjoying this, that he perhaps even relished what had happened. Scott dropped the instrument to the table before him and allowed his hands to fall to his sides. Connor was dead on the table. . . .

Also by Howard Olgin, M.D.
LIFEBANK

FOR JOY YVONNE BEHRENDT
   (THE JOYSTER) AND
        THE CUBSTER
        THE BEARSTER
        THE FOOTSTER
        ALPHONSO

     WITH LOVE ALWAYS,

     THE DUCKSTER

ADDITIONAL THANKS TO QUINTON SKINNER
FOR HIS CONTRIBUTIONS TO THE BOOK

REMOTE INTRUSION

Howard Olgin M.D.

This title first published in Great Britain 1997 by
SEVERN HOUSE PUBLISHERS LTD of
9–15 High Street, Sutton, Surrey SM1 1DF.
First published in hardcover format in the USA 1997 by
SEVERN HOUSE PUBLISHERS INC., of
595 Madison Avenue, New York, NY 10022,
by arrangement with Dell Publishing,
a division of Bantam Doubleday Dell Publishing Group, Inc.

British Library Cataloguing in Publication Data

Olgin, Howard A., 1939-
      Remote intrusion
      1. Thrillers
      1. Title
      813.5'4 [F]

    ISBN 0-7278-5221-3

Typeset by Palimpsest Book Production Limited,
Polmont, Stirlingshire, Scotland.
Printed and bound in Great Britain by
Hartnolls Ltd, Bodmin, Cornwall.

Prologue

He was alone. Here the present day did not exist, and the past could be brought to life on command. The equipment was all in place: the headpiece, the earphones, the hand control. Nearby was the computer, which processed information at the rate of millions of items per second.

He took a tentative step forward and activated the virtual reality program. In an instant his vision blurred beneath the visor, the blackness exploding with a meaningless jumble of images. A cacophony of sounds filtered through his earphones: voices, animal noises, a warped fragment of speech.

The program was working better than ever before. All around him danced the brightly colored ostriches and the ducks. They were both representations of physical robotic models designed in a far-off laboratory—her laboratory. He winced at the thought of her.

He closed his eyes and opened them again. The animals' animated faces contorted into surreal smiles of pleasure as they skipped through the sketched green landscape blending into an unreachable horizon.

To his right an orange ostrich tripped—an imperfection in the program's motion sequence—and fell headfirst into the imaginary ground. Its upper body disappeared, with only its flailing legs still visible. He would have bent over and picked it up, but he couldn't touch anything here.

A school of ducks waddled by his feet, their bodies blue and yellow, their bills turned upward in anthropomorphic delight. Their quacks sounded like delightful laughter, the comical stuff of imagination. With his hand control he sped up the program, and the school sped off toward a lone patch of trees on a nearby hill.

Behind him now the sounds grew louder, the colors

more vivid. As though from behind a curtain six robots emerged, performing exquisite synchronous backflips, their movements designed to imitate water ballet. But one robot fell, conflicted between his programming and the constraints of this virtual world.

Enough.

He stripped away the virtual reality visor and headphones, and dropped the hand control into its matte black case. He had to return to this world, the one everyone called real.

He picked up his phone and dialed an international line. It was two in the morning in Japan, nine A.M. in California. No matter. The people he needed to speak to would wake for him.

November

MAPHEX DOCUMENT DECODER RUNNING

FROM: 82152@MC.COM
TO: MT GROUP
103096

OUR FACTION'S DEVELOPMENT PLANS HAVE MET WITH AN
UNFORESEEN OPPORTUNITY. AN OPERATIVE WITHIN
CENTRAL MANAGEMENT HAS MADE IT KNOWN TO US THAT
OUR TARGET WILL SOON PLACE HIMSELF IN A POSITION
OF EXTREME VULNERABILITY.

OUR GLOBAL OUTREACH PROGRAMS OF THE PAST SEVERAL
YEARS HAVE PUT US IN AN ADVANTAGEOUS POSITION TO
CAPITALIZE. OUR ACTIONS IN THE NEXT TWO MONTHS
WILL DETERMINE OUR FUTURES.

INDIVIDUALS RECEIVING THIS MESSAGE WILL BE
CONTACTED SHORTLY WITH SPECIFIC ASSIGNMENTS. ALL
TASKS WILL BE OF IMPERATIVE URGENCY. FAILURE OF
AN INDIVIDUAL WILL RESULT IN FAILURE FOR THE
COLLECTIVE.

REWARDS WILL BE CONSIDERABLE WHEN OUR GROUP
ASSUMES POWER. YOUR ALLEGIANCE MUST BE BEYOND
QUESTION. ANY DEVIATION OR OUTSIDE CONTACT WILL
RESULT IN IMMEDIATE TERMINATION.

MAPHEX DOCUMENT DECODER QUIT
FILE DELETED
DISK SCAN RUN—82152T@MC.COM NOT FOUND
SIGN OFF

1

SCOTT GOLDMAN FELT THE SWEAT GATHERED BENEATH HIS powder-blue surgical scrubs, already forming rivulets of anxiety that, he knew, would soon begin to run south. By the time this was over, he would be soaked.

"Repeat the patient history to me, Dr. Goldman."

The voice came from behind Scott. As usual, the leverage of power was placed firmly on the side of Dr. Kyle Jefferies, assistant professor of surgery at the Pacific University School of Medicine.

"The patient is Frank Connor, a fifty-seven-year-old male with a history of ulcers who was admitted to the ICU with apparent internal bleeding. He has a history of arthritis and has been on cortisone for ten years and gold shots once a month. These have knocked out his marrow and impeded his ability to clot."

"And what would you have recommended at that point, Dr. Goldman, if you had admitted this patient?"

Scott felt the cold steel surgical instrument in his hand. He desperately needed to gather his every inner resource for this operation—it would be a difficult one, probably the toughest of his surgical residency.

It was impossible to pull himself together while forced to answer the clinical, hectoring voice of his professor. Jefferies's voice pierced his resolve like an arrow; with each question, each roundabout probe with its intimation that a wrong answer was tantamount to unforgivable failure. Scott's own heart rate rose. He hoped Jefferies couldn't see his knees shaking.

"Bright red blood was pouring out of the NG tube in the patient's nose as quickly as the ICU nurses could replace it intravenously. There was obviously a severe bleeder."

"And you would have stood there pondering these fascinating details instead of taking action? Not in my hospital, Dr. Goldman."

Jefferies was doing it again: breaking him down, making him feel foolish. *Don't take it personally,* Scott thought, allowing himself the luxury of two deep breaths. *He does this to everyone.*

"I would have ordered a stat NG endotracheal tube and a gastroenterological workup. And scrubbed in for surgery."

"Fine, Dr. Goldman. And what would you have said to the doctor administering the endotracheal tube?"

Scott's mind raced. Jefferies was still behind him—he could have been preparing Scott for one of his ill-timed jokes, or he could be asking the question on which he would base his entire evaluation. There was no way to tell, and even if he could have seen Jefferies's face, he wouldn't have known for certain. The man's intentions and feelings were as difficult to decode as those of a sphinx.

"Sir?" Damn, he just wanted to start the surgery.

"You would have told him to cover his ass and yours by making sure he put the tube into the right hole. You'd tell him if he stuck it into the patient's esophagus instead of the trachea, and you found out twenty minutes later the patient was dead because no air had reached his lungs, that you would personally kick his ass."

"That almost never happens, Dr. Jefferies."

The silence behind Scott was so charged that, for an instant, he felt a pulse of fear, an irrational worry that Jefferies would do something to him from behind—kick him in the kidneys, stab him with a scalpel. Scott took another set of deep breaths. This was getting ridiculous. Jefferies was a respected man, a renowned surgeon. He might want to kick Scott in the backside for talking back to him, but he would never do anything so outside the bounds of professional propriety.

"Dr. Goldman, let me remind you of something. Assume that everyone is an asshole. Assume that they went to the University of Northern Mongolia and that they spent their residency working on yaks instead of humans. If you want to stay *in* practice and *out* of malpractice court, you'll assume that you're the only one who knows how to do anything properly. Have I made myself understood?"

"Yes, sir."

"Good, now, get to work. Everyone who matters has reviewed the case and they all agree that you need to open the patient and stop the bleeding. Time is wasting."

Scott now allowed himself a clandestine but profoundly deep breath, the kind that his wife taught him from her yoga classes. He looked down at the middle-aged man's shaved, exposed abdomen, which protruded from blue surgical drapings like a pink raft floating on placid waters. The rhythmic beeps of monitoring machines and the repeated hiss of the respirator gave Scott a comforting sense of familiarity. He opened the patient with a broad midline incision and saw the muscles on either side of his scalpel suddenly quiver and tense.

"More relaxation. Put him deeper," Scott barked hoarsely.

Jefferies's voice cracked like a shot into his ear; the man was standing right behind him, almost touching. "You have to keep him as light as possible. He's too sick to tolerate a deep level of anesthesia for a prolonged period."

"I have to take the risk," Scott said. He felt a surge of confidence pass through his heart, his veins. He knew what he was doing. "I won't be able to stop the bleeding unless he's completely under."

Scott paused and waited for his order to the anesthesiologist to be obeyed. He watched the patient's musculature relax and then continued cutting into the abdomen. In a few moments he held the patient's stomach in his hand. The organ felt strange and unfamiliar; he tried to ignore the sensation.

"Retraction," he ordered, and began to explore down to the end of the stomach, the pyloris, and farther into the first part of the duodenum. Instruments were at his disposal almost as quickly as he could request them: hemostats, the metz, scissors. It was almost as if the nurse were superhuman. Finally, he thought, someone who can live up to Jefferies's standards.

"Here it is," Scott said. He peered a little closer and saw the eroded blood vessel pumping bright red blood directly at him. "The bleeder. Right where the scope indicated."

Jefferies stepped back and Scott felt a welcome coolness at his neck replacing his teacher's breath.

"So the gastroenterologist did his job," Jefferies said coolly. "Continue to do yours."

"Blood pressure 100/70, pulse 94." The anesthesiologist was yet another disembodied voice coming from a place Scott couldn't see: this OR layout seemed designed to befuddle and alienate the surgeon.

"Long needle holder," Scott said. "2-0 silk." He felt the instrument in his outstretched hand and prepared to stitch shut the open vessel. But something was wrong. His movements weren't quite natural, and his stress had become so great that he felt his own heart pounding under his gown. He felt as if his hand couldn't move quickly enough to match his will, as if it were someone else's hand. Sweat poured out from under his cap and stung his eyes.

"Wipe," he said, and felt a hand reach up from behind him to mop his forehead. With a mixture of shock and an inexplicable shame he realized that it had been Jefferies.

Blood continued to pour out of the artery and into the stomach, flooding everything. This was the crucial, make-or-break moment in the case.

"Retract," Scott said, hearing his voice break. He tried to adjust his grip on the needle holder as he looked into the mass of blood and organs before him. He needed only to make these stitches and it would be over: the patient would live, and Jefferies would be pleased. Scott at that moment wanted nothing more of the world than for those two things to occur.

"Pressure down, sixty over forty. Pulse is thready."

Scott thrust the needle into the flesh, beginning to pull together the structures. He had miscalculated the case, thinking he would have more time to work.

"Pulse is very erratic, Doctor."

"Give him more blood, Goldman."

The first stitch was in, and Scott delicately manipulated the holder into place for the second. The flesh moved as he tugged, and he could see that the vessel was taking shape. Then he felt an elbow softly jostle his spine.

"Damn it, Mister. I said give him more blood. Two units, stat. Don't flake out now, son, this man's life is in your hands."

The flesh covering Scott's spine burned where Jefferies had bumped him. He ordered the blood and continued to stitch, pulling the needle through the flesh.

"Look at the monitor, Dr. Goldman. The pulse is falling. Don't wait for someone to tell you what to do: react. Do it now, or he's going to die on the table, in your hands." Jefferies's voice rose in pitch, reflecting his own obviously mounting anxiety.

No one spoke as Scott began to tie in the critical suture. He deftly placed the figure-eight stitch around the bleeding vessel and gave it a slight tug. He held his breath and applied more pressure, pushing down on the knot with his instrument to secure it in place.

"Pressure's still falling," said the anesthesiologist in a dispassionate voice.

Suddenly the spurting, pumping vessel was quelled. Scott was shocked at the sudden visibility within the abdomen, and ordered suction to remove the pooled blood. He rationed himself another deep breath and thought briefly of the images his therapist had suggested, after working with Jefferies had driven Goldman to panic attacks and weight loss: a beach, a golden sun, cool blue waters shimmering like the surface of a beautiful perfect marble.

"It's not holding, Goldman. Do something." Jefferies now sounded almost panicked, and Scott shifted his attention back to where he had tied the stitches: two of them were faulty, and blood pushed against them and began to spill anew into the cavity. Soon they would all give way, and he would be back to where he had started.

"No pressure. Apparent cardiac arrest." The anesthesiologist sounded unconcerned; this was beyond his power to change, out of his reach. Scott reached into the cavity and pulled in vain at the stitches. The attached flesh tore slightly, and blood flowed out with more force than before.

"That artery is ripped to shreds," Jefferies said. "You're losing him."

Scott felt a pain run from his chest down to his left hand. A moment of dizziness overtook him as suspicion became hard reality: the patient was as good as dead.

"Help me, Dr. Jefferies," he said, struggling to control his voice. "I can't do this alone. I don't have the training."

"You know I can't do that, Dr. Goldman. This *is* your training. Any interference on my part will destroy the integrity of your evaluation."

The heart monitor rang out with a sustained high-pitched tone, indicating a flatline. Blood spurted from the artery irregularly now, and with less force.

"You're on your own, Dr. Goldman. This one is your responsibility."

Scott Goldman's field of vision dissolved into a disorienting play of colors. His body turned cold, and he felt the dampness on his back like ice water poured from a pitcher. This was grotesque: crucial minutes had passed in which something could have been done, however desperate. In Jefferies's voice was the suggestion that the older surgeon was enjoying this, that he perhaps even relished what had happened. Scott dropped the instrument to the table before him and allowed his hands to fall to his side. Connor was dead on the table.

"I hope you've learned something from this," Jefferies said. "Specifically that you can't count on anything. I'll have to evaluate those stitches, but sometimes even perfect stitches will give way. As for your performance, I have to say—"

"I have to say that the system needs work," said a woman's voice through the room's intercom. "I can see the delay time on the monitor from up here, and I don't exactly have an intimate view."

Scott hurried to remove the heavy, wire-lined helmet and to extricate his hands from the virtual reality surgical-instrument workstation, stunned to hear anyone speak so boldly to Dr. Jefferies. He looked around the small theater, which housed the university's primary surgical simulator; he saw the gear he had just taken off, which fed him visual and verbal stimulus from a powerful computer system that analyzed and responded to his movements, and he saw the small video monitor flanked on either side by larger, twelve-foot screens—which enabled spectators to watch the simulation as if it were really happening.

But of course none of it had. Scott had endured the onset of a particularly nasty anxiety attack and felt horrible loss and failure that came from having a patient die at his hands, but Frank Connor was the fiction of a computer designed to test Scott Goldman's mettle. So real was the experience that only now did Scott feel his heart and circulatory system begin to return to normal.

Jefferies also looked around the room, at the massive wire hookups leading to the main computer center, at the screen, at the empty chairs often used by spectators. Finally his gaze turned upward, to the dark observation gallery. He was obviously angry.

"Who is that? Turn on the lights up there and tell me what special expertise enables you to criticize my evaluation of this student's performance."

The lights came on, and there stood a young woman of

about thirty, dressed in an attractive plum suit. Scott's view was obscured by a glare off the glass booth, but he could see her wavy auburn hair pulled back into a knot, and her smooth skin and delicate features. For a moment he forgot about the scathing review he would no doubt receive from Jefferies.

"You," Jefferies said. "I might have known."

"Sorry, Kyle," the woman said with an apologetic shrug. "I wish we could have met again under better circumstances, but I just happened by. Look, I'll be right down."

She disappeared, and Jefferies began shuffling his feet on the floor, clearing his throat repeatedly. He looked around with a withering gaze, settling his attention on Scott in an instant that made the younger man freeze with a powerful sense of fear and intimidation. Scott noted the older man's thinning hair, double chin, deep-set eyes and severe features, and noticed that he appeared to be composing himself. Then she entered and, Scott thought, she looked even better close up.

"Pick your tongue up off the floor, Goldman," Jefferies said, looking at him disdainfully. "Depending on the allocation of residents under the impending restructuring, you might find yourself working for this woman."

She looked quizzically at Jefferies, apparently put off by being referred to in such a fashion, then extended her hand to Scott.

"Holiday Powers," she said. "I have a background in medical virtual reality simulators and robotics. I interrupted Dr. Jefferies because I thought I saw an unacceptable lag time on the system. Did you get the feeling that your virtual movements weren't keeping up with the actual motion of your hand?"

Scott looked at her in confusion, then turned to Dr. Jefferies, who folded his arms and retreated into a stoic pose that rendered him as impassive as a granite monument. Scott didn't know how to play this situation, or which side he wanted to come out on. Jefferies was so political that any slight to his authority, no matter how innocuous or unthreatening, was always repaid eventually. Always.

She continued her questioning. "What I'm asking is, did you feel that the computer-generated reality moved slower and responded less quickly than actual reality? That's what I saw, and if so, it means that your performance has to be evaluated with that in mind."

"When I was preparing to apply the stitches to the artery," Scott said quietly, looking at the floor, "I felt something like you described. It distracted me, and it's a delicate motion—"

"Dr. Powers knows it's a delicate motion," Jefferies interrupted. "She's a trained surgeon, and a very good one. Next week she will start work at Pacific University as . . . what is it, Dr. Powers? Empress? Princess?"

Jefferies's icy sarcasm chilled the conversation, and Scott looked uncomfortably at his shoes. Anyway he was too embarrassed at the moment to look back at her: just because she was a beautiful young woman, he had talked to her as if she knew nothing about medicine.

"I've been hired as an associate professor and chief of advanced surgical technologies," Holiday said, her own tone becoming distinctly chilly. "As you well know, Kyle. I must say, I didn't expect you to start in on me so quickly. I don't see any need for it."

Jefferies ignored her. "Dr. Powers started in Boston as one of my residents," he said. With sudden shock Scott realized that his professor was talking to him. "This was in the days before these technological toys were used, you see. Still, she finds it justifiable to make excuses for young surgeons such as yourself, on the grounds that the technology isn't up to speed. Try that excuse when your real patients die, Dr. Goldman, and see how far it gets you. In any case Dr. Powers will be running these simulations in the future. She's taking my place and, as far as I'm concerned, she can have it."

Holiday folded her arms in front of her chest and began

to speak. She checked herself, shaking her head. "Same old Kyle. I'd like to say it's good to see you. . . ."

She let her sentence trail off, then turned brightly to Scott. Her smile sent him spiraling off into further distraction. "Dr. Goldman, I don't know which residents will be assigned to me," she said. "But it would be a pleasure to have you on my staff. Keep up the good work."

Jefferies pursed his lips petulantly, forming them into a heart shape that strangely softened the man's harsh appearance. "So you start tomorrow," he said. "I'll see to it that we have an honor guard ready to throw rose petals at your feet as you enter the building."

Holiday looked at Jefferies; a moment of sadness crossed her features before it was quickly replaced with cool resolve.

"It doesn't have to be this way, Kyle. It really doesn't."

She turned and walked out the swinging doors of the simulation room. Jefferies waited a moment, then also left, without a word. Scott stood in silence until the computer technicians arrived to check the equipment. They ignored him, lost in their world of private codes and the labyrinthine details of technology.

He hoped he would be assigned to her, that he would be able to work with her. He really did.

2

HOLIDAY WONDERED WHAT KIND OF STUDIES HAD BEEN performed on the brain's ability to digest new logistical data. Maybe, she thought, she should offer herself as a test subject. It felt like the first day of school. All this information—names, numbers, protocols, privileges, and restrictions, all the codified ways of doing business within an institution—the brain could take only so much before it shut down.

"Dr. Powers," Pam Lincoln said, a note of exasperation creeping into her voice. "You aren't listening anymore, are you?"

Holiday looked at her new assistant: a black woman in her midforties with fine hair and dark skin that lent her features a mature dignity. Pam had been lecturing with the authority of a staffer who knew the place inside and out. Her words rang with a pride of control that Holiday immediately recognized as a sign that she was a committed, efficient worker. Holiday also admired the way Pam's orange-striped sneakers peeked out from under her slacks; it was a welcome hint of irreverence.

"Sorry, Pam," Holiday said, pushing a stack of welcome notes and agendas to the far corner of her desk. She swiveled her chair a hundred and eighty degrees and took in the fifth-floor view of West Los Angeles. The city baked in the heat of a southern California autumn; palm trees in the parking lot below swayed roughly from the arid Santa Ana winds.

"You have one of the better views in the hospital," Pam said, conceding for the moment that their orientation was on pause by clicking shut her leather notebook. "This place wasn't built to keep people sane and happy. Most of the people around here get a view of three walls and their cubicle doorway."

"I noticed that. Well, this is the nicest office I've ever had. In Boston they stuck me in a room with a hissing radiator and windows that were painted shut. And the desk took up half the room."

"You won't have that problem here," Pam said. She looked around the office, at the stained-wood book-shelves and credenza containing advanced video equip-ment. The carpet beneath their feet was aquamarine, thick and sound dampening. "This place was renovated just for you, you know. They really wanted to give you the red-carpet treatment."

"And I suppose you're part of that red-carpet treat-ment," Holiday said. She met Pam's eyes and tried tacitly to communicate, *Hey, I'm not here to take over the place. I want us to work together.*

Pam smiled, disarmed. "That's right. They brought you the best in the business. I've been here for twelve years, so there's nothing that gets by me. People here try to stay on my good side."

Holiday laughed, not so much at Pam's bravado but at the obvious good nature behind it. "I'll remember that."

Silence fell over them. Pam was suddenly serious. "Dr. Powers, before things get hectic, I just wanted to say that your appointment to this job . . . well, it means a lot to a lot of people around here."

Two men walked by Holiday's open door, laughing in deep-throated, beer-commercial bellows. They peeked in the door as they passed and were instantly silent. She knew she was an object of curiosity, and as so often in the past, people seemed to find her unapproachable. She re-turned her attention to Pam.

"What do you mean?"

"Well, you're young. It's going to be good to have some fresh blood and energy in the department. But what's more important is that you're a woman. You're going to find out pretty quickly that there aren't any women with positions as high as yours in this department, or anyplace else in the hospital. We've been talking about it since the appointment was announced last month. It's like a victory for all of us."

Holiday's smile froze, and she sat back in her chair with a sigh. "I appreciate that, Pam. I really do. I just don't want to make too big a deal of my gender or my age." She suddenly felt terrible: Pam's gesture had been so genuine, so obviously unrehearsed, and Holiday could find no appropriate way to respond. What could she tell her: that her quick rise in the Boston medical community had been filled with more trouble than triumph? That she was always the object of stares and curiosity but rarely the recipient of true friendship? How male and female colleagues alike assumed she was a bitch until she proved otherwise? That standard mentor relationships were psychic minefields for her because of the rumors that she was sleeping her way to the top?

"Of course," Pam said. "I'm just glad you're here, and I'm glad to be working with you."

Holiday extended her hand, and they shook for the second time that morning. "The feeling's mutual. Now I think I'm rested enough to go over that agenda you tried to show me earlier. I already have appointments? That's—"

"You can deal with that crap later. I've blocked out twenty minutes to show you around." Pam and Holiday turned. The doorway was filled with the burly figure of a dark, curly-haired man in surgical scrubs, his thick mustache perched over a broad smile full of irregular teeth. With his huge hands and aggressive, almost hyperactive bearing, he looked like a cop or a linebacker for a pro football team. Only his surgical attire and the stack of files in his hand indicated differently.

"Dr. Hermoza," Pam said, standing.

"Phil!" Holiday sprinted around her desk like a schoolgirl and embraced the huge man, her hands barely encircling his shoulders. "You look great. I'm so happy to see you again."

"I look like shit. My gut's getting bigger every day and my hair's falling out. My wife says I'm turning into a beach ball. Thanks anyway." He extricated himself from Holiday's embrace, still grinning. "Now, come on. I'll show you around the place and get all the administrative shit out of the way early. I'm going to put you to work, young lady. Pam, I'll get her back to you in a few minutes."

With this he strode intently down the hall, obviously expecting Holiday to follow. She watched his wide, muscled back recede, and felt as though she had been looking at it her entire life, beginning with her residency at Boston General.

Hermoza had been a department head then, years before his appointment as dean of medicine at Pacific University and his unexpected move west. He hadn't changed: he still retained the trace of a Mexican accent that became thicker when he grew excited, even though he was born in San Antonio. He still carried himself like a man of physical menace, though he was paradoxically full of gentleness and fairness. He was in his early fifties now, but Holiday could see the form of the Harvard wrestling champion that he once was.

He was one of the most honorable men she had ever met, more so than her father, her brothers, or any lover. The politics of high-level medicine came easily to him: he immersed himself, extracting what he needed and caring for those under his authority, then brushed the rest aside like so much detritus.

Hermoza became Kyle Jefferies's mentor in the early eighties, making him his chief resident and working him like a field animal. Then, as now, Jefferies was ambitious to the point of heartlessness; Hermoza had smoothed over the rough spots and trained him in the art of selective diplomacy to reach his ends. When Phil went to L.A., Jefferies followed. Now Hermoza had hired Holiday—

who was still a medical student when Kyle was a resident. In typical fashion Hermoza recognized no conflict in hiring her for a position a grade more powerful than Jefferies's.

"You haven't lost a step, Powers. Excellent," he said when they reached the operating suites. True, she could keep up with his long stride and bulldozer way of moving through crowded corridors. But he was panting slightly, and grunted when he moved. Phil was starting to go to fat, she realized: the middle-aged big man.

"How's Jacqueline, Phil?" Holiday remembered his wife, a small-boned, demure woman who always seemed in a state of amused outrage at her husband's bulky clumsiness and profane vocabulary.

"Fine, fine. She's taken to L.A. like a goat to a tin can." They moved through the impressive OR suites, lined with equipment and bustling with ordered purpose. Hermoza stepped over a box of surgical gloves, ignoring a nurse who politely motioned for his attention. "The kids are good, too. Emily's in a private school, which wasn't my idea. She brings home the Beverly Hills kids and I get to embarrass the shit out of her when they see that her dad's a big old Mexican, running around with his belly hanging out, cussing at the dogs. Here's an open suite."

Hermoza held the door open for Holiday. Inside she saw a tiled room and a gleaming steel operating table. The room was ample, with plenty of room to house surgical equipment. In Boston one of her main headaches had been the lack of elbow room in the ORs. Obviously Pacific University had built these rooms recently, and with modern needs in mind.

"This one's empty, but you'll be happy with what we have. We've got technology coming out of our assholes. Pardon the expression." Hermoza took a handkerchief from his scrub-suit pocket and blew his nose. "CAT scan, PET, MRI: all in-house. With the HMO patients you'll play hell getting authorization sometimes, but any consult or test you'll ever want can be done right in this building.

There are a few specialists at the Bartholomew that we don't have, but that's basically why we're in bed with them now. They're also drooling over the possibility of getting at our VR labs."

Hermoza introduced Holiday to a few gawking surgeons in the surgical lounge. They seemed to have heard about her. Holiday, at thirty-three and a woman, had been brought into Pacific University administration because she had distinguished herself in two areas in which Hermoza needed expertise: noninvasive surgery and advanced medical technology. The university recently forged an alliance with the Bartholomew Institute, a private-practice hospital catering to the relatively affluent citizens of West Los Angeles, and both sides were naturally wary of what effect this joining of forces would have on their finances and talent pools.

"All the bed space is in the West Wing," Hermoza said, picking up his pace. He rapped on the white corridor wall as he walked. "You'll find your way around."

They boarded an elevator with a young couple bearing flowers and an orderly pushing an elderly man in a wheelchair. "We'll head by the research labs, then to the computer center." Hermoza's voice boomed and resounded in the confined elevator. Holiday felt a distinct sense of relief among the other passengers when she and Phil disembarked on the seventh floor.

Hermoza led her quickly down a long corridor. "Bioresearch is down that way." He waved his hand dismissively in the general direction of a long hall. "We have pharmaceutical work going on upstairs somewhere. The people downstairs on six are doing surgical work, trying out instruments and putting together test data. You'll deal with them eventually. Light a fire under their ass and they're all right."

They came to a corridor sealed off by a wide glass door. Hermoza fished around for his pass-key card, cursing softly. Holiday watched him for a moment, then produced her own, sticking it into a small grooved slot. The door clicked and hissed, and Phil pushed it open. It was at least two inches thick, made of shock-resistant glass.

"We need the security. For what these computers cost, they could hire hundreds of people at our salaries." With this, Holiday realized that the tour was even more efficient than she had thought: from the surgical suites to the computer labs, he was spending time only where he personally needed Holiday's services.

The computer laboratory walls were glass from waist-high to the ceiling, affording passersby a clear view inside. Holiday was impressed with the technological array she saw: in one section alone were two of the processing units she had campaigned for unsuccessfully in Boston. Several technicians looked up from their screens and wires to peer at her. Some of the more astute among them must have realized that their new boss had arrived.

They stopped before another glass door leading into the main research area. Phil nodded at the key-card slot, and Holiday inserted her pass. A silence pervaded inside that rang of recently ceased conversation. Holiday looked around at the technicians, a little annoyed. She felt like an intrepid anthropologist who had just discovered a rare and isolated tribe; these men behaved as if they had never before seen the likes of her.

"Dr. Hermoza," said a young black man who emerged from a doorway pinned in by two large computer units. "And you must be Holiday Powers. Gregory Hampton, good to meet you."

He extended his hand, first to Holiday, then to Phil. He looked her in the eye as they shook. This was the department head of the advanced computer research program. She hadn't expected this: he was in his late twenties at the oldest, and he carried himself like an undergraduate, with high-top basketball shoes and a rumpled Oxford shirt. An intelligence gleamed in his dark brown eyes, but he somehow managed to seem friendly without projecting any real warmth at all.

"As you know already, Gregory is our resident genius and boy wonder."

"I prefer 'wunderkind,' Doctor," Gregory said. "If you aren't old enough around here to have rolled in the mud at Woodstock, it blows their minds. They can't get over it."

He flashed an easy smile at Holiday and Hermoza, who gave him a short burst of raucous laughter. "I used to goof on the old fat asses who were my bosses, back when I could still see my own shoes. Now I am one. Go figure."

Phil patted Holiday on the back. "Stay and talk to Gregory. Talk about how much grant money you're going to get for us. Let him smooth-talk you for a while." He checked his watch. "Gotta run. Seriously, kid, it's good to have you here. If there's anything you need, don't hesitate—"

"To ask someone else first. I remember, Phil."

"We're gonna get along great," Hermoza said. His mustache bristled under his enthusiastic smile. "See you, Greg."

"See you, Dr. Hermoza." Gregory watched Phil lumber out of the room and down the hall, then turned to Holiday.

"First thing, Dr. Powers, I don't like to be called 'Greg.' Second, I don't care about grants except to know the dollar figures I have to work with. So don't expect me to go out and play the good soldier at all the fund-raisers I'm sure you're going to be having."

Holiday sat on a vacant desk. The other technicians had gone back to their work, but were obviously eavesdropping on Hampton's impromptu harangue. When he was finished, he took a deep breath, as if bracing for a fight. Holiday found herself smiling.

"Fine," she said. There was something charming about the way he simply started in on his grievances and demands. He obviously wasn't a political man, not in any practical sense. She realized how ironic Phil's "smooth talk" comment was intended to be.

"That's it? 'Fine'?"

"That's it." Holiday folded her hands. This was an environment she liked, her favorite after the operating room itself—the computer labs, isolated from power players and bureaucracies. Medicine was once like this, she mused, before administration and bureaucracy became the ruling orders. But that was a time before her own.

"I brought five million dollars in grant money from the Mitsuyama Corporation in Tokyo with me when I took this job," she said. "They gave it to Pacific University instead of Boston General because I've worked with them as medical technologies liaison for the last few years at Boston General and MIT. They want to continue to work with me. I want the money earmarked for R and D in VR simulators and telepresence. Does that interest you?"

Gregory shoved his hands in his pockets and looked searchingly into her eyes. His intensity made Holiday uncomfortable.

"That interests me. I already know about the money, and you have a good rep from your work in Boston. A couple of old college buddies of mine are working at MIT."

"You did your homework on me." Holiday felt herself relaxing. He reminded her of her brother, Calvin, a New York stockbroker who summered in the Berkshires but somehow maintained a true glimmer of a youthful, outlaw spirit.

"Word gets around. I'd be a fool not to check out my new boss."

"You're the boss in here, Gregory. We both know that. I know the medical side, and I have enough knowledge of computer systems to follow you if you dumb things down for me. All I can do is try to make the hospital's needs clear to you, and try to make your job easier."

Gregory's attention was fixed on the other side of the room, where a young man in glasses and a Western-style string tie was immersed in a set of wires leading to a pair of black goggles.

"No fund-raisers? You promise? I want to stay as far away from that crap as I possibly can," he said.

"I never force anyone working for me to do any kind of extracurriculars. Especially you computer guys. I learned that lesson a long time ago."

Gregory stuck his tongue in his cheek, suppressing a chuckle. "Yeah, well, it's not the most outgoing profession in the world."

"And you don't have to be a social butterfly. You know how to do something that very few people can understand, much less do."

"Like you surgeons." Gregory paused, as if holding himself in check. Holiday waited for him to continue. If she guessed right, he would want to bridge the gap between them by showing her his world: technology.

"Well, come on," he said decisively. "Let me give you a quick demo of our telepresence project. I know you guys were starting this in Boston, but the real breakthrough is taking place here."

"I thought you'd never ask," Holiday said, following Gregory to the technician in the string tie.

"Holiday Powers, this is Bill Epstein, my right-hand man. His title is assistant projects coordinator, and he works directly with me on everything. If you can't reach me for any reason, talk to him."

Holiday shook Epstein's hand. He stood to his full height, much taller than he seemed sitting down. He gave Holiday a shy smile. "It's a pleasure to meet you."

"Likewise. My office door is always open. As I told Gregory, I'm here to work *with* this department, so let me know if you have any problems."

Holiday wondered how much morale boosting she would have to perform before people realized they no longer worked under Kyle Jefferies.

3

"Now that we're all friendly, let's get our new boss hooked up for a demo sequence," Gregory said, motioning to the goggles. "You got the focus worked out on that thing?"

"Absolutely," Epstein said, picking up the device. "It was purely mechanical; nothing wrong with code or linkup." The eyepiece was thick, like a scuba-gear visor. Wires ran from it to a patchwork grid of plugs that in turn ran to a computer. Epstein untangled several of the wires and handed it to Holiday.

"I'm sure you know how to put it on," Gregory said. "Are you familiar with your field of vision within the system?"

"Pretty much. But where's the robot?"

"In the next room. We have everything powered up. The demo only runs on a plastic steak for now. It's the price we pay for working in the real world."

Gregory wheeled over a plastic stand containing a plastic penlike device. "Here's the manual instrument," he said. "I'll go to the robot and play nurse."

He left through an unmarked door. Epstein nervously checked the board of cables and wires, then settled down in front of a computer monitor displaying rows of numerical code. "Go ahead and put it on," he said.

Holiday donned the visor. She was immersed in complete blackness. Earphones slid into place and shut off noise from her immediate surroundings. She could hear only a vague static hiss. Then her vision cleared. She saw a field of multicolored dots.

"Bill, are these dots I see part of the system initialization, or are my eyes just playing tricks on me?"

Suddenly Gregory's voice rang out in her ears: "Just

your own eyes doing their thing, Dr. Powers. I didn't want to turn on the visual hookup until I rolled the robot into place. The motion makes some people nauseous."

Holiday felt an odd sense of dislocation and a momentary chill of fear. She knew she was in a room, standing before a plastic instrument, and that Bill Epstein was only feet away from her. She tried to sense him there, to feel her feet on the linoleum floor and the objects around her, but found that the noises—bumping, an odd mechanical whir, and the sound of Gregory's breathing—made it impossible for her to find her own sense of place.

Then the machine was activated. She looked around slowly and saw that she was, for all purposes, in another room. She looked down, expecting to see her own hands and feet, and saw instead two brass-colored robotic arms attached to a dull metal base. She looked to her right and saw Gregory, who smiled and waved.

"Welcome to telepresence, Dr. Powers," he said. "As you can see, you are not in 'virtual reality': what you are seeing is real, and taking place about thirty feet away from you. You are seeing what our surgical robot 'sees' through a wide-angled camera designed to duplicate human peripheral vision. Reach up to your right ear, where you will find a plastic arm. This is your microphone."

Holiday did as she was told, moving her head to the left as she put the microphone in place. Her field of vision rotated to take in an empty corner of the neighboring room, which held a vacant desk and a wall clock. A twinge of nausea made her catch her breath as she swiveled her head back to face Gregory; the world she saw moved slightly slower than the "real" world. The effect this created was akin to seasickness.

"There's a little delay in keeping up with my head movements," she said.

"I know. It's a little sickening." Gregory looked perfectly natural addressing the robot as if it were Holiday: in a sense, it was. "It's a function of the turning radius of the robot, not a delay in the computer processing information. You see, the computer isn't inventing a reality for you to see, it's only transmitting a camera image and matching it to your head movements and the position of your eyes as determined by infrared scanners. Anyway once the surgeon is working, there isn't much need for broad head movements."

"Right," Holiday said, focusing her eyes and positioning her head squarely forward. "You guys have done an incredible job. You're right: you're way ahead of everyone."

"We aim to please," Gregory said. "Now, request a surgical instrument and reach out straight ahead for the multipurpose instrument tray in front of . . . well, in front of your real body."

Holiday reached out and felt a hand touch hers: Epstein. He guided her hands until she felt cold metal in her hands, the familiar feel of a surgical instrument.

"Move the instrument in your 'real' hand, and your motions will be duplicated by the robot. The difference is, you'll be moving your instrument in thin air, while the robot will perform the actual surgery. Now request an instrument and look down."

"Scalpel," she said. She saw Gregory reach for an instrument tray, heard a slight clatter, then felt pressure on the instrument she grasped as he fitted the scalpel into the robot's mechanical "hand."

"This is incredible. I can feel the pressure through the instrument. It's like someone is pushing on it."

"No one's pushing on it," Gregory said. She looked up to see him grinning. "Not where you are. The instrument you're touching is wired to the robot's hand. We even got Dr. Jefferies to admit he couldn't tell much of a difference between the telepresence sensations and real life. When you're operating on a patient, you ideally will feel absolutely no clues that what you see and feel aren't as immediate as anything you've ever experienced. Now, cut the plastic steak."

Holiday looked down and saw the robot arm holding a

scalpel. She moved the instrument and was quickly able to forget that the robot arm wasn't her own; focusing on the scalpel itself sealed the illusion. Before her, on a plastic tray lit by surgical lights, was a plastic replica of a steak. She cut into it and was amazed by the delicacy of the robot's movements. The system responded to every nuance of her eye movements, the way she held her head, and the subtlest delicacies of the way she moved the instrument.

She looked up at Gregory. "I'm impressed. Let's quit the demo."

Holiday released the surgical instrument and moved the microphone away from her mouth. She felt a hand on her shoulder, and the visor was pulled off her face. Bill Epstein stood there, smiling warily. The effect was jarring, no matter how many times she experienced it: in a moment, without physically moving at all, she had gone from one place to another. Gregory returned, beaming.

"The practical applications for this are amazing," Holiday said, trying to put her hair back into place. Her own voice sounded odd to her.

"That's right," Epstein said. "Theoretically a surgeon could be anyplace in the world and could perform surgery at any other site, if there are fiberoptic hookups available to connect the robot and the surgeon's console."

"For noninvasive surgeries you would see the image transmitted by the microcamera," Gregory added, biting on the end of a plastic pen and staring at the computer console screen.

This was a real breakthrough. Laparoscopic surgeries—procedures performed without making broad cuts in the skin, done instead with scopes and instruments pushed through one-inch incisions—were limited because the surgeon had to watch her own actions on a television screen. In effect, now she could go into the patient's body and look around as though she were shrunk to the minute size of the camera itself.

"Gentlemen," Holiday said, "thanks for taking the

time for a demonstration. I'll be back around to let you
know when we'll have our first planning meeting. In the
meantime it looks like everything is going well around
here. I'll leave you to it."

She turned to leave. Just as she opened the door, Gregory's voice called her from behind.

"Thanks," he said, his expression serious.

Holiday paused.

"Thanks for leaving us to our work, and for respecting
what we do," he continued. "We haven't had that privi-
lege for a while."

On the elevator back to her office Holiday pondered
what Gregory had said. Obviously Kyle was still a lousy
boss. No one made a secret of it. Still, she hoped that
people didn't pin too many hopes on her. She wanted to
treat people humanely, and to allow them to exercise
their abilities, but she also knew well that as an administrator she had to juggle many sets of priorities. Not everyone could be happy all of the time.

Holiday returned to her suite, greeting Pam and heading
toward her own office. Pam was busy assembling a pile of
documents.

"These are rules and regulations for your membership
in West Coast Health," Pam said. "I'm trying to get it
together into one stack. You have to sign off as an expert
on their rules before you can even begin to think about
treating any of their patients."

This was one of the conditions of Holiday's new employment: that she be granted membership in one of California's largest HMO plans, which would give her a
patient base and also enable her to treat cases from the
Bartholomew.

"Thanks, Pam. I'll plow through it. The rules can't be
much different from ones I've already dealt with."

Pam looked at her as if she were incredibly naive. "Are
you serious? They change the rules so much that doctors
working under the plan for years have a hard time keep-

ing up. You're lucky—I have a memory for this kind of thing. I'll keep you from doing anything you'll regret."

Holiday laughed, but Pam was serious. Holiday accepted a handful of papers and took them into her office. Her phone rang.

"It's me," Pam said. "You can ignore most of the messages on your desk. Just people wanting to greet you and get in your good graces. There's one important thing. A memo was just distributed from Dr. Jefferies. I think you should have a look at it."

She hung up. "What *is* this?" Holiday pulled the paper closer, scrutinizing it. It was a memo from Kyle Jefferies, circulated to department heads in surgery, nursing, and to various head residents in the surgical program. It claimed that there was a need to standardize pre-op procedures for minimally invasive surgery at the hospital, and contained a new set of policies.

Holiday read it again. It was about laparoscopic surgeries. The memo said that henceforth all such procedures were to involve a standard protocol: an upper GI series, mandatory pre-op lab tests.

"But I was hired as chief of advanced surgical technologies," Holiday said aloud. "He's setting policy in my department."

She picked up the phone, intending to call Phil Hermoza. No, that was no way to handle it, going over Jefferies's head the first day on the job. This memo was vintage Kyle: political, backbiting, an open challenge.

"If anyone calls while I'm out, tell them I'll be right back," Holiday said, striding quickly past Pam's desk. Holiday heard her assistant's voice over her shoulder as she left.

"I figured that memo would make your day. It's people like that who—"

Holiday didn't bother to listen to the rest. *It's people like that who: turn fulfilling work into a battlefield; who personalize everything into a senseless struggle; who turn a good job into a living hell. Take your pick,* she thought.

Kyle's office was on the other end of the floor. She passed other doors on the way, and ignored several people who tried to catch her attention. She would meet them all later.

The secretary was immersed in her computer screen. Her nameplate read: Robin Franks. "Yes, can I help you?" she asked.

"My name is Dr. Powers. I want to speak to Dr. Jefferies immediately."

Robin swiveled away from the typewriter, obviously wary. "Dr. Powers, it's a pleasure to meet you. I had hoped to speak under more pleasant conditions."

She knew about the memo, knew that her boss was issuing a challenge. Holiday relaxed a little, trying to keep it in perspective. Kyle had always been able to push her buttons and send her into a fury.

"Dr. Jefferies is in surgery," Robin said. "He has two procedures lined up back-to-back. I can have him call you when he gets out."

"No, thanks, that's fine," Holiday said. She felt an electric charge of tension move through her, then out, leaving her burned-out and tired.

Instead of returning to her office, Holiday took the elevator downstairs to the surgical suites. In the nurses' locker room she changed into a blue scrub suit and donned a mask and paper boots to cover her shoes. She entered the long corridor.

"Which room is Dr. Jefferies working in?" she asked a nurse.

The woman stopped for a moment. All Holiday could make of her face above her mask was a pair of dark, Asian eyes. "Number seven. Do you want to have him paged?"

"No, thanks. It's not important."

The nurse shrugged and began removing sterile towels from a small stack. Holiday walked slowly down the hall, stopping at the closed door of OR Seven. She peered through the oval glass window.

There he was: the same intense eyes peering down at his patient. A video monitor displayed the patient's inner anatomy and the tiny instruments moving inside, controlled by Jefferies. He was performing a laparoscopic appendectomy, where the instruments were pushed through holes in the patient's skin and controlled by triggerlike handles. Holiday saw on the screen that the appendix, apparently just isolated, was inflamed and probably ready to burst. The patient was safe, she thought, and in good hands.

Holiday stood there a moment longer, watching the way the assisting surgeon and nurses deferred to Jefferies's authority, obeying his orders as quickly as he could bark them. They all knew he was one of the best.

It had begun. She knew this would turn into a battle, and Kyle had wasted no time starting it. *Why?* she wondered. Because Phil Hermoza hired her into a better position than Kyle's, after all the years Kyle dedicated to working under Phil in Boston, then L.A.? Did he think all he had worked for had been spit upon by Holiday's presence?

Was it because they had been lovers in Boston when they were years younger, when the bitterness and naked ambition in his eyes was all mixed with a kindness that now seemed entirely gone? Maybe she reminded him of what he used to be, or what he wasn't now.

"I don't know what it is, Kyle," she whispered, looking deeper into the window. She wasn't sure, but for a moment it seemed that Jefferies glanced up and looked at her.

Eight years ago Kyle hadn't even told Holiday that he'd been offered a job in California. She'd learned it from someone else who worked with Kyle and overheard him on the phone in the surgical lounge. She hid her shock and disappointment at the time, but hours later when she was working in the ER, she felt something inside her turn cold.

The ambulance technician had to call her name twice before she responded, turning to look through the automatic door at the stretcher being wheeled into the hospital by the paramedic crew and an orderly. It was one of the coldest nights of a particularly frigid Boston winter; snow danced in the bright lights around the hospital entrance, and from the portico above the doors hung thick icicles like stalagmites in a cave.

"This little girl got caught outside for almost an hour," the paramedic said as they wheeled the patient to an open area. A stocky nurse pulled white curtains around the girl as Holiday helped the orderly move her to a waiting gurney.

The little girl was about eight or nine, with clear ebony skin and wide brown doe's eyes that were transfixed with fear. She was conscious, but trembled under the bright examination light.

Holiday bent over her as the nurse took the girl's temperature and started to remove her soggy clothes. "What's your name, honey?"

The girl turned to look at Holiday; thankfully her eyes were clear and focused. She had come in wearing only a cloth coat over her child's pants and sweater—no hat, gloves, or scarf. The paramedic stepped into the enclosure, rubbing his hands together, chilled from his brief time outside.

"Man, it's down to about ten out there, with a hell of a wind," he said, glancing at the little girl.

"What happened?" Holiday asked. The man was dressed in a bulky hooded parka, which he unzipped.

"Found her on the front porch of her house after we got an anonymous call," he said, shaking his head. "I guess she got locked out, and her parents were gone. Some neighbor thought to call the police, but they didn't think to bring her inside; anyway the police are looking for the parents."

He looked at Holiday, and she knew what he was thinking—another instance of carelessness and neglect, and too often children were the victims.

The girl grabbed Holiday's white lab coat. "My name is Kimberly," she said, her gaze enveloping Holiday with need.

"I'm Dr. Powers, but you can call me Holiday." The girl had been stripped, put into an adult's hospital gown that was too big for her, and covered with a thin wool blanket. Holiday began to examine her face and hands.

Kimberly whimpered as Holiday touched her ears and fingers, but she didn't cry out. "Holiday. That's a funny name," she said.

Holiday finished her examination. "I know it's a funny name. But it's the only one I've got."

Kimberly looked pleased. She wiggled on the gurney, doing a little squirmy dance of delight. Holiday knew the girl must be in some pain, but she didn't seem to care.

The nurse handed Holiday the chart containing Kimberly's blood pressure, body temperature, and vital signs. "Frostbite?" she asked.

Holiday led the nurse away from the gurney, speaking in a low voice. "This was a bad night for her to get locked outside. She's got transitory hyperemia on the ears, cheeks, and fingers. Those rubber boots seem to have protected her toes."

They joined Kimberly again. "Am I sick?" she asked. Her face was heartbreakingly serious.

Holiday touched the girl's cheek. "Does that hurt?"

"A little."

She touched her ear, which was still red and hadn't turned as pale as her fingers and nose. "How about that?"

Tears filled Kimberly's eyes. "That hurts more."

"We need to warm the affected areas in hundred-and-five-degree water, get her tetanus prophylaxis and anti-inflammatories. I don't think we're going to have any tissue loss."

The nurse jotted down the orders. Kimberly watched

with respectful quiet, then spoke in a wavering voice. "I'm cold."

Holiday turned to the nurse. "Also let's get her a cup of cocoa from the lounge." She leaned over Kimberly and lightly kissed her soft, braided hair. "You're going to be just fine, honey. You have what's called frostbite, but we'll take good care of you."

Kimberly listened wide-eyed, nodding at everything Holiday said. She sat up on her elbows. "I like hot chocolate, Dr. Holiday," she said, looking reverently at Holiday. "You're nicer than my mother."

Holiday saw a watching figure out of the corner of her eye; it was Kyle. "How long have you been here?" she asked.

He smiled at Kimberly for a trace of a second, his expression turning serious when he turned to Holiday. "Just a minute or so. Do you suspect formation of vesicles?"

"No. She was outside for a while, but she was on a porch. She didn't get too much wind exposure, from the looks of it. She was wet, but at least she was out of the heavy snowfall."

Kyle nodded and shoved his hands in his pockets. He winked at Kimberly, but she turned away, taking hold of Holiday's hand.

"Kimberly, I have to speak with Dr. Jefferies. Will you be good until I get back?"

"I promise, I'll be good. Please come back soon."

Kyle watched Kimberly intently as she spoke; Holiday knew what he saw in the little girl's behavior—"frozen watchfulness." It was a trait that had nothing to do with the cold, or frostbite; it was the hopeless stare of children who were physically or mentally abused.

She and Kyle stepped out of the enclosure and sat in chairs near the nurses' station. He brushed a stray lock of brown hair away from his face, his thick cheeks pale and fleshy in the yellow overhead lights. He was only in his early thirties, but his severity and tendency to carry extra weight added at least five years to his appearance.

"Are her parents here?" he asked.

"The police are looking. She was found locked out of her house."

Kyle drew his breath sharply. Of any doctor Holiday knew, Kyle always seemed the most personally offended by child abuse. Holiday wondered if something had happened in his own past, but that was a part of himself that he always kept hidden.

"Some people shouldn't be allowed to have children. They should be neutered like animals," he said in an icy voice.

"That's a strange opinion for a doctor to have," she said softly, not wanting to make him combative—which he always became when dealing with abused children.

"You saw that look in her eyes. I'd bet a thousand dollars her parents beat her. Or worse."

Holiday tucked a lock of Kyle's hair behind his ear. He seemed comforted by the familiar gesture. "She's a beautiful little girl, and sweet," she said. "I'll talk to the police when they get here and see what I can do."

He looked away down the hall, where orderlies wheeled an elderly ER patient toward the elevators. Holiday had treated the grandmotherly woman a half hour before for an erratic heartbeat, recommending she be kept overnight for observation.

"We have to talk about my job offer. I'm sure you've heard about it by now," Kyle said. She was used to his abrupt shifts in conversation; Kimberly was now forgotten to him.

"I did hear. I needed to hear it from you. And before now."

"I'm sorry about that. I just needed time to think on my own."

Holiday watched the corner of his mouth; it was trembling. "That's a lie," she said. "You wouldn't think twice about a job like that. Phil's offering you a department-chief position. It's what you've been working for your entire career."

He couldn't look her in the eye. "I know it is. And I probably didn't tell you about it because I had to decide whether to ask you to come along."

"You didn't think to ask me whether that's what I wanted?" She felt a tightness in her throat, and a feeling of helplessness. They both knew how this would end.

"I'm asking you now," he said, turning to her. He put a hand behind her neck, softly caressing the skin beneath her pulled-back hair.

Some of the ER staff were watching them; their romance had been fuel for the gossip-hungry, and everyone must have known what they were talking about. She wanted to rise and drive them off, but instead she turned her back so that they couldn't see her face.

"You're not asking me. You're telling me. I know you're going no matter what I say."

"I know it means finding another job for you, but Phil and I can get you something at Pacific University. They have better research facilities there, more money to spend."

Holiday pulled away from his touch. "I don't want a job as your wife, or whatever you're saying."

He leaned closer. "Maybe that is what I'm saying."

She shook her head, fighting off tears. "You can't ask me like this, Kyle. I don't want to be part of your ambition."

"Is it so damned important to you to do everything on your own?" He glanced over his shoulder at the watching staff and lowered his voice. "What are you asking, that I stay here and give up the opportunity of a lifetime just so that we can be together?"

She paused a long moment, then spoke in an unsteady voice. "No. I just want to know that you could even imagine doing it."

"What about your Swedish boyfriend? What did he ever sacrifice for you? He went home and didn't look back."

His voice had turned caustic; she knew she had backed

him into a corner by trying to get him to feel, to rise above the psychological straitjacket his ambition had created within him. "That was two years ago, Kyle. That doesn't have anything to do with this."

Kyle stood up, straightening the crease in his slacks. "I need your decision, Holiday."

"Just go, Kyle. I have to get back to my patient."

His expression sealed his feelings from her, as though he had become another person. "I'm leaving in two weeks, Holiday. With or without you."

"You've made your decision, Kyle. And I didn't factor into it."

She turned and walked back toward Kimberly's enclosure; the nurses and residents all looked away in unison.

Kyle called out from behind her, "I love you, Holiday. Don't ruin this for me."

She turned to respond but saw only his back as he turned a corner to resume his rounds. Inside the enclosure Kimberly's extremities were being heated with hot water. She looked up at Holiday with a mixture of fear and awe.

"Why are you crying, Dr. Holiday?" she asked.

Holiday had just opened the lab results that morning, after keeping them on her dresser for two days, too afraid to read them. She and Kyle had been careful, but not careful enough. She had come within a second of telling Kyle that she was pregnant, but she saw now that it would only hold him back. Or else she would have to follow him, and give up the career she was trying to build.

Holiday sat beside Kimberly and caressed her hair. "Everything's fine, darling. Just be still."

"I'm feeling a little better." Kimberly spoke with the stern seriousness of a child denied the carefree license of being young. Holiday looked into her wide, staring eyes.

"That's good, Kimberly. Don't worry about a thing. I'll take good care of you."

* * *

Now Holiday had come to L.A. after all. Their child would have been seven years old if she hadn't aborted it.

"You left me," she whispered, "and expected me to follow. When I didn't, you hated me. You don't even know how much we both lost when you left. Damn it. You're not going to take my life from me."

Holiday looked around her; the Asian nurse had been listening, but quickly returned to her towels when she was noticed.

Enough is enough, Holiday thought. *If he wants a fight, I'll give him one.*

4

SO THIS IS THE PLACE, HOLIDAY THOUGHT, WHERE I'M GOING TO spend at least the next several years of my life. She pulled a sweatshirt over her head and silently calculated the passage of time: in two years she would be thirty-five, probably still living in this Los Angeles high-rise apartment building.

She looked down at the spectacular view below. From her new fifteenth-floor home she could see the low-lying sprawl of the city, a solid mesh of concrete construction dotted with clusters of tall buildings, each batch a miniature downtown. She recognized some of the places out there: to her right, Beverly Hills and Westwood; straight ahead, Santa Monica flowing into a marble blue sea now partially obscured by the haze; to the left, Century City, then the low green hills around Loyola Marymount University.

Pulling herself away from the window, she looked over the apartment again. Pacific University had leased the unit to her; they owned about thirty in the building. She had six spacious rooms and a terrace—far more luxurious than the second floor of a dilapidated Victorian in the Back Bay neighborhood of Boston she had moved from—but this felt like someone else's home. The stacks of unopened boxes in every room and the helter-skelter furniture arrangement didn't help.

She had to start somewhere, so she ripped the tape off the nearest box. It contained framed photos wrapped in tissue paper. There she was, graduating from medical school, her mother and father flanking her on either side. She wore her hair longer now and, she hated to admit, in photos now she looked more rigid, without the blind optimism of the youthful prodigy who received her M.D. at twenty-four. She dropped the photo back into the box and sat down on her blue and white pinstripe sofa.

She had passed through an accelerated medical program at Boston University in record time. Holiday was always the one willing to stay late, to sacrifice her social life (what social life?) for her work. Her colleagues in Boston weren't surprised when she announced her departure; it was as if they had expected it long in advance, and had kept their distance because her hyperaccelerated career track would take her away to the best jobs, the most advanced research. She knew people her own age who still bummed around, playing in rock bands and writing poetry in coffeehouses. And she also knew people who played tennis and sipped tea every afternoon as if that were a vocation.

Which reminded her: she had promised to call her mother.

The wall phone dialed direct to the building's parking valets, and security and maintenance crews. It bespoke the kind of luxury she hadn't experienced in years—and had trained herself to abhor.

A familiar voice answered on the second ring. "Powers residence." That low, even voice, with a vaguely Continental accent.

"Mr. Arnold, it's me. Holiday."

"Miss Powers, what a pleasure it is to hear from you. I take it you have arrived in Los Angeles?"

"I'm trying to get settled in. How are things there?"

"Very well. Your father is in New York on business, and your brother Philip is planning a visit next week."

Philip. Holiday's youngest brother and the closest thing she ever had to a lifelong confidant. He had moved to Vermont a year ago to live in the country with friends, following a messy six months of on-again, off-again rehabilitation from cocaine and alcohol. Holiday felt a stab of sadness. She hadn't been there for him; she was focused on her work, completely immersed in round-the-clock development of a virtual reality anatomy lesson designed to allow medical students to work on cadavers that existed only in computer memory. She felt she shouldn't ask how Philip was, as if she had ceded a right of intimacy.

"That's great. Be sure to say hello to the rest of the staff for me: Marie, Henry, Paul."

"I will, Miss Powers. And I assume you would like to speak with your mother. I'll get her for you."

She heard the phone receiver placed gently on the familiar antique stand in the front hall, and closed her eyes to picture the quiet evening on the grounds outside. Every time she called home, it was as if time had ceased to exist. Nothing had changed, not even Mr. Arnold with his cultivated accent. Holiday alone knew that he had really grown up in Baltimore; that was a secret he'd divulged to her one night years ago when they'd stayed up talking while he wrote a letter home and she reviewed patient files.

The sound of the phone being picked up made her draw her breath in with the combined sense of dread and pure childish glee that comprised her feelings about her mother.

"Hello, Mom. I just wanted to say hi."

"Holiday, darling, You sound positively depressed."

"No, I'm fine. It's just been a long day for me and there's a lot going on at the hospital. I'm home now, though. The view's beautiful."

"That's nice. It isn't too sterile and Californian, is it? When I was out there, it felt like they'd built the place the week before I arrived. It's no wonder earthquakes knock everything down."

"It's a nice place, Mom. It's fine for me."

"Fine for you, yes. I'm sure that's right. Oh, by the way, I saw Brian Lloyd on the golf course today. He asked about you."

"That's nice, Mom. I really—"

"You know, we don't get to talk much. That's why I feel I have the right to bring things like this up. Talking to Brian reminded me of how you and he used to play tennis every afternoon in the summer when you were young. He's only three years older than you, you know, and still single. I could tell just by the way he said your name that he still carried a—"

"Mom. That really doesn't matter to me. That's not my life."

"Of course it isn't. Sitting in that apartment in that horrible city all by yourself is your life. Working so hard that you developed a nervous condition when you were twenty-five, that's your life."

"I'm over that, Mom. I'm fine."

"Of course you are. I'm not saying you should be like me, for heaven's sake. I'm no model of perfection. Remember, my mother told me that a lady never touches money. Can you imagine that? All I'm saying is that your suffering and hard work . . . we're proud of you, darling, your father and I. You've accomplished more than most people do in their entire life. But you don't have to completely ignore your background. If you want to take a year or two off, just to travel, you can. Take advantage of the opportunities your father and I are still willing to give you."

The sun had begun to descend in the west, turning the sky a brilliant orange that bled into violet. The endless procession of cars now lit their way with beams that cut through the twilight haze. She hated this conversation. But she was also loath to hang up. There was no one else to call, nowhere to go.

"Holiday, dear, are you listening to me?"

"Of course I am, Mother. You want me to quit medicine, come home, marry Brian Lloyd, and raise little caddies for charity golf tournaments."

Silence. Holiday tried to picture her mother: thin and perpetually tanned, even in the gloomy New England winters. Her sandy hair, which she once bragged contained at least ten different shades of blond, had recently begun to look washed out and monochromatic. It was fall;

she would be wearing a white skirt and a tennis sweater, with her glasses on a chain around her neck.

"Every time you call me 'Mother' rings an alarm in my mind that you're about to attack. It's not that I don't deserve it, I'm sure."

Elena Powers was the sum of her parts, nothing more and nothing less: born into the Boston aristocracy, she married a man who had inherited and built upon a successful financial concern and banking interest. She then raised children and refined her taste until her life was static perfection. But it was Elena and not Holiday who had been there for Philip, who had lost his way and spent years secretly numbing his inner suffering with drugs.

A knock on the door intruded upon Holiday's thoughts; she pulled the cord as far as it would go and reached for the knob.

"Hang on, Mom. I have a visitor."

She cupped her hand over the mouthpiece. Holiday had been too harsh. It always turned out this way.

She pulled open the door. A woman stood there with a bottle of white wine. Holiday looked at her quizzically, then pointed at the phone. The woman nodded and leaned casually against the doorway.

"Mom, there's someone here to see me. I have to go."

"Someone to see you? Whom do you know in that city? That's another thing, darling, there really is something to living around your own kind. I know how that sounds, but—"

"*Good-bye,* Mother. You have my number. We'll be in touch."

Holiday walked to the kitchen and hung up the phone. The woman let herself inside: she wore a sharp blue suit, with white hose accenting slim, toned legs. She was diminutive, and her blond hair was cut short and neat, giving her an overall appearance of control and precision. She extended her hand.

"Kate Fisher," she said. "You don't know me, but I live next door. I saw the movers yesterday and wanted to say hi, but I got caught at the hospital on an emergency case repairing something I had done, which wasn't really my fault. But you know how it is, being a surgeon, too. I work at the Bartholomew, by the way." She paused. "God, I know you one minute and I'm already talking my head off. Here, take this wine. I bought it as a housewarming present, but I hope you don't mind if I have a glass. Or two. I've been on my feet all day."

Holiday closed and bolted the door and walked to the living room, where Kate opened the wine with a corkscrew she produced from her shirt pocket.

"By the way, my name is Holiday Powers," she said, trying to infuse some humor into her voice. Somehow Kate's spontaneous appearance served to show her how stark and gloomy her own mood had become.

"I know," Kate said. "Hey, I hope I didn't come at a bad time."

Holiday sat heavily in her favorite chair, its brown leather worn and scuffed by years of use. "Not at all. You came at a really good time."

Kate tossed the cork aside. "Mother driving you nuts, huh?"

"It's that easy to tell?"

"I know all the signs. Do you have any wineglasses?"

"God, somewhere. I haven't unpacked anything." Holiday fruitlessly looked around. In her haste to pack she had barely taken the trouble to label any of the boxes. The kitchen utensils could be in the bathroom, maybe in the extra bedroom. In any case home elegance had never been her strong suit; she spent so much time at work, she never even bothered to collect a set of matching plates.

"Don't worry about it, sugar," Kate said, walking into the kitchen. "There's some old coffee cups in here."

"Sugar?" Holiday leaned back in the chair, taking a dripping cup from Kate when she returned. "You're Southern, aren't you?"

Kate gave her a brief look of astonishment, as if trying to determine if she were being put on. "Well, I guess the accent's pretty toned down these days, but yes, I was born and raised in Augusta, Georgia." She settled heavily on the sofa, looking much smaller on the large piece of furniture. Holiday guessed that Kate probably stood five-two in her stocking feet.

"I'm from Boston. Actually, it's the only place I've ever lived."

They took long drinks of the sweet, mellow wine, both looking around the wreckage of the apartment.

"You're pretty young, aren't you, Holiday?" Kate said. Her tone was neutral.

"Thirty-three," she said.

"You look younger."

Holiday smiled awkwardly. She liked this woman. Still, she felt defensive, as if Kate controlled the ebb and flow of conversation between them. The comment about her age made her feel very young—perhaps even out of place in this new job and new life. She took another drink of wine.

"I'm forty-five," Kate said. "I know what you're thinking—'but she's so well preserved!' " Kate laughed. "But I'm jealous of you. You know how many people applied for that job of yours?"

A sudden gust of wind blew through the open window, clattering the metal blinds and sending copies of Holiday's rental agreement flying from the coffee table between them.

"A lot, I know," Holiday said. "I happened to have the right combination of skills, or else they picked my name out of a hat."

Kate replaced the papers on the table and slammed the wine bottle on them like an ersatz paperweight. She walked to the window and pulled it half shut. "Well, you probably know there's lot of pissed-off old boys now that you're here. They can't handle a high-level appointee unless it's a wrinkled white male, well-off, with a pedigree to die for. But I guess you have all those things, except you're not a boy, and you're certainly not old."

Holiday pulled a box to her and ripped it open. It was full of old sweaters and coats, useless in southern California. She felt a rush of embarrassment; these clothes were out of style, unfashionable. It was years since she'd given much thought to her appearance. Packing in Boston, she had realized that nearly her entire wardrobe was fit for a charity drive.

"Enough about me, Kate. I'm still in culture shock and might give away all my secrets." Her flippancy earned an appreciative smile from Kate. "Tell me about yourself."

"Oh, let's see." Kate stood up straight, holding her glass thoughtfully in the air. "Georgia. U. of Virginia med school. Marriage. Divorce. Everything required to turn a girl into a cheerful cynic. I got the hell out of the South and came here about six years ago."

"You said you're a surgeon. What kind?"

Kate smiled mischievously, pouring refills for herself, then Holiday. "I'm a urologist. Things are going pretty well."

"What kind of work do you get?"

"Mostly, shall we say, well-off gentlemen of a certain age. My particular bread-and-butter procedure these days is the penile implant."

Holiday couldn't help grinning. "You mean—?"

Kate turned no-nonsense. "That's right. I go directly to the seat of the male intellect and make it bigger and better. It's a dirty job, but I have the most grateful patients in town."

Holiday burst out in laughter, spilling wine on her sweatshirt. Kate also giggled as if she had perpetrated some sly prank, though it was obvious that she had used her punch line before.

"I also address more serious plumbing problems. I'm hooked into the HMOs like everyone else, scrambling for a patient base and trying to keep up a steady practice."

Kate's last comment hung in the air between them; lately so much conversation among physicians revolved around the consequences of America's shift toward managed care.

"So," Kate said, looking out the window. "What do you think of the view? You know, I have some extra plastic chairs I can loan you for your patio. You can help me lug them up from the basement."

Kate slowly walked toward the kitchen, quiet and thoughtful for the first time since entering the apartment. Something in the cut of Kate's suit, some severity in her hair, reminded Holiday of the differences between them; their ages, their backgrounds, their personalities were so different. It made her feel uncomfortable, but who didn't she feel this way with? The luxury of her youth, the casual friendships, the scattered relationships with men—aside from her career, she had kept everything in her life at a distance, never feeling the ease she sensed in others.

"So, young lady, are you seeing anyone in L.A.?" Kate returned to the living room and pursed her lips with a friendly smile that stripped years from her features.

"No. To tell you the truth, I only know a few people here."

"Name some names, I'll give you the dirt."

"Um . . . Phil Hermoza of course. I've known him since I was in medical school."

"I like Hermoza," Kate said, pushing back an errant shock of hair. "He's a sweetheart. We knocked back a few drinks about a year ago, when the Bart and Pac U were just starting to play footsie. I thought he was going to smash a table or something, but he just kept talking about his kids."

"He's a good man," Holiday said, sensing the formality in her own voice. She suddenly remembered a vivid image from the past. "You know, he once evacuated a five-bed ICU in Boston when there was a chemical leak in the air system?"

Kate met her eyes. "What do you mean, he evacuated the unit?"

"It's just what it sounds like. He picked up the beds,

with three people holding the other end, and carried them to another wing."

"You're shitting me. He must have given himself a hernia."

"No one could believe it, but he was fine. He had nurses running beside the beds holding the IVs, trying to keep up with him. One patient was asleep and didn't even wake up."

"You saw this?"

"Just the end of it. It was quite a sight."

They shook heads simultaneously. It was a memory that Holiday hadn't evoked in years.

"All right, who else do you know?"

"Well, the guys working under me in the computer labs. Bill Epstein, Gregory Hampton."

Kate's eyes lit up. "I like the way you say his name: 'Gregory Hampton.' What did you think?"

"Well, he's nice. A little defensive. Do you know him?"

"Missy, he lives two floors below us. I've seen him around. Wait until summer by the pool; now *there's* a sight for sore eyes. I always thought computer guys had emaciated bods, but he certainly drove that notion out of my mind."

"He lives in this building? I had no idea."

"*Look at you!* Don't worry about it, honey. He's a sweet guy. Want me to set you up with him?"

"Kate, come on, I don't—"

"Oh, I was just kidding. Don't get nervous. Just admit he's cute."

"Kate." Holiday searched for another box to open. *"Holiday."*

Holiday looked up at Kate's beaming face and let out a giggle. "All right . . . I think he's cute. Are you happy?" She felt relaxed for the first time that day.

"I'm happy. Just checking for a pulse, honey."

"I have one. It's just that . . . I haven't had the best experiences with men. It's always turned out bad for me."

"Tell me about it. We should swap war stories soon."

Kate looked at her watch and frowned. "Look, I've got to go home. You polish off the wine, because you're buying next time."

"Oh, fine." Holiday suddenly felt frightened of being alone.

"One more thing. I have to ask. Where'd you get the name?"

She felt herself blushing. "Family tradition. It's supposed to be a last name."

Kate laughed. "Well, at least it wasn't Beauregard or something. Hey, that's your phone."

Holiday brushed past Kate and flipped on the kitchen light. It was dark outside, and the apartment was now filled with shadows. It took her a few quick glances around the kitchen walls to recall precisely where the phone was located. She found it by the refrigerator and picked it up.

"Don't say anything. Just listen."

Kate had picked up her purse and stood peering into Holiday's box of photos.

"You made a big mistake, bitch."

Holiday extended the cord and stepped into the hall. "Look, whoever this is, you can just hang up."

"Shut up. I told you not to talk." Kate looked up from the box. She silently mouthed: *Who is it?* Holiday shook her head and pulled the phone closer to her ear. Her hands were trembling.

"You shouldn't have left Boston."

The voice was muffled, unrecognizable. He had no discernible accent, nothing familiar, but the malice in his tone was unmistakable.

"You're going to get hurt if you stay here."

"Holiday? What's going on? Who is that?" Kate stepped up close as if trying to hear through the plastic receiver.

"You've been warned."

He hung up. Holiday stood staring at the phone.

"Holiday, talk to me. Who the hell was that?"

Kate took the phone from her hand, listened to the tone, and replaced it on its base. She took Holiday's hand and led her into the living room, seating her on the sofa.

"I . . . I don't know. Some man making threats."

"I'm sure it's nothing. There are a lot of freaks out there, probably a lot more than where you're from. Just forget about it. The guy probably just dialed a random number."

"No, Kate. That's impossible." Holiday took a deep breath, trying to control her voice. "He knew me. He knew I was from Boston. He said I was going to have trouble here."

"What kind of trouble?"

"He didn't say. He just . . . God, Kate, he sounded so hateful. I think he wants to hurt me."

Kate sat on the sofa and put her arm around the younger woman. "Come on, now. So he knew about you. Like I told you, a lot of old boys are pissed off about you getting the job. Maybe one of them's got a screw loose. That doesn't mean you're in any danger."

"I guess so." Holiday sat still. She felt that if she moved at all, she might burst into tears. She never cried in front of anyone. Ever.

"It'll be fine, sugar. I'm a yell away if you need me. Remember that. Look, I want to give you something." Kate fished about in her purse, clucking with approval when she found a silver key. "Here's a spare to my place. If you need to come by or if you get scared and I'm not home, just let yourself in. All right?"

Holiday looked at the silver object and felt a measure of safety. At least she had options now; she wasn't trapped in her apartment with nowhere to go.

"I have an extra, too," she said, looking through papers on the coffee table, finally finding a small ring with a single key. "Take this. The same goes for you."

Kate took the key. "Thanks. Now we're like dorm roomies." She smiled ironically. "By the way, if you let yourself in and I'm not there: feed my fish. I always forget."

Holiday nodded gravely, making a mental note.

"And don't be so serious. Believe me, everything's fine. It's just some pervert with nothing better to do. He's sitting somewhere scared to death you traced the call."

"You're probably right."

"So you made some enemies. Fuck 'em. Be a brass-balled bitch like me. It's the only way to go."

Kate began moving toward the door and Holiday followed. Kate talked as she walked. "Say, do you have any ex-boyfriends or anyone who might pull something like this? My ex-husband used to pop up for a while after we split up. I had to get a restraining order on him."

Holiday opened the door for Kate. "Well, the only real ex-boyfriend—if you could call him that—works at the university."

Kate stopped at the door, interested. "You don't say? Who?"

"Oh, Kate, I don't think he . . ."

"Of course you don't. Who is it?"

"Kyle Jefferies."

The mention of Kyle's name stopped Kate where she stood, her mouth open as if she had been slapped. "Jefferies? You used to go out with Jefferies?"

"A long time ago. He's not very friendly to me anymore. Since I got this job, in fact, I think he hates me."

Kate regained her composure. "So you have a political enemy and an ex-lover rolled into one."

"I guess, but I don't—"

"I don't either. He's too ambitious, too political. This kind of thing would dust his career."

"Where do you know Kyle from?"

"It's hard not to know him. He acts like he runs surgery at the Bart, in addition to his kingdom at Pac U." Kate smiled ruefully. "But he's good. That's how he gets away with it."

Kate stepped into the hall. "It was nice to meet you," she said. "I think we'll be great friends."

"Me, too." Holiday smiled, and shut the door. Her apartment was dark and silent, the corners filled with shadows. The sky outside had turned a bruise-colored purple, and for all the action and tumult below, she could see only indistinct lights and movement. She had to get out, if only for a while.

The supermarket was another choice bit of culture shock for Holiday. She had stood puzzled in the produce aisle— *jicama? radicchio lettuce? edible flowers?*—at a variety of goods she never saw in Boston. The entire place was bigger, breezier, faster, and more open than what she had grown up with in New England. She stocked up on comfort food and things she could easily cook: fresh bread, yogurt, a chicken breast, and a pint of double chocolate ice cream.

She pulled her car, a German sedan the university leased for her, out of the underground garage and blended into the stream of traffic. It was a fifteen-minute drive home, but Michael Waters at the high-rise security desk (who was gruff at first but warmed to the opportunity to show off his knowledge of the area) claimed that this market was more convenient and safer than a nearer store.

The rhythm of traffic soon allowed her mind to wander, and she shut off the radio and opened her window, letting the night air fill the car. She had heard about L.A. pollution, but the air that night was fresh and had a slight odor of sea salt.

She thought about Philip, feeling that she had let him down. For the first time in his troubled life his big sister was more than a few hours' drive away. She had known about his drug use before anyone else in the family, and had made the classic mistake of believing his promise that he was dealing with it on his own. And now, by moving away, she had perhaps failed him again. No longer could he show up at her house unannounced at three in the morning and crash out on the sofa. And he could no longer expect the no-questions-asked loans from her, not after it became clear that he had spent the money on cocaine over the last eighteen months.

On a whim she kept driving, trying to unwind. Moving north on Bundy Drive into Brentwood, she took a left at Sunset. If she remembered correctly, the winding street led all the way to the ocean.

She was right. The ice cream in the trunk would melt, but this was part of why she had come to California: after parking in a roadside lot and crossing the highway she found a stretch of beach, the sand white in the moonlight and the surf gently easing against the shore.

Holiday walked with her head back, feeling the breeze and looking up toward the sky. A seabird·cried out loud overhead, circling the shore in search of food. She kicked off her shoes and stood there for a moment, her eyes closed, feeling the cool night and the water's presence and the blissful beauty all around her. Then she gasped.

Someone was watching her. She looked around but saw only an old couple walking hand-in-hand down along the waterline. Still, she couldn't shake the feeling.

The moment was ruined, so Holiday put on her shoes and trudged back to her car, still looking around, watching the shadows. Her heart beat hard in her chest, and she felt the fine hair on her arms stand on end.

She drove fast on Sunset, back to Bundy, now in a hurry to get home and lock the door behind her. About a mile from home she heard tires squeal. She checked the mirror and saw a long black American sedan racing through the curve behind her.

That's weird, she thought. She had seen that car parked in the beachside lot. She was sure of it.

A left turn came, leading to the high-rise. She took it, and the car sped to stay behind her.

"You shouldn't have left Boston."

Holiday gunned the engine, pulling past a Mercedes

and cutting it off. Home was near; she could see her building up ahead. She checked the mirror. The sedan had duplicated her move, and the Mercedes's horn blared at the double indignity its driver had suffered.

"You're going to get hurt if you stay here."

She took the left turn into the driveway cul-de-sac far too fast, her tires losing traction for a moment as she skidded to a stop before the valet parking kiosk. Turning her head so forcefully her neck hurt, she saw the sedan accelerate and speed off down the road.

"You've been warned."

The valet approached her car warily, opening the door for her with a nonplused expression. Holiday handed him the keys and stood in the drive, watching the street. The car was gone.

Once inside, Holiday knocked on Kate's door. There was no answer. She quickly crossed the carpeted hall to her apartment and took the phone off the hook. This was ridiculous. She'd calm down, have dinner, and go to bed early.

She slept with a chair wedged under the bedroom doorknob, like a scared character in some old movie. Her dreams were of familiar, warm things: Boston townhouses, the Charles River at night, the relief in her patients' eyes when they awoke from delicate surgery. When she awoke, she found she had wound the sheets around her neck and at some time in the night had pulled the blinds down over her bedroom windows—sealing herself in absolute quiet and darkness.

5

OUTSIDE THE WINDOW THE SAN FRANCISCO BAY GLITTERED with crescents of reflected sunlight—like knife edges against the undulating water. Alcatraz, in the center of the vista looking like a luxury villa, took in and let out its daily complement of tourists. To the north were the green rolling hills of Marin County, crowned by the peak of Mount Tamalpais. Gregory Hampton allowed his gaze to linger for a moment, intoxicated by this view of perhaps the most beautiful place he had ever seen, then focused his attention again on the speaker at the front of the room.

He was spending only one day in his favorite city, and hated to waste it in the cheaply paneled conference room of TelStar Technologies—attending a conference on virtual reality advances, listening to a middle-aged man speak in a low, incomprehensible voice to a room full of drowsy technicians and engineers. Gregory checked the program: the man was named Foster Meyerson, and he was talking about digitally enhanced imaging systems and their potential use for the sight-impaired. Well, he could have fooled Gregory. The subject was interesting, but Meyerson was so stage-shy that his voice barely rose above a whisper.

There were perhaps thirty men and five or six women in the room. The field was still dominated by men, but more and more female faces appeared at gatherings such as this. Gregory, in charge of hiring and firing at his department at Pacific University, was painfully aware of the dearth of women in his department. He wasn't opposed to hiring them, but the best candidates for the last few job openings had invariably been men. This would have to change, he knew. This Holiday Powers had all the earmarks of an administrative activist. He might find his ass on the line if he didn't "catch up with the times," or whatever they would say to get him to do what they wanted.

Meyerson loaded up a slide, and the audience's interest palpably slipped farther away. It wasn't that they weren't interested. These people were all dedicated to exploring new technological frontiers, but they felt the hot breath of competition on their necks every day. The field had become so specialized that people tended to group together in their little camps, ignoring other disciplines.

The slide depicted a plaster model wearing a pair of thick green oversized sunglasses, attached by a cable to a small black device that looked like a stereo speaker. Meyerson explained that the system could be used to enhance human vision, making it more stark and vivid to compensate for damaged or faulty eyes. Gregory yawned. It was interesting, but he was concerned only with surgical technology at the moment—not ophthalmology.

The sky outside was vivid blue. The grass in Golden Gate Park looked like a pile carpet. Gregory fantasized about the nap he wanted to take, then saw that the talk was over. He checked the program: lunch, then two afternoon talks on motion-based technology. This material, focusing on reciprocal motion and pressure responses between machines and humans, would be useful to him. If he could remain awake.

The group filed out. Gregory knew a couple of people there from previous conferences, and even spotted an old classmate from Stanford. He wasn't in the mood to talk. He remembered his interaction two days ago with Holiday Powers, wondering if he had played it right. She was young, smart, good-looking—there had to be a catch. He needed to keep his leverage and political power, protect his people, and get the job done. He had to serve notice to her that he wouldn't be stepped on. It was the only intelligent thing to do.

Of course there was always the possibility that he had

acted like an asshole. That had certainly crossed his mind and now, sitting alone in a quiet cubbyhole before a communal computer terminal, that interpretation seemed pretty valid.

"Gregory Hampton! I've been waiting for you to show up."

Gregory swiveled in his chair to see the imposing form of an obese bearded man in a short-sleeved pinstripe shirt and khaki pants. He felt as if he had been greeted at a party by someone he had, until then, carefully avoided.

"Pete Willis. I was going to look you up, but I got here late."

Willis smiled with the condescension of someone who, mistakenly, felt he was innately more intelligent than everyone else around him. Gregory found it incredibly irritating, and always had, ever since he met Willis in college. Gregory had since moved on to pure research, while Willis ended up running the computer room at TelStar—which was, in reality, a minor player in the business.

"Sure, Gregory. My feelings weren't hurt. I knew you'd be in to check your E-mail on the community terminal. Isn't this where we always meet?"

"Like clockwork, my man. So how's the love life?"

The question was calculated to irritate Willis. As far as Gregory knew, Pete's love life had, to date, consisted of a series of unrequited crushes on young women in TelStar marketing.

"Stellar as always. And how are things at the Pac U snake pit?"

"Interesting actually. I have a new boss, this thirty-year-old, overachiever baby-doll type." Gregory hated himself for this remark; he was trying to be clever, and he had succeeded only in making a sexist remark about someone he barely knew. Nice work.

Willis nodded sagely, resting his hands on his considerable paunch. "I'm sure it's only a matter of time before you add her to your collection."

Gregory shook his head. "Get with the times, my friend. Workplace romance is out, especially with the boss. Now, if you don't mind, I'd like to view my E-mail."

There were only forty-five minutes left in the midday break, and Gregory still hoped to grab some lunch. Also, talking with Willis had made him feel that he was compromising himself—as always.

"Indeed, Gregory." Willis sniffed. He still hadn't taken care of his sinus condition. "Care to have a drink or two after the conference?"

"No time. I'm heading back to L.A. at six. Thanks, though."

"All right, see you, then."

Gregory shook his head and turned to the computer terminal. He had never been friends with Pete Willis, but still the man acted slightly offended when Gregory didn't want to socialize. There were enough clichés about the social backwardness of computer types without people like Willis proving them true.

He looked around and saw that he was alone in the small room. Quickly, in a routine he had performed thousands of times before, he logged into the Internet and accessed his account in the Pacific University computer system by using his personal access code and password. He quickly passed through a series of menus and loaded his E-mail. He clicked a box for the first of his three messages, which came from Bill Epstein:

```
HOPE YOU'RE HAVING A GOOD TIME. IT'S QUIET AND
BORING HERE. RUNNING THROUGH THE SEQUENCE ON
THE ROBOT, PER YOUR IMPERIAL DEMANDS. HOLIDAY
POWERS HASN'T BEEN AROUND AND JEFFERIES IS
LEAVING US ALONE. AT LAST! FREEDOM. DON'T
FORGET TO PICK UP BROCHURES, ETC. FOR ME. WISH
WE HAD BUDGET FOR ME TO LOLLYGAG AROUND LIKE
YOU. HAVE A SAFE TRIP BACK, BUDDY. BILL.
```

Gregory clicked an option box and deleted the message, loading the second. His eyebrows raised when he saw that it came from Phil Hermoza:

NO ONE TOLD ME YOU WERE GOING TO A CONFERENCE TODAY. BAD TIMING, I WANTED TO GET YOU AND HOLIDAY POWERS FOR A MEETING. YOU ARE PROBABLY UP THERE PLAYING VIDEO GAMES OR SOMETHING, YOU CAN'T FOOL ME. CALL ME FIRST THING TOMORROW. UNIVERSITY ADMIN IS PRESSING ME AND POWERS TO GET A FULL WORKING DEMO TO IMPRESS ALUMNI AND ALL THE OTHER ASSHOLES WHO GIVE MONEY TO THE SCHOOL. JEFFERIES IS COMPLAINING ABOUT THE SIMULATORS FOR HIS RESIDENTS. SAYS HE CAN'T GRADE THEM AS WELL AS ACTUAL SURGERY. I KNOW, I KNOW. INDULGE HIM.

Gregory shook his head. Hermoza, in political code, had just informed him that Kyle Jefferies was bitching again about the virtual reality training simulators. Nothing was ever enough for Jefferies; though Gregory's department had, after years of work, created a simulator that was being heralded in the industry as a prototype model for the future, Jefferies had nothing but complaints. Now that the computer labs were taken away from Jefferies, he would no doubt complain all the more, just out of spite.

This was serious business to Gregory. His job was, after all, at a university hospital—so high-ranking surgical staff naturally had more clout than computer technicians. On more than one occasion, after he and Jefferies fought with dogged acrimony over some element of a system (usually pie-in-the-sky demands by Jefferies that couldn't be satisfied with current technology), Jefferies had tried to fire Gregory and most of his staff. Hermoza had always intervened.

Outside the small room a discussion was heating up.

"*Star Trek*," Gregory reflected in disgust. *They're arguing about "Star Trek." You people need to get a life.* He eagerly loaded the last message, shutting his colleagues out of mind. The transmission was from Holiday Powers:

I DIDN'T KNOW YOU WERE OUT OF TOWN. PHIL WANTED
US TO GET TOGETHER FOR A MEETING, BUT IT CAN
WAIT. I HAVE MY HANDS FULL ANYWAY. I GAVE PHIL
MY VOTE OF CONFIDENCE IN YOUR DEPARTMENT AND
TOLD HIM WE SHOULD CAVE IN TO ALL YOUR DEMANDS
HOWEVER UNREASONABLE. ALSO I WANT TO WORK WITH
YOU ON A PROPOSAL TO PUT TOGETHER TWO MORE VR
SURGICAL SIMULATOR WORKSTATIONS: ONE FOR US AND
PERHAPS ONE TO SELL TO THE BARTHOLOMEW. LET ME
KNOW WHAT KIND OF PERSONNEL YOU CAN ALLOCATE FOR
THIS. WE'LL TALK WHEN YOU GET BACK. ENJOY SF.

Gregory pondered for a moment, then hit the "respond" prompt on his E-mail menu. He began to type:

SORRY YOU DIDN'T KNOW I WAS LEAVING, BUT IT'S
ONLY FOR A DAY. THANKS FOR PUTTING IN A GOOD
WORD FOR ME. IN TERMS OF YOUR PROPOSAL, WE'LL
HAVE TO TALK AS SOON AS POSSIBLE. IT CAN
CERTAINLY BE DONE, BUT WE MAY HAVE TO BRING MORE
PEOPLE ON STAFF. SEE YOU WHEN I GET BACK TO THE
OFFICE.

Gregory sent the message, then deleted Holiday's. He pondered whether he should load up his personal calendar, to see if he had failed to inform anyone else that he was out of town, then decided it wasn't worth the bother. Instead of messing with it, he logged off the computer and gathered his papers. He could grab a sandwich on the run and still have time to pick up pamphlets and brochures for Bill Epstein.

Stepping into the hall, Gregory looked back into the room. There was no sign of Willis, which was just as well. With luck Gregory would get through the day without seeing him again.

The line at the TelStar cafeteria was clogged with employees on their lunch break. They eyed Gregory, an outsider and an unfamiliar face, with curiosity. Waiting for his shot at the sub stand, he ran through his messages in his mind, finally grasping the full impact of what Powers had written. Two more workstations? Was she out of her mind? The first one took more than six months to put together, and at the expense of all other priorities. He laughed softly. The lady had a soft touch, but she certainly knew what she wanted.

Pete Willis emerged from his office, a slip of paper in his hand. He removed his glasses and wiped them on his shirt, savoring the satisfaction of the moment. It had gone perfectly—Gregory Hampton, a true creature of habit, had arrived at the break and logged into the communal terminal—just as he did every time he came for a conference.

So it had been easy to do what they asked. Why they had asked him to do it—and who they even were—were other questions entirely, mysteries that he didn't care to ponder at all. For now all he had to worry about was calling the international phone number he had been given. He would tell the person who answered that the plan was a success, and pass on the information. Then he would concern himself only with what to do with all the money they paid him.

"This surgery is specifically designed to address the plight of, shall we say, the mature man. They can have ejaculations, but can't achieve an erection. If they can get it up, they can't keep it that way, if you know what I mean. Not enough blood gets to the old scepter, and we have vascular impotence."

Holiday looked around the small operating room. The assisting surgeon, the anesthesiologist, and the nurses all ignored Kate Fisher. Apparently this lecture was aimed at Holiday, who sat on a creaky stool in a corner of the room, waiting for the operation to begin.

"Delicately put, Doctor," the anesthesiologist said, looking up from a spiral-bound stack of reports. The patient, on the table and surrounded by the team, had already been put under. His body was completely draped in blue surgical cloth. Holiday could see his gray hair and his eyes covered with cotton and taped shut.

"Hey, Patterson, what other way is there to say it? You're no spring chicken yourself. Maybe I'll be getting a look at you before long." Kate's eyes narrowed and gleamed over her surgical mask.

The anesthesiologist shifted uncomfortably in his chair. "Don't hold your breath, Fisher," he said.

The circulating nurse draped a surgical robe over Kate's outstretched arms, tying it behind her. She repeated this process with the assisting surgeon, a Latino with stark brown eyes.

Holiday waited for the penile prosthesis surgery to begin. She probably shouldn't have taken the afternoon off to witness Kate's procedure, but her third day at work had been much like the first: a slew of impromptu meetings and an ongoing policy wrangle with Kyle.

"Excuse me, have you ever watched surgery before?" Holiday turned her attention from the instrument tray to the head nurse, who waited for a reply.

"Forgive them, Holiday. They know not what they say," Kate announced. "Jane, everyone, forgive me for not introducing our guest. Meet Dr. Holiday Powers, new associate professor at Pacific U. She also has this big long title, so treat her nice, y'all."

Kate delivered the last half of her introduction in a drawling parody of her own slight southern accent. Holiday sensed her friend growing loose and excited as the surgery drew near. It was a sharp contrast to many other doctors, such as Kyle, who always bristled with tension and made biting remarks to his assistants.

"Sorry," the nurse said. "I didn't want anyone passing out."

"If anyone is going to pass out, it's Patterson over here when he sees what fate has in store for him in a few years," Kate said, blowing the anesthesiologist a kiss.

Holiday watched in silence as Kate drew back the double sterile drapes covering the patient's penis, which then lay exposed amid the blue cloth field. A small mountain of sterile towels rested on the patient's abdomen.

Kate requested a scalpel and made a quick incision on the penis shaft, opening the corpus spongiosa, the vascular layer of the penis.

"We use one of two types of prosthetic inserts for the procedure," Kate said, continuing to work. "Inflatable or semirigid. It depends on the specifics of the patient's condition."

The head nurse, following a mumbled command, handed Kate a steel rod. The assisting surgeon held the penis, and Kate drove the rod into the exposed shaft.

"There's something for you to dream about tonight, Vasquez," Kate said to the assisting surgeon without looking up. She fastidiously and gently jiggled the rod, ensuring that it was in place.

Vasquez chuckled, still grasping the penis. "I just let it wash right over me. Nothing bothers me."

"Vasquez is our resident Zen master," Kate said, glancing at Holiday, who had moved forward a few steps to get a better view without violating the sterile surgical field.

"Number fourteen dilator, Karen," Kate said to the nurse, then delicately used the device to expand the penis, affording room to insert the implant.

"Wipe, please," Kate ordered. "I'm sweating like a pig. Too much coffee. Say, Holiday, will you turn on the radio?"

"Got it," the anesthesiologist said, resting his log book on one knee.

"Good man, Patterson," Kate said. "Always on the ball."

Patterson shook his head. "Another lousy pun."

"It wasn't intentional," Kate said. "But I'm on a roll today."

Patterson switched on the radio; a rock ballad played softly.

"Switch it!" Kate yelled. "Uh, Karen, number nineteen prosthesis please. Nineteen plus one." The nurse sorted through a row of implants on a nearby tray. "I hate that stuff. I want some mood music. Let's see . . . how about 'I've Got You Under My Skin'?"

" 'I Get By with a Little Help from My Implant,' " Vasquez offered.

"Not bad," Kate said. Karen handed Kate the implants, which Kate placed into the penis shaft. "Holiday, have a look. This little button is what the patient will use. It's right here, beneath the skin on the underside of the penis. He'll push the button, and the penis will go up and down on command." Kate activated the mechanism; the penis slowly became erect.

" 'A Hard Day's Night,' " Holiday said, breaking into a smile under her mask.

Kate looked up from her work, her eyes aglow with warm surprise. "My dirty-minded little sister," she said to no one in particular.

The button was pressed again, and the penis collapsed. Karen sewed the implant into place to the strains of country music selected by Patterson. Within forty-five minutes the incision was closed and the dressing was applied. A palpable feeling of relief filled the room; despite their levity, the team had obviously taken the work seriously.

"You know, Fisher," Patterson said, adjusting the flow of anesthetic to begin bringing the patient out of deep unconsciousness so that he could be wheeled to post-op, "there is a theory that patients can subconsciously hear things said around them while they're put under. I read a report on that."

Kate snapped off her surgical gloves. "God, I hope not. I'd be in deep shit," she said, yanking on the strings holding together her gown.

Holiday waited for Kate in the surgical lounge. She read the business section of the *L.A. Times* while a group of male doctors boisterously watched a college basketball game on a big-screen TV. It was like a fraternity house; she received a lot of interested looks from the men, but none had the maturity to approach her like an adult and introduce themselves.

Kate finally emerged from the nurses' locker room, dressed in a deep-green suit with impeccable tailor-made lines and folds. Her blond hair swirled in a perfect wave down to her ears. Without thinking, Holiday ran a hand through her own long, curly, and increasingly unruly mane. She tried to dress like a professional—today, in a skirt and silk blouse—but she doubted she would ever pull off Kate's easy elegance.

"Lost in thought again?" Kate asked, grabbing a muffin from a snack tray and looking briefly at the basketball game. "I'll give you Kansas if you give me nine points," she said to a bearded man, who simultaneously studied a patient chart and watched the game.

"No way, Fisher," he said calmly. "You must be out of your mind."

"Never hurts to try." Kate shrugged. "Come on, Powers, let's take a walk. Do you have to go back right away?"

"I was thinking of calling it a day," Holiday said, checking her watch. It was nearly four-thirty. "But no, I should get back and check my messages. Pam, my assistant, seems to stay every night until about seven. I'm getting a huge case of shame for cutting out early."

"Can't set a bad example for the troops," Kate said. They stepped outside and stood in the balmy southern California afternoon before the stone facade of the Bartholomew; above them the gleaming twin towers of the complex shot eleven stories into the sky.

"So. What did you think of the prosthetic surgery?" Kate asked.

"I'm impressed. Do you have a lot of problems with infection?"

Kate shook her head vigorously. "Not really. Not now at least. At first we got some post-op infection, and we had a couple of malfunctioning prosthetics that we had to go in and fix. But the manufacturer has really got their act together in the last couple years, and we've refined the technique."

Holiday nodded. Kate's self-assurance and pride reminded her of her own satisfaction when she became expert with laparoscopic surgeries developed in the last decade: cholecystectomy, inguinal herniorrhaphies, bowel resection, vagotomy, Nissen funduplication. She had been fortunate enough to participate in formative research at Boston General, working with Kyle.

"You were enjoying yourself in there, weren't you? Straight-ahead surgery, no politics. No ulterior motives." Kate leaned over, searching in her purse. "I know I have a cigarette in here somewhere."

"I enjoyed it, sure. The Bart seems like a great place to work."

Kate shrugged. "Upscale clientele. Pac U takes a lot of the general cases from the area, we get the private-care patients. Which is why Pac U wanted to join up with us."

Holiday grimaced. "Let's not spoil a perfectly good afternoon by talking politics."

"My thoughts exactly. Come on, I'll walk you to your car while I sneak a smoke."

"I walked here, actually."

Kate was aghast. "You *walked*?"

"Sure, it's only about a mile."

"We've got some work to do with you, girl. Nobody walks in L.A. Well, I'll at least walk you out to the street after I have my cigarette."

Holiday glanced at the doctor's parking lot, which was

filled with expensive imported cars. One vanity plate
read: #1MD.

"What are you thinking about?" Kate asked, lighting
up her cigarette and leaning against a white wall. Just a
few feet away from her was a sign reading No Smoking in
three languages.

"That since I've moved here I've felt almost as if I'm
acting or something. It's hard to describe."

"It's called impostor syndrome, sugar. We all get it
from time to time. You feel like you don't deserve to have
people's lives in your hands, that you shouldn't be the one
making the important decisions."

Holiday adjusted her purse. "It's not really that. I feel
like *other* people don't think I deserve to be where I am. I
want to tell everyone I meet about the years of work I've
put in."

"You're for real, honey. People will figure it out. Just
give them time to get it through their thick heads."

She barely heard Kate, transfixed instead by a silver-
haired man climbing out of a royal-blue Mercedes convertible in the doctors' lot. In his light linen suit and
wraparound sunglasses, he looked as if he wouldn't be out
of place walking into a Monte Carlo casino or a trendy
Hollywood hangout. There was something about him that
she couldn't place. She recognized him somehow, but
couldn't find a context in which to place him. He drew
nearer.

"It's a bitch being a woman in medicine. Not only that,
but law, government, any line of work that men think of
as their own private domain. All the old boys complaining
about welfare and entitlements won't own up to the fact
that they're the ones who have the biggest entitlement
attitude of anyone. Sometimes I . . . Holiday, are you
even listening to me?"

Kate stamped her cigarette out on the pavement and
blew out a final cloud of smoke. Holiday snapped out of
her reverie, about to apologize, when the man reached
them. He nodded at Kate.

"Afternoon, Bo," she said.

Bo? Holiday felt a wave of recognition and memory that disoriented her long enough for the man to make his way into the hospital. Then she gave chase, leaving Kate utterly befuddled.

"Bo Swenson?" Holiday called out. She heard Kate's footsteps following her. The man stopped and turned, taking off his sunglasses to reveal his striking blue eyes.

He gazed at Holiday for a moment, confused. Then a smile crossed his tanned features. "Holiday Powers!" he exclaimed in a Scandinavian accent. He stepped forward and took Holiday in a long embrace, kissing her once on each cheek.

"Bo knows Holiday?" Kate asked ironically.

"Yes, from long ago," Bo said. He stepped back, still smiling. "And Holiday knows our finest urologist?"

"We live in the same building. Where do you two know each other from?" Kate asked, bristling with gossipy curiosity.

From a lifetime ago. Holiday had been another person then, barely out of her teens and buffeted by her accelerated medical studies—in which she had enrolled despite her parents' protests. There was so little color to life then, it was a world painted entirely in washed-out grays: the sky, the muddy banks of the Charles River, the walls of the classrooms and the hospital.

She had been shy and awkward, virtually friendless save for a Swedish exchange student named Lars Swenson. They worked together to get through exams, and both excelled, their grades earning them passage into an advanced computer technology course for medical students. Lars then was both innocent and hard to know; Holiday was one of the few fellow students he spoke with.

In the last months before Lars returned home, they became lovers. He was her first: before Kyle, before anyone. Life became electrical, both trying to catch up on everything they had missed in life. They had a shared intensity, and both felt at odds with the world. Still, there was something about Lars that went beyond a drive for success. The word she used secretly to describe him was *haunted*.

Lars returned to Sweden, and Holiday eventually met Kyle. But after she and Kyle split, she met Lars every winter break—once in Mexico, once in Boston, another time in Italy. These once-yearly meetings felt strange, even forced, as they tried to rekindle a love very much tied to a specific time and place. Holiday had begun to come to terms with life, and the world, and Lars had not. If anything, he was changing for the worse, becoming bitter and withdrawn.

Lars finally broke off the relationship, walking out of their hotel in Rome one December without a word, never calling again. The sting of this hurt came alive again within Holiday now; she remembered her desolate loneliness and feeling of loss that season. She had never spoken to Lars again.

"We met in Boston," she told Kate, feeling guarded. "His son was a friend of mine. How . . . how is he now?"

Swenson nodded warmly. "Fine, fine. He still refuses to leave Sweden. He is currently practicing in Stockholm, but the King's Committee is due to rotate him elsewhere soon."

Bo's accent evoked many memories for Holiday, most of all of Lars's contempt for his father. Bo had decided in the late seventies to come to America, to escape the oppressive conditions and lack of financial rewards within the Swedish socialized medical system. Lars's mother demanded a divorce, and kept her only child with her in Stockholm. Father and son reconciled later, in a fashion, but Lars never recovered from his perceived abandonment, always painting his father as a money-hungry villain.

Holiday wanted to know more about Lars—how he truly was, what had happened to him since their last meeting—but she didn't ask.

"Well, kids, I've got to run," Kate said loudly. "I've got

a patient coming in for a consult, so I'll give you two a chance to catch up. See ya, Bo. Holiday, give me a call, sugar.''

Holiday waved good-bye to Kate and smiled guilelessly at Swenson. She saw so many changes in him—his deep tan, the fine gold chain around his neck, his gleaming, polished teeth—that sharply contrasted with the dowdy, traditional Scandinavian she remembered. *It's unbelievable, Bo Swenson's turned into a swinger.*

"Perhaps we should sit down," Swenson said. "We have so much to talk about."

Holiday stammered apologetically. "I'm sorry. I have to get back to work. I'm at Pacific University now."

"As chief of advanced technologies, yes, I know. It is very impressive." He nodded and smiled at a pair of men passing by in surgical scrubs.

"You knew already?"

"Yes, I read it in the hospital bulletin. I was very, very pleased for you. I thought about giving you a call, to see if you were interested in speaking with an old friend, but . . . *here we are!*" He laughed, perhaps too eagerly.

"You're still in general practice?"

"Indeed. My work has made me very comfortable." He paused, perhaps remembering, as Holiday now did, the fight he had had with his son when visiting Boston years ago. Toward the end of an excruciating drive back from a day trip to Maine, Lars denounced his father as a callous mercenary who had destroyed his family for greed.

Holiday felt pressed for time, though she wanted to savor the familiarity of Swenson's presence. He was a lot like Lars, not in his actions or appearance—though he had the same brilliant blue eyes. He had a physicality, a jittery intensity, that he shared with his son. "Give me a call at my office sometime, Bo."

"I will do just that," Swenson said, rocking on his heels. "But why wait? If you have no plans tonight, perhaps you will meet me at one of my favorite restaurants. You can tell me all about what has become of you since we met in Boston."

The formality of Bo's speech put Holiday off its meaning for a moment. He was a different man from the man she knew before, at least outwardly: outgoing, even charming. And he might become a friend. "Sure, Bo. Jot down the address and I'll meet you at eight."

"You're very kind to take the time," he said, producing a pad and pen from his jacket pocket. He wrote down an intersection and restaurant name, handing her the paper. "At eight, then."

"All right, here's the skinny," Pam said.

Holiday leaned over Pam's desk and whispered, "Who's that? I don't have any appointments." A young Asian man sat quietly in Holiday's office reception area, thumbing through a magazine.

"I'll get to him in a minute. First off, you have an eight o'clock senior faculty meeting tomorrow. Your big showdown with Jefferies."

Pam smiled slyly. She was obviously enjoying having a woman on staff willing to do battle with Kyle. *You can fight him if you want to; in fact be my guest. Take my place.*

"And at nine forty-five you're meeting with Sandy Stein, the head resident in your unit."

Holiday frowned ruefully. "They're going to expect me to start teaching soon, aren't they?" In six weeks Holiday's get-acquainted period would end; then she would assume daily duties with students. It was one of her favorite parts of working on a faculty.

Pam sensed Holiday's irony. "You love it," she said with mock dismissal. She looked across the room to the Asian man, whom she had studiously ignored while briefing Holiday.

"Mr. Hyata, Dr. Powers will see you now."

He rose and extended his hand, lugging a large black valise. "Mike Hyata, Mitsuyama Corporation."

Holiday turned to Pam for an explanation.

"Mr. Hyata has been waiting for an hour," Pam said pointedly.

"I'm so sorry, Mr. Hyata, did I forget about—"

Hyata smiled and took Holiday's elbow, leading her into her own office. "No problem. I didn't have an appointment," he said in a calm, modulated voice. "I don't mind waiting."

Holiday followed his lead, glancing back at Pam, who pulled an expression of mixed curiosity and confusion.

Seated behind her desk, Holiday was aghast at the small stack of phone messages that had accumulated while she was at the Bartholomew. "Mr. Hyata, I—"

"It's rude of me to keep interrupting, Dr. Powers, and rude to come by without an appointment." He remained standing. "I apologize for both, but I needed to reach you immediately. Mitsuyama has concerns about your research here in virtual reality and robotics."

Hyata opened his leather case and produced a black laptop computer that bore the Mitsuyama logo in shiny silver lettering.

Holiday remained silent, waiting for Hyata to explain. "You're not from Japan, are you, Mr. Hyata?" she said. His English was precise and unaccented, and he carried himself like a young, up-and-coming executive. His black double-breasted suit hung like a model's. It seemed that everyone she saw that day was better dressed than she.

"I'm Japanese, but I was born in Long Beach." He smiled disarmingly, and switched on the computer. It hummed quietly, the bright color screen coming to life.

"Let me check the charge on this thing, and then we'll get going," he said. "Tokyo headquarters needs to talk to you immediately."

Hyata paused and looked into Holiday's eyes. It was impossible to gauge his intentions, and he obviously expected her to wait to find out. A corporation such as Mitsuyama did nothing without a reason: Hyata was here for something important. For reasons she couldn't explain, Holiday felt an unpleasant foreboding.

Is he trying to intimidate me?

6

MIKE HYATA CROUCHED FUSSILY OVER THE COMPUTER. "This'll just take another minute," he said, tucking his tie between the buttons halfway down his shirt. "Sorry for all the mystery, but I got word from Tokyo around noon today. I've been working for Mitsuyama for four years, and it's the first time my orders have ever come direct." He smiled apologetically.

"What do you do for Mitsuyama, Mr. Hyata?" Holiday tried to keep her voice in check, pretending to look out at the gathering shadows of late afternoon. She checked her appearance in the window's reflection and raked her hand across her hair, trying to fluff it a bit; the polluted air of L.A., even stirred up by the fall winds, made her feel grimy and slightly unkempt.

"Call me Mike, please. All right, I've got this thing working." Hyata stood up and pulled his tie out of his shirt, straightening it. Without a trace of self-consciousness, he ran his hands through his silky black hair. "I'm a liaison officer. I coordinate project management between headquarters and the main American office. I do lot of international recruitment, and I work with organizations affiliated with Mitsuyama, getting them up to speed and reporting on their progress."

"And what is this all about? Am I supposed to be reporting on my progress, and whether I'm 'up to speed'?"

Holiday finally succeeded in maintaining eye contact with Hyata, who looked a little lost now that he had no gadget for a diversion. Though she hadn't meant to sound accusatory, she detected a patronizing chauvinism in his comment.

Hyata seemed to pick up her intimation immediately. He must have been well versed in all the forms of both

Japanese and American business and social chauvinism. He pulled a pen out of his pocket and began drumming nervously on Holiday's desk, choosing his words carefully before speaking.

"Sit down, Mike." She motioned to the empty chair before her.

"All right, Dr. Powers, let me tell you what I know before we call in." Hyata continued his annoying drumming. "I don't have any specifics on what this is going to be about. But I have some ideas."

Holiday stared at the pen for a moment, watching it tap away a small shard of veneer from the wooden desktop. Hyata suddenly realized what he was doing and stopped.

"The Mitsuyama Corporation has dedicated considerable resources over the last five years to virtual reality research in America, primarily in Boston and Los Angeles."

Holiday nodded rapidly, growing impatient with this preamble. *Tell me something I don't know.*

"A lot of the work in Boston, through the technical universities, has been very theoretical and without many immediate applications—except for architectural simulations and the like. The program at Boston General Hospital that you headed for the last three years yielded better results, though."

Holiday nodded again. Mitsuyama had provided critical funding on the virtual reality simulator for anatomical studies, which was now being used at a number of universities.

"But the work here at Pacific University is of more interest to Mitsuyama. The surgical simulator is impressive, but the real hot-ticket item is telepresence robotics. Mitsuyama is traditionally a consumer electronics company—stereos, cellular phones, TV equipment—but since the U.S. began putting pressure on these areas of trade, Mitsuyama has tried to diversify farther into medical technology. Telepresence is our hottest item."

Hyata told her nothing she didn't suspect already. The

funding she brought to Pacific University was earmarked
for telepresence technology. If she had stayed in Boston,
the money would have stayed with her, but she would
probably have been pressured to accelerate telepresence
research there as well. Gregory, with his advanced skills
and well-cultivated department, was a singular variable
that made the move to L.A. a better choice than staying
put.

"So here's the inside dirt," Hyata said, sitting forward
and staring at Holiday conspiratorially. "Whom have you
dealt with most of the time in Mitsuyama management?"

"Either Phil Jackson from your office, or Keiko Suda
from Tokyo," Holiday said. "As well as other representatives who came to the various labs for status reports and
planning meetings."

"Mitsuyama has kept you and your researchers on a
pretty loose leash," Hyata said matter-of-factly. Holiday
stiffened at his choice of words. "Jackson and Suda don't
make high-level policy decisions, they merely make reports. Like me." Hyata grinned with self-deprecation. "I
mean that as no insult. But I know you've never been to
Tokyo headquarters. You haven't seen the real corporate
power structure."

This condescension was growing unbearable. "I know
that Han Takamoto is the president, and that the board of
directors includes nine other individuals," she said. "You
should keep in mind that I don't work for this company."

"Point taken." Hyata leaned back. "But you should
know that Takamoto has been under fire for many recent
business decisions. Including his approval for funding
projects that fall under your supervision. He's the one
who wants to talk to you today."

"Under fire?" Holiday knew that they were moving
into the real substance of this visit. "In what sense?"

"Look, I don't agree with the critics. In my opinion this
is a standard power play, trying to get the old man out
and replace him with a different faction. It's corporate
politics."

"Fine, I can understand that," Holiday said. She couldn't keep her eyes off the computer, as if it might suddenly spring to life, making the video link without warning.

Hyata checked his watch. "Kyle Jefferies's commitment and attitude toward virtual reality research and telepresence was spotty and antagonistic, on a good day. Takamoto is fighting to maintain funding for your research because it fits in with his personal vision. My guess is he wants reassurances from you so that he can appear to be under control and to have made the wise decision."

Holiday sighed loudly. *That's it?* She had to give a big thumbs-up and generally convince a funding source that she was in control?

"So let me initiate the link," Hyata said, turning serious. "I'll rotate the screen to you when I get Takamoto."

"Do you need to plug that thing into a phone line?"

"No way. It's completely wireless."

Hyata swiveled the computer away from Holiday, dialing up an international connection. The modem within the machine beeped and hissed, and Hyata typed a few characters on the keyboard.

A woman's voice speaking Japanese rang out from the computer speaker. Hyata responded and there was a moment of silence. He kept his gaze fixed on the screen.

After a moment a gravelly voice emerged. Hyata bowed and spoke Japanese in deferential tones, giving extremely brief answers to what sounded like a series of questions. Finally Hyata stood up and turned the computer to face Holiday.

On the small screen was a Japanese man, perhaps sixty years old, seen from the chest up. She first noticed Takamoto's elegant black suit, then his hair, its thickness and luster belying the wrinkles around his eyes, which were dark and focused directly on her. His image was clear, without the breakups and distortions common to computer video links. Glancing down at the computer, she saw it bore no model number. It was experimental technology.

"Dr. Powers," he said in impeccable English. "I have known about you for some time. It is indeed a pleasure to finally speak to you."

Takamoto spoke with the casual intensity of the wealthy and powerful. Holiday willed herself to remain still. Fighting off an urge to bite her lip, she said, "Mr. Takamoto, the pleasure is mine."

Holiday searched her memory, trying to recall details from a Japanese business etiquette seminar she took a few years ago. Protocol required that she maintain a pleasant and unassertive demeanor, waiting for the older man to bring up the business behind the call.

"Dr. Powers, Michael Hyata called me while I was engaged in a meeting with the Mitsuyama board of directors. They are in the room with me and will monitor our conversation."

Holiday peered into the video display. Behind Takamoto she saw a wood-paneled room and a long table, at which sat several men in suits. Some of them wore headsets; they were probably receiving an instantaneous English-to-Japanese translation. One man in particular, who wore no headset, stared into the screen from beyond Takamoto's left shoulder. His hawklike eyes seemed to look into Holiday's.

"Mr. Takamoto, I send my regards to the board and thank them, as well as you, for your ongoing support of our research projects."

"Very good." Takamoto broke into a grandfatherly grin. "I would like to express my personal pleasure that you have taken a position at Pacific University. Dr. Jefferies's contributions will be missed, but we are pleased to see a familiar and competent face in his place."

Holiday thanked him. She quietly put her hands under her stockinged thighs in an effort to keep them from roaming. Hyata watched dispassionately from the corner sofa.

"And work is proceeding with the telepresence project? I'm sure you were impressed by the demonstration you saw this week."

Holiday smiled and nodded, confused.

"I talked to Epstein earlier today," Hyata whispered. "And told Takamoto about it."

"I was very impressed, sir. I invite you and any members of your board to come here for a demonstration. You will see that your funding and support have been put to good use."

Takamoto's features tightened slightly. "I'm sure that's so," he said neutrally. "If I may, I would like to address a question to you in your capacity as a surgeon."

"Certainly." A surge of electronic interference made the man's image waver within a band of static. "I have seen my personal physician for a series of recent discomforts." Takamoto's voice became easy and casual. "It is nothing to be overly concerned with: some discomfort in my stomach area, nausea, a slight . . . yellowing of my eyes."

"You mean jaundice?" Holiday leaned forward in her chair, but the video image wasn't clear enough to verify what he was saying. His eyes were couched in a fine film of pernicious static.

"Yes. Jaundice, that is the word. Dr. Mishima, my personal physician, ordered a test. My gallbladder contains a number of stones."

"You have cholecystitis," Holiday said cautiously. She squinted at Takamoto. He needed treatment right away.

"That is the word. Thank you for pronouncing it for me." He gave a self-deprecating smile. "Dr. Mishima recommends removing my gallbladder. Do you agree that this is an appropriate course of action?"

"I can't say without examining you myself."

"Please, venture an opinion."

"If your symptoms are as you have described them, there is a very good chance that you're cholecystic. Depending on your state of general health—"

"Other than this condition I am in perfect health." He spoke a tone louder, as if for the benefit of those in the room with him.

"Then you're probably healthy enough to undergo surgery. If I were treating you, I would perform a laparoscopic exploration, and if my suspicions were confirmed, I would remove your gallbladder with a laser." Takamoto stared blankly, his mind far away.

"If I were you, sir, I would pursue treatment before your case becomes more acute. With current technology the surgery can be quick, safe, and efficient."

Takamoto nodded rapidly as she talked, as if he already knew what she was going to say. *Then why ask?* "Medical technology is indeed amazing," he said, grinning beatifically.

Holiday could think of no response. She glanced at Hyata, whose attention was diverted by the diplomas on her office wall. Abruptly he stood and walked to one, inspecting it.

"In fact is it not the case that such laparoscopic—" Takamoto halted as he pronounced the word. "—surgeries can be performed using telepresence technology?"

Holiday cleared her throat, feeling her foreboding return. "That's right. The surgeon uses virtual reality equipment to control a robot at another site."

"If I understand correctly, the robot would work through a series of small incisions, and the surgeon would see and feel everything the robot did?" Takamoto glanced briefly over his shoulder at someone behind him. He whispered something and turned back to the screen.

"That's how it would work," Holiday said.

"So I could be the first man operated on by this robot. And you could be the first surgeon to operate on a patient who would lie under anesthetic on another continent."

His deep, calm voice contained only a hint of a query, as though his question had a predetermined answer. Hyata blanched with alarm.

"You could be, Mr. Takamoto." Holiday winced. "Of

course the technology hasn't been quite perfected. My advice is for you to have your surgery through conventional means. After all, I'm sure your doctor would be very upset with you for not following his orders."

"I see," Takamoto said. He stared intently from the screen; for an instant Holiday felt, strangely, as though the small device actually contained the executive, shrunken down to fit within.

"I do recommend that you explore your alternatives as soon as possible," she added.

Takamoto appeared not to hear her. "I am a bit fearful of doctors. I don't take well to the idea of being cut open and . . . interfered with."

"That's not uncommon," Holiday said quickly.

"I have taken the liberty of checking your reputation as a surgeon and have found it exemplary. I would be pleased and honored if you would consent to perform my surgery."

Holiday struggled to hide her emotions. Hyata sat astonished and mute on the sofa, shaking his head. He began to look through a stack of files in his briefcase.

"I . . . don't know if that's possible. Mister Takamoto, I would be honored to perform the surgery, but I—"

"Yesterday I sent a complete copy of my medical records to Michael Hyata. Have him give them to you."

Hyata tossed a stack of manila folders onto Holiday's desk, his expression worried and apologetic.

Takamoto continued, "I have been informed by my physician that the surgery can wait only two weeks. I believe we should schedule our 'appointment,' then." His smile vanished, replaced by a tight-lipped expression that Holiday instinctively knew was an entreaty.

Takamoto was giving her no opportunity to back out. A refusal would be tantamount to an admission that telepresence wasn't a viable property. It was easy to imagine that Mitsuyama might then pull future funding. The old executive, Holiday realized, was making the ultimate power gambit, using his own body as the stake, and she was merely caught in the middle.

"Mister Takamoto," she said. "I don't know that I have the authority to do what you're suggesting. There are approvals that have to be obtained, tests that have to be validated."

Takamoto gently shook his head. "My legal staff had informed me that there is no true precedent for what we are going to do. As is often the case, regulations have not caught up with technology. Our success in this endeavor will be a historic event."

Holiday picked up the stack of files. They were written in English and, she could tell at a glance, extended back several years. She felt as if she had lost the power of speech. *Two weeks to prepare for surgery six thousand miles away?*

"On behalf of myself and the Mitsuyama board of directors, I thank you for your cooperation and enthusiasm. We shall coordinate our staffs in the next days. Please inform me if you have need of any unforeseen financial assistance."

With this, Takamoto hit a switch on his computer: the image dissolved. In that fleeting last instant Holiday thought she saw a frailty and fear in the old man. The board member with piercing eyes behind him stared into the screen until it was blank.

"Oh, man," Hyata said, slouching back on the sofa. "I was worried this might happen."

Holiday walked to her coffeemaker. A black, sludgy residue coated the bottom of the pot. She poured one for herself and offered another to Hyata.

"God, no," he said. "I'd explode if I had any coffee."

She sipped the bitter, lukewarm liquid. "He looked worried," she said. "But there's no reason to be afraid. It *will* work. My technical people are the best. If they give the go-ahead, we'll do it."

The laptop computer's casing gave a brittle crackle as Hyata stuffed it into his case. "I don't know what the hell's going on," he said. "I heard rumors, but I didn't think anything of it. Takamoto must have been planning this since his initial diagnosis. The man does nothing on the spur of the moment."

Holiday felt calm and cool next to the obviously bewildered Hyata. "Come back here at about eleven tomorrow, Mike. I have some early meetings, then I'll clear my calendar."

"You're actually excited about this, aren't you?" Hyata said. His helplessness had shifted to dismay. "Fame and glory, right? Well, you'll get it. You can be sure that the media will have a field day with this."

"It's not that," Holiday said. Though it partly was.

She drained the last of the coffee. "Mike, how often do you have a chance to do something no one has ever done before?"

"I don't know, I don't think about things like that," he said quietly, gathering the last of his things. "I'll leave the files."

"Thanks."

Hyata buttoned his jacket and stood stiffly. "Tomorrow, then."

Holiday smiled at the young executive; his world was obviously shaken. Any shift in the status quo was a threat to him. It was impossible to explain that this represented to her everything she relished about medicine: the chance to go forward without a safety net, to create something that others would use to heal and to preserve life.

She suddenly remembered something taught to her by a karate instructor in her college days. "Remember, Mike, the Chinese character for *disaster* also means *opportunity*."

Hyata frowned. "I'm Japanese," he said, walking out the door without looking back.

Before Holiday left the office, she sat at her computer terminal. She logged on to the system with her password and selected Gregory Hampton's E-mail address from a long list of names. She typed quickly, remembering her date with Bo Swenson and wishing now that she could somehow cancel it without seeming rude.

YOU'RE NOT GOING TO BELIEVE THIS, BUT HERE IT
IS. I JUST SPOKE WITH HAN TAKAMOTO OF MITSUYAMA
ON A VIDEO LINK. (HE'S THE CEO, IN CASE YOU
WEREN'T AWARE). HE REQUESTED A HUMAN DEMO OF
TELEPRESENCE WITHIN 2 WEEKS—A GALLBLADDER
SURGERY. THE KICKER IS THAT THE PATIENT WILL BE
TAKAMOTO AND I WILL BE THE SURGEON. SUBTEXT:
FUNDING IS IN DANGER UNLESS WE DO IT. WHEN YOU
PICK YOUR MOUTH UP OFF THE FLOOR, COME TALK TO
ME RIGHT AWAY.

She hit the return key and sent the message. Gregory might react in any number of ways: by resigning, by going apoplectic, by relishing the challenge. She would have to infect others with her own enthusiasm—which would be difficult, now that she began to feel her own resolve, invulnerable a moment ago, fading as she looked at the cold text on the screen.

"Holiday? I'm going home early. I hope you don't mind."

Holiday wheeled her chair around to face the door. Pam stood there, a pen tucked behind her ear.

"Going home already?" Holiday said sarcastically, checking the wall clock. "It's only six!"

Pam stared at her for a moment. Holiday guiltily realized she hadn't yet acknowledged Pam's routine of staying until nearly seven.

"I have a doctor's appointment for my son. He has to get some tests for some headaches he's been having."

"I hope it's not serious." Holiday felt a second wave of guilt; she didn't even know that Pam had a son. There were pictures on Pam's desk, but Holiday hadn't bothered to look at them.

"The doctor says it's probably just lactose intolerance,"

Pam said calmly. "Anyway I'll be in bright and early to-morrow."

"I have meetings all morning, so why don't you come in an hour or two late—and catch up on some sleep? Things are going to be pretty busy around here the next few days."

Pam narrowed her eyes wearily. "It has to do with Hyata from Mitsuyama, doesn't it?" Holiday nodded. "I knew it. Anyone who sits and waits that long must have something important to say."

"We're doing a full demonstration of surgical robotics in two weeks. With the Mitsuyama CEO as the patient."

Pam sighed and shook her head. "Now I've heard it all. It took fourteen years here, but it finally happened."

Holiday smiled at the warmth she heard in Pam's voice. "It'll all work out. It's going to be exciting."

"Just keep telling yourself that," Pam said. "Good night."

When Pam was gone, Holiday turned to her computer screen; the E-mail program was still loaded. She selected Phil Hermoza's address, copied the message she sent to Gregory, and added:

I KNOW YOU'LL HAVE SOME INTERESTING THINGS TO
SAY ABOUT THIS, PHIL. KEEP THINKING ABOUT THE
PUBLICITY FOR THE DEPARTMENT. ALSO I WANTED TO
TELL YOU ABOUT SOMETHING. AFTER MY FIRST DAY
HERE I RECEIVED AN ANONYMOUS THREATENING PHONE
CALL AT HOME. THE PERSON KNEW THINGS ABOUT ME
THAT LED ME TO BELIEVE THE CALL WAS MEANT TO
INTIMIDATE ME ABOUT MOVING TO L.A. AND TAKING
THIS JOB. I KNOW THERE'S NOTHING YOU CAN DO, BUT
IT MAKES ME FEEL BETTER TO TELL YOU ABOUT IT.
I'LL SEE YOU AT THE MEETING TOMORROW MORNING.

She sent the message on its way, questioning the wisdom of telling Hermoza about the phone call. He might think her paranoid, or expecting persecution. Men were allowed rational worries—women were labeled hysterics.

If it had been anyone but Phil, she would have kept it to herself, but he was protective and would want to know. And he would be willing, if it became necessary, to help her. Though she didn't do it anymore—it didn't seem appropriate now—she used to call him "Papa Phil" for good reason.

7

THE CALIFORNIA GARDENS RESTAURANT LIVED UP TO ITS NAME. Palm trees and tall flowering bushes obscured the dimensions of the spotless white stucco building. Handsome young uniformed men waited to whisk visitors' cars to a hidden parking lot. When Holiday stepped inside, she was momentarily stunned by a profusion of light shining from recessed lamps.

As her eyes adjusted, she saw a long, crowded bar populated by a flock of young, attractive men and women—all of whom looked as if they had just returned from a particularly restful and satisfying vacation in the Caribbean. Deep tans and exquisite clothes were the norm; Holiday stood for a moment in the entryway, feeling very much out of her element.

A young couple in black—black jeans, cowboy boots, and matching silk shirts—bustled by Holiday, pressing her against the wall. She straightened her skirt (which seemed embarrassingly dowdy) and heard her name called out in a familiar accent.

"Holiday Powers! I must admit, I entertained the sad notion that I was being stood up."

Bo Swenson walked swiftly to her and took her arm. He spared a quick glance at the couple in black, who had found friends at the bar.

"People are so eager to come here that they will run over you to get inside," he said with a laugh.

"So I see," Holiday said. She pulled her arm away from his grasp and self-consciously ran her hand through her hair.

Swenson led her to the dining room, which held tables and long black leather booths running along all four walls. The decor was stark black and white, with thick patches of greenery installed atop plaster stands. A low din of voices filled the room with an indistinct murmur that was quickly absorbed and diffused in the high stucco ceiling.

"Did you have any trouble finding your way?" Swenson asked solicitously as they were led to their table by a young hostess who could easily have stepped from the pages of *Vogue.*

"Not at all. I just followed the flow of beautiful people."

Swenson chuckled. "I know the glitz is a bit extreme here. You must think I've changed very much from the man you met years ago."

A dark-haired young man with high cheekbones appeared to fill their water glasses. "Maybe," she said, then paused. "Well, definitely."

"It's a matter of appearances," Swenson said, rotating his glass and watching the water swirl inside. "Perhaps it's a matter of a foreigner becoming a bit too enthusiastic about enjoying the gold-lined streets of America."

"I'm not criticizing you," Holiday said quickly. "You look very good. Life here obviously agrees with you."

Swenson warmed visibly to the compliment. "You're very kind. In any case I didn't bring you here to talk about myself. I want to know about you. Tell me everything."

Even his mannerisms had changed; he had a sort of glib humor about him. Still, she felt a warmth and sincerity she remembered from meeting him in Boston. Somehow this guilelessness beneath his polished exterior made him endearing.

"There's a lot to tell," she said. "It's been a long time."

A waiter arrived and stood silently. Holiday couldn't be sure, but she thought she recognized him from a car commercial. He smiled at Swenson with familiarity.

"Good evening, Raymond," Swenson said. "This is my old friend, Dr. Holiday Powers."

Raymond gave her a theatrical stare. "Hello, Doctor," he said.

"This evening I would like the beef tenderloin with red pepper coulis. Holiday, what might you like?"

Realizing that she hadn't even looked at the menu, Holiday peeled back its padded cover. "I'm not sure," she said. "I'm sorry. Something light, I guess."

"Dr. Powers will have the fresh halibut with lime butter and fresh herbs, Raymond. And I will leave the wine selection to you, if you can find something that goes tolerably well with both," Swenson said. Raymond left without writing down the order.

"Does it bother you that I ordered for you?" Swenson asked. "I forget sometimes. What I grew up thinking of as good manners can now be taken for boorish chauvinism."

"No, no. Not at all. What you ordered sounds delicious."

Holiday took a drink of water and looked around the room. The diners had the polish and easy manner of the wealthy, but they were light-years from the New England aristocracy she had grown up with. They gleamed with youth and vigor, like Bo.

Swenson opened his napkin and laid it on his lap. "It's so good to see you, Holiday. Though I only met you briefly, I've always thought of you as my American niece of sorts. Tell me all about yourself."

"Well, I completed the accelerated M.D. program soon after we met. I stayed with the university, practicing as a general surgeon at Boston General and maintaining my academic affiliation."

Swenson nodded. "I knew you would become a talented surgeon. Lars spoke with awe of your talent and endurance for work."

She wasn't comfortable talking about herself this way, but Swenson seemed genuinely interested. "Well, in a few years I took on increased administrative duties. I studied laparoscopy and computer applications in school, and when these areas became advanced enough to warrant their own departments, I was there to head them. I guess it was a matter of being in the right place at the right time."

He waved his hand. "Hardly. Don't undervalue your own talents."

"Well, thank you. I was offered the job here a few months ago, partly because the dean of medicine is an old instructor of mine."

Raymond slipped up to their table with a bottle of pale red wine. He poured a small glass, which Swenson sniffed, nodding his approval.

"To hear you talk about yourself," Swenson said, "It's as if you wish to give the impression that things have happened accidentally for you. I know that's not the case. To be in your position at your age, your talents must be considerable."

Holiday looked into her wineglass. "I appreciate that," she said. She was unsure how to react, and realized how little she knew him.

"So tell me about yourself, Bo," she said.

He smiled ruefully. "I have a successful practice. I enjoy this lifestyle." He glanced around the room. "Though it is expensive. I was married for two years in the late 1980s, to a younger woman."

Holiday leaned forward. "What happened?"

"We divorced," he said plainly. "We discovered quickly we didn't have much in common. She is a dance critic for the newspaper here."

A recently healed pain hid near the surface of his words. Holiday drank her wine, waiting for him to speak again.

"But," his voice rang out, a little too loud, "that is that. And as for this lifestyle, I am afraid that I will soon have to kiss it good-bye."

Raymond appeared with their food. Though it hadn't occurred to her before, Holiday was ravenous, and the halibut smelled delicious. She dug into the rice. "What do you mean?"

"These HMOs are going to mean the end of the medical profession as we know it. I am strangulated with rules and regulations, and my patient base is being taken away by the bureaucracy. Patients are now told where to go, instead of choosing by merit or loyalty. Physicians are paid less money for the same services. My bank statement dwindles every month."

The savory tang of mint combined with fresh fish distracted Holiday for a moment. She realized that Swenson was waiting for a response.

"I've heard this a lot recently. Most of my income is drawn from a salary, so it doesn't affect me much. Still, I think some kind of reorganization is necessary. The American system can't go on without some kind of change."

"Yes, of course," Swenson said morosely. "But consider my perspective. I practiced for years in the Swedish socialized medical system, and saw firsthand how degraded the physicians felt. We were automatons, technicians, without the stimulus of financial reward."

Holiday nodded neutrally. She knew many doctors who agreed with this viewpoint, and in some ways she concurred. Bo's mention of Sweden, though, distracted her. She wondered how to bring up Lars.

"And the final irony," he said, oblivious to Holiday's drifting attention, "is that I came to America fifteen years ago, underwent the hardships of going through residency—even though I was a full M.D. in Sweden—just so that I could have the opportunity to enjoy the benefits of the American system.

"Now"—he raised his glass in a mock toast—"that system has followed me across the Atlantic."

"Everyone in the health care field is concerned with where things are headed," Holiday said cautiously. "Including me. But we have to be responsible for a bigger picture than our own wallets."

"You are right of course. But it can be more than that. I have a colleague, also from Sweden, who came here after I did. He had an excellent surgical practice. Then a managed-care group took over his entire patient base and gave it to other doctors who were willing to work for less money."

"What happened to him?"

"He took a job at half pay in rural Virginia, moved his wife and children there. Without an HMO contract he had no work in Los Angeles. He found fool's gold in America."

Swenson gripped the table with both hands. "I'm sorry. I'm being rude. I didn't invite you here to listen to my complaints."

"It's fine," Holiday said. His tirade had obviously gestated within him for some time. "And dinner is delicious."

"So," Swenson said, pushing his food from side to side on his plate. "I'm sure you are curious about Lars."

"Of course I am." She paused. "I saw him last in Italy five years ago. We haven't spoken since then."

"That might be for the best." Raymond approached their table, his eyes averted. Swenson waved him away.

"What do you mean?"

"Lars has had difficulty in recent years. It's very sad, but then, he no longer tells me much about his life."

Holiday took a long drink of wine. "You see," Swenson said, "his mother died five years ago."

In the moment she heard these words, Holiday saw an image in her mind: herself and Lars walking the banks of the Charles River, watching the sailboats drifting lazily across the waters in the spring chill. She was young then, younger than her years. The shell she constructed in her childhood—a shield of indifference that kept everyone at bay but her younger brother—had barely begun to weaken.

She lived constantly with an inner desperation then, rejecting the life her parents had cultivated for her and finding nothing to replace it with. When she and Lars had worked together as friends for several months, they began to open up to each other.

Once they started, they couldn't stop. They stayed up late at night divulging their inner secrets like teenagers. She kept one secret from Lars, one day by the Charles: the night before had been the first time she had made love. They sat together on a bench, holding hands, huddled together for warmth.

"My mother," he said in a voice more accented than his father's, "she is everything to me. When Father decided to move to America, she resisted. They fought bitterly for a time. And then he left."

She had heard the story before, several times. She ran her hand through his long blond hair. "I know."

Smiling, he said, "You remind me of her, Holiday. Very beautiful, very caring. Too nice to live in a world of bad people."

Tears glistened in his eyes and he wiped them away. "I cannot forgive my father," he said in a husky voice. "He left us all alone. That is why when he calls me, I hurry to get off the phone. I have to respect him, but sometimes I wish he were dead."

The last time she saw him, in Rome, they had been together two days, sightseeing and spending time together in their room. One afternoon, after taking a call at their hotel, he packed and left. She thought at the time it was another woman, that he may even have married without telling her. Five years had passed since that December.

Holiday realized her breathing had become labored. Bo Swenson stared at her with grievous calm. "How did she die?" she asked.

"She killed herself by hanging. Lars was very upset."

"No," Holiday said, a catch in her throat. "Five years ago . . . what was the date?"

"She killed herself on December thirteenth," Swenson said. "Santa Lucia Day. It had been of great significance to her and Lars, ever since she was a child. He was apparently out of the country at the time."

If Swenson knew that Lars had been with Holiday then, he showed no sign. That had been why Lars left so abruptly—his mother was dead by her own hand. She thought of him packing in that tiny hotel room, his expression vacant.

"Anita was my wife," Swenson continued. "Not any longer, but we once loved each other. It was very difficult. Lars refused to speak to me at the funeral ceremonies in Stockholm."

"I'm so sorry, Bo." Holiday reached across the table and squeezed his hand. To her surprise he pulled it away.

"Would you like more wine?" he asked. Holiday put her hand over her empty glass and shook her head.

"There is something else you should know," he said, looking into her eyes with a deadened expression. "Two years ago—three years to the day after his mother's death—Lars tried to kill himself with a narcotic overdose."

Holiday's first reaction was one of intense discomfort. She felt the distance between her younger and her current self, and between herself and the stranger that Lars Swenson had become in the last five years. That he had attempted suicide sounded surreal, something she might read about in a book.

Bo turned completely ashen. "He survived, thank God. But there was some damage to his nerves."

"What do you mean?"

"The injection went into the antecubial fossa. It clotted blood vessels and blocked off nerves. There was infection and paralysis. He survived, but his hand is deformed and paralyzed. He was a practicing surgeon at the time, but now of course that is impossible."

She was speechless. The loss of an arm or a hand was a surgeon's worst nightmare. She tried to imagine the depths of Lars's loss, the grief that drove him to try to destroy himself. For five years she had felt abandoned by her first lover. Now she wondered if there was anything she could have done to save him.

"Lars is now practicing as a general physician."

"How is he? Have you talked to him lately?"

A low air of classical music suddenly sounded from hidden speakers. The restaurant lights were dimmed a fraction, bringing a faint nimbus of gray shadow to the edges of objects. Bo looked around as if perplexed that this had happened.

"Not for several months. I am trying to bring us together, to talk him into moving here to be with me. I think"—he paused—"he needs care. The death of his mother affected him terribly."

Unanswered questions lay unvoiced. How did Lars function with his injury, and what kept him from trying again to kill himself? What had Bo endured, living alone in America while this drama unfolded within his abandoned family?

They sat in uncomfortable silence until the check came, which Bo insisted on paying. She felt as if part of her had withered and died away. Her old passion for Lars, the insistent ache—she had allowed it to fade, shoved it into some hidden emotional compartment. He had insisted on living in Sweden, he had ignored her, he had . . . this spiral of thoughts was unbearable.

The sky outside shone with a crimson radiance as they waited for the valets to retrieve their cars. Holiday stared straight ahead, trying to imagine the man she had known, full of intensity and idealism, determined at any cost not to become his father. Everything after that was couched in a gossamer film of sensuality without context, their yearly meetings an inadequate substitute for the life they had once hoped to share.

Swenson took her hand and squeezed it. "Thank you for coming to dinner with me. I can't tell you how much it means to talk with someone who knew Lars."

"I'm sorry for what you've gone through," she said. She realized she could easily judge him—he was responsible for so much damage, for the wreckage of his family.

He kissed her cheek. "The next time we meet will be happier. If you like, you pick the place."

Holiday climbed into her car. She pulled out into the

flow of traffic, pausing for a moment and looking into the mirror: he still stood there, alone and waiting, staring off into space as if in no hurry for anything ever to happen again.

1:30 A.M.

"You are positive that our conversation is secure?" Moshiro Tamo stared hard into the camera mounted over his computer. A mistake now would be the end for him, and for those who worked under him. Did these young men, with their swagger and their Western attitudes, understand the severity of what they were about to attempt?

"Sir, I've taken the strongest security measures available to us."

"I will hope that is enough," Tamo said. Ironically, he was never comfortable with technology. The computer in front of him in his darkened office connected him with men in two far-off continents—one was his employee, the other an unknown factor. It seemed strange and unnatural, and made him ill at ease. He understood that, even at this early stage of events, he would be forced to put trust in men who were perhaps unworthy.

"Mr. Tamo, are you ready to speak to our operative?"

"Go ahead."

Tamo stared into the screen. It was always advantageous to meet the eyes of the other person first, in any transaction. He knew his own gaze to be direct and withering.

Then came the disappointment. The third man appeared in the small open box in one corner of his computer display, above Tamo's employee. He was shrouded in darkness.

"Why can't I see you, sir?" Tamo asked. "It is unfortunate that we cannot meet in person, but this is unfair. You can see me."

"Never mind," the man said. "We can still talk."

This was not encouraging. "Please give us some privacy," Tamo said to his young employee. "But keep the connection open. I will want to speak with you in a few moments."

"Yes, sir," the young man said, and his image disappeared.

"You have received the password and protocol codes?" Tamo asked. "You know what is expected next."

"I have them here," the man said neutrally. "I am ready to act."

"You should know that we obtained them at a great deal of trouble and expense."

"That doesn't matter to me," the man said.

Tamo stared into the screen, trying to make out a face amid the dark forms ringed in static. He saw only blue eyes, which were piercing, offputting. "But you are ready?" he whispered.

"I have put the plan in motion."

"And you have spoken to no one?" Tamo asked. "You are aware of the penalties you would face?"

"Of course I am," the man said venomously. "What you want will happen, and then I'll take my reward. That's all I care about."

Of course, Tamo thought. A man motivated by need, by loss. He was perfect: manipulatable, petty, a man of deep sorrow.

"We will speak after you have succeeded," Tamo said. "Until then, you know how to contact my employees."

The man switched off without saying good-bye. It was just as well. Tamo typed a command into his keyboard, and his employee reappeared. "You have found a good one," Moshiro Tamo said. "He cares about nothing."

8

IN HER DREAM SHE SPRINTED THROUGH A LANDSCAPE OF SHAPES and people with hidden faces. A ringing noise filled her ears. "I belong here," she said, without knowing why.

She awoke in her bed, holding the phone. It rang again. The sky was dark outside the window. She turned to the luminous clock dial; it was just after five in the morning.

"Hello," she said weakly, startled by the tremor in her own voice. With her free hand she vigorously rubbed her eyes, confirming to herself that she was truly awake.

"Dr. Powers?" A young man's voice, full of doubt and worry.

"Yes, this is she."

"This is Andrew Jacoby at Pacific University Hospital. I'm the on-duty emergency room resident right now. We just got a severe trauma case in here."

"I see," Holiday said, shaking her head to fend off the tempting urge to fall asleep again.

"Dr. Powers, are you still there?"

She cleared her throat and got up. "Yes, I'm sorry. What do you need?"

"You're on call this evening, Dr. Powers. Or, I guess I should say, this morning."

She hadn't even realized that she was on call for emergency cases. The notification probably sat on her desk amid other messages ignored in the wake of Mike Hyata's visit.

"All right." She slipped out of her sweat pants and T-shirt, searching in a suitcase for something to put on. "Tell me about the case. Please."

"It's a woman, thirty-six. She was hit by a car on her early-morning jog. Initial examination suggests a ruptured liver. Paracentesis was positive, and a quick liver-spleen scan confirmed. We've got her on two pints of blood, but someone has to get in here quickly."

"I'll be right over," Holiday said, pulling on a pair of slacks and searching for a blouse. "Get the patient to surgery and I'll meet you there in twenty minutes."

She hung up the phone and switched on the overhead light, catching her reflection in the mirror. Her hair was wildly twisted into chaotic auburn waves and curls. For a moment she remembered a dark, frigid plain in her dreams and a figure off in the distance.

There was no time to think about it. Fetching her purse, she called the valet to retrieve her car and quickly caught an elevator downstairs. On the way out she passed the security booth, which was empty, silent except for the crackle of an unattended radio left on a desk behind an open glass partition. She glanced inside and saw a row of security monitors flickering through assorted camera shots of the building's exterior and interior.

Within fifteen minutes Holiday had parked her car and strode through the quiet hospital halls to the surgeons' lounge. Don Angstrom and Jake Sammler, a pair of surgeons she had met earlier in the week, sat staring at an early-morning news program on the big-screen TV. They wore standard powder-blue surgical scrubs and white tissue caps.

"Good morning, guys," she said, relieved to find fresh coffee on the snack counter.

Angstrom looked up and nodded, quickly returning his attention to a feature story on L.A. gangs. Sammler, a short man with a dark beard and thick glasses, joined Holiday at the coffeepot.

"Why are you here so early?" he asked, raising a well-muscled arm that belied his slight stature. "It's only five-thirty."

"I'm on call and got a ruptured liver in the ER," Holiday said. She reached down into the freezer to fetch some ice to cool her steaming coffee. "How about you?"

Sammler ran a hand through his beard and smiled

warmly. "Got a six A.M. knee job. I don't usually like to keep farmer's hours, but I had to schedule it quick." He leaned forward and whispered into Holiday's ear. "It's a professional tennis player. You'd know him if I told you who he was. He wants to get his knee scoped out so that he can get back on the tour."

Angstrom, a ruddy-faced, bulky man, stood stiffly and yawned. "Jake with his big secrets," he said with fond sarcasm. "I know who you're talking about—he'd be better off taking up something he's got a future in. Like garbage collection."

"Hey!" Sammler said. "He got to the fourth round at the Australian Open. This guy serves to you, you don't even see it." He made the sound of a tennis ball hitting a padded surface. "Right in the mat, and you're saying, 'Come on, serve the damn thing already.'"

Holiday drank her coffee while the men argued. She had a good impression of Sammler; at lunch he had talked about his kids and his practice with an earnest good nature. Angstrom, however, carried himself with a surly aura of aggression that reminded her of the piggish frat boys at college. It was just as well to her that he remained on the other side of the room.

A phone rang. Angstrom gazed lazily at it and, though it was sitting at his side, let it ring three times before answering. He listened for a moment, nodded, and hung up without a word.

"Powers, they're ready for you in OR Three," he said laconically, returning to his television viewing.

After quickly changing in the nurses' locker room, donning scrubs, a cap, and mask, then washing in at a stainless-steel sink in the corridor, Holiday entered the operating room. The lights within were dimmed save for a bright beam focused on the patient's naked abdomen. The familiar hiss of the anesthesiologist's respirator and the steady beeps of body-function monitors filled the room.

Holiday extended her arms for the head nurse, who

quickly wrapped her in a surgical gown and snapped rubber gloves onto her hands. A second nurse was positioned before an instrument tray, absorbed in counting and cataloguing the various devices.

"I'm Phyllis James, Dr. Powers," the nurse said. "We met in the hall a couple of days ago, but you probably don't remember."

"I'll let you know after we're out of masks and gowns," Holiday said, only able to see the nurse's eyes.

"Right. This is Ben Franks," she said, pointing to the anesthesiologist at the patient's head. Franks, a lanky man in glasses, looked up from his log books and nodded.

The OR door opened for a tall young man with striking green eyes. She instantly remembered him.

"Scott Goldman," she said. "You were the first resident I met here; you were on the VR simulator."

Goldman cleared his throat nervously, extending his hands for Nurse James to pull a robe over him. "Dr. Powers. Sorry I'm late. I hope I didn't keep you waiting."

Holiday sensed the younger man's nervousness. "Don't worry about it. Let's get started—you're here to assist, right?"

"Of course," Goldman replied apologetically, moving to his station, nearly stumbling over the operating table.

Holiday asked Phyllis for a scalpel and made the initial incision. "How's the pressure, Ben?" she asked, glancing at the anesthesiologist.

"One hundred over seventy-six, Dr. Powers. And holding."

"Fine. Second blade, Phyllis." Holiday used the instrument to split skin and subcutaneous fat. The midline fascia of the linea alba fell to either side of the incision, and she entered the abdominal cavity.

Goldman leaned forward. "Jacoby told me the paracentesis was very bloody. It's probably going to be a bad one."

"We'll pull her through," Holiday said. "Just pay attention to the job at hand." She heard Goldman draw a sharp breath. The chaotic nature of trauma work, she remembered from her own residency, was often daunting for those accustomed to the controlled setting of workaday surgery. She remembered his failure on the virtual reality simulator and reminded herself to be kind and supportive—he had already been sufficiently badgered by Kyle.

Her incision revealed a startling gush of bright red blood mixed with clotted material. "Three pints of blood in the right upper quadrant," she said.

Holiday scooped the clots into a large steel sterile pan that Phyllis James held near the patient. "Four more units. She's lost a lot of blood. Type and cross her for four more units, stat."

"Got it," Ben Franks answered, wheeling his chair behind his ether screen. "I've got four on hand and three more coming."

"This liver is completely shattered," Holiday announced. She began to pick out large pieces of liver tissue with her hands and forceps. "Scott, help me get these pieces," she said, pointing with the forceps.

She watched him work with approval. "Good. As you can see, we basically have to debride the organ and remove the damaged sections. Fortunately for the patient, the liver will regenerate a good deal."

Goldman replaced the forceps on the steel tray beside him.

"All right: suction, vascular clamps. Scott, let's get some retraction in here," Holiday ordered. She watched Goldman and was pleased with his work. From what she had seen in the simulator, she recalled, he seemed to have good hands and a cool head. Unlike many medical professors, she didn't think an instructor had to make residents nervous wrecks to test their mettle.

Phyllis smoothly passed the vascular clamps: large steel instruments that fit snugly over the portal vein and hepatic artery running in and out of the liver. This slowed the patient's internal bleeding enough for Phyllis to insert a suction tube to clear away some of the blood.

Holiday sighed when the visibility improved. "We've got some damage in the portal vein and the hepatic artery, at least a branch of it. We'll have to resect at least half the liver and close the holes in the blood vessels. Let's get a little more retraction, Scott."

Goldman struggled and twisted to push aside the flesh and organs impinging on the damaged area. He called harshly for a wipe; the younger nurse reached up with a towel and wiped off his profusely sweating forehead.

"Hang in there, Scott," Holiday said soothingly. "Do you know if they caught the driver?"

He looked up, his eyes open wide. "Pardon?"

"The driver. The guy who hit this poor woman?"

"Oh, the driver." He sighed deeply, as if angry with himself. "LAPD was in here to try to get a statement from her, but she was out of it by then. Apparently they don't have any witnesses."

"A hit and run," the younger nurse said ruefully. Holiday glanced at her. "I'm Isabel Perez, Dr. Powers," she said.

"Hit and run," Franks said in a deep, sonorous voice, shaking his head. "There are some real bastards out there."

Holiday had isolated the hepatic artery and the portal vein. "Hemaclips, please, Isabel," she said, extending her hand. She applied the metal clips to the bleeding vessels around the portal vein, then doubly tied off the tissue with 2-0 silk ties.

"Pressure, Ben?" Holiday asked.

"One hundred over seventy-six, Doctor. Holding steady."

"Good. Scott, retract a little more and tell me what you see," she said. "Tell me what you would do if this were your case."

The respirator and life-signs monitors continued their steady accompaniment of hisses and beeps. Goldman quietly peered into the patient's abdomen for a long, awkward moment.

"I think the hepatic artery is fine now," he said in a steady voice. "But the portal vein is going to need intensive repair. It's about as bad as I've ever seen."

Holiday was pleased with his response. "Right." She reached into the cavity with forceps and removed more fragments of liver and pieces of dead tissue that had been exposed by the further retraction. "You're going to repair the portal vein. What are you going to use?"

Goldman answered immediately. "5-0 vascular silk sutures."

Holiday extended her hand. "Phyllis, the sutures, please." She received the silk sutures on tiny, delicate needles; Phyllis held the silk taut in the air.

"Steady, Phyllis," Holiday said, beginning to place a neat, continuous row of stitches in the portal vein while Goldman took over on the vascular clamp.

Slowly the vein came together. "I know my line of questioning might seem simplistic for your level of learning, Scott," Holiday said. It was her habit to keep talking while performing the most delicate aspects of surgery; somehow the rhythm of conversation kept her relaxed and her hand steady. "But you'll find that you have to approach each situation as if it were unique. Try to always see surgery with fresh eyes. Think of every procedure as an opportunity to learn something."

She didn't notice Goldman's reaction, so intent was her focus on the fragile row of sutures. Finally she tied a last knot in the gossamery silk and removed the clamp that had held together the torn vein.

The surgical team all craned their necks for a look inside the abdominal cavity. A palpable sense of relaxation spread through them when they saw that there was no bleeding: the vein held together.

"Great," Goldman said. "Great work, Dr. Powers."

Holiday glanced up at him, unsure for a moment whether this was sincere praise or mere ass-kissing of the sort she knew Kyle encouraged. For the moment it wasn't important.

"Thanks," she said in a neutral tone. "But we're not finished."

Over the next half hour Holiday explored farther, finding two holes in the small intestine, which she sutured shut, and a nick in the pancreas. When she was done, she left the job of closing the patient's skin to Goldman and sat in a corner filling out postoperative reports.

"We'll need some heavy drains," Holiday said to Phyllis. "That pancreatic leak is a little touchy, but she's going to pull through."

"You did a great job, Doctor," Phyllis said. "It's going to be a pleasure to work with you." Her eyes wrinkled into a smile. She stepped back and, to Holiday's dismay, began to applaud quietly.

The rest of the operating team joined in: Ben Franks, Isabel Perez, and Scott Goldman, who left off tying up a stitch for the moment. Holiday took a small, self-deprecating bow. She was embarrassed as hell but, she realized, a familiar feeling had settled over her. She was home.

She burst into the meeting room to the unwelcome sound of Kyle Jefferies rattling harshly about pre-op protocols. Around an ovoid circular table, replete with platters of Danish and coffeepots, were a group of men and women dressed in suits. Holiday, wishing she hadn't had to rush out that morning in a wrinkled blouse and plain skirt, tried to move inconspicuously to the only open seat.

Jefferies stopped talking the moment she entered, effectively focusing all attention upon her late entrance.

"Sorry," she said, picking up an agenda. "I had an emergency trauma case. I was on call this morning."

Phil Hermoza, dressed in a typically slipshod version of business wear—a short-sleeved yellow dress shirt bulging at the buttons topped by a thick ebony tie that hung down only to his midsection—glanced absently at her. "It's fine, Powers. We hadn't done anything worth a damn, any-

way." Jefferies stared intently at Holiday as if offended
by her interruption.

"I guess I'm the host here, so let me make sure you
know everyone's name," Hermoza continued, ripping off
a strip of strawberry pastry. "You know Jonathan Landry,
head of University Hospital Administration."

Landry, a silver-haired man with a gaunt face, nodded
in acknowledgment. She had met him during her interviews a month ago, and he had struck Holiday as utterly
unimaginative and officious. They had haggled on the
phone for two days prior to her departure from Boston
over how long she could keep her rental car.

"Jonathan," she said, realizing that she was unconsciously mimicking his grim, tight-lipped smile. "Good to
see you."

Hermoza bit into the pastry. Landry, seated next to
him, sat back in his chair a little as if afraid of being hit by
flying food fragments. "And Sandra Jeanette, head of
nursing," Hermoza said. "She was on vacation last week,
so I don't think you've had the pleasure."

Jeanette, a heavyset black woman in a blue suit that
begged to be described as sensible, gave Holiday a bright
smile. "Very good to finally meet you," she said in a melodious voice. "If you're free for lunch soon, I'd like to
give you some background on my department."

"I'd like that very much," Holiday said, sensing that
she had found an ally.

"And Xavier Schulze, whom you also know." Hermoza
waved a hand vaguely at the other side of the table, an
offhand gesture that he didn't seem to realize seemed dis-
missive.

Holiday had also met Schulze during her interview process; he was the chairman of the corporation that ran the
Bartholomew, and also oversaw West Coast Health's Los
Angeles division. Part of her job now was to maintain
links between his bureaucracy and the university surgical
department, a duty shared by Hermoza and Jefferies.
Though he was perhaps in his early fifties, Schulze af-

fected the look of a younger corporate player, sporting a blue double-breasted suit with crimson silk tie and suspenders. He peered at Holiday coldly behind tortoiseshell glasses.

During these introductions Kyle maintained a petulant silence. He obviously was waiting to resume speaking. "If we're all together now," he blurted, "I want to finish. I can't stay here all morning."

"This is your first administrative meeting, Holiday, so we'll forgive you if you show any enthusiasm," Hermoza said dryly. "We generally like to keep things on the grim side."

Jefferies glanced angrily at him, then resumed his diatribe. "All right. As I said, my intention was to set a standard policy regarding laparoscopic surgeries, specifically pre-op policies including an upper GI series and a standardized series of lab tests. If you'll turn to page four of today's agenda, you'll see the proposal written up. We all need to sign off on it to make it policy."

Holiday turned to page four and saw the proposal. She cleared her throat and raised her hand, instantly regretting it; the gesture made her seem unsure of herself. She was reminded that, years ago, when she was just preparing to enter her internship, Hermoza was her teacher and Kyle was a seasoned resident.

"I don't know if all this is necessary. Do we need to go to the bother of setting policy like this?"

"The whole point of setting this policy is to cover all the bases before we perform these surgeries. We've finally got the HMOs to consider laparoscopic technology normal and routine." Kyle glanced once briefly at Schulze. His tone bordered on condescension, as if he were running through rudimentary material for a slow student who was holding up the class.

"But most of these tests are standard." Holiday found herself staring at Sandra Jeanette as she spoke. "If the surgery is going to affect gastric function, the gastroenterologist is called in. These lab workups are standard as well. It's all just common sense."

"Look," Jefferies said. "We want to have a policy in place so that new staff have guidelines."

"But in some cases these tests would be unnecessary," Holiday said. "And not all lab tests are part of this proposal. This looks like a personal preference set into policy." She understood that Jefferies's reference to "new staff" was a way of setting her apart from the group, and a way of intimating that she brought different, perhaps unsound surgical practices with her from Boston.

Jefferies sat back in his chair and scratched his chin. As in his youth, he had a perpetual shadow of beard stubble. "Maybe you have another suggestion," he said, his voice tinny and harsh.

"Well, an upper GI series is an integral part of vagotomy preparation, but do we need it for a simple appendectomy? And this part about patient selection. I mean, there's always a degree of judgment and subjectivity."

"So you like the idea, but you want to argue over the specifics," Jefferies said, pouring cream into his coffee. He seemed to be making a display of his calm detachment.

"I don't want to argue at all, Dr. Jefferies," she said. They were playing the same cat-and-mouse game that typified the last days of their relationship, and it angered her. "I just won't be willing to sign this until we make some changes."

"It's nitpicking," Hermoza said, staring at his folded hands. "But it's necessary. If we're going to set a policy like this, we have to make sure it's something we can all live with."

"Additionally," Holiday said, examining Kyle's proposal, "as chief of advanced surgical technologies, I need to see this kind of thing before we bring it to the general board."

Jefferies unbuttoned his collar and loosened his tie. "I see. Keep in mind, Dr. Powers, that chief of advanced surgical technologies was a post that I held when I drew up this proposal." He pursed his lips. "It's a field of surgery that I'm also very familiar with."

And taught you a lot about, he seemed to be saying. "Of course, Kyle." He stared at the table, obviously uncomfortable with her familiarity. "I just feel that this should be settled within the Department of Surgery before we bring it to a full vote here."

"I don't know about that," Xavier Schulze said. "It's important for me to know what kind of patient selection and pre-op protocols you're going to implement. If we're going to send patients to your doctors, we need to know they're going to receive the best care possible."

Holiday knew a little about Schulze: "Wouldn't know a scalpel from a butter knife," Hermoza said of the administrator after she first met him. He was a businessman, interested in the financial bottom line; his technical knowledge of medicine was negligible. She sensed that Schulze had nonetheless found a kind of kindred spirit in Jefferies. They glanced at each other occasionally, as if seeking reinforcement for their positions.

"Point taken, Xavier," Hermoza said, looking contemptuously at another strawberry Danish, as if offended by its temptation. "Kyle, Holiday, get together on this and work out a solution. Bring it to next week's meeting."

Jefferies frowned. "If Dr. Powers would type up her requests, I'll incorporate them into the proposal. It's not my department anymore, but as a department head I expect to have some input. Anyway," he continued in a quieter voice, "I brought it up. I'll finish the homework."

"Thank you, Dr. Jefferies," Holiday said quietly. She somehow felt that she had embarrassed Kyle. This was his old pattern: create a conflict, then back down and claim injury from the defeat.

"And kids, work together. *Play nice.*" Hermoza held his hands out in a magnanimous gesture and broke into a wide, utterly sarcastic grin. "After all, it's only work, boys and girls."

He picked up the agenda and flipped through its pages.
"A lot of this shit." He coughed. "Pardon my language. A
lot of this is self-explanatory. Does anyone have any business they want to discuss while we're here?"

Holiday saw that Phil was staring at her. For a moment
her memory flashed on the E-mail message she had sent
him the day before. Did he expect her to bring up the
telephone harassment in this forum? What would be the
point? Then she realized that he must have been thinking
about the Takamoto surgery. They hadn't had a chance to
discuss it yet.

"Actually, I do," Xavier Schulze broke in. He opened
his briefcase and looked through its contents, exposing a
circular bald spot on the crown of his head. Despite herself, Holiday felt a shiver of visceral repugnance for the
man.

Schulze pulled out a folder. "This is in regard to Dr.
Powers's appointment to the Pacific University Hospital
surgical staff," he said. "As part of the package offered to
Dr. Powers, she was promised access to both cash-paying
and HMO patients from the Bartholomew, as part of the
Bart–Pac U liaison."

He smoothly reeled off his phrases in a rehearsed manner. Holiday stared at Schulze, though he seemed unwill-
ing to acknowledge that she was even in the room. Kyle
Jefferies folded his arms and listened intently.

"In my opinion Dr. Hermoza was a bit presumptuous
in extending this offer. We are happy to have access to a
surgeon of Dr. Powers's ability and experience, but it's
not as easy as waving a magic wand to integrate her into
our staff pool."

Phil Hermoza stared at an invisible fixed point on the
wall, running his fingers through his mustache.

"So let me get down to it. As far as access to cash-
paying patients goes, we'll have to take it as it comes.
We're fortunate to have a patient demographic that af-
fords such opportunities; many hospitals don't."

"We certainly don't here," Jefferies said. His flat tone

betrayed nothing; he could have been defending Schulze's drifting argument or making a counterpoint.

"So it follows that our own staff are *extremely* reluctant to allow these patients to drift over to your hospital. Your surgical department has some good people in specialties we can't offer, so our deal works out much of the time."

"Isn't one of those specialties noninvasive surgeries?" Holiday asked. "I only want to take on patients who fall within that range. And I know you're already sending patients over here for advanced laparoscopic procedures."

"Right," Schulze said with finality. "But those cases have until now gone to Dr. Jefferies, for the most part."

Schulze let his words hang in the air. This *had* to have been rehearsed; Kyle was making a play for keeping a patient base that no longer fell directly under his administrative authority. This was about money, she thought, then corrected herself. Kyle never cared about money, not enough to fight for it. This was about power.

"Look, that's neither here nor there. Dr. Jefferies doesn't have a God-given right to any patients. No one does," Hermoza said. He crossed his thick fingers into a steeple.

"I don't think I expressed any such sentiment," Schulze said. He began looking through the file. "In terms of the HMO, let me put it simply: It's full. We can't make a place for Dr. Powers at the moment."

"What do you mean 'it's full'?" Holiday said, instantly regretting the shrillness she heard in her own voice. Sandra Jeanette stared at her with raised eyebrows. "I met with you when I first came out here, and you said there wouldn't be any trouble."

"If you would let me finish, Dr. Powers, I could explain what I mean." Schulze took off his glasses and rubbed his eyes. "A verbal commitment isn't the same as a written contract, and you know that."

Holiday suddenly realized that none of this was serious. There was no way they could bar a surgical department head from access to patients; this was a little boy's game, a way of serving notice that she wasn't going to just come in and take over the playhouse.

"We will find a way to get you into West Coast Health as quickly as possible," Schulze said. He put his glasses on the table and looked at her through red-rimmed eyes. "But it might take a little time. And as for the cash-paying patients, I—"

"Xavier, I get sick enough of hearing doctors talk about cash-paying patients like they were some goddamned pot of gold under the rainbow," Hermoza said, staring intently at Schulze. "Without having to listen to it in an administrative meeting."

"Phil, there's no need to make this personal."

"Fuck that, Xavier. Noninvasive surgery is Dr. Powers's department now, and all such cases will go through her office for determining surgical assignments. That takes care of that, doesn't it?"

"I assumed there would be some kind of probationary period," Schulze said, drawing in his cheeks.

"You were wrong. Send them all through her and leave it at that. If you want to discuss the basis of our agreement for sharing patients, we can do that. Make an appointment with my secretary."

Schulze replaced his glasses and sat silently, obviously struggling to contain his irritation.

"And as for the HMO, that's bullshit and you know it. Fill out the papers and get her on. Do I need to remind you that we've been talking about eventually bringing all our patients under West Coast Health's umbrella? What do you think this little display says for the flexibility of your operation?"

Jonathan Landry, completely silent until now, broke in tentatively. "Let's not get inflammatory here. I'm sure Xavier isn't going to be difficult about this."

"Same old Phil," Schulze said, smiling sardonically. "Yelling everyone down to get what you want."

"No, Xavier, this is the new Phil." Hermoza grinned

devilishly. "You notice I haven't pounded the table or busted any heads. I'm turning into an old pussycat, so take advantage of it. Be reasonable.

"Sorry about my language, Sandra, everyone," he added, taking a deep breath. He stared coldly at Jefferies. "But I'll tell you, I'm really fucking tired of all these politics."

Kyle smiled, his eyes blank. "Oh, come on, Phil, you love it."

Hermoza looked up at the ceiling, then back at his former protégé. "Jefferies, you asshole," he said, then exploded with hearty, affectionate laughter.

"I have something I need to discuss," Holiday said. She thought about bringing up Takamoto's surgery, but decided to wait until she had talked to Hermoza. Instead she remembered a case just sent to her. "I have a patient who needs a laparoscopic Nissen. She was told by a West Coast Health representative that the surgery was unnecessary."

The Nissen procedure was still relatively new and radical—the patient's stomach was literally wrapped around the esophagus to prevent acid reflux. Holiday had performed the procedure laparoscopically—through small incisions—several dozen times in Boston, a number that put her near the front of her field.

"How bad is the patient?" Schulze asked suspiciously.

"She's in a lot of discomfort. She's been to the emergency room three times in the last year."

Phil glanced at Schulze. "Is she on omeprozol?" he asked Holiday.

"Twenty milligrams, once a day for nearly two years. You know the studies—there's a cancer risk. If not from the medication, then from the acid burning the esophagus. This woman needs surgery."

"It's an expensive procedure—" Schulze began.

"But necessary," Holiday interrupted.

Schulze sighed and glanced at Phil. "Fine. I don't want

to start a war here. You can have your expensive, exotic surgery. But understand we go on a case-by-case basis."

Holiday thanked Schulze, feeling she had won a minor victory. The remaining agenda moved quickly—Sandra Jeanette's concerns about time allotments for nurses splitting their time between Pacific University and the Bartholomew, Jonathan Landry's criticism of the timeliness of chart filing in the Department of Surgery (with an ironic comment that senior faculty were among the worst offenders, earning a bored sigh from Phil Hermoza)—and the meeting broke up with muted good-byes. Kyle and Xavier Schulze stayed behind, conferring silently at the far end of the room.

Hermoza motioned for Holiday on the way out. "Come on," he said. "I'll walk you to your office."

In contrast to the static stuffiness of the conference room, the daily life of the hospital crackled with energy: nurses and orderlies moved swiftly past Holiday and Phil, and as they passed through the wing, Hermoza bumped through two separate groups of faculty-led rounds, with residents in tow.

"Ready to start teaching?" Hermoza asked.

"Very," Holiday said, taking long strides to keep up with him. "I finally got into the OR this morning. It reminded me why I got into this line of work in the first place."

Hermoza stopped before the elevators, his finger nearly covering the circular plastic "up" button. "I heard about that hit-and-run. Sounded nasty."

"It went well," Holiday said. "I had a good resident assisting."

On the crowded elevator Hermoza spoke in a loud voice as if they were completely alone. "Don't worry about Schulze, by the way. He's just a bureaucratic asshole. You've seen his kind before. They're like cockroaches."

Stepping off the elevator, Hermoza turned to her. "Tell me about this business with Mitsuyama. You agreed to

perform telepresence surgery on Han Takamoto? It's nice
of you to let me know."

Holiday wasn't sure how to take this. Hermoza had the
authority to veto the surgery. She hadn't asked for his
approval, and now she realized she shouldn't have taken
his support as a given. "It's a matter of funding, Phil."

"What about ownership of intellectual property?" he
asked.

"The same as before. When a full prototype is developed, they pay Pac U for patent rights."

He frowned, adjusting his tie. "So you're positive
Takamoto might yank funding if you don't go through
with this?"

"It's motivated by politics on their end, but we're
ready. It's simply a matter of moving our schedule
ahead."

His features darkened and he leaned back against the
wall to let a male orderly pushing an empty wheelchair
pass. The orderly wore headphones blaring music and was
blissfully oblivious of his surroundings. Phil started to say
something to him, but he stopped himself. "Doing things
for other people's reasons gets you in trouble, Powers.
I'm sure you know that as well as I do."

"I can think of three reasons to do it, Phil: first, the
technology is solid and ready, and I'm dying to see it in
motion; two, we'll establish ourselves on the ground floor
of virtual reality surgery. We'll be in a position to dictate
its future, and how it's developed and sold."

"That's only two."

"And it'll be fun as hell."

He laughed. "Fair enough. I won't deprive you of that.
But one thing." He folded his arms. "My ass is going to
be on the line as well as yours. If this thing fucks up, I
. . . I don't even want to think about it. The chancellor
will put our heads on spikes outside the fucking gates of
this place. You haven't been around here long enough to
know what a bastard he can be, and you don't want to
find out."

Holiday smiled at his hyperbole but quickly realized that he was completely serious.

"I want reports every step of the way," he said. "And I want to be involved when it goes down. Understand?"

She did: Phil, in his own way, was maneuvering for position and a share of the credit and publicity.

"Now, about these calls. You might want to get the police to put a bug on your phone. Has it happened again?"

"A few hang-ups." She paused. "Look, Phil, there's nothing you can do about it. I just wanted you to know."

Hermoza scuffed his feet on the floor. His black rubber-soled shoes left skid marks on the white tile. "Powers, I don't know what kind of son-of-a-bitch would hassle you like this, but if it's anyone at this hospital, I will personally beat the shit out of him."

Again she felt the force of his protectiveness, his male bluster. He was like a force of nature seeking an outlet for his fury. She sensed, as she had in years past, that he sought out conflicts in which he could exert this restless energy.

"Keep me posted on telepresence," he said. "You should know, my first instinct was to say you're out of your mind on this. But you sold me on it."

She watched him turn the corner, his hands clenched at his sides like a boxer heading for a collision with his opponent.

Pam sat at her computer terminal with a look of vague dissatisfaction. "Gregory Hampton called while you were out. I told him you'd get back to him as soon as possible."

She handed Holiday a paper slip with Gregory's phone extension. "I'd say he sounded weird, but it wouldn't do him justice. Out of his mind is more like it."

Holiday looked at the clock. "You came in at the regular time this morning, didn't you?"

Pam sighed. "I know, you told me to come in late. I wasn't really comfortable with that."

"What do you mean?" As they spoke, a young man with longish dirty blond hair wearing a white lab jacket strode into the room.

"Let's just say that I want us to get to know each other for a while, then we can talk about favors."

This declaration was so direct and blunt that it shocked Holiday. Pam obviously felt Holiday had shown too much caprice in her willingness to play loose with Pam's hours. Many doctors showed excess largesse to their support staff one moment, then made unreasonable demands on them the next. Pam had evidently lived it.

"Fair enough," Holiday said. "I'll trust your judgment. Just remember that the offer's open. As far as I'm concerned, you have a few hours' off-the-clock time coming to you."

Pam nodded, and turned to the young man, who stood watching their interaction with undisguised interest. "This is your resident, Sandy Stein. He's here for his appointment."

Holiday took him into her office, leaving the door open. She motioned for him to sit.

"First of all, Sandy, I'm glad to meet you. I hope I'll be a good supervisor, but for the next two weeks I'm going to be a lousy one. I have to oversee a project in the computer labs that's going to demand all my attention."

Stein's face was etched with premature sun-wrinkles; he had a bit of a surfer look about him. He probably was only five, maybe six, years younger than her.

He looked at her with shy appraisal. "I'm glad to meet *you*," he said. "When I heard you were coming on and that I'd be reporting to you instead of Jefferies, I was pleased. To say the least."

"I've been hearing a lot of that," Holiday said, not wishing to add more. "Look, why don't you drop off the transcripts and performance files on your group sometime soon? I'll need an idea what everyone is about."

"Very good," Stein said, jotting a note in the margins of his notebook. As head resident, Stein would have the best academic record among his colleagues, Holiday knew. She had served in the same capacity at Boston General.

"I wanted to tell you about one thing," Stein said.

A beam of sunlight broke through the dark morning clouds outside. The morning was already slipping away. "It's Dr. Jefferies," Stein said in a low voice, casting an eye over his shoulder as if half expecting Kyle to be there listening. "I know all about his history and his skill. I'd be the first to admit that I was excited as hell when I first found out I'd be working under him."

Holiday sat through this preamble impassively. Stein obviously knew he was going out on a limb.

"And he's harsh, demanding, unfair sometimes. Fine, whatever. But the last couple days he's been ripping into me every chance he gets." Stein's eyes widened, as if he were implying secret knowledge of some exotic conspiracy. "It all started when they posted my transfer to your supervision.

"This morning, just because I hooked some EKG leads on backward, he said he was going to see to it that I never finish the program. Over that!" All youthful flippancy was gone from his demeanor. "He can't do that, can he? I mean, I don't need any enemies here. I've worked too hard to go through this crap for nothing."

Holiday tried to think of a way to assuage Stein's anxiety. This was ridiculous—Kyle was turning people into basket cases just to attack her however he could.

"Sandy," she said, trying to sound at once stern and soothing. "There is no possibility that your place in this program is in any jeopardy as long as your overall work is up to par."

Stein nodded eagerly. "That's only fair, isn't it?"

"Right. And you should know that Dr. Jefferies is simply using you to get at me, and it's going to stop. In the meantime just cooperate with him when you have to, and *don't worry*."

The head resident seemed immensely relieved.

"Don't worry, huh? You're pretty calm for someone

who just ordered an entire tech unit to push their schedule ahead six months."

Holiday looked up, startled, and saw Gregory Hampton leaning in her doorway. She was relieved to see that he regarded her with a mixture of amusement and an eager, inclusive respect. She had him on her side.

"You're with me, then?" she said. Stein jerked back in his chair, perplexed when he saw Gregory.

"Sorry to interrupt, man," Gregory said to Stein. He turned to Holiday. "You're completely crazy. And of course I'm with you."

Holiday stood up and extended a hand to Stein. "Remember what I said, Sandy. Just stay focused on your work."

She smiled at Gregory. "Now, if you'll excuse us, Mr. Hampton and I have to get down to some serious work."

December

```
**MAPHEX DOCUMENT DECODER RUNNING**
```

FROM: 92448T@MC.COM
TO: MT GROUP
120296

NOTE PROTOCOL REGARDING ELECTRONIC MESSAGES:
ACCOUNT NUMBER CHANGING EVERY TWO HOURS FOR
ACCESS TO RESTRICTED INFORMATION. USE NUMBER-
GENERATOR PROGRAM TWO TO FIND CODES FOR FURTHER
MESSAGES.

AS YOU KNOW, WE HAVE NOW PASSED BEYOND ANY
POSSIBILITY OF RETREAT. THROUGH NORTH AMERICAN
CONTACTS WE HAVE OBTAINED CODES AND PROTOCOLS FOR
FULL ACCESS. OUR OPERATIVES HAVE BEEN DETERMINED
TRUSTWORTHY AND HAVE BEEN GIVEN FULL
INSTRUCTIONS. MISDIRECTION GOALS HAVE ALSO BEEN
PUT IN PLACE. OUR LIKELIHOOD OF DISCOVERY IS
MINIMAL.

OUR TASK WILL BE TO MOVE QUICKLY FOLLOWING
CULMINATION OF STAGE ONE. AT THAT TIME, ALL
SECTOR MEMBERS WILL RECEIVE INSTRUCTIONS.

AS ALWAYS, ANY ACT TO JEOPARDIZE OUR GROUP
OBJECTIVES WILL BE MET WITH SWIFT AND IMMEDIATE
TERMINATION.

```
        **MAPHEX DOCUMENT DECODER QUIT**
              **FILE DELETED**
    **DISK SCAN RUN—92448T@MC.COM NOT FOUND**
              **SIGN OFF**
```

9

GREGORY HAMPTON LEANED BACK IN HIS CHAIR AND CROSSED his feet on the desk. Patchy stubble covered his face, his eyes were ringed with fatigue, and his red Stanford sweatshirt and black jeans were limp and wrinkled—but his expression was one of complete triumph.

"So, everyone's gone for the day. And we did it. We're ready."

It was seven o'clock at night. Mike Hyata had just departed with his team of inspectors and technical assistants from Mitsuyama. Gregory and Holiday now stood alone in the computer labs before a polished, tested, and ready-to-use telepresence system. It was a moment that seemed almost unreal now that it had arrived.

Holiday popped the lid off a diet soda and undid her top blouse button, relishing Gregory's contagious sense of relief. "We're ready, but we haven't done it yet. I really could use a good night's sleep."

He folded his hands on his belly: a stout man's gesture, though he was well toned and lean. "Are you going to use my little speech with the TV people?"

"If I get a chance. They'll probably just take footage and run five seconds of it on the news. It's not like we're a top story."

Gregory chuckled deeply. "They'll be all over it. We're going to get more publicity than this place has had in years."

It had been two weeks since they started work preparing for the telepresence demonstration on Han Takamoto. The work had been hard and rushed, and ensuring total safety meant round-the-clock work and fourteen-hour shifts—even on Thanksgiving—for her and Gregory.

First were the tests coordinated between the Pacific University staff and their counterparts at Mitsuyama. It took three days to hone the fiberoptic link through preexisting cables running across the ocean floor. Then Holiday performed in-lab surgeries on test animals. This stage was exhausting and painstaking—Holiday performed laparoscopic examinations on two dozen pigs in six days, each time growing more and more confident that the system would work perfectly.

In that time Gregory relaxed enough to accept Holiday as an equal in his own world. They gained a familiarity that would have taken months to develop, if ever. She began to think of him in a different way. He cared more about his work than anything else, that much she knew for certain, but there was an easy humor about him, and a sensitivity and sophistication that she didn't expect. He often reflexively retreated behind an emotional shell, but she wanted to get inside that barrier, to learn as much about him as she could.

Her attraction was growing, she could admit it to herself. The timing couldn't have been stranger. Kyle was a constant reminder of her past, and Bo had brought Lars's specter back to her mind. Gregory was different from either of them. He burned with intensity, as they did, but Kyle and Lars had both been aflame with something else, something hurt and injured. Gregory emanated strength and solidity.

She stared at him for a moment, the words almost reaching her lips: *Can I trust myself enough to have these feelings?*

"Hey, what's the matter? You're spacing out." Gregory pushed against the desk and rolled his chair to a video display monitor. "Come on, indulge me. *If* you get a chance to talk about the technology to the media tomorrow, and *if* you decide to use my genius all-purpose public-relations speech, what's the central idea?"

Holiday joined him at the processing station, a small cluster of white plastic-shelled computer units linked by a jumble of cables. Her worries and attraction for Gregory disappeared, as though someone else had felt them. She was about to take the life of a billionaire into her hands the next morning. That thought brought everything into focus.

"The central idea is that this system is like a crowded room."

He smiled and stroked his stubble. "Very good, Doctor Powers. Please continue," he said in a burlesque Viennese accent, like Doctor Freud probing for hidden secrets.

"The 'system' as such exists as an abstract reality. In truth, it's the sum of its parts and inhabits no real physical space. You have the hard disk"—she pointed to a unit humming nearby—"which stores much of the relevant information the computer uses to put the pieces together. Here is the main display, a screen and a keyboard, which is the human being's way of communicating with the system."

"Let's get to the sexy stuff," Gregory said.

Holiday punched him lightly on the arm. "Okay. The surgeon works at the operator console, which consists of two gloves, a headset, and a workstation with a multipurpose plastic surgical instrument suspended in a ready position. The surgeon receives input from the computer, which shows the visual image as seen by the off-site robot, as well as tactile pressure transmitted from sensors built into the robot."

Gregory took Holiday's soda from her and had a sip. "Diet," he said, frowning. Then, with little-boy innocence, "Don't let me interrupt."

"This," she said, pointing to a Mitsuyama computer unit hooked up by multicolored cables to a thick black box, "is the output device, which relays my motions to the robot, which then duplicates them. It also receives visual and tactile information from the robot itself."

"And what is the magnificent instrument that brings it all together?" Gregory smiled, staring into her eyes with obvious pleasure. To him, she realized, this speech was akin to a list of his own most appealing personal qualities.

"The central processing unit," she said with ceremony. "The CPU does nothing else but pass on information from place to place in the system. It's the schoolmaster and the translator all rolled into one. So, in a sense, this system is like a crowded room at a party. Except that everyone waits his turn to speak, and then only one at a time."

"Of course they speak so quickly that they get their message across in millionths of a second," Gregory said.

"Right. My surgical operating console takes information from my actions and goes to the CPU. There it shouts out: 'Hey, listen, I have something to say.' The CPU, being very polite, listens carefully and then sends the information to a memory space, where it is picked up by the output device and sent to our robot in Japan."

"Which receives it and sends it back in a tenth of a second."

"A tenth of a second," she repeated. "So, do I have it down?"

Gregory mused for a moment, his expression darkening. "Yeah, great," he finally said. "You know, the delay time really has me concerned about this operation."

"What are you talking about?" she asked. His manner had changed. He looked almost disdainfully at his equipment.

"I've had you performing simulation tests with a one-eighth-second lag time between your actions and your seeing them duplicated by the robot through the goggles."

"And the pigs were very grateful that I was able to apply surgical staples without harming them," Holiday said, smiling.

"I'll bet they were. The reason I was having you work with so much delay—which didn't seem to present any problem for you—wasn't because it takes my system that long to process information. It's because that information won't be traveling twenty feet like it did here. It'll be traveling from L.A. to Tokyo."

Why was he so concerned? An irrational case of cold feet? Their tests had been absolutely exhaustive, and even with a severe time limitation, they had brought the system up to a standard that any doctor or scientist would have to consider completely safe.

"But the data will be going through fiberoptic wire," she said. "Which means the information will be traveling at the speed of light."

"I just wish we could make light go faster. It goes a hundred and eighty-six thousand miles per second, and it's about ten thousand miles from here to Japan and back. Light takes about one-twentieth of a second to travel that distance."

Holiday looked at the clock: it was almost eight. Gregory's train of thought had begun to sound more and more irrational. "Well, that's fine," she said. "We can't do anything to make light move faster."

"Yes, but those wires aren't going to run only ten thousand miles. I haven't seen the precise route they're using to run that cable, and I wish to hell I would have asked. It's not going to go in a straight line—there are too many trenches on the ocean floor. For all I know, the cables run all the way up to Alaska and around the coast of Siberia. We could add another five or ten thousand miles to the total estimate."

Gregory folded his arms, obviously angry at himself for this eleventh-hour apprehension.

"Gregory, listen," she said. "Even if the delay runs up to a half a second, we'll be fine. I'll notice the difference, but my contribution to this surgery will involve making an incision here and there and pulling the gallbladder out through the laparoscopic trocars. The real delicate stuff will be done by the assisting surgeon in Japan."

"Yeah, and you were smart to set it up that way." Gregory stood up and pulled on his worn denim jacket. "Because I think I fucked up. Those damned Mitsuyama technicians never brought it up, either.''

Holiday tossed the near-empty soda can—which Gregory had left perilously close to the main computer terminal—into a recycling bin. "Don't worry," she said. "This system is brilliant. We're making history tomorrow. You're acting as if you were getting married tomorrow.''

Gregory turned, adjusting his jacket cuffs. "Bite your tongue, young lady. That'll be the day that I die.''

What was that all about?

His tone softened, and he hooked his arm in Holiday's a little too quickly, as if he realized how oddly he was acting.

"I know we're up early tomorrow, but let me take you to Venice Beach for a quick burrito. I'm buying. It's my way of thanking you for putting up with my ass all week.''

She thought of her quiet, empty apartment. "You're on.''

They drove in separate cars to Venice. Holiday, following Gregory's directions, found herself in the long alley corridor of the former Venice Speedway, and steered herself into a parking lot that charged six dollars a space. She waited for Gregory to arrive; he had at the last minute returned to his office to pick up his beeper.

This was the third straight evening they had gone out to eat together after a long day in the labs. Each successive night their spirits grew higher as the surgery grew nearer and their successes in animal tests and safeguard trials became routine. And at the end of each evening they had left their cars with valets and walked together into the high-rise, picking up their mail and lingering in the lobby before taking separate elevators to their own apartments.

And each night, after she turned on the lights, looked through her mail, made herself a cup of tea, and turned on the television, her phone had rung. Whoever was on the line always hung up.

She spotted a pay phone and decided to check her messages. Locking the car door, she remembered that the rental car's return was three days past due. She wondered if Jonathan Landry would make her pay for the late charges.

The answering machine emitted a string of annoying beeps after Holiday entered her remote access code. She waited for the tape to rewind and heard a signal indicating that she had two messages.

"This is Kate. Up late at the labs again, I see, with the mad scientist. At least he has a cute butt. Give me a call tomorrow night and let me know how everything went. If you're not *busy,* nudge nudge, wink wink, we can have some dinner or something. Take care. Bye."

Holiday rolled her eyes. If she stretched the phone cord to its limit, she could see between a pair of buildings the gentle Pacific waves crashing on the shore under pale moonlight. It was magnificent.

"Bo Swenson calling for Holiday Powers. I hope that you are well and that I didn't upset you with my troubles. I fear I may have—I've called three times without a response. If you wish, I'd enjoy taking you to dinner again. Good-bye."

She hung up, Bo's words barely registering. The rhythmic wash of the ocean lulled her into a momentary sense of relaxation, almost a trance. The darkness of the quiet parking lot enveloped her like a shaded room.

She felt someone grab her shoulders from behind.

At once Holiday spun and clenched her fists. She cried out and stepped back, nearly tripping on a concrete parking divider. Gregory stood before her, frozen.

"Jesus, Holiday, I am so sorry. I should have known that would scare you. Oh, man, I'm such a spastic."

"No, it's all right, it's just that I was . . . no, it's not all right. What the hell do you think you're doing?"

A burly Latino man in a Dodgers baseball cap stepped warily out of the parking-lot booth. Holiday waved to signal that she was fine; the man leaned against the booth, unconvinced.

"I was just playing around, acting like a kid. I'm really

sorry." Gregory extended his hand. "Come on, let me buy you that burrito."

Winter darkness had descended over the Venice Beach boardwalk. A row of shops, stands, and restaurants lined the promenade, facing benches and landscaped knolls that gave way to white sand descending in a gentle slope to the sea. Holiday felt overdressed in her business suit, silk blouse, and heels—everyone else, including Gregory, was dressed in casual, bumming-around clothes.

"Me and my friends used to come here every weekend in the summer when we were kids," Gregory said. They walked slowly, breathing the cool, salty air. "We'd come down here and act rowdy, pick up girls. But we never really got in any trouble, not like today. It seems like everyone's packing a gun these days."

Holiday felt calm and secure in his presence. Gregory, unlike her, seemed closer to the energy and willfulness of youth. She tried to recall ever feeling young, unfettered, perhaps even reckless, and realized that she never had. Gregory somehow made her feel closer to whatever glimmer of that freedom still lived within her.

"You never told me about your childhood," she said. A small group of bicyclists sped by on a concrete path. "I know you grew up around here."

Gregory began buttoning his denim jacket. "Yeah, I grew up in a black suburb. My family still lives there. It's not the 'hood, you know, just a regular middle-class neighborhood. I went to Stanford on scholarships and stayed until they kicked me out."

"Until you received your doctorate in computer engineering at the age of twenty-seven," she corrected.

Gregory smiled. He had nice teeth. "Hey, Doctor, I've got an image to uphold. Young, black, and gifted."

"An iconoclast, a firebrand. Takes shit from nobody," Holiday said, warmly mocking his tone.

They reached the Mexican restaurant, actually a counter jutting from an old brick building's facade. They ordered burritos and sodas, Holiday following Gregory's lead, and took their bags of food to an empty bench under a streetlamp facing the ocean.

Gregory dug into his food with fervor. "So, Doctor," he said, washing down a huge bite with a long slug of soda. "You haven't told me too much about yourself, either."

"I'm from a suburb of Boston."

"Not a poor suburb, I'll bet."

She started to take offense, but he attacked his food anew as if there was no significance to his comment. Anyway he was right.

"No, not a poor one. I grew up with country clubs, servants, the whole package. I got away from it all as soon as I could."

Gregory regarded her with mild skepticism. "Sounds all right to me. But I guess you'd have all the Buffys and Chads to contend with."

"It wasn't just that. I . . . I knew that I wouldn't be able to find myself there." She paused. "I know that sounds corny, but it's true. There was a whole life mapped out for me. All I had to do was make the right choices. When I got into medicine, it was the first time I found something that was completely mine."

"You've done well with it." He handed her an extra napkin. "Here. These things are sloppy."

"Thanks." They sat in silence for a moment, watching a dog running in circles in the distant sand, barking happily. A young woman followed in jogging shorts with long, flowing red hair, running gracefully over the small, compacted dunes.

Finally Gregory broke the silence. "Well, I could tell from the way you talked that you were from back East. And I could tell by the way you acted that you hadn't exactly gone hungry your whole life."

Holiday stopped eating for a moment. Her worst vision of herself was that she might become, without knowing it, a younger version of her mother, moving through life with the hauteur and selfish ease of one who knew nothing about want or worry—or about having to fend for herself in the world.

"Hey, don't look like that. I didn't mean you act like a snob or anything. It just seems like you know you'll always have a place, no matter what. That's not a bad thing."

"I guess you're right. I've tried to forget my safety net. I've seen what it does to people. They either spend their lives trying to keep what they have or they waste their time doing nothing."

Gregory pondered this for a moment, then pointed to Holiday's burrito. "You'd better finish that before it gets cold."

When they finished eating, Gregory bundled the greasy wrappers and tossed them in a nearby garbage can, nodding to a homeless man who sat in the dark under a palm tree. Gregory returned and settled heavily on the bench.

"It's not the lightest food in the world," Holiday said, sipping the last of her soda.

"No, but I wanted you to have a 'cultural' experience. I know you don't have food like that back in Boston."

She shook her head. "Nothing close to it. We have Mexican food, but it tends to be a lot blander."

Gregory folded his hands behind his head and leaned back. "Good. I figure we won't be having any dinners together for a while, so I wanted to show you a taste of what I like."

His comment sent a momentary wave of disappointment through Holiday. Tomorrow the hectic work would be over, and so would their casual meals together. Why did this seem not to bother him, and why did she feel such sadness at the passing of this brief phase in her life?

As if he had sensed a change in her mood, Gregory sighed heartily. "This is great. The beach at night. You know, I lived here my whole life, and I think I've only done this three or four times."

"I appreciate your bringing me here," she said. "You know, starting a new job in a new town is hard enough without being the boss. And I've never made friends easily." Her words came out in a fast monotone, as if infusing them with her feelings would kill them. It was suddenly vital that Gregory understood how she felt.

"I can see your point," he said. "It must be tough."

"I'm not complaining," she said quickly. "I have opportunities now that I never dreamed of a few years ago."

"Sure," he said calmly. "And you pissed off Kyle Jefferies. Any opportunity to do that is golden."

She wondered how much he knew. Had Kyle spoken to anyone at the hospital of their affair years ago?

"I'd really prefer if he went his way and I went mine. I've had to deal with the consequences of his bitterness since I took this job. I just wish it would stop." She hesitated, wondering if she should go farther, if she should talk about the personal history behind their increasingly public conflict.

"I've heard about some of that stuff. It's too bad you can't get him to really step out of line. You could slap him with a harassment charge or something."

"He's never done anything like that, it's all political and work related. Besides, the last thing I want to do is hurt his career."

Gregory stared up at the sky. "One thing about L.A.," he said, his voice distorted by a yawn, "I wish I could see the stars. The pollution and the lights drown them out."

"You're right. I hadn't even noticed." She looked up; the horizon was shaded pink, reflecting the illumination of the vast city.

"You know, I should get back home," Gregory said suddenly, pulling himself upright. "I've got to check on my cousin."

"What do you mean? You have to call your family?" The thought of ending the evening so suddenly jarred her.

"No, I mean I have to get back to my apartment." A tight, self-deprecating expression crossed his features. "I have a cousin staying with me. His name's Shawn."

"So you're a parental role model now? I wouldn't have guessed."

"Hey, don't joke. The kid was getting messed up at home. He was living alone with his mother in a bad neighborhood—a lot worse than the one I grew up in. His mom, my aunt Beverly, looked in his room about a month ago and found a pistol. The kid's only fourteen, and he's mixed up with gangs. Beverly completely freaked."

Holiday watched him intently. His angular face became creased with concern as he spoke; it made him look ten years older, burdened with responsibility.

"So I thought, hey, I live on the West Side, we can get him enrolled in school out here, keep him out of trouble. It took me a while to convince him that I wasn't going to be one of the boys, you know, just letting him do whatever he wants."

"So how is he adjusting?" Holiday asked. She studied his face, his eyes gleaming with quiet intelligence, his ears stark against his close-cropped hair. She suddenly realized that, like her, he lived alone in a world removed from that of his youth. They shared a unique frustration and isolation and, now, understood this about each other.

"Not bad, I think. I've got him doing his homework and helping keep the place clean." He shook his head, looking out at the dark sea. "He's still catching up from when he switched schools. The same grade, the same age, but the school on the West Side is about a year ahead of the school in his neighborhood."

"That's sad," Holiday said. "Those kids aren't going to find a lot of opportunities to make up for lost time."

"Most of them won't. Anyway," Gregory laughed quietly. "I told him if this thing didn't work out, his mother was going to send him to military school."

"What did he say?"

"He said his mother can't afford it. I said, 'No, but *I* can, and it'd be my pleasure to ship you off to boot camp if you don't straighten up.' He knows I was putting him on, but I think he got my point."

Gregory stood up and stretched. "It's getting chilly," he said, extending a hand to Holiday to help her off the bench.

"And we have a big day tomorrow," she said. She buttoned her suit jacket collar against the mounting chill and followed Gregory back to the boardwalk. The Mexican stand had pulled down its shutters for the night. Only a café attached to a small bookstore remained open.

Past the café there were few people, only some indistinct figures sitting in the grass that ringed the bicycle trail. The repetitive waves made their restless activity heard, and Holiday closed her eyes for a moment as she walked, savoring the indolent feeling coming over her. She felt adrift in a gauze of fatigue, along with warmth and comfort. She opened her eyes and saw Gregory watching her.

"Feeling all right?" he asked, smiling gently. "You looked like you were in dreamland for a moment there."

"I think I was."

They walked off the strip to an empty lot, heading back to their cars. A series of thin metal poles protruded from the blank asphalt, the skeletons of tents that would be set up to cater to weekend tourists. At the dark end of the lot they had only to pass through an opening in a tall wooden fence to reach their cars.

But there were three men standing there.

"Maybe we should go around," Holiday whispered, trying to see the men in the shadows. They looked up and quickly turned to each other, forming a small circle with their bodies.

"Don't worry," Gregory said. "It's mellow here."

Holiday tensed. One man passed something to another. As her eyes adjusted to the light, she saw that it was a paper shopping bag.

"Seriously," Gregory said. "Come on."

When they were ten feet away, the men turned, exposing their faces. They had donned black ski masks, leaving only their eyes and noses exposed. Before Holiday or Gregory could react, the men were upon them.

They split up: one man grabbed Holiday's arm while the other two descended on Gregory. In the instant before the man grabbed her head and shoved her to the ground, Holiday saw Gregory square off in a fighting stance, his fists held before him.

Holiday hit the ground hard, tearing her suit and scraping her elbow. She lay there for a moment, feeling the cool damp touch of the asphalt, then heard the sound of fists striking flesh and a man's deep muffled voice cry out in pain.

Someone tugged on her shoulder. She was gripped with terror. She realized how isolated they were, that no one could see what might happen to her. To them.

She screamed and received a hard slap to her face. Holding her jaw, she felt her purse being tugged away from her shoulder. That's all the man wanted, she realized.

"Take the money," she whispered hoarsely, and lay very still on the rough ground.

Sheltering her head with her arms, she tried to locate Gregory. Now two men held him, one on each side, while the third punched him with frantic brutality in the face and abdomen. Gregory's head lolled, and the men pulled hard on his shoulders to hold him up.

Then the third man reached into his pocket. A shiny blade glinted in the dim light.

Holiday screamed again, and the man turned to face her. "Shut up, bitch!" he yelled in a deep, raspy voice. "Or I'll cut you, too, just like your nigger boyfriend."

Hot tears of terror and sadness gripped her; her breath caught with a series of spasms. Her senses erupted with detail and sharpness, the scene caught in a horrible focus, as if they were actors frozen for an instant in the spotlight of a stage.

"Hey! Drop that guy and get the hell away from here!" The sound of clamping feet echoed through the vacant lot. Holiday rolled on the ground to see five men running hard toward them. In her confusion and terror, she couldn't tell whether they had come to help or to hurt them more. She put her head under her arms and waited for whatever was to come.

10

". . . I'M A DOCTOR, PLEASE LET ME SEE HIM."
Holiday stood in the emergency room of St. Luke's Hospital in Santa Monica outside a cordoned-off cubicle. An officious orderly, tall and lanky but with broad shoulders and an aggressive mien, stood between her and Gregory, who was receiving treatment within.

A white-haired man in thick glasses and a short-sleeved blue tunic stuck his head through an opening in the curtain. "It's all right, Franklin, let the lady in. Our patient wants to see her."

Franklin shrugged and stepped aside. Holiday parted the curtains; there was Gregory, sitting upright on an examining table with an expression of hurt defiance.

The doctor extended his hand. "Walt Moseby. I understand you're on the surgical faculty at Pacific University?"

"Holiday Powers, pleased to meet you." One of Gregory's eyes was swollen, and Moseby had applied a bandage and splint to Gregory's broken nose.

"How are you feeling, Gregory?" Holiday spoke tentatively. He had been full of rage in the Venice parking lot, and gave his police report in a manner that the officers repeatedly reminded him was verging on belligerent. He had refused to go to Pacific University Hospital, insisting that Holiday drive him to St. Luke's. He was afraid that someone he knew would see him.

"I'm a lot better," he said. "Did you call Shawn for me?"

"I woke him up from sleeping. He was worried about you."

"Mr. Hampton is going to be fine. There's no permanent damage." Moseby stepped back and put his hands on his hips, regarding Gregory with the air of a parent whose son had come home scraped up from an essentially harmless fight.

Holiday sat on the examining table. "You're lucky you don't have any broken ribs," she said, gingerly touching the inflamed area around his eye. When he blanched at her touch, she continued in a softer voice, "I'm so glad you're all right."

Moseby completed his report and signed with a flourish at the bottom of the sheet. "Be sure to pick up these painkillers and antibiotic cream for your eye. Other than that, just stay out of trouble." He smiled as if he had made a particularly charming joke.

They drove back to the parking lot to retrieve Gregory's car. It seemed a point of pride for him to drive home under his own power. Gregory sulked in silence on the way, his head turned toward his passenger window.

"You're sure you're okay to drive? I'm positive nothing will happen to your car if we leave it there overnight."

"I'm fine." He turned to face her for the first time since leaving St. Luke's. "Look, I'm really sorry I wasn't able to defend you."

"Defend me? Come on, Gregory, you were outnumbered. Anyway I took karate in college, I know how to handle myself. I just froze up."

He gave her a look packed with irony. "Karate's fine, but those guys were street fighters. They were vicious."

Holiday was silent. She knew her karate classes, which had only lasted two years, had long been a psychological defense mechanism of sorts for her. She always assumed that she could debilitate a larger man with a kick or a focused jab to the eye. But this evening, under fire, she had simply given up.

"I'm sorry they took your wallet. I don't know why they left mine in my purse."

Gregory shrugged. "It doesn't matter. I'll call to cancel my credit cards tomorrow morning."

"They only took my address book and my personal calendar," Holiday said.

"Maybe they mistook it for a big wallet. It was dark, you know."

Holiday steered right, into the narrow speedway. She drove slowly through the dark, her headlights illuminating looming apartment buildings and old, three-story homes on either side.

"I had a good time with you tonight," Holiday said quietly. Gregory didn't respond. "And I just want you to know that I think what happened may have been my fault."

Gregory's head jerked around as she pulled into the nearly vacant parking lot. "Your fault? Why? For being out with a black man?"

Holiday shook her head. "No, not that. It's because I—"

"That's what was going on. You know that, don't you? That guy would have stabbed me if those men hadn't scared him away. And you heard what he said. He was going to stab me for being a black man with a white woman."

"I know that's what he said." Holiday reached across the gear shift and took Gregory's hand. "But I don't think that's all of it. I've been . . . someone has been harassing me. Ever since I moved here."

Gregory shifted restlessly, as if he suddenly felt pent up and confined. "Threatening you? How?"

"I got a phone call telling me to get out of town, from someone who seemed to know a lot about me. Then some hang-up calls. And I'm not entirely sure, but once I thought I was being followed."

"Did you call the police?"

"I don't have anything definite to tell them. And a phone tracer is hard to get. You have to fill out reports, and I haven't had time."

"So you think this attack might have had to do with those calls? I don't see it."

"Maybe I'm wrong. But I've had the feeling that someone is trying to get me away from Los Angeles. From the hospital."

"Who would want that?"

"I don't know. I know a lot of senior staff and faculty were upset that I was appointed above them, but no one has said anything directly to me." Holiday sighed, feeling the weight of her worries vanishing as quickly as she could voice them, as if they possessed a tangible substance and weight that she was finally rid of.

"What happened tonight probably wasn't part of it," Gregory said. "But it sounds like someone's really trying to rattle you."

He paused, choosing his words. "And I want you to know that I'll be there for you. Boss or no boss. I'm right downstairs. Call me and I'll be up in ten seconds."

A homeless man pushing a shopping cart wandered through the parking lot, pausing to look into Gregory's car, which was parked under a streetlight. He bent over, hands on his knees, and inspected its contents before wandering away, completely uninterested.

"See, I told you. You could leave your car here and no one would mess with it. One look at all that junk in the backseat and anyone can see it isn't worth the bother of breaking in."

Gregory stared at his car for a moment and laughed. "I didn't think you noticed. I'd better clean it out."

"Bad for the image."

"Right."

Holiday looked at her watch. "It's eleven-thirty," she said. "It's getting really late."

"We have to be in the labs by eight at the latest," Gregory agreed. "They're going to start prepping Takamoto at around ten our time."

A police car cruised slowly down the alley, slowing when it neared the parking lot. A spotlight shone from within the cruiser, lighting the dark asphalt and the shadowy corners in the distance with a rude yellow glare.

As the police drove off, Holiday began to speak, but

stopped herself. Gregory unbuckled his seat belt and was obviously ready to leave. She held a hand out to stop him, feeling an inner tension mixed with eagerness. *I'll be so disappointed with myself if I don't go through with this. I just have to ask, I just have to ask. I . . .*

"Gregory, I want you to come home with me tonight."

She felt as though the effort of speaking this simple phrase had completely exhausted her. At this point, she realized, she didn't care whether he said yes or no. She felt only relief that she had taken the step her heart dictated, that she had taken the risk. That she was alive, with a beating pulse.

He looked as if he had just been slapped in the face. The sight of him—with his puffy eyes and nose splint—staring in unabashed shock was inexplicably hilarious. She began to giggle.

"Hey, what's so funny? Were you kidding me?"

With a hand over her mouth to suppress her laughter—aimed at herself, at him, in an odd way at life itself—she shook her head. "No, Gregory. I'm not joking. I would like . . . I'm inviting you to spend the night with me."

Her laughter was contagious, and he smiled. "Good, because, you know, this is . . . I take this kind of thing pretty seriously. And with you I take it very seriously."

Suddenly the laughter stopped, borne away with the tension that had sustained it. "I do too," she said. "Really."

The elevator hummed softly as they rose through the heart of the apartment building. Only Holiday's floor number was illuminated on the brass electronic button panel. Halfway to the seventeenth floor Gregory reached over and took her hand, squeezing it tightly. She stared straight ahead, as if they existed in the bubble of a mutual wish that could be destroyed with a word, a gesture, a thought.

Once within the apartment she flipped on only essential

lights—the kitchen, the living room lamp, the recessed lights running along the hall to the bedroom.

Gregory stood in the middle of the living room. "You've barely unpacked," he said.

"I don't really feel like I live here yet." She unbuttoned her jacket, looking away from him. "Can I get you something to drink?"

"Just water, thanks. We have to be up and out early."

She went to the kitchen, digging through the cupboards for a water glass. A mirror above the stove caught her reflection; she looked as if she had aged years in the last week. Under her eyes were dark purple patches, and her mouth was dry and taut.

Gregory appeared in the mirror. "Do you mind if I tell you I think you're beautiful?"

She turned and smiled at him, laughing nervously and handing him the glass. "No, not at all. I'm not sure I believe you right now, but it's nice of you to say."

"I know this has been a rough time for you," he said gently. "Especially after what you told me tonight. I understand if you just want a friend for now."

She folded her arms. "It's all right. I . . . I don't want you to feel like you can't say no to me. I know I'm your boss, your supervisor. Tomorrow is so important, and it's already late."

Smiling for a second, as if entertaining an amusing notion that he left unvoiced, Gregory leaned back against the kitchen wall. "If you hadn't asked me home tonight, I would have just had to dream about you alone. I know you're not the kind to mix your personal affairs with your work. I'm not worried about anything like that."

"Thank you," she said. "For giving me some credit."

Gregory frowned. "What do you mean?"

She pulled him into her arms, crushing her lips against his. He responded, tightly embracing her, his fingers tracing hard paths against the back of her silk blouse. The comical mask of his nose splint filled her vision, and after trying studiously to avoid it, she kissed him hard, grazing his nose and swelled eyes. It seemed not to hurt him.

They pulled apart for a moment; she saw his searching expression, as if he were trying to look past her exterior to what lay within. She pulled him close again, this time kissing him longer, harder, with a passion that surprised them both.

"Doctor," he said quietly, still holding her. "I would like to accept your invitation."

They moved silently to the bedroom, Holiday turning out lights as they went. The phone rang in the kitchen, unattended, and finally stopped. She opened the blinds to her darkened room, letting in the light from the moon and the city below.

He began to undress her, first gently unbuttoning her blouse, his eyes gleaming in the darkness. Then his hands moved lower, to her skirt, which she allowed to fall to the floor. She reached out and pulled away his jacket, then his shirt, revealing his dark torso and hairless chest.

The bed squeaked under their weight as they held each other in a tight embrace, first kissing slowly and furtively then holding to each other longer and longer. She heard herself groan softly as he unsnapped her bra and slowly circled his fingers along the soft contours of each breast. From the side he kissed each nipple gently, then traced a path lower and lower along her naked stomach.

She stared at the ceiling in the quiet of the room, feeling suddenly alone until she felt the softness of his touch, then his mouth upon her. She closed her eyes and allowed her body to abandon itself to what it felt, breathing deeply, trying to banish worry and consequence. A vivid pulse of energy ran through her body, and she heard herself call out his name in a high voice. Moments later he was next to her again, kissing her softly.

"I don't usually do that," she said, surprised at the girlishness in her voice. A moment of anxiety came over her, as if she had lost her sense of control. She felt ageless and ungrounded, and wondered if she knew this man well enough to allow him to be so close.

"Do what?" he said, moving to kiss her neck.

She put a finger over his lips and shifted over him, settling above his hips. He cried out in an unfamiliar voice as she guided him into her, rocking gently with her hands on his chest and looking into his eyes. In the darkness he looked younger, more boyish. She moved quicker, his hands pulling on her hips and caressing her stomach.

Leaning forward over him, her hair falling into his face and covering his broad shoulders, she allowed herself to let go. An electric tightening came over her, and she felt his body tense beneath her. They cried out together as her movements became more intense; he also moved beneath her, thrusting upward and holding her shoulders.

When it was over, she lay in the darkness, her back to his chest, the smell of him on her hands and in her hair. She heard his breathing deepen.

"I didn't set the alarm," she said, pulling loose from his embrace and feeling in the darkness for the clock. He mumbled unintelligibly.

She set the alarm for early the next morning and returned to his arms, letting his warmth settle over her, seeking security. Thinking about him, she allowed her thoughts to wander. Unbidden, her mind raced, seeking the meaning of what had happened. *What have I done?* she thought, then pulled herself closer to him. She had done what she wanted to do. Nothing else mattered.

"Gregory?" she whispered. The moon shone through the blinds, casting irregular shadows.

"Yeah?" he mumbled, pulling her closer.

"Can I trust you?"

There was a moment of emptiness and complete silence. Then he kissed her hair, her neck, humming in a low, comforting voice.

"You can trust me," he said.

11

HOLIDAY LAY STILL IN BED, HOLDING HER BREATH AND listening. In her murky, barely awake haze she heard a noise in her apartment. It sounded like the heavy creak of her front door, but it could have come from an apartment down the hall.

"Gregory," she whispered. His inert form gave no sign that he had heard her; his chest rose and fell with the deep breaths of heavy sleep. Barely conscious herself, Holiday's mind drifted for a moment to the man next to her. They had only been sleeping a few hours.

An indistinct sound, like footsteps in her kitchen, jarred her to full consciousness. She quietly folded the blankets over Gregory and pulled on a cotton nightshirt.

This is ridiculous, she thought. I've lived in apartments for years, heard all kinds of noises that turned out to be nothing. She looked at the glowing red numerals on her clock radio: it was just after five. She had to get up anyway.

Holiday walked out of her bedroom and trod lightly in the hall leading to the living room, pausing for a moment. It was no wonder her nerves were shot, that she was hearing odd noises. The violence last night in Venice had disturbed her deeply. And this morning, though she had suppressed the thought until now, she was going to perform surgery that would either put her at the forefront of medicine or permanently damage her professional standing.

You can trust me, Gregory had said, in the last glimmer of a long night. She exposed herself to him, showed him recesses of herself that she had hidden for years. She had let others believe that her drive and dedication were all there was worth knowing about her. And now, though she hated to admit it, she thought about Gregory and was filled with worry. What did she really have to offer him? Their lovemaking might not have meant anything to him—in a way she hoped so.

But she knew that wasn't true. It had meant something.

She heard a tinkle of glass from the kitchen: the dishes settling in the sink? After a couple of steps she was out of the hall to the landing leading to the kitchen. Holiday squinted, trying to wake up. Sidling up to the wall, she peered around the corner, listening.

A form moved around the corner at the same time, bumping into her before she could react. Holiday screamed and threw her hands up in defense.

Gregory rushed from the bedroom, the sheet wound around his waist. Struggling to focus his eyes, he sprinted past Holiday into the hall. There he was greeted by a second woman's scream, which sent him leaping into the air with insensate shock and surprise.

"Jesus!" Kate said, rushing away from Gregory, leaning heavily on the wall and holding a hand over her heart. She was dressed in jogging shorts and a T-shirt. "You scared me to death."

Gregory, his eyes bulging with shock, looked from Holiday to Kate, as if they held answers and were keeping them from him. He pulled the sheet tighter around himself, blinking and scowling over his nose splint and bandage.

"I'm so sorry," Kate said, holding her hand over her mouth. "I came back from my morning run and thought I'd stop by and wish you luck on your surgery today. I knocked and rang the bell, and when you didn't answer, I thought you'd overslept. I got your extra key and let myself in. Sugar, I had no idea—"

She looked at Gregory. Suddenly remembering he was naked under the sheet, he tried to rearrange it for maximum coverage. "I'll go get dressed," he said sullenly.

Holiday suddenly erupted with laughter at the sight of

her two friends lost in a world of mutual embarrassment. She kissed Gregory's cheek, then led Kate to the kitchen.

She got out filters and coffee, catching Kate staring at her out of the periphery of her vision. She turned to see her friend wearing a knowing grin, shaking her head.

"I guess I'll call first from now on," Kate said. "I hope you're not upset. I didn't mean to invade your privacy, but I know how important that surgery is today. I just wanted to be a friend."

"It's all right, Kate. I'm glad you were looking out for me. It's just that I . . . well, you know, with Gregory . . ." Holiday stammered. She felt suddenly full of conflict. Some part of her was proud to be found in the morning with a handsome man, living life and enjoying herself. But another part felt helpless, exposed, and out of control.

"Hey, come on. You look like you're getting upset. Did anything bad happen?" Kate cast an eye out of the kitchen, checking to see if Gregory was near.

"No. Well, yes. We were attacked by three men in a parking lot."

"Is that what happened to him? Are you all right, sugar?"

Holiday slid close to Kate so that they could speak softly. She felt tall and ungainly next to her diminutive friend. "I'm fine. Gregory got a broken nose. We stopped at Venice for dinner after work and . . . well, it was weird."

"That's a weird part of town," Kate said. She lowered her voice. "So then you brought him home with you?"

"Yeah. I guess I did."

Kate held her hand over her mouth to contain her excited laughter. "You vixen," she said. "Any 'morning after' regrets?"

The sound of running water came from Holiday's bathroom. She thought for a moment, then softly smiled. "No. Not really."

Kate rolled her eyes. "All right, I get it. It's a long story."

"It's not that, it's just that I . . . I don't do this kind of thing very often, you know. Bringing someone home that I barely know."

"Gregory's a decent guy," Kate said, suddenly serious. "Look, I have to scrub in by eight, so I have to go. But let's get together tonight or tomorrow. You *have* to tell me about this. I'm not letting you off without some serious girl talk."

"Thank you, Kate," Holiday said. "I'm glad to have someone to talk to."

Holiday's reply seemed to take Kate by surprise; she suddenly stepped forward and took the younger woman in a tight embrace. "You take things way too seriously, sweetheart," she whispered.

When she pulled away, Gregory was standing in the doorway fully dressed, his embarrassment faded to sheepish reticence. "Holiday, I'm going down to my place to make sure Shawn's out of bed and getting ready for school." He paused for a moment, then smiled shyly.

"Good morning, Mr. Hampton," Kate said dryly. "And, may I ask, what are you intentions with young Holiday?"

Gregory's jaw dropped; he looked supremely uncomfortable. "Don't answer that," Kate said. "Or we'll probably be here all day, and I have to go. Give me a call, sugar," she said to Holiday. "Remember, next time the Chablis is on you."

Holiday closed the door softly behind Kate. Gregory was behind her, ready to leave. "I guess I'll meet up with you in the lab," she said, avoiding his eyes.

He took her hand. "It's going to be a big day," he said softly.

She stared at the floor, suddenly overcome with awkwardness. "Gregory, will we—was what happened last night something real?" She heard a beseeching quality in her voice. *Why can't I handle this the right way?*

"Of course it was," he said softly. "Of course."

"So it . . . it wasn't just two bodies that happened to be in the same place, was it? I don't do things that way." Her gaze remained fixed on the floor. *Why am I doing this?*

"Me either. I promise. Look, we should talk about this later."

Holiday stepped aside to let him pass. "Right," she said, more caustically than she intended. "We'll talk later."

Gregory opened the door. "Hey, what does that mean?" he said. "You sound like you—"

"Just go," she said. She looked up into his eyes. "Look, it's me that has a problem, not you. We'll talk later, that would be good."

He paused for a moment, looking at her as though he had seen some facet of her he didn't expect.

"Everything's fine," she said. "Really. I've got to get ready. I'll see you in the labs. We'll make history."

She led him into the hall and closed the door softly, listening to his footsteps receding toward the elevators.

He was sixty-one years old. It was two in the morning in Tokyo. He lay in a plush silk robe, the hospital staff buzzing around him. At the other end of the secured corridor, past his bodyguards, his technicians prepared the operating room and double-checked the fiberoptic links to the laboratory at Pacific University. Han Takamoto leaned back on his pillows and sighed. A lifetime of work and struggle, and he was using his own body as gambling stakes in business battles he thought won long ago.

Last evening he lay in this bed and thought of his wife. In the four years since her death he lived in their home like a man waiting for the house's rightful owners to reclaim what belonged to them. The classical music always playing softly; the fresh flowers, plants, and trees for the enclosed stone garden; the aroma of foods and oils: these things were gone now. He had always worked late and now he worked even later, striving like a ghost to keep Mitsuyama a dominant force in the international electronics market—and to ensure that he remained the center of decision making and power.

With a slight wave of his hand Takamoto indicated that everyone should leave his room. The nurse informed him that they would begin readying him for surgery in ten minutes. He looked for doubt in her eyes, and saw only the subservience of an employee attending to a man whose power was beyond question. It was a look he had seen on thousands of faces.

Mitsuyama sent a small delegation of representatives to witness the surgery, mostly people loyal to Takamoto. Even now he worried that someone at the corporation might be working against his interests, that someone would take advantage of his absence to implement a plan to undermine him.

Takamoto had grown up in the shadow of World War II, his family devastated and adrift by the time of the Japanese surrender. In the decades since he became president of Mitsuyama in the early seventies, he had seen the world and enjoyed the benefits of his position. But he never lost sight of his goal—to win his battles, always to move forward. From transistor radios to cellular phones and computers, he had played a crucial role in a technological revolution unprecedented in human history.

What had changed? His competitors—from within and without—whispered behind his back that he was old, that his committed drive into surgical technology was folly, that he was trying to relive his lost youth. When he committed expenses to hire American researchers, they said a more conservative course was in order. He was accused of pursuing personal goals at the expense of the corporation.

Outside the hospital window the terminal congestion of greater Tokyo sprawled and sputtered, fighting with itself for space in which to breathe. Perhaps he *was* too old. His resolute commitment to his vision had fallen prey to doubt. His wife would have scolded him for his bluster and stubbornness.

Dr. Mishima, his personal physician, stepped into the room, a slight man with pockmarked skin who always chided Takamoto for eating steaks and smoking. Mishima regarded his longtime patient with a look of compassion mixed with an almost imperceptible disappointment. "The robot is ready," he said. "We will take you to the operating room."

Takamoto stepped into a waiting wheelchair, trying to hide the pain in his abdomen. Mishima had recommended surgery a week ago, saying it was foolish to wait. And he was right, undoubtedly.

"It is good of you to be here," Takamoto said, arranging his robe.

"You are more than my patient, Han," Mishima said. "We have become friends."

Takamoto turned in the chair as Mishima began to push. "And you've made your feelings known about this operation," he said.

"I have," Mishima said, with a trace of melancholia. "And now I will watch. And wish you luck."

When they reached the operating room, the equipment was ready. Mishima retreated to a corner. Takamoto's executive assistant entered quickly, his hands held together, his expression stoic.

The anesthesiologist waited by his cart of monitors. The room was packed with wires and cables and a bank of computers. The team of technicians, absorbed in their minutiae, failed even to note the entrance of the man they all worked for. The small team of nurses and the surgeon bowed silently, their reverence mixed with an obvious air of apprehension.

Takamoto felt that he no longer existed; he was a body, a factor in an experiment. He felt a tingle of irony. All his adult life had been spent achieving mastery over technology. Now he would lay prostrate before the power, and potential, of science.

"I want to speak with the surgeon before I am put under anesthetic," Takamoto said with the air of a man who expected to be obeyed. The surgeon in the room, misunderstanding, stepped forward before catching himself and rejoining the nurses.

"They are ready. We will have Dr. Powers on-screen in a moment," his assistant said.

Takamoto wheeled himself to the video device set up near the computers. In a moment the visual link was established, which would be maintained throughout the surgery.

There she was: young, beautiful, and supremely competent. It was superstition to want to see her, he knew. Still, he looked at the screen, into her eyes and for a moment wondered who she really was. Would she have understood his doubts, his need for these extreme measures, if he had had the opportunity to explain them?

No matter. "Dr. Powers, hello." He fixed a look of rigidity on his face, allowing the hint of a confident smile to appear. "It appears that we are ready to begin."

"Mr. Takamoto, good morning. It's good to see you." Even on the screen the man had an intense aura of authority. Holiday suppressed the automatic urge to bow.

"Our surgical team is prepared," Takamoto said, his voice flat. "And I am prepared to be rid of this bothersome illness."

Holiday smiled, but Takamoto's severe expression didn't change. "Sir, you have my assurance that our technical team is among the best in the world and that I have personally overseen our tests. In an hour you'll be ready to begin your brief recovery."

"Very well. I will arrange to speak to you tomorrow. Good luck." Takamoto pursed his lips and disappeared from the screen, his image replaced by a waist-level view of the operating room. Holiday saw the prototype robot that had been flown to Tokyo, a squat device with a thin, four-jointed arm. It waited motionless on its metal pedestal.

Another face appeared on the screen: Andy Shale, one of Gregory Hampton's assistants. A ruddy, long-haired man of forty, he had to bend down to face the screen.

"Dr. Powers," he said quietly, obviously uncomfortable with being part of the small American contingent in Tokyo. "Our people are all accounted for. Can I talk to Gregory?"

"Good morning, Andy," Holiday said. She wanted to speak with him confidentially about the state of mind in the OR, but could see that the room was full of curious eavesdroppers. "Gregory stepped out for a moment. Do you want me to give him a message?"

Shale looked confused. "Just tell him that we have everything running, and all the diagnostics are perfect. We're ready to go as soon as they have Mr. Takamoto on the table."

"Good, I'll tell him," Holiday said. "Everything's on schedule."

Mike Hyata turned off the linkup's speaker. "I can't complain with the way you handled that. If they knew Hampton hadn't showed up yet, they'd be very upset."

Phil Hermoza stepped away from his examination of the surgical workstation and joined Holiday. "And they damned well should be." He lowered his voice to a whisper. "They've set up the closed-circuit monitors for the media in the next room, so they can hear what we say unless we speak quietly. So pretend I'm yelling when I say this: where the fuck is Hampton?"

"I don't know, I—" She paused for a moment. "I spoke with him this morning. He said he'd meet me here."

"How many times have we had him paged?" Hermoza asked.

"I paged him three times," Hyata said, checking his watch. "And there's been no answer."

"I don't get this," Hermoza said. "Hampton is a pro. He's the last person I'd expect to flake out like this."

"It's starting to worry me," Holiday said. This day was as important to Gregory as it was to her. She had to hope he'd had car trouble, something that wouldn't delay him past the starting time.

"We're going to be ready to start in half an hour," Hyata said. "We can do this without him if we have to, can't we?"

Holiday rubbed her eyes. "Hold on a second."

She walked quickly to the computer setup, passing by several assistant technicians until she found Bill Epstein. Over her shoulder she heard Hermoza's booming voice, complaining. "What a fucking mob scene. Can't we get some of these people out of here?"

Epstein was dressed in his standard Western tie and sported a new close-cropped, slicked-back hairstyle. "Still no word?" he said.

"No, and I don't know what's going on." She took a chair next to him. "Bill, at this point we have to operate under the assumption that Gregory's not going to show up this morning."

"Do you think something happened to him?" Epstein stared into his computer monitor and pecked nervously at the keyboard. A three-dimensional chessboard appeared on the screen. He looked shyly at Holiday. "It helps me relax."

"You've got half an hour, so don't think too long about any of your moves," she said. She leaned forward to whisper to him. "Bill, I'm putting you in charge if Gregory doesn't make it in time. I don't know what's happened to him, but it's too late for us to back out or try to delay. You can run this system yourself, can't you?"

"I can run it. You're the one with the hard job." He sighed heavily. "I was worried that something like this was going to happen."

Holiday pulled away, perplexed. "Why?"

"Because it always does."

Half an hour. She would have to go next door and give a brief talk to the press—local news, a couple of network affiliates, a twenty-four-hour cable surgery channel—outlining in broad terms what she and the technical team faced. It would be even more of an ordeal than the surgery itself.

The small surgical arena had been converted into a nest of technology. A row of thirty-six-inch screens displayed a series of images: an overview of the room, a closed-circuit linkup to the Tokyo OR, a blank display that would show the robot's view in Japan, which Holiday would see through her visor, and a close-up of the station at which she would work.

The theater seating above the room was dark and empty; the press and hospital administrators would be led in when it was time to begin. The only friends Holiday had in L.A.—Kate, Bo Swenson, a few other doctors she barely knew—would be unable to attend. Holiday had discovered, days before, that her surgery was a hot ticket. Nearly everyone at Pacific University wanted to view her failure or triumph.

This would be the strangest place she had ever performed surgery. There was no table, no patient, no medicine. Everyone wore street clothes. She realized she would have to work hard to achieve the concentration she needed to operate—a level that normally came by instinct, cued by the sights and sounds of the operating room.

"We should get over there and talk to the media," Hermoza said, startling Holiday out of her reverie. He looked at the camera crew, who sat idly near their cases of equipment, waiting for the action to begin. "Look at those assholes. Five hundred bucks an hour to shoot the room and make sure the monitors and recorders are working. I should be paid so much for sitting on my ass."

Holiday smiled thinly, watching one of the cameramen pull a sloppy sandwich from a black case full of equipment. "Quality costs, Phil. But it's worth it."

He scrutinized Holiday for a moment. "That's right,"

he finally said. "So let's get on with it and start earning our own obscene salaries."

Outside the theater Hermoza stopped and extended his arm for Holiday to take. She was touched by the gesture; even though she had suspected, perhaps wrongly, that he knew she was hiding something about Gregory, he was trying to calm her and lend her some confidence.

In the hall they ran into Kyle Jefferies, who stood alone reading one of the press releases distributed by Pacific University Public Relations. He looked up and leveled a flat stare at Holiday.

"Dr. Powers. Phil," he said.

"Glad you could make it, Kyle. I thought you had surgery this morning," Hermoza said, stopping Holiday's stride with gentle pressure on her arm. She sensed the emergence of the political Phil, trying to reconcile his two resentful charges.

"I canceled it. I'm really curious to see how all this works out," Jefferies said, folding his arms. He wore a long white lab coat over a powder-blue shirt.

Jefferies turned to Holiday. "So how do you feel? Ready to make your big splash?"

This was the first time since Holiday arrived in Los Angeles that Kyle had spoken to her casually, as an equal. His eyes remained cold and appraising, as if looking for a weakness.

"I'm nervous," she said. "But the system is virtually flawless. All in all I'll be glad when it's over."

Jefferies chuckled softly, politely.

"Gregory hasn't showed up yet," Phil said to Kyle. "We don't know where he is."

Jefferies arched an eyebrow in surprise. "Really? Do you want me to have my secretary page him?"

"No, no. We've already done that about ten thousand times," Hermoza said. "It's going to take about a dozen people to pull me off him when he does show up, though. You can bet your ass on that."

Phil unconsciously tightened his grip on Holiday's arm.

She remembered the nickname his students had given him in Boston: El Hermoza the Mauler. An anonymous artist had sketched him in a wrestler's colorful tights and mask, leaving the picture on a hospital bulletin board. It had been, in fact, a good likeness, and Phil tacked it on his office door when he discovered it.

"Well," Jefferies said, folding the press release. "I just got out of the media room. They're in there chomping at the bit."

"We'd better go in, Phil," Holiday said, checking her watch. Twenty-five minutes. She hoped Gregory had arrived, and with an excellent excuse.

Jefferies pointed to the amphitheater. "I'll see you guys in there. I'm going to be hanging out on ground level, since they didn't have any seats for me. Holiday, good luck. This never would have happened when I was in charge of the department."

She wondered for a moment precisely what he meant. Then she was pulled down the hall by Phil's viselike grip, quickly finding herself in a bright conference room serving as an impromptu media center. There were about twenty reporters and cameramen, with bright handheld lights and a batch of microphones taped to a podium. Holiday followed Hermoza to the front of the room.

The lights glared in Holiday's eyes. She stood still, her hands at her side, and waited for Hermoza to begin.

"All right, folks, greetings," he began, running a hand through his hair. "I'm Phil Hermoza and this is Holiday Powers. Our titles are in that release on the table with all the Mitsuyama brochures. Dr. Powers will be performing the telepresence surgery today, and I'll be taking all the credit."

A low titter of laughter surged through the room. Phil smiled eagerly, obviously enjoying the attention. "We've been planning a demonstration of telepresence robotics for some time, and we—in partnership with the Mitsuyama Corporation—finally have the system ready for development and marketing. What you are going to see today is the future of medicine—the capacity to perform off-site surgery with a minimum of expense and preparation. Pacific University and I are extremely proud to be associated with this undertaking, and we're very happy to have Dr. Powers on our staff."

He stepped away from the podium and leaned over Holiday. Whispering, he said, "Pretty good, huh? I got through it without swearing. The chancellor's going to shit his pants."

"You're incurable," Holiday said. She stood there for a moment, noticing that everyone appeared to be waiting for something to happen. Everyone, she realized, was waiting for her.

"We'll be starting in about twenty minutes," she said after stepping to the dais. "The procedure will be an enhanced laparoscopic cholecystectomy, in which a small assisting team in Tokyo will anesthetize the patient, then insert the plastic trocars and put the cameras and instruments in place. Once this is done, I will guide the instrument from here to isolate and remove the diseased gallbladder."

Her eyes had adjusted somewhat to the bright lights; she saw the reporters below her, a small group of men and women staring up as if she were the most boring part of the show. She opened the conference up to questions.

A young blond man in a double-breasted suit held up his hand. "Brett Sanderson, Channel Five. Dr. Powers, what are your plans in case something goes wrong?"

Holiday paused. "We'll be in visual and audio communication with Tokyo at all times. If anything at all seems wrong, we have a trained surgeon on hand to finish the operation there."

"Melanie Powell, with the Surgery Network," a middle-aged black woman said. Holiday didn't even know there was such a channel until she was told days ago that the network had bought rights to broadcast recordings of the surgery at a later date.

"What do you have to say," she continued, "to allegations that this surgery has been rushed, that insufficient trials have been performed?"

"I'm not aware that anyone has said that," Holiday said evenly. "We did extensive trials, and the system has been tested to everyone's satisfaction. We were able to circumvent some regulatory delays because of the unprecedented nature of what we're doing. But to answer your question, I would say that those doubts, however benign, have no grounding in fact."

Who has that woman been talking to? Holiday wondered. She thought of Kyle lingering in the hall. Was he spiteful enough to plant that kind of bad press, even though it was a strike against the hospital's reputation?

"Tony Lee, *Pacific Rim Monthly.*" A handsome Asian man in a linen shirt held a microphone toward Holiday, evidently denied access to the taped-up mass affixed to the podium. "I'm curious: why is this surgery being performed on Han Takamoto? He's a famous, powerful man—is this a kind of publicity ploy?"

"Well, if it was, it apparently worked," Holiday said. She smiled at Lee, who laughed uneasily. "Seriously, though, we're operating on Mr. Takamoto because he has a diseased gallbladder that needs to be removed as soon as possible. He volunteered to be the first human subject and, candidly, I was impressed with his courage."

Tony Lee jotted some notes on a spiral pad. Holiday suddenly thought of her parents watching her on Boston TV that night. Her mother, all protestations of Holiday's lifestyle to the contrary, would surely tape the broadcast to show to all her friends. The notion gave her an odd mix of warmth and discomfort.

"All right, folks, that's it." Hermoza waved his hand toward the door as if encouraging an uninvited guest to leave. "We'll be available later for questions. Go down the hall and follow the signs to the theater. We'll have someone there to check your credentials."

The reporters filed out, packing up their gear and talking quietly among themselves. Phil smiled vacantly at

Holiday, suddenly tense. "Well, kid, go do it. I hope to hell this thing works out."

Holiday punched him lightly on the shoulder. "Come on, Phil. We'll be done in a few hours, and I'll buy you a beer." Her own voice sounded hollow and tentative to her. "We're the best, remember?"

"Yeah, the best," he said, putting a hand on her shoulder and squeezing. "Either that, or we're out of our fucking minds."

They walked together back to the amphitheater in moody silence. When they arrived, Phil made his way to a row of folding seats placed unobtrusively in the corner at floor level.

Holiday glanced one final time around the room. Gregory wasn't there. The members of the press were assembled in the observation seating above, speaking in whispers. In the middle of the room were the computers, ranging from a four-foot-high white box to small console units placed on long tables. The technical team had settled into their seats, each charged with specific responsibilities. One technician was engaged in conversation with the video crew, pointing at a stack of computer cables taped to the floor.

Bill Epstein sat nervously in the central position behind a pair of computer screens. He looked at Holiday and ran a hand nervously through his hair. She gave him a thumbs-up, provoking a grim smile.

Something must have happened to Gregory. He would have been there if he'd had to crawl. She wondered if they should send someone to his apartment, or if they should call the police. Perhaps his injuries the night before were more severe than they seemed. But he had seemed fine. *God, I slept with him, I should know he was fine.*

Mike Hyata appeared at her side. "They have Takamoto under anesthetic. As soon as you're in the telepresence system, you'll have audio connection to the OR. The staff there are instructed to recite his pressure and heart rate in English upon request, and they'll be able to hear and respond to any of your needs." He straightened soberly. "Of course you know all that."

"I don't mind being reminded," Holiday said.

"Well, here. Put this on." He handed her a blue lab coat, emblazoned with the logos of both Pacific University and the Mitsuyama Corporation: a quill ascending over a cloud bank and an abstract minimalist representation of the Japanese island chain, respectively. The combination was surreal and slightly ridiculous.

"I didn't know anything about this," she said. She eyed the logos. "I'm going to feel like a race-car driver in this thing."

Hyata's eyes narrowed. "You don't want to wear it? I know I should have mentioned it, but the regional office just put it together yesterday. I didn't think there would be a problem."

His sudden burst of anxiety perturbed Holiday. Since the initial pledge was made to perform the surgery, Hyata had been a swinging pendulum ranging between disaffection and an all-out panic attack. But she had come to like him: despite his slick corporate style and obsession with appearances, he was honest and forthright. She didn't want to upset him, so she quickly put on the lab coat.

"It fits fine," she said. "I'm surprised the shoulders are big enough. A lot of off-the-rack stuff is too constrictive on me."

Hyata sighed with relief. "I stole one of your lab coats from your office and had this one made to order."

A loud throat clearing echoed in the quiet room. Holiday turned to see Bill Epstein staring at her. "Dr. Powers, we're ready to begin."

She glanced at the floor-level seats as Hyata scrambled to get out of the way. Along with a few representatives from Mitsuyama's California office were Hermoza, Jefferies, and a few Pacific University department heads. Kyle stared at her unemotionally, his arms folded. She turned away from him.

Epstein walked to her with the telepresence headpiece. She felt oddly as if she were in a theater, acting out the opening scene of a play that she hadn't read through to the end. Closing her eyes to shut out the world, she nodded in acquiescence. The equipment was placed gently on her head, shutting out all sound and vision.

She was suspended in a ghostly world of distorted lights and garbled sounds. It reminded her of the frightening images she had seen in her sleep when she was in her twenties and jangled by medical school: voices and ethereal colors playing in her ears and eyes. Then she heard a click and the voices cleared. They were speaking Japanese.

The visual field came into place a moment later. She saw the operating room from the robot's vantage point: Takamoto lay still before her, his body obscured by drapery. His abdomen was inflated with gas, distended and stretched until it resembled the girth of a very pregnant woman. His midsection was covered with orange jelly and grease-pen marks indicating incision sites.

She turned her head to the left and saw the anesthesiologist speaking quietly with a nurse. As her hearing grew more acute, she heard the hiss of the respirator and the gentle clatter of instruments being picked up and laid down.

When this technology was in everyday usage, the surgeon normally wouldn't have the luxury of looking around the room. Her view would entail only that of the laparoscopic camera, and would be activated only after it was inserted in the patient's body. Holiday had requested this get-acquainted period earlier in the week, knowing that it would help her orient herself. This prototype system was costly, however, because it used both a laparoscopic camera hookup and a traditional wide-angle television camera. It would have to be abandoned in the future.

Holiday held her head motionless and watched the assisting surgeon make four half-inch incisions with a scalpel through the black ink crosses on Takamoto's skin. Small quantities of dark blood oozed from the cuts, which a nurse efficiently wiped away. The surgeon, a short, stocky man in thick glasses, requested trocars—the word was the same in Japanese. He stared down at the patient, conspicuously avoiding looking at the robot.

The trocars were plastic tubes that tapered on one end into an edge, which the surgeon now used to push roughly through the incisions and into the patient's inflated abdominal cavity. From here instruments would be inserted into the trocars and moved around within the body.

The surgeon pushed in the microcamera. Holiday felt like an intruder, watching the life-and-death process of surgery from a comfortable observer's view. But now the camera was in place, and her view would change. She took a deep breath, realizing that she was about to move from the grandstands to the very center of the action.

"Jesus, that's what she's seeing through that helmet?" Brett Sanderson said to his neighbor in the observation seating. He looked closer at the large monitor below: on it an amplified and enlarged image of the inside of a human body appeared. It was full of reds and greens and dominated by the ochre lobes of the liver. The picture suddenly became clearer as the light at the end of the laparoscopic camera was turned up another notch. Sanderson could see a slow, convulsive throb—the patient's pulse.

"Of course that's what she's seeing," his neighbor said. "Usually the surgeon sees that image on a TV screen, not as their entire field of vision, but she's very familiar with what she's looking at."

Sanderson snuck a glance at his neighbor; Melanie Powell worked at that surgical cable network, where they gleefully displayed open-heart procedures, hip replacements, complicated bowel-obstruction removals—all in color, twenty-four hours a day. Sanderson shuddered. The sight of gore nauseated him, and the crash medical overview course he had taken for this job had been a disgusting ordeal.

Powell turned to him. "So you're from Channel Five, huh? Worked there long?"

"No, I just got out of broadcasting school a year ago."

Powell nodded. "You know, I think this is a bigger story than any of us realize."

"What do you mean?" Sanderson said. She was at least fifteen years older than he, and exuded the authoritative reporter's mien that he was trying so desperately to cultivate.

"Did you see her face when I asked if they were rushing this? She knows they are. I got an off-the-record statement from someone at Mitsuyama to confirm it."

"But why would they do that?" Sanderson asked eagerly.

Powell looked at him with muted disdain. "You're a reporter, just like me. Let me know if you find out."

All right, she's not talking, he thought. What did it matter? He would take the press release back to the station with some footage from the after-surgery press conference. The anchor and the weatherman would shake their heads and comment about how fast technology was progressing, and everyone would go home.

Come on, concentrate. He looked down at the row of video screens. In addition to the goriest one, containing the image that filled Dr. Powers's vision, there were the more generic views. He saw an overview of the room, including the screen he was looking at—a worlds-within-worlds effect. And he saw the rather attractive figure of Powers (even in that stupid coat) standing before a clear plastic stand, holding a device that looked like an elongated ball-point pen, moving it delicately through thin air.

In Tokyo they had wheeled the robot close to the patient and attached a grasper device to its hand, which they then inserted through one of the surgical trocars near the patient's navel. There were too many things to watch at once: Powers, moving her instrument and staring into her helmet; the robot in Tokyo, duplicating her movements with amazing delicacy; and the laparoscope's view, in which the instrument in Takamoto's body pulled lesions away from the bloated, distended sac of the gallbladder.

Dr. Powers was younger than he thought she'd be, and better-looking. She seemed a little aloof, though, probably full of herself. It was always that way with over-achievers.

In Tokyo the nurses watched the robot arm pull out of the patient's body, taking its cue from Holiday's similar motion. She said something into the microphone attached to the helmet, and a nurse stepped forward to take the grasper from the robot's mechanical "hand," replacing it with a tiny surgical stapler. Powers raised her elbow. The robot arm plunged through the trocar again, moving carefully through Takamoto's body and affixing staples to a thin structure held in place by the assisting surgeon.

"What's she doing?" Sanderson whispered to Powell.

"Tying off the cystic duct," Powell said. She sat back in her chair. "You know, I'm amazed. This thing is really working. Look at what she's seeing—it's like she's shrunk down tiny enough to get inside this guy's belly. It must be an incredible experience for her."

"I guess," Sanderson said, shrugging.

"You guess? What did they teach you in broadcast college—how to ignore anything interesting?" Powell spoke without looking at him, her attention fixed on the monitors.

Sanderson didn't answer, instead glancing to his right at the old boy from CNN who had remained silent throughout the morning. The man had heard Powell and chuckled softly.

Damn, Sanderson thought. She's just pissed off because she has to work for some cable station that no one watches. She'd give her own gallbladder to work for a network affiliate like Channel Five.

Now, this was good. Powers asked for another instrument, holding her hand steady and motionless in the air.

The Japanese team handed the robot a thin, pencil-like device. She, along with substantial help from the assisting surgeon, had isolated the gallbladder and sealed off its connecting structures. All that remained was to carefully slice it away from its bed of surrounding tissue.

"That's a laser, right?" Sanderson said, leaning over to Powell. The older woman ignored him.

Feeling rebuffed, Sanderson focused on Dr. Powers. Something was happening: she held the instrument in place and swiveled her head from side to side. Brett could sense her frustration. It looked like she was trying to see her actual physical surroundings and was completely hindered by the VR helmet.

An odd-looking guy in a string tie leaned forward and spoke into a microphone. Dr. Powers nodded; the technician had broken through into her audio reception and delivered a message.

Sanderson looked back up at the screen. Whatever the problem was, it was gone now. He felt a moment's thrill as she activated the laser and carefully began to cut away the gallbladder. The tissue parted as if gently torn in half by the thin orange beam.

They were about to wrap it up. Brett fidgeted in his seat. He had to admit, this was pretty amazing. He turned to Powell, about to explain to her that he wasn't the blasé moron she took him for. Tapping her on the shoulder, he watched as her expression turned to one of horror. In an instant of complete confusion, the entire spectator section erupted with cries of anguish and astonishment. Someone stood up and cried out, "God, stop that thing!"

Sanderson stood up. He saw the interior of Takamoto's body, and realized with disgust that the liver had been cut in half. Blood and fluids coursed through the cavity. The laser hovered in the air a moment, then fired a thick orange beam wildly into the body.

The second blast sliced through the two major carriers of blood in the middle section of the body (the aorta and the vena cava, Brett would later learn). They exploded with a torrent of pulsing blood, bathing the ruined liver and inner structures with a viscous spray.

Downstairs pandemonium erupted. Phil Hermoza leaped from his chair, screaming obscenities in a startling wail.

Dr. Powers stepped completely away from the console, leaving her surrogate surgical instrument dangling in the air. She tore off the headset and threw it to the ground, scattering ruined electronic equipment across the sparkling floor.

"I can't control it!" she screamed, looking at Hermoza. "It's not responding!"

The laser, now burning with an even greater fury, hovered in Takamoto's body, searing through tissue and organs. Smoke and blood filled the image on the monitor as the laser cut again, deeper. Through the obscuring mist of the shredded anatomy, Sanderson could see a bony mass appear, only to be neatly sliced in half. Brett's stomach rose in his throat when he realized it was the man's spinal cord.

On the closed-circuit monitor the Japanese surgical team looked on, their faces turned to pitiful masks of terror. Those poor people, he thought, watching them struggle with the robot to wrest the laser out of its grasp and pull it from Takamoto's body. But by then the device had ceased firing. The monitor showing the laparoscope's view went blank. The assisting surgeon stepped forward with a scalpel and began cutting a huge incision across Takamoto's belly. He screamed at a nurse, who stepped over to the camera and cut off the transmission.

In the room below, initial shock had turned to numb disgust. The man had been butchered, cut in half from inside as if by a buzzsaw. The reporters sat in stunned silence, looking at one another before running for the stairs.

Dr. Powers stood alone. She stared at the headpiece she had destroyed, then sank to her knees, her skin pale and lifeless. Hermoza ran to her. The big man's body obscured Sanderson's view until he turned to take a wet cloth someone had fetched.

In that instant he saw Holiday's face. It was terrible, contorted into a grimace of uncomprehending pain. Hermoza cradled her head in his hands, looking around the room with an expression of unabashed, dumbstruck grief.

12

THROUGH THE OPERATING ROOM'S GLASS WINDOW GREGORY could see only the indeterminate shapes of the surgical team: the trauma specialist, visible only as a pair of concerned eyes over a blue mask, and the nurses leaning tensely over the patient. The surgeon requested another instrument, pausing for a moment and stretching his spine before resuming his work.

Someone bumped into Gregory, jostling him. He turned, angrily, to see a nurse standing beside him. "Excuse me, sir. I need to get in there." She held a box of surgical gauze in her hand.

"Wait a minute," Gregory said. "What's going on in there? How bad is the injury?"

"I'm sorry, sir, but we don't know yet. Are you a relative?"

"I'm his cousin. I'm on staff here."

"I think you should have a seat in the guest lounge. It's going to be a little while." Her eyes creased over her mask; he couldn't tell if she was offering a smile or a grimace of sympathy.

"Dr. Allston is one of the best," she said, her hand on the OR door. "Your cousin is in good hands."

He walked numbly down the hall to the lounge, a small, private room decorated in soothing pastels and offering a row of padded vinyl seats. An elderly couple occupied the far corner of the room, holding hands and staring grimly at the floor. Gregory sat quietly in a chair near the window and put his head in his hands.

He tried to reconstruct what had happened. When he'd returned home from Holiday's apartment, he turned on his computer. Then he saw he had a phone message, from Pacific University Hospital, saying that Shawn was in the

ER. The boy had been shot in South Central, in a park known to be a gang meeting place, and they'd found Gregory's phone number in his pocket. They had helicoptered him to West L.A., because he needed the best trauma specialists in the city.

It was now ten o'clock, almost the precise moment the telepresence surgery was due to begin. He leaned back in the chair. The hell with it. He belonged with his family. Bill Epstein knew the drill, he could run the show.

Of course, they'll probably fire me. But how could they, when he had just slept with the boss? *Why in hell did I let that pampered, privileged, neurotic woman take me home for the night? I should have been at home, I should have been responsible.*

He was being stupid. It wasn't Holiday's fault. He rubbed his aching nose and searched his memory for the tenderness of the night before. In a way he was frightened of her, of what she might mean to him.

He checked his watch again, wondering when his aunt Beverly might show up. The telepresence surgery had begun, but his beeper lay unattended in his car. He was on crisis time, a line of events beginning with playing his phone messages that morning.

Shot in the back. Gregory had pretended that they were a pair of guys sharing a sports-and-junk-food fraternity of two, that catching *Baywatch* and *Monday Night Football* with Shawn was enough to convince him the straight life was worth living. He had fooled himself.

"Gregory. They told me to look for you in here. Oh, God, Gregory, what happened?"

His aunt was standing in the doorway, her hands clasped over her mouth. She began to shake, and Gregory went to her. There wasn't anyplace private to go, so he led her into the lounge, ignoring the discreet stares of the old couple.

Beverly was thirty-six and worked as a secretary for a downtown city government office. She had driven straight from work after receiving his call, and was dressed in a blouse, skirt, and tennis shoes. This image of the working commuter filled him with an inexplicable sadness. He took her hand, unable to think of anything to say.

"Gregory, I got here as soon as I could. You must have called when I was on the way to work. What happened to my son?"

He tightened his hold on her hand. "He was shot late last night," he said plainly. "There were complications, so they had to bring in a trauma specialist. But that's good. I know him, he's a good man."

Beverly nodded, holding out hope that some force of nature could make things right.

"What happened to your nose, baby?" she said gently, touching his nose splint. "He didn't do this to you, did he?"

"No, me and Shawn got along . . . get along great, Aunt Beverly. I just had an accident last night. It's nothing."

His aunt nodded, looking at him strangely. Living with the willful Shawn had made her wary. She was looking for lies everywhere, and he had just told her one.

"Did he sneak out? Did he sneak out on you like he did me?" she asked, pulling a plastic packet of tissues from her purse.

"Yes," Gregory said quietly.

She balled her small, delicate hand into a fist and drummed on her thigh. "Damn. I really thought it was over. I thought I had done something about it."

Gregory ran his hand along the length of his chin, feeling the soreness under his stubble.

"Beverly, I need to tell you something," he said. She took both his hands in hers. "I didn't come home last night. I called to check on Shawn, and he told me he was going to bed. I didn't come home until this morning. That was when I got the message from the hospital."

She blinked several times, then she sighed.

Tears began to well up in his eyes. He willed them

away, wanting to be strong for her. "I'm so sorry. It was the first time. I thought it was all right."

"It's not your fault," she said, glancing at the institutional drapes drawn across the window. "You have your own life to live. You've been good to him. He tells me all about it. You've been a good influence, and I can't fault you for staying out one night and enjoying yourself."

If she had been angry with him, then he would at least have had the luxury of self-pity. But this reaction, with its undertow of resignation and loss, hurt even more.

Takamoto's surgery would be well under way by now. Soon he would have to face Holiday, having let her down. It was too complicated now; he wondered if they could separate this professional disaster from what happened between them in her apartment.

A tall black man in surgical scrubs stepped into the room, pulling off his mask and leaving it dangling around his neck. Gregory was used to seeing this wiry frame dressed in shorts on a racquetball court in one of their infrequent lunchtime games.

Michael Allston stepped slowly toward Gregory and Beverly, his expression grim.

"This is my aunt Beverly," Gregory said. "She's Shawn's mother."

Allston shook her hand. Beverly looked into his eyes and began to cry again. Gregory thought she would never stop.

"No! No one comes in here! Get them the fuck out of here and lock those doors!"

Phil Hermoza's voice boomed in the amphitheater as he ran toward the double-door entrance, where the agitated pack of reporters shouted questions at Holiday.

She stood up, brushing off her skirt. Phil locked the doors, leaving them sealed inside with the technicians and the small group of spectators at floor level. People sat still and shocked, staring at Holiday yet keeping their distance. Mike Hyata sat on a table and frantically punched numbers into his cellular phone.

Holiday clenched and unclenched her fists, struggling to put the last few minutes into any kind of sane chronology. She had isolated the gallbladder with the assisting surgeon's help. She had stapled the hepatic duct and the cystic duct—carefully, fastidiously, working with the slight time lag between her movements and their execution. It had all been going well, until the laser . . .

She had fired it once into the gallbladder's connective tissue, noticing that the beam was slightly stronger than it should have been. So she shut it off. Then it fired on its own, as if it had come to life with its own deranged, murderous will.

Hermoza joined her. "Get yourself together," he said harshly. "We have to figure out what happened here, or we're finished."

He approached Mike Hyata, his body tensed with anger. Hyata still sat, pale and drained, listening on the cellular phone.

Finally he hung up. "Takamoto is dead. They opened him up, but the damage was too extensive."

Holiday dropped her head to her chest, swaying slightly. Bill Epstein rose from his seat and led her to a metal chair near his station. She took a deep breath, wanting desperately to explain what had happened. But there was no answer, just a horrific loss of control worse than any operating-room nightmare she had ever endured.

"They . . . they don't really know what to do," Hyata continued, looking at Hermoza and shrinking back as if fearing the big man might strike him. "Mitsuyama is going to notify the police and start their own investigation. But right now it sounds like everyone is . . . I mean, that thing *cut him in half.*" He stared at Hermoza, his straight black hair clinging to his forehead with sweat.

"The police," Hermoza muttered. "Give me that damned phone."

Holiday turned to the small group staring at her: Sandra Jeanette, Jonathan Landry, Xavier Schulze, Kyle Jefferies. They gaped as if she were a condemned woman about to hang on the gallows. Epstein kneeled on the floor beside her, shaking his head.

"Bill," she said. "Can you review what happened? Can you tell what went wrong?" She reached out and grasped his shirtsleeve, pulling at it nearly hard enough to rip the fabric.

"I can try," he said. "But what can you tell me? Did you have any indication this was going to happen?"

Holiday tried to ignore the trace of accusation in his voice. "Just the laser. It blinked on me, so I thought there might have been a problem with the hand-trigger control. I asked you about it and you said everything looked fine."

"I know. And everything *was* fine," he said, his voice turning cold. "I know the system inside and out. There's no way that robot could have gone haywire like that. There are too many safeguards."

Hermoza clicked the cellular phone shut and tossed it on the table next to Hyata. "All right, the police are coming. They couldn't understand what the fuck I was talking about, but everyone has to stay until they get here."

He sighed, digging his fists into his eyes. "Epstein," he said quietly, removing his hands to expose his bleary, sagging features. "What can you tell me?"

"Dr. Powers has asked me to review the transmission records," he said, stepping toward the headpiece that Holiday threw to the floor.

Epstein carefully picked up the device. A plastic attachment dropped to the floor, the visor and microphone hung askew. "This thing isn't going to be much help," he said sullenly. "It's completely ruined. The computer's hard drive will have saved all the information we need, though. It's just a matter of finding it."

"How long is it going to take?" Holiday asked.

"It depends on what went wrong," Epstein replied,

pulling a chair to his keyboard. Four morose technicians stood in a circle behind him, silently peering at the screen.

One of the hired camera crew approached Hermoza. "We stopped the recorders when the signal ended," he said. "I assume you're not going to release the video right away to the media, like you planned?"

For a moment Hermoza's eyes widened and his cheek pulsed wildly. Then he collected himself. "Pull all the tapes and give them to me," he said. "The police might want them for evidence. And don't touch anything you don't have to touch."

Holiday felt a wrenching helplessness. There was nothing she could do, no way to apply her knowledge or expertise. For all anyone knew, this was all her fault; she had been in command of a device at the time it killed a man. She thought of Han Takamoto, of his mastery and his self-assurance—and of the doubt she had thought she saw lurking behind his dark eyes.

She began to pace in a slow, nervous circle, trying to stay calm. Could she possibly be arrested for this? She wondered, *Should I be?*

Holiday's gaze wandered to the back of the room, where Kyle and Xavier Schulze were speaking in low voices, casting glances at Epstein and his technicians. Jefferies turned, sensing he was being watched, and met Holiday's eyes. Holiday broke away.

"I'm really sorry to see this happen, Dr. Powers." She felt a hand on her shoulder. Jonathan Landry, his silver hair topping his tanned features, wore an expression of genuine concern.

"Thanks, Jonathan," she said, pulling away. He looked into her eyes meaningfully for a moment, as if he expected her to provide some kind of perspective on what had happened, to neatly tie up the package of this disaster. "I . . . I don't know what to say. All the trials were perfect. The system had no bugs."

He looked at her as if she were his daughter and had

officers and now left together. Most of the spectators were gone now; only the small group near the computers remained. Hermoza sat next to Hyata, both stunned and morose, watching the technicians with blank languor.

Gregory rubbed his eyes. "You checked all the idiot possibilities, right? Cables, cords, plugs, just to see if anything came loose?"

"Of course. Those were the first things we checked," a young technician in glasses said. "It's all fine."

Pete Miller, a relatively older technician, cleared his throat shyly. "What about checking the compiled code size from last night?" he said in a nervous voice. "If it doesn't match up with what we ran today, then we'll know something changed."

Epstein nodded enthusiastically. "That's a good idea," he said. He looked at Gregory. "Want to check it out?"

"Go ahead," Gregory said. "You know it as well as I do."

Epstein began typing into the keyboard. He ran through a series of number blocks, inspecting them and occasionally commenting to Gregory, who looked barely interested.

Detective Harper took Holiday's arm and led her away from the computers. "At this point you're the closest thing we have to a suspect," he said in a reedy voice. "All we have is your word that you didn't fire that laser yourself."

She pulled her hair away from her face, staring at the rings and depressions around Harper's eyes. "Does that mean you're going to arrest me?" she asked.

He bowed his head slightly, looking up at her. "For now I just need a statement. Until we complete the investigation, don't leave town. Are you planning a vacation or anything?"

"Of course not," Holiday said. "I want to know what happened more than anyone else. You have no idea what it was like. There was nothing I could do."

Harper regarded her sympathetically. Holiday smelled

a lilac floral odor from his old-fashioned hair tonic. "One time I had to deal with a fifteen year-old kid hopped up on PCP, waving a Saturday night special at me," he said slowly. "I shot and killed him. That was eleven years ago and, no, I haven't forgotten it. So maybe I know what you're talking about."

She looked into his brown eyes. "But shit," he said, turning away, "by the time this really gets going, the feds'll probably get into the act, maybe even politicians. I don't think you did it, to tell you the truth, but my opinion might not matter. Just don't take any vacations. It won't look good."

Holiday felt his momentary intimacy turn to something harder and unknowable. She joined him at the computers, where Epstein had begun to type rapidly.

"What is it?" she asked, trying to get a response from Gregory or Epstein. Both were immersed in a rapidly flowing series of numbers and codes.

"Something weird," Epstein finally said. "The compiled code size is different from last night. That doesn't make sense—there were no last-minute changes."

Hermoza stood up, leaving Hyata looking forlorn and alone. "What do you mean, it doesn't make any sense?" he asked loudly, wedging his large frame to the fore of the group.

"I mean . . . Gregory, look at this," Epstein said, his face pallid in the monitor's light. "There's extra code in here, no doubt about it. I remember the program size from last night. Someone added something to the system since then."

Gregory squinted at the screen. "It's not in the start-up codes," he said. Epstein typed rapidly at the keyboard.

"It looks like something tacked on to the remote system." Everyone in the room grew quiet, listening to Epstein with anticipation. "It's set to work only when the computer is hooked to an off-site linkup."

"What the fuck are you talking about?" Hermoza said

impatiently, leaning over the screen as if trying to make sense of hieroglyphics.

Epstein rested his hands on the keyboard, stunned. "I think there's a subroutine command in here, built to feed into the laser when the surgeon works on a live patient through a fiberoptic link. I'd have to read the source code, but my guess is that it told the laser to fire at maximum intensity regardless of Dr. Powers's instructions."

Harper stepped next to Hermoza, both men elbowing each other to get the best view of what was going on. "So you're saying someone sabotaged the computer?" Harper said. He cocked his head in confusion. To Holiday it seemed that he might be playing dumb.

"Exactly," Epstein said, typing again, faster this time. Gregory sat in sullen silence.

"I can get a user ID from when this change was made," Epstein said. "And here it is." He suddenly stopped typing.

A sense of suspended time filled the room. "You mean you know who did it?" Harper asked, his hands on his hips.

Gregory started from his torpor and stared at the screen. Suddenly his eyes grew large. "No," he said. Then, louder, "No!"

Detective Harper put his hands on Gregory's shoulders, roughly holding him in the chair. "What does it say?"

Bill Epstein stared at Gregory for a moment, then turned to Harper. "Gregory Hampton made the change early this morning."

Hermoza inhaled sharply. "Are you sure, Epstein? Did you make some kind of mistake?"

Holiday for an instant saw slivers of light playing before her eyes, and the men's voices came to her as if passing across a long distance. She felt her breath catch in her chest and reached out to grab a chair to keep from falling.

"There's no way anyone else could have logged on under Gregory's name. This system is too secure. He put this instruction in," Epstein said, pulling away from Gregory as if he suddenly posed a physical threat. "He killed Takamoto."

Hermoza turned to Gregory, his rage of a moment ago replaced with a sad look of entreaty. "Say something, Hampton."

"Collins, Banks, get over here and arrest this man," Harper said, pushing down harder on Gregory to keep him from moving. "I'd recommend that you don't speak, Mr. Hampton. Everything you say from this point onward can be used against you in a court of law."

The two officers pulled Gregory out of the chair and roughly cuffed his hands behind his back. He remained silent and expressionless. They led him to the door and waited for Harper.

"I didn't do this," Gregory said, his voice almost inaudible.

"Dr. Powers, your statement has become even more important." Harper took a card from his jacket pocket and handed it to her. "I expect to see you by five o'clock this afternoon. That should give you time to recover from your shock."

Harper began to walk out. "Wait a minute," Hermoza cried out. "I'll come with you and deal with those fucking media jackals."

Before he left, he turned to Holiday. "Until we get this figured out, you're on indefinite leave. Your surgical privileges are suspended."

She looked at him, at the man she had known since she was a young, frightened woman just out of high school. There was still familiarity and compassion in his eyes. And there also was a wariness, a reserve, that hurt far more than anything else.

"Phil, I didn't know," she said, reaching out to him.

"We'll talk later," he said, stepping away from her. "Go out the back way. Talk to this detective, then go home and ride this out."

"I didn't know, Phil."

He paused. "I believe you, Holiday. We'll get through this, all right? Just do as I say."

Then he was gone, leaving her alone with the small group of stunned technicians and Hyata, who frantically spoke Japanese into his cellular phone.

Gregory. *You can trust me,* he had said.

10:15 P.M.

Kyle Jefferies took a booth in the back of the place, as agreed, and ordered a bourbon on the rocks. He almost never drank, as a rule, but today he would have one.

If it were up to him, he never would have picked such a seedy bar to meet. Tucked into an alcove off Fourth Street downtown, the Mutineer was a dingy, run-down dive full of old fishing nets hung from the ceiling and tackle nailed to the walls. The clientele was one step above the occupants of a holding pen in the county jail.

Which is where they took Gregory Hampton. Jefferies searched his feelings as he felt the alcohol warm his insides. Satisfaction was one of the things he felt. He wouldn't deny it.

The front door opened, and the half-dozen other customers in the bar looked up briefly and then returned to their drinks. Jefferies didn't wave or signal to Clay Simmons. He simply waited.

"Doctor," he said as he took a seat opposite Jefferies. Simmons was young, maybe thirty, but he looked worn from hard living. His hair was long, and his pockmarked brow shaded his darting eyes. Beneath his denim jacket Jefferies could see Simmons's strong, wiry frame.

"Simmons," Jefferies replied. "You picked a nice establishment."

Clay Simmons cast a look around. He wore his usual chilling smile. "Guess this isn't the kind of bar you'd find a rich doctor in." He looked into Jefferies's eyes. "This place got you scared?"

"Don't be stupid," Jefferies said, and instantly regretted it.

Simmons laughed softly. He turned to the bar and called out for a beer. The Mutineer apparently didn't boast table service, and at the sound of the order the bartender shot a withering look. Within moments, though, he had brought the drink, giving Simmons a wary, almost frightened glance. They knew him here.

"What's the matter?" Simmons asked, lighting a cigarette. "You look like someone ran over your dog."

Jefferies took a deep breath. "I asked you to meet me because it's time for you to stop. I brought some more money for your trouble. But it's over."

Simmons blew a smoke ring across the table; it disintegrated before Jefferies's face. "What's over?" he asked innocently.

It was like dealing with a child. Jefferies felt an overwhelming sense that he had made a terrible mistake. "Don't play dumb," he said. "Dr. Powers. I don't want you to call her anymore. Something important happened today, and I . . . I have everything I need."

"So what you're saying," Simmons asked, moving his beer glass in a small circle of condensation, "is that I'm fired?"

Feeling a tight knot in his throat, Jefferies took a blank envelope from his jacket pocket and passed it to Simmons under the table. "There's two thousand in there," he said. "It's yours. You don't have to do anything more."

Simmons sat up slightly and stuffed the money down the front of his jeans. He looked down at the table, a slight smile flickering across his lips. "I hate taking money for doing nothing."

"You've done enough. You've done plenty."

"Does this have anything to do with that colored guy?" Simmons asked. He was nearly finished with his beer, and Jefferies saw that his eyes were already runny and bloodshot. "Me and a couple of my boys played around with him last night."

Jefferies felt his face growing hot. He pushed away his half-finished drink. "Hampton. He had a bandage on his face this morning. You had something to do with that?"

"Well, Doctor," Simmons said, obviously pleased to have given Jefferies a surprise. "You told me to mess with her head a little. She and the colored guy looked like they were having a pretty good time. I thought I'd put a little fear in 'em."

"I never asked . . ." Jefferies paused. He definitely had made a mistake. "Just stop. Don't do anything. It's all under control."

"Think so?" Simmons signaled for another beer. The bartender was quicker this time. "Well, I'm not so sure. You came to me, remember? I did what you asked. And I think I did a pretty good job."

"You did fine," Jefferies said eagerly. "She's gone. I don't think it's a problem anymore. So just lay off."

Simmons snorted derisively. Jefferies had spent a month during his residency in a clinical psychology ward. In an instant he catalogued the nature of Simmons's psychosis: he was manipulative, racist, a misogynist, and preoccupied with creating fear. He certainly would have violent tendencies.

"You don't know what it's like, Doctor," Simmons said. "I have to look into those security monitors at her apartment building forty hours a week. It's my job. I see her coming and going, all the time. And she's a *fine* one. You and her used to have a thing going, didn't you?"

"You heard me," Jefferies said, trying to sound intimidating. He felt more weak and ineffectual than he ever had in his life. He stood up and leaned close to Simmons. "It's over. Take the money, don't expect any more, and forget you ever met me. Do you understand?"

Simmons leaned back. His eyes were wild now, and he spoke like a man in complete control of everything around him. "Oh, sure, I understand," he said. "Problem is, I got a pretty good memory. I can't forget a face like yours."

"I'm leaving," Jefferies said. He had never felt so help-less. "Don't do anything more to her, or so help me—"

"Go on, Doctor," Simmons said, laughing. "I'm tired of talking to you. You go on home and don't worry about a thing."

Outside the Mutineer Jefferies leaned against a lamp-post and tried to catch his breath. Takamoto's death would work for him, and Holiday would almost surely leave the hospital.

Jefferies would have what he wanted, although now he had to wonder what the final cost would take from him. As for Simmons . . . he was drunk, and stupid. He was just trying to get under Kyle's skin. He wouldn't try anything more. Would he?

13

SHE LAY WATCHING TELEVISION ON HER LONG BLACK SOFA, propped on a haphazard mound of pillows. Looking around, she saw the evidence of her existence for the past two days: take-out food wrappers, dirty glasses, unopened mail, newspapers that had arrived and been left unread.

In the light that seeped through the blinds she saw unpacked boxes still stacked around the apartment. They made the place look as though it was inhabited by someone who didn't plan to stay long.

Which was a tempting thought. She had nowhere to go. Her job was effectively in limbo, and her only human contact since the failed surgery had been with Detective Harper. Harper was sympathetic, listening intently to her explanations without interrupting. Gregory was being held without bail, until federal authorities could confer with Japanese law enforcement to decide what he might be charged with. Gregory clung obstinately to his innocence, and Harper suggested she call him if she "remembered" any additional information.

He made her feel guilty somehow. She hadn't told him that she and Gregory had become romantically involved. It was private, her own business. She felt at the time, illogically, that she was protecting herself at Gregory's expense.

She felt terrible. She hadn't exercised in weeks, she was eating junk and taking Valium to sleep. Without the drug she would lie awake, imagining she could still feel Gregory next to her, thinking of Han Takamoto's dark, haunting eyes.

The television sprang to life with a noisy hiss; she had inadvertently nudged the volume control. Puzzling for a moment over the remote controls, she pressed the button that would play the tape sent by the Pacific University Public Relations Office.

Winding through the recording, the machine finally produced an image of Dan Rather. The tape had been edited to show only his story on the bizarre, bloody death of Mitsuyama's CEO. She wondered: had her story been second, fifth, last in the program? How large in the scope of world disaster were her problems?

She stared at the image of herself standing before the telepresence workstation, dressed in the blue lab coat that now lay draped over a dining chair. Her video likeness moved the penlike instrument. She looked hunched and tense and—as the camera panned back to take in the video screen, the computers, and the small crowd of spectators—she seemed enclosed and isolated by the headpiece.

Rather's voice was soothing and familiar. "Authorities have taken a suspect into custody, having found evidence linking him to the computer malfunction that resulted in Takamoto's death. The surgeon has not at this time been charged with any involvement."

The image of the surgery disappeared just as the laser fired: it was too revolting for television. The anchorman appeared again, a photo of Takamoto appearing over his shoulder. He pursed his lips meaningfully, intoning, "Han Takamoto, dead at sixty-one."

More stories followed: the other networks' coverage, followed by local news stations' analyses, with hastily rendered illustrations and freeze-frame images of Holiday standing before the workstation. One report froze her just before she put on the headpiece; she saw herself offer a grim smile to Epstein at the computer station.

The phone rang, amid clutter on the coffee table. She had kept it unplugged for days, but had decided to plug it in perhaps a half hour before. She waited a moment, then answered it.

"Dr. Powers? This is Sandy Stein."

It was her head resident. He sounded anxious.

"Yes, Sandy."

Stein hesitated. "I hate to bother you, but I thought you would want to . . . it's about Mrs. Alacia."

Holiday searched her memory. She had been seeing Rose Alacia on an outpatient basis for acute esophageal reflux. Holiday had fought with Xavier Schulze to perform a laparoscopic Nissen procedure—when was it, weeks ago?

"What's wrong, Sandy? Has her condition grown worse?"

"Not really. It's . . . it's Dr. Jefferies."

"What about Dr. Jefferies?"

"He has her on the schedule tomorrow morning for seven-thirty. He's doing the operation himself. Even though there's no real emergency, he said he thinks there is. Since your privileges are suspended, he's going to take over the patient."

"I see."

"Is there anything you want me to do?"

Holiday considered. Kyle had stolen her patient, taking advantage of her predicament and undermining her position at the hospital. She knew this was probably only one of many incidents.

"No. Thanks, Sandy. Thanks for telling me."

"I'm really sorry, Dr. Powers. I know you spent a lot of time with Mrs. Alacia. That is, before . . ."

She thanked him again and hung up. The phone rang almost the instant it was placed back in its cradle.

"Dr. Powers? Wow, I can't believe I finally reached you. My name is Brett Sanderson, and I'm with Channel Five News."

Holiday hung up. It rang again. She wasn't sure why, but she picked it up.

"Dr. Powers. You haven't been answering your phone."

She knew the voice instantly: deep, breathy, insinuating. "What do you want?" she asked quietly.

"I saw you on the news. Now, didn't I warn you to get

out of town? You could have gone back to Boston, back to Mom and Dad and your little brother Philip."

"How did you know that? Who are you?"

"I know everything about you, bitch."

She hung up and pulled the cord out of the wall. For an instant she considered tossing it off the balcony. *I'd probably hit someone and end up on the news again.*

She told Detective Harper about the calls, hoping he would respond, maybe even validate her paranoia. He merely told her she could apply for a phone tap if she wanted. When he began to recite the list of technicalities and difficulties involved, she told him it wasn't necessary.

She sat up, her muscles tight from atrophy. The kitchen offered only dirty dishes, stale coffee grounds, and stuffy air. Wreckage, she thought, the place looks like wreckage. Like the other damage: Takamoto, dying in his sleep, never knowing what happened. Shawn, in the hospital recovering, a paraplegic before he could grow out of a tumultuous adolescence. Gregory, alone in jail, waiting to be charged.

She didn't know if she believed Gregory was guilty. She thought about his anger, always just beneath the surface, and how oddly he acted the morning she woke up with him. She put her hands on the kitchen counter and looked down at the floor. One moment she thought he did it; the next, it was impossible. It was as if her feelings were on the far side of a flooded river, its banks swelled with chaos. She had believed in him. Perhaps she wanted to punish him for that.

She washed down a sedative with a glass of water and reclined on the sofa. She wasn't precisely sure how many pills she had taken that day, and she didn't care. Groggy from earlier pills, she closed her eyes. Within moments she felt herself slipping.

When her awareness returned, she was in the dark somewhere. She wanted to cry out, but her voice wouldn't come. There were hands on her, someone was shaking her and saying something, but she just wanted to be left alone in this soft, comfortable place.

She opened her eyes slightly, feeling her head against the sofa cushion. Wait, she thought, I'm here, I'm awake. Through her half-closed eyes she saw a dark shape looming over her, pressing down on her shoulders and shaking her back and forth. In an instant she was back in reality. Someone was in her apartment.

Holiday lashed out at the shape, striking it. It had to be the man on the phone, coming for her, she thought. She couldn't focus her eyes. The room was a dim canvas of shapes and noises, and she couldn't be sure what was real.

"Stay awake, damn it!" Hands held her shoulders again. Holiday felt a light slap across her cheek.

"Holiday, it's me. Wake up, or I'm going to throw you in a cold shower."

This warning brought her to consciousness. Kate Fisher knelt before her, one hand on Holiday's shoulder and the other held over her own forehead, which had sprouted a light cut.

"Oh, Kate, did I do that?" she said, sitting up.

Kate raised up and sat on the nearby chair. "You've got long nails for a surgeon, kid," she said ruefully.

"I'm so sorry. I didn't know it was you."

"It's my fault. Every time I let myself in, I start a panic." She leaned forward. "You look like shit. Do you want me to get you something? Want some coffee?"

"Please." Holiday watched her friend recede into the kitchen, her slight frame enveloped by a draping silk pantsuit. She called out, "You cut your hair."

Kate's voice sounded metallic from the kitchen, echoing on the linoleum and tile. "I got depressed. I always cut my hair shorter when I don't know what to do with myself."

Holiday rose from the couch, feeling stagnant and unwashed. It was embarrassing to be discovered looking like this. "What were you depressed about?"

The tap running drowned out the first part of Kate's

sentence. "—so I took the last couple of days off. Everything's been a mess. I tried to call you, but your line was
busy."

"What did you say?" Holiday asked, leaning in the
kitchen doorway, watching Kate unfold the coffee filter.

Kate looked up, and for the first time Holiday noticed
that her friend looked haggard and spent. Her fair skin
showed violet rings under her eyes. "Oh, sugar, I'm being
silly. My ex-husband called to tell me he got married to
his little girlfriend last week. I didn't think I'd take it so
hard, but it just got me feeling old. Anyway I took some
time off and went to stay with a friend."

"A friend?"

"You don't want to know. I don't mean to sound like
. . . look, I'll tell you later. That's another can of worms,
at least lately. I would have come by this afternoon, but I
went to the beach to sort things out."

"This afternoon?" For the first time Holiday realized
that it was night. Outside the window was the red-
smeared night sky. The kitchen clock read 9:30 P.M. "I've
been asleep longer than I thought," she said.

"That's an understatement," Kate said harshly. "You
look like you've been in those pajamas for a couple of
days."

Holiday looked down at her wrinkled nightshirt. "I
know I'm a mess," she said. "I've just been . . . it's been
hard."

Kate folded her arms. "I'm sure it has, but you can't let
yourself go like this."

Holiday felt scolded. "Everyone's talking about what
happened, aren't they? Everyone knows."

"It was on the news, sugar, of course they know." Kate
leaned back against the counter. "Do you really care what
people think?"

"It's my career, Kate," Holiday said, suddenly angry.

"You have to take care of *yourself* before your career,"
Kate said. "Remember that. And do you know what people are saying—other than the usual jealous assholes?

They're saying it was a terrible thing that happened. No one blames you. People are hoping you're all right."

"I hope that's true," Holiday said. She felt sleepy again. "We finished the system in a hurry, but it was solid, Kate. We didn't take any unnecessary risks."

"Everyone knows that, Holiday," Kate said, almost sadly.

Kate made a tremendous amount of coffee. The machine sputtered and hissed, producing a brimming potful. Kate shrugged at Holiday. "You looked like you needed to wake up."

Walking to the living room, an overly full cup held delicately to keep it from dripping on the carpet, Kate paused at the dining area. "What are you doing with these?"

Holiday paused in the kitchen doorway. Kate held the vial of Valium as if it were contraband.

"I had an old prescription," she said slowly. "My nerves were shot, as you can imagine. I just need to relax and sleep."

"For two days?" Kate stared at the label. "These things are high-dosage. What in the world were you thinking? No wonder I had to slap you to wake you up, sugar. You're lucky you woke up at all."

Holiday placed her cup on a coaster, avoiding Kate's eyes. "I had a nervous condition when I was younger," she said. "I'm stronger now, but I just needed . . . not to have to cope with things."

"Listen, I know you've been through a lot."

"You made things sound good, Kate, but I know what people must be saying about the operation." Holiday froze for an instant and wondered if Kate had mentioned to anyone about discovering her and Gregory together that morning.

"Look, honey, monks in Tibet are probably talking about it. So what? You're going to have to put it behind you eventually."

They sipped their coffee. "Look," Kate said. "Lay off

the pills. When I was breaking up with my husband, things got pretty crazy."

There was a world of experience, most of it bad, behind this terse statement. "I got pretty down and out," she continued. "I started taking sedatives to help me sleep. Before I knew it, I *needed* them to sleep. Then I needed one when I had a bad day at work. After a while I took them just because I liked the way I felt with them better than the way I felt without them."

"All right," Holiday said. "You're right. No more pills."

Kate appeared satisfied. "You might have been scared and messed up when you were younger, but you're not a kid now. You're stronger than you give yourself credit for."

"Thanks. I guess I just needed to be reminded." Holiday felt an urge to reach out and embrace Kate, to demonstrate how much these words meant to her.

"Tell me about Gregory," Kate said. "I guess giddy girl talk is out of the question at this point."

"I'm not sure what I think," Holiday said, speaking quickly, forcing the words out before they were lost behind her barricade of mixed feelings. "We had a wonderful evening together. I thought he was someone I might . . . fall in love with, if that doesn't sound too ridiculous."

"That's not ridiculous."

"We made love and it was . . . it was really good." Kate's eyes widened. "It was a little strange the next morning, after you left, but I thought it was more me than him. But now *this,* this thing he's supposed to have done."

Holiday caught Kate's gaze and fixed on it. "Do you think he did it, Kate?"

Kate took a deep breath, shifting uncomfortably. "Sometimes you don't know someone as well as you think you do. Which is not to say you can't know someone after one evening, because I think you can, if you're smart and lucky."

Holiday digested this. "Have you gone to see him in jail?" Kate asked quickly.

"No. I don't even know for sure if he's still there."

"Well, I can understand that. If he is guilty, he had to know what his actions would do to you."

"One minute I think he did it, and the next I know there's no way he could do that to anyone. He just isn't like that. But I think if I went to see him, I'd just be more confused than I am already."

"You're probably right." Kate put down her cup and walked to the window. The breeze had turned starchy and arid, a final blast from the Santa Ana season. A strong gust blew through the window, sending the blinds clattering against the windowsill.

"These damned winds aren't supposed to come around this time of year," Kate said distractedly. As if in response, a stronger gust sent the blinds in motion like metallic sails, heedlessly billowing in accordion folds. "But I guess you never can tell."

Holiday suddenly realized how much her friend's visit had helped her. She felt selfish. "Kate, we've only talked about me. I'm really sorry about your ex-husband."

"That bastard put me through the wringer." Kate's mouth tightened; she still stared out the window. "In terms of him getting married, I feel sorry for the girl. I don't know . . . it just felt like something died, like some part of my life had been cut off. Does that make any sense?"

"Of course it does," Holiday said, thinking of Kyle, of Lars. "What about this friend? Is it a boyfriend?"

"Yeah, I think so." Kate said. "Lately he's been weird."

"Do I know him?"

"Just plug your phone in, all right?" Kate said, turning to Holiday and smiling ironically. "Enough with the hermit bit."

She sat down and put an arm around Holiday, pulling her close. "You're young, talented, and beautiful. You'll be all right."

In Kate's embrace Holiday felt her older friend physically surrender, as though her own worry had ground her down. They held on to each other for a long time.

After Kate left, Holiday turned on the kitchen phone. It immediately rang. She ignored it, turned down the volume on her answering machine, and walked slowly into her bedroom. Kate was right. She could survive this.

14

PAM LINCOLN SAT AT HER DESK, TAPPING AT HER COMPUTER keyboard. "There are plenty of messages on your desk," she said. "As usual I prioritized them. There are about ten calls from Mike Hyata at Mitsuyama. And your head resident, Sandy Stein, wants to get hold of you. Remember, you start teaching after the first of the year."

Holiday listened to this onslaught of information with growing irritation. For the first time in three days she had gone to the office, ignoring her administrative suspension. When she arrived, Pam had poured fresh coffee for her, something she never did.

Then the honeymoon was over. Pam seemed to harbor an unspoken grievance against Holiday's absence. Holiday stopped just short of reminding Pam that she was her assistant and not her keeper. If things ever got back to normal, she would take Pam to lunch, or give her a day off.

"That's it," Pam said. "Other than the million other things I'm not telling you about." Her features softened. "Look, I know about your suspension. Don't worry. You're too valuable to lose."

"Thanks, Pam." Holiday felt the tension between them evaporate. "I hope everyone else agrees. Now I'll go make the calls."

"You do that." Pam turned back to her computer screen.

Holiday closed her office door behind her and opened the blinds. The sky was a crisp blue, casting bleached-out light on the dry trees and grass below. This time of year it would be snowing back home; here people were in their shirtsleeves. It could have been any time of year, any season, and she would see the same view from her window.

The air was stale, but the hospital, built in the flush of postwar modernism, had windows that wouldn't open. The steady ambient purr of the atmospheric control system rang in her ears as she dialed the phone. Maintaining her will made her feel like Atlas holding up the heavens. She wanted to go back to her apartment. Everything was still half packed, she could be out of L.A. in a day.

Mike Hyata answered on the first ring. "Dr. Powers, how are you?" He sounded cold and distant.

"As well as could be expected. How are things with you?"

"You can imagine. I don't have much time to talk, but I have a request. Could you send me internal personnel files on everyone involved on the telepresence project at Pacific University?"

"What for, Mike?"

"To save my ass, that's why." He paused. "I'm sorry. But you can't imagine what it's been like for me lately. The company is in a state of shock. The board of directors wants to conduct a private investigation into Takamoto's death."

"I don't know if I can send you those files," Holiday said. "I'd have to check on the personnel policy here."

"Do what you can, Dr. Powers. I appreciate it."

She waited a beat, then asked, "Mike, what's going to happen with Mitsuyama now?"

"In terms of your funding, I don't know. Everything's in a state of flux. Moshiro Tamo, who runs international management, is going to be announced as the new chairman next week."

"International management? So he was your boss."

"Technically. I've never even met the man. It's one hell of a lousy way to have your boss rise to power."

After hanging up, Holiday headed out of her office. "Leaving already?" Pam asked.

"I'm just restless," Holiday said. "I'll be back in a while."

The hall was crowded with a small group of residents

on rounds with Ron Bagghasian, a tall, wild-haired doctor she had met during her preliminary interviews. In a low voice he was berating a young student for misdiagnosing a patient's recovery speed after a foot amputation. A few students in the group glanced at Holiday as she waited for the elevator, nudging one another.

She was relieved when the elevator doors finally closed. Arriving at one of the research floors, she strode down the antiseptic hall, looking directly ahead, trying to ignore the minor stir she caused as she headed toward the virtual reality lab.

At the door Holiday produced her security key card and jammed it into the slot. She waited for the familiar buzz authorizing her entry, but it didn't come. She realized that her security code had been deleted from the system.

"Damn." She walked to the laboratory's glass wall. A small group of technicians were gathered in a corner, conversing by a water cooler. She pressed her face to the glass until she saw the person she was looking for: Bill Epstein, his feet up on a near table, reading a thick spiral-bound log book.

Holiday stepped back and rapped hard on the Plexiglas. It gave a hollow thump, absorbing the sound and force of the blow. She hit it again, harder this time.

Epstein looked up from his book, cocking his head curiously. Angry now, Holiday rapped on the window harder, not stopping until Epstein swiveled in his chair, his eyes wide when he saw her standing outside. He frowned and pointed to the doors.

"Dr. Powers." He opened the door and looked up and down the hall, blocking her from coming inside.

"Let me in, Bill. We have to talk." Holiday folded her arms, feeling a faint sting of humiliation.

"I don't like this any more than you do," Epstein said, staring over her shoulder. "But Dr. Jefferies is back in charge of the project. He told me I can't let you into the labs."

"I'm on suspension, Bill. I haven't been fired. I still run this department." She glanced past him. The water-cooler conversation had ceased, its participants now slowly drifting toward them to hear what was going on.

"I know that, Dr. Powers," Epstein said. "And, believe me, I can't wait until you're back." He looked into her eyes. "Have you heard from Gregory?"

"No, I haven't," she said. It felt painfully ridiculous to stand there begging to be let inside. She didn't even know why she had gone there, beyond feeling that Epstein might make some sense of Gregory's arrest for her. She saw now that he knew nothing, and that Kyle had intimidated him about speaking to her—to the point where he was behaving like a grade-school hall monitor.

"I haven't either," Epstein said. "I know why you want to talk to me, but I don't have any answers. No one but Gregory could have accessed the system with his password, and not many people would have known how to make the laser do what it did. I don't know why, but he did it."

His lips trembled with tension and his cheeks reddened. "There's no reason to be angry with me, Bill," Holiday said.

"The hell there isn't," he said coldly. "I thought we were finally going to have some sanity when you came in here, so that we could concentrate on our research. Instead we got rushed into that operation. Now our reputation is shit."

"I was trying to keep funding coming, so that you could stay in your safe little lab and keep tinkering on your machines." Holiday felt icy inside. "And tell me—how could one man ruin the system like that?"

"Because he's the one who created the fucking thing," Epstein hissed. "We don't do miracles here. Any results we get come after busting our asses more than you can even imagine."

Holiday stared at Epstein. "Did Kyle Jefferies put you in charge of the department, Bill?"

Epstein closed his eyes. She could see he wasn't angry at her specifically. He was merely hanging on in adversity, striking out at random to express his frustration.

"I'm the acting department head," he said. "Even if Gregory isn't convicted, I seriously doubt they'll hire him back."

"We'll be working together from now on, then," Holiday said calmly. "There's no need for us to be at each other's throats."

Epstein looked at her curiously. "I hope that's true, I really do." He took a step back. "Stay in touch." The door shut slowly. Epstein stepped away and walked deliberately down the hall to his office.

When he was gone, Holiday turned a corner so that she couldn't be seen by the lab workers. What was wrong with him, she wondered. While they were speaking, it seemed as if he were frightened of something. She realized she hadn't actually seen the evidence against Gregory; it existed as an interpretation of electronic data that she barely understood.

But all the technicians had agreed, and Gregory's eyes had bulged with shock when the information was called on the screen. It had to be real. Gregory's surprise seemed that of a guilty man who thought he couldn't be discovered.

Wandering now, Holiday found herself at a long desk staffed by a bored-looking young man. No doubt underpaid and probably overqualified, he sat stiffly at a computer station, probably wondering how he'd found himself working in a hospital records department.

He looked up, his thin face partially obscured by a scruffy goatee. "Can I help you?"

"Pardon me?" Holiday asked.

The young man sighed as if speaking to a particularly dull child. "This is Records and Billing. Did you come here for something?" As he spoke, his expression changed from impatience to vague befuddlement. "Are you going to answer that?"

"Answer what?" Holiday asked, realizing that he was staring at the pager on her hip. She unclipped it to see an unfamiliar number on the readout. "Thanks," she said quickly.

At a nearby phone she looked back to see the young man staring at her. He turned away when their eyes met, shrugging and returning to his screen. Holiday dialed the number displayed on her pager.

"Hello? Holiday?"

It was Kyle's voice on the other end, partially drowned out by the sound of heavy traffic. Quick anger flowed through her as she thought about her humiliation at the computer labs.

"Kyle? Where are you?" she said.

"Um . . . Close to Wilshire and La Cienega. I'm on my car phone."

He sounded familiar and easy, which only irritated her more. At every turn, she thought, there was Kyle. With every obstacle and debacle, he would appear.

"Kyle, I just got back from the tech labs. They wouldn't even let me in. You owe me an explanation for that."

He was silent. She heard the great swoosh of a truck passing him. "We can talk about that later."

It was as if they were chatting on a Sunday afternoon. "Then why did you have me paged?"

"I wanted to see if you were all right."

"I just told you, Kyle, I'm not all right. My access to the labs is cut off. And what about Mrs. Alacia? You stole one of my patients." Her voice sounded shrill. Without thinking, she had slipped into her old role with him: the acolyte, the young girl who had to cajole to get what she wanted.

"That's not what I'm talking about," Kyle said. He was silent for a moment. "Fucking traffic. I talked to Kate about you, and she said she was worried."

"Kate?" Holiday asked. "Kate Fisher?"

"We've been dating, you know." Kyle sounded

strangely proud. She wondered if he was trying to make her jealous.

"I didn't know that."

"Well, Kate didn't want to say anything for a while. She thought you might not understand, in light of our past."

"That's over, Kyle," she said.

"Of course it is," he said. A little too quickly, she thought. "That's what I told her."

"She also told me you two were having problems."

Silence. "I've had a hard time lately. What happened with you is part of it. You know how it is when your responsibilities are increased."

She tried to picture him and Kate together, but saw only their separate images spliced together like two photographs united with glue and tape. "I know how you are about your work," she said.

He sounded as if he didn't hear her. "I just wanted to see how you were. I've been worried about you. Worried about . . . I don't know, I'm worried that something might happen to you."

"What do you mean?"

"It's stupid," he said dismissively. "But I worry. I still care about you, Holiday. I know it's hard to believe, but . . . now I really want the best for you. I'm trying to let go of some hard feelings I had."

It sounded almost like something Kate would say. She wondered if her friend had been coaching him. "I'm glad, Kyle," she said. "There's no reason we should be enemies."

"I'm glad to hear that." She heard a horn blare, probably someone the hyperaggressive Kyle had cut off. "And I promise I'll do what I can to make things all right for you."

There was something strange in his tone. There was something he wasn't telling her. Her mind flashed on the voice on the phone, the man who kept calling her, but that wasn't Kyle. She would always know his voice.

"You can help by restoring my access to the labs," she said.

"As I said, we'll talk about that later." His voice went cold. "Take care of yourself, Holiday. I think you're going to be all right. And"—he spoke quickly—"even though we've both moved on, I still love you in my way."

He hung up then, cutting any link that might have been restored between them. Holiday looked around; the young man at the billing desk was staring at her again, no longer trying to feign disinterest. She turned away, not wanting him to see her tears.

15

HE HAD WAITED IN THAT DAMNED PARKING LOT FOR TOO LONG.
The car was stuffy, and the longer he waited for her, the
angrier he became. Looking inside the supermarket, he
saw that the place was crowded. No wonder she was taking forever.

Sitting back in the seat, pretending to relax, he thought
about how he must have looked. He wasn't a young man
anymore, but he kept in shape. Dressed in nice jeans and
a polo shirt, sitting in a black sedan with the radio playing
low—people must have thought him a husband waiting
patiently for his wife. It pleased him to fool them.

Holiday Powers wouldn't give him the time of day in
most situations, he knew that. Young, talented, beautiful,
with those legs he had watched from afar and up close,
that trim figure he longed to wrap his arms around—she
would never give him a chance.

He squirmed, suddenly uncomfortable. He thought he
caught a glimpse of her through the supermarket window,
but it could have been anyone. He had only caught a flash
of long, dark, curly hair. Like a pony's, he thought, that
hair. Beautiful.

It was starting to get dark; the lights in the parking lot
switched on. He took out her address book, which he had
stolen in Venice the night they mugged her. There was a
photo of her standing in a summer dress in front of a huge
house with a rolling green lawn. He could see her bare
shoulders in the picture, and he wondered if that was
where she had lived as a girl—while he'd lived in a dirty
little house with only three rooms and a drunken father.

He got some useful information out of that address
book. She was going out on dates with men. Swenson was
one of them. He lived in Santa Monica. And Hampton,

the colored guy—he had paid for touching her, though maybe not enough. If those people hadn't interfered . . . He wondered if she'd slept with Hampton, or this Swenson. Or with both. The thought made him angry, and he slapped the dashboard with a clenched fist, crying out in nameless pain.

Looking around to see if anyone had seen him do that, he finally saw her coming out of the store carrying three heavy bags of groceries. She was domestic. He liked that.

She pulled out into traffic, and he knew she was going home to the apartment that was so high above the city. High above it all.

Make a few calls. Put a scare into her. We'll see what happens.

Mister, he thought, I did all that. But it's like introducing me to your sister at the dance and expecting me to go away when it's over. You can't just hire a man for something serious and expect nothing to happen. It was like a rock rolling down a hill: sometimes it's going to find another path it wants to take. And there's nothing you can do to stop it.

Holiday stood alone in the elevator, staring at her reflection in the mirrored door. An elderly woman carrying a growling poodle stepped off at the fifth floor, leaving her to ride in silence. Holiday wasn't sure, but she thought the woman was the fifties film actress who was said to live in seclusion in the building's penthouse, leaving home only to walk her dog and visit the cemetery.

The doors opened to the long, silent hall. As usual, it felt as if she had the building to herself. The insistent television chatter from the apartment nearest the elevator provided some comfortable familiarity. Everyone on the floor complained to the middle-aged accountant inside about his TV and stereo volume, but now his sonic pollution was like the warm lights of home.

Her apartment was dark and lifeless until she switched on the foyer light. Dropping the bags heavily on the kitchen sink, Holiday saw there were no phone messages for her. Apparently the media had moved on. Somehow she had expected Kyle to call again.

She didn't know exactly where Kyle lived, somewhere in the beach community of Playa del Rey. She imagined a bachelor's apartment on the water, filled with diplomas and photographs taken at conventions and awards ceremonies. Even when they were together, years ago, he had always seemed like a lonely man.

Her groceries came primarily from the supermarket freezer section: pasta and chicken, ice cream, a bag of peas, two frozen gourmet pizzas. Holiday opened a bottle of French table wine and poured a glass, enjoying the silence.

The phone rang. Cursing, she glared at it for a moment. *I'm not on call for surgery, I don't have to answer it. I could just stay here in the kitchen all night. Make a campfire.*

"Hello?"

"Holiday, how are you? I've been trying to reach you."

Bo Swenson's voice was thicker, deeper than she remembered. She didn't want to talk to him, or anyone else.

"Bo, I'm not feeling well. I need to lie down and watch some TV or something." *God, I sound like I did when I was a teenager, when Brian Lloyd wanted to take me to the movies.*

"Holiday, I haven't spoken to you since your surgery. I want you to know, I'm very sorry."

Holiday suddenly felt irritated. "Don't say you're sorry."

His voice turned humble. "Of course, you're right. Perhaps I'm not very good at saying the right thing."

"Bo, I want to have some wine and relax. We should talk later."

"I want to come visit you. Would you allow that?"

She was feeling petulant—probably an inappropriate response to her only friend in town who wasn't caught up in personal problems or in jail. "I don't know, Bo."

"Holiday," he said, reminding her of her father. "I'm worried about you. I won't stay long, just allow me to see how you are."

Fighting him took too much energy. "All right, Bo. Come over." He assented and began to say good-bye when she hastily interrupted. "Wait, Bo. Come over in an hour. I need some time to myself."

"Of course. I look forward to seeing you."

Holiday finished the wine in a single gulp and ran cold water over a washcloth. She made her way to the sofa, turning on only the lamp above her head, and lay back on a pillow and closed her eyes.

Crises, she thought, her mind reeling into the comfortable zone on the threshold of sleep. What crises had she known? Medical school, that was one big crisis, it seemed. And she had survived. She had ended up in University Counseling Services, explaining to an alarmed psychiatrist how her hands shook and her back sometimes felt as though someone were plunging a knife into it. And the nightmares, the mood swings. The counselor said she hadn't admitted to herself that she was very young to be so far into medical school, that her body and mind were reminding her to respect them and not use them as tools. That had been very sound advice.

What was I just thinking about? Crises. And now: Takamoto's death, the phone calls, Venice. Taken together, they added up to a respectable crisis. But she wasn't shaking, her thoughts hadn't turned to self-destruction or escape. She thought about abandoning everything and going home, but she didn't.

Something had changed within her. She had grown, become stronger. As for Gregory . . . Holiday frowned and burrowed deeper into the pillow's plush luxury, deeply asleep within seconds.

That was a strange noise, she thought, turning over on her side. She opened her eyes. The place was quiet and empty, as usual. She strained to focus her vision through a fog of pain centered in her eyes. The cold washcloth: she had left it on the coffee table. She would go to the kitchen, run fresh water on it, and doze on the sofa until Bo arrived.

Holiday grabbed the cloth and stood up unsteadily. Some animal sense told her something had gone wrong. But it was too late; strong arms wrapped around her from behind, pulling at her with frightening strength. Still trying to wake up, she turned her head to the side, trying to see behind her. In that instant his hand grabbed the washcloth and he tried to shove it into her mouth.

She began to struggle. She could see only the living room in the pool of light coming from the kitchen. It was hard to breathe. Bo was coming. When? She had been asleep a minute, a half hour, a full hour—how long?

The man's hot breath fell on her neck, and she felt his hand moving. He was under her dress now, rubbing between her legs, roughly caressing her inner thighs with a callused hand. She could feel his erection against the small of her back.

He held tighter, one arm pinioning her arms to her sides. She relaxed and let her body go completely slack. She felt his hand reach into her underwear, touching her eagerly. *I've given up,* she thought. *Think that, you bastard. I've given up.*

When she felt some slack between her body and her attacker's, she whipped her head backward with all the force she could muster. He cried out when her skull struck him hard in the chin. His grip loosened and she raised a leg and kicked backward into his kneecap.

His scream was guttural and frightening. She turned to look at him. He was tall, with a thin build and sinewy muscles. A woman's stocking was pulled over his head. Jeans and sneakers, she thought, trying to put together a description for the police, when he slapped her with his open hand and knocked her to the floor.

She tried to crawl away, but he grabbed her bare legs and pulled her toward him. The rug burned her calves and pulled her skirt up around her waist. He stood there for a moment, staring down at her, then looked around as if he had heard something. His gaze passed several times between the door and her exposed legs. She was too frightened to move when he leaped past her prone body and ran for the door. Before Holiday had time to feel relief, he was gone.

She lay breathing slowly on the floor and waited for her breath to stop catching in her ribs. Her cheek stung from where he had hit her.

A bump was already rising on top of her head. She hoped his chin had fared even worse. Walking to the phone, Holiday realized she would never feel safe there again. He had slipped inside while she slept. And she knew she had locked the door behind her.

The phone rang several times. "Security. Michael Waters speaking." He sounded bored and tired.

"This is Dr. Powers in Seventeen-oh-five. I've just had an intruder."

"What? Where is he?"

"He left a few minutes ago," she said. "I want you to call the police for me."

"I don't see anything on the security cameras. Was it anyone you know?"

"Mr. Waters, call the police and have them meet you up here."

Waters's voice was respectful. "Of course," he said. "Have you been injured? Do you need first aid?"

"He hit me," she said quietly. "But I'm all right."

"I'll be there in a minute," Waters said. "Sit tight."

He hung up. *Sit tight.* In an apartment that obviously wasn't safe. A minute passed, then another, without Waters's arrival.

The hallway was empty, she saw through the peephole in the door. Hesitating a moment, wishing someone would arrive, Holiday turned the doorknob and pulled on it. Nothing happened.

She pulled again, harder this time, with no result. Stepping away from the door, full of frustration and rage, Holiday kicked at the door with her bare foot. It clattered on its hinges but didn't budge.

The knob turned from the outside. She looked through the peephole and saw Michael Waters pushing on the door. He knocked, calling her name.

"I'm in here," she yelled. "I'm fine. I just can't open the door."

A rustling noise, accompanied by swearing, came from outside. Finally it opened. Waters stepped into the apartment holding a long sliver of metal, staring at it with grudging admiration.

"Someone jammed this in the door," he said, turning the dark object over to inspect it in the light. "Lodged it in the frame. Locked you right in. That was really smart."

"Great," she said. "We had a rapist in the building, but at least he was clever."

Waters's craggy features drained of color. "Oh, shit," he said. "I'm sorry. Are . . . you said you were all right."

"I'm fine." Waters was certainly concerned—for her, or for his job, she couldn't tell. In his blue jumpsuit and California Angels baseball cap, he didn't inspire much confidence.

"I've been on duty all night," he said. "And I haven't seen anyone unusual come in, or anyone on the security cameras. I don't know how this happened."

Holiday rubbed her cheek. From the feel of it, it would probably bruise by morning. "Mr. Waters," she said quietly. "I have nothing against you personally, but you're not doing your job. You and your staff are here to keep this building safe."

"I know, I know." He sat heavily at the dining table. "What did the guy look like?" he asked.

"I don't know. He was wearing a stocking over his head." Holiday peered out into the hall just as two police officers arrived. She introduced Waters, whom they regarded with haughty superiority.

"What happened here?" One officer, with a military-style haircut and thin mustache, scanned the apartment suspiciously as he spoke, as if felons might be lurking behind the curtains. His name tag identified him as Officer Mazilli.

Holiday explained what happened while Mazilli walked around the room. The other officer, obviously the junior partner, took notes.

Toward the end of Holiday's explanation, Bo Swenson arrived with a bottle of wine and a plastic take-out tray with Chinese characters emblazoned on the side. He stood there dumbfounded.

"Who is this, lady?" Mazilli said, staring at Swenson.

"He's a friend. I was expecting him."

The younger officer rattled off a message into his radio. He kept an eye on Swenson, apparently unconvinced that the gray-haired man wasn't going to produce a gun and start taking hostages.

"What happened here?" Bo asked, taking Holiday's arm and looking at Waters, who silently stared into space at the dining table. "Who is that man?"

Running though the story again seemed hopeless, and Holiday was almost relieved when Mazilli interrupted. "Dr. Powers, I have your description and your statement," he said. "Is it possible that anyone you know might have tried . . . something like this?"

"No one I can think of," Holiday said.

"Well, then, if you have any more trouble, give us a call." He glared at Waters. "You come downstairs with me. I want to see what kind of security you're running."

Waters looked up at the officer in shock. On the way out the door, he turned to Holiday. "Dr. Powers, I just want you to know that nothing like this will happen again. Not in my building."

"I'm sure that makes the lady feel real safe, guy," the younger officer said, his close-set eyes narrowing. "You've obviously done a great job so far."

Mazilli chuckled, noticeably pleased that his partner slammed Waters—whom they clearly both regarded as far below them on the chain of law enforcement. They led him out the door like a prisoner.

When the door was closed, Swenson stuck the bottle of wine in the pocket of his thin cloth overcoat. "Holiday, I don't want you to stay here tonight. Come home with me."

"No, thanks," she said, walking away into the living room. His paternal tone again reminded her of her father. *It's unsafe for a woman to live alone and unprotected, Holiday.*

Swenson followed. He looked tired and gaunt. "Please don't be stubborn. You can sleep in my bed and I'll take the sofa. It would be better for your peace of mind, not to mention mine."

She had to admit he was right. Her apartment apparently afforded all the safety and security of a cardboard box. "All right," she said. "But I'll sleep on the sofa. I'm not going to kick you out of your own bed."

"You can do whatever you wish," Swenson said, smiling.

Holiday changed into jeans and a Cape Cod sweatshirt, quickly packing a business suit for the next day while Bo waited on her sofa. When she returned to the living room, he seemed tired and distant, more his age than the energetic dining companion of weeks before.

They took separate cars to his house, Holiday following and losing track of him only for a moment on a busy stretch of Bundy Drive. The traffic was light, given the hour, except for the congested stretch near the freeway, which bustled as always with cars streaming through the corridor between Orange County and the San Fernando Valley.

Off Bundy, Swenson led the way in his Mercedes convertible to a secluded enclave of good-sized houses and apartments set off from the street behind tall palms. Bo turned into the driveway of one of the larger houses, a two-story stucco place with flower beds and neatly trimmed hedges set in contrast by discreet semiburied lights. It was a big place for one man to occupy alone.

By the time she parked, Bo was out of his car with the wine and Chinese food. He smiled generously and led her inside.

Flipping a dimmer switch that illumined the long, high-ceilinged living room, Bo hung up his coat in a closet. "Make yourself at home," he said. "I'll open the wine. Do you want Chinese food as well? I can heat it up in the microwave." He slid open the carton, releasing the savory smell of spiced chicken.

"Please," she said. He disappeared down a hallway. "Thank you, Bo, you're too good to me," she called after him.

His laughter receded into the house, and she soon heard rustling from the kitchen. She descended the three set-in steps into the living room and looked around.

The place was full of quality furniture that looked as if it had been tended to with great care. Mixed with the cloth chairs and thin-legged end tables were odder items: a brown leather sofa hunched at one end of the room like a snobbish relative; and an entertainment center with an expensive, high-tech stereo and glossy TV. It was the decor of a man living with two conflicting impulses, between the sensible Swede he was and the L.A. bachelor he had become.

A long series of photos lined one wall, near a rolltop desk that housed a portable computer. She leaned over the desk to look at the pictures of landscapes and buildings. None of them featured people.

"Oh, my pictures," Swenson said, walking quickly into the room holding two wineglasses in one hand. He handed Holiday one. "Do you recognize any of them from your time with Lars?"

"Not really," she said, wondering why Swenson displayed no pictures of his only child.

"This is the Riddarholm Church," he said, pointing to a photo of a sprawling brown building on a tiny island connected to land by two thin roads set at sea level. "The island is Riddarholmen, near Old Town Stockholm. Swedish kings and queens are buried there."

Holiday folded her arms, feigning appreciation while thinking that the large color picture looked like a postcard that had been blown up and framed.

He pointed to a photo of a large, tree-lined square, where people were gathered to watch two men play chess on an oversized board, each piece two feet tall. "This is Kungstradgarden, which means King's Garden. It's also in Stockholm. As you can see, it is a beautiful city."

"It is," she agreed. The other pictures featured similar generic city scenes, and a few depictions of the rugged green Scandinavian landscape. "But, Bo, why don't you have any pictures of people here? It's a little—"

"Impersonal?" he said. "I've been told that. Perhaps when your past is unpleasant, you gravitate toward things that don't reflect your personal life. I loved my country, and I like to be reminded of it."

"I didn't mean there's anything wrong with it," Holiday said quickly, sensing that she had saddened him. Before she could continue, a beep came from the kitchen—the microwave oven—and Bo set off to fetch her dinner.

They settled into a pair of loveseats next to a curtained window, Bo watching while Holiday hungrily wolfed the Chinese food. Finally he caught her eye and his cheeks creased with pleasure. "You don't eat enough, I can see that," he said. "I will have to feed you more often."

"I'm sorry I was rude to you earlier," Holiday said between bites. "It's a poor excuse, but I've been under a lot of pressure."

"You don't have to apologize. I'm just glad nothing happened to you tonight." He shook his head in disgust. "What kind of a man does something like that? He is an animal. You know, I could help you find another place to live. There are many places around here that you could surely afford. This is a lovely neighborhood."

"Thanks, Bo, I appreciate it. I might take you up on that."

Bo unlaced his shoes and rested his feet on a leather ottoman. He sighed. "I had the feeling earlier you don't want to discuss what occurred in your telepresence surgery," he said. "I just wanted to tell you I think this Hampton is the worst kind of criminal. He abused the trust of the university, and your trust as well. I only wonder why he did such a terrible thing."

"It hasn't been established that he was responsible," Holiday said. She put down the food, suddenly not hungry.

"In the papers they said there was conclusive proof."

"It's likely that he—" Holiday paused. "I don't know. I can't understand why he would do it. I probably never will."

Swenson sipped his wine. She checked her watch; it was nearly midnight. "Bo, I'm so sorry to be keeping you up like this. I should get ready to go to sleep."

"No, it's fine," he said, motioning for her to stay seated. "I don't have guests often enough. It's pleasant to talk to you."

He sat back on the sofa and exhaled deeply. He was obviously struggling to stay awake. "I never did get Lars's address from you," she said. "I'd still like to get in touch with him."

"Of course," Swenson said. His eyes brightened as if he had just remembered something. "When I talked with him a few weeks ago, we agreed to speak again around Christmas. If you don't reach him by then, I'll remind him to call you."

"I'm sure he's heard about Takamoto's surgery. It's got to be all over the world by now."

Swenson shrugged. "He hasn't mentioned anything to me."

Holiday looked away, her heart beating faster. Bo said at California Gardens that he hadn't talked to Lars in several months. A few moments ago he said they spoke more recently; now he seemed to imply that they had been in contact since Takamoto's death. *Stop it. This is paranoid.* Bo tilted his head at her querulously, sensing her change of mood.

"Is something wrong?"

"No . . . well, yes." She tucked her legs beneath her. "It's been a hell of a week, that's all."

Bo rubbed his eyes. "You've had more bad fortune than you deserve. But things will change for you, I'm sure of it."

"Lars was well a few weeks ago?" Holiday asked.

"He is still very depressed about the injury to his hand." Swenson fussily brushed some lint from his pants. "But he is being transferred to Umea soon to practice there for the next two years. The change in climate might help him."

"Umea? I've never heard of it."

"It's in the north," Swenson said. "Near the Arctic Circle. I was rotated there for a time once, when I was much younger."

"God, it must be bleak and depressing." Holiday pictured swirling winds and ice floes drifting through frozen seas.

"In the summer it's very pleasant. The winters, however, are harsh." The phrases flowed as if he were a travel agent or tour guide. All emotion seemed drained from him now. She felt an urge to break through his distance and reserve.

"Bo, why do you really think Lars tried to kill himself?"

Swenson looked down at the floor. "His mother, obviously. My own deeds." His voice was low and formal. "Everything that happened to him in his life, along with his own morbid and overly dramatic sense of things. He may blame me, and why not? I am a convenient target. But the responsibility lies within him, within his own heart."

Holiday sat still, feeling an icy wave of deep regret and perhaps resentment from the older man. She said nothing.

"Each man must answer to himself. That is the one truth that I have learned in life. What everyone else thinks does not matter. No one has the right to punish others in the way that . . ."

His voice trailed off. Holiday waited for him to continue, but he stood up. "I need to sleep now," he said plainly.

At her insistence Holiday took blankets and a pillow and dressed the sofa into a makeshift bed. He said good night over his shoulder as he shut off the lights and disappeared into the house, to his own dreams.

Though the sofa was plush, comfortable and—most importantly—long enough to accommodate Holiday's long legs, she couldn't sleep. Talking about Lars had stirred memories and emotions that she had thought were behind her long ago.

They had been lovers throughout the winter he was in Boston, spending nearly all their free time together, never speaking of the time when Lars would have to return home to Sweden.

One night, late after a day of grueling exams designed to track their progress in the medical program, she lay in Lars's bed. The small dormitory room seemed like a cocoon with the lights off and the shades open to reveal the snow swirling in the sky outside. Though they had just made love, she still felt a physical yearning for him. She pressed close to him under the blankets, their skin touching.

He stared up at the ceiling, his angular profile casting a shadow on the wall. "What are you thinking about?" she asked.

"The winter snows remind me of home," he said.

"Then why don't you go outside and run around naked?" she asked. "I heard you Swedes like doing that."

In response he growled like a bear and nuzzled her

neck, biting her. She laughed and pulled him closer, savoring his touch.

"Are you coming home with me next weekend to meet my parents?" she asked when he had rolled over onto his back.

He frowned. "I don't know. I may have to stay and study."

"*Lars!*" she said. "You promised. Mother wants to meet you."

He shifted to face her, kissing her bare shoulder. "I wish you could meet my mother," he whispered. "She would like you."

"Someday I will."

"In two weeks it will be Santa Lucia Day," he said. She heard the shift in his tone; he would be lost to her for the night, set aside in favor of his memories. It seemed as though she always had to struggle to keep him with her, to fight off the drifting of his mind.

"Santa Lucia was a little girl, a Christian martyr," Lars said. She closed his eyes, feeling the enthralling timbre of his voice, as though he spoke from a dream. "Every year in Sweden we commemorate her."

"Do you go to church?" Holiday asked.

"The Swenson family?" he laughed. "Never. Mother was a nurse and father was a doctor at the same hospital. There the celebration started at five in the morning. I would get up early and ride my bicycle over the ice to get there in time."

Holiday stopped asking questions, knowing the momentum of his memories would take on its own life. "There would be a procession through the halls," Lars said. "The nurses would dress in white robes with red sashes, and my mother every year would be Santa Lucia. She wore a crown of burning candles with her robes. The nurses would sing: *Santa Lucia. Santa Lucia.*"

His voice was haunting. "They would walk to where the men were, singing. I can see Mother's face when I close my eyes: her hair was always longer and more shining than the rest. She was the most beautiful, and she would always smile when she saw that I had come. She knew I would. I was there every year."

"What about your father?" she asked, knowing she shouldn't.

"Father," Lars said. "He was always there, too. But when he saw me, it was, 'Anita, look at our son. His pants are wrinkled.' Or, 'Look, Anita, this is the little boy who says he wants to be a doctor. He can't even pass his math classes.' "

She could hear the sting in her lover's voice. "Your father was hard on you?"

Lars tensed in the dark. "He would call me a little fool, tell me I was stupid. Mother was the one who cared for me, who told me I could be a doctor."

That night Holiday held tight to Lars, feeling his body quake with the force of his recollections. She knew then that he could never let go of his past, and that he would always return home to his mother.

It was a decade later, and Holiday adjusted her pillows on Bo Swenson's sofa. She had to get some rest, but her mind replayed these old scenes like a projector that couldn't be shut off.

Like anyone else, she wanted love. For a time she loved Lars, then Kyle Jefferies. Both had left. She wasn't a woman willing to abandon her ambitions for a man, nor was she prone to tallying her losses and wondering what might have been.

But there, in the silent night, she remembered the times in her life when she had loved, and had been loved. And she wondered if she would ever feel that way again.

16

HOLIDAY AWOKE STIFF AND TIRED ON BO SWENSON'S SOFA. Bright sun shone in a beam through the closed curtains. She arose and found a note from Bo on the coffee table where she had left her overnight bag:

> *I must apologize again for my rudeness. I talked last evening of grim subjects, when you had just had a very bad experience. I hope that you will forgive me, and consider allowing me to help you find another place to live.*
> *I will be at the hospital all day, but please feel free to stay as long as you like. I fear there isn't much to eat in the kitchen, but you are welcome to what I have.*
>
> *Yours, Bo Swenson.*

She felt in an inexplicable hurry to leave, and showered and dressed quickly. Thinking about the night before, she relived her sensation of violation following the attack. She had moved into the high-rise in part because it was a security building. It now felt as though security were an illusion. Even Bo, who had provided her with sanctuary for the night, had been evasive and contradicted himself when he spoke about Lars. It seemed increasingly as though there was no one she could trust, no place that was safe.

Her options for the day were open: she could return to her apartment, she could even drive around and finally see the city that was her new home. But her mind felt ragged, and restless tension burned at her shoulders and neck. There was really only one place for her to be, as always.

* * *

Holiday's first stop at the hospital was the Supply Department. There she requisitioned a plastic model of a human abdomen complete with laparoscopic surgical instruments that pierced the clear plastic skin and reached the vinyl organs inside. This was a standard device that she had used in Boston; housed in her office, she would use it to demonstrate to future patients precisely what would be done to them when she performed surgery.

If she ever did again. Normally she would have asked Pam to handle such a task, but without her operating privileges she was effectively at loose ends. A suspension such as hers also meant that she wasn't covered by malpractice insurance; as a result she was restricted from even seeing patients in her office.

In the hallway by the stairwell she saw a familiar, stocky figure approach and wave for her to stop. Sandra Jeanette, the head of nursing, shook her hand warmly.

"It's good to see you here," Jeanette said in a bright voice. "We haven't had a chance to have that lunch yet."

They stepped into a small curtained foyer, out of the traffic of doctors and orderlies. "I'm glad you remembered," Holiday said. "I was afraid no one would want to be seen with me."

"Please," Jeanette said. Her tasteful burgundy suit hung loose over her rounded body. "I'm really sorry about what happened. Everyone knows now that it wasn't your fault."

Holiday thanked her. She recalled hearing that Jeanette had been on the long list a few years before when a sub-Cabinet position in Health and Human Affairs opened up in Washington.

Jeanette gently put her hand on Holiday's shoulder. "You've got to get over it, and you will. Give it time," she said. "Anyway, while I have you here, what are you doing about your problem with Kyle Jefferies?"

"My problem?" Holiday asked. "You mean—"

"I didn't want to put any fuel on the fire during the

senior staff meeting, but some things around here have to stop." Jeanette stepped into a ray of sun that emerged through the window. "It's mostly Jefferies, as far as I can tell. But your little feud with him is starting to affect my staff. If there's anything you can do to defuse the situation, I'd appreciate it."

Holiday thought of Kyle's strange call the day before. Though she hadn't thought much of it, he had sounded worried about more than her emotional well-being. It was almost as though he—

"Dr. Powers?" Jeanette said. "I don't want to put any pressure on you now, but I wanted to make my feelings known."

"I'm sorry," Holiday said. "My mind was drifting. But I talked to Dr. Jefferies yesterday, and I think his attitude might be changing. For what it's worth, I certainly didn't come here to fight a war every day."

"I heard *that,*" Jeanette said, smiling. "You know, it's naive to think we can get along with everyone. But really, it's not such a terrible goal."

As she spoke, Kyle Jefferies emerged from a hallway that led to a series of conference rooms. He spotted Holiday and Jeanette talking and walked toward them, stopping a respectful ten feet away. Jeanette looked over her shoulder and invited Kyle to join them.

"I hope I'm not interrupting anything," he said.

"Not at all, Doctor," Jeanette said, shooting Holiday a smile. "We were just discussing how to make the world a better place."

Jefferies smiled politely. "Can I speak to you for a moment, Dr. Powers?"

Jeanette squeezed Holiday's shoulder. "Give me a call about that lunch," she said, walking away.

Kyle walked to the windows and parted the curtains, allowing the sun to strike his face. "Sandra has a good mind," he said. He stared out at the small scrubby courtyard outside. "I'm sorry about that call yesterday. I may have said some things that were out of line."

Holiday couldn't get him to look her in the eye. "What kind of things, Kyle?" she asked.

"Do you want me to repeat them?" he asked. "I simply was concerned. I know how hard—"

"Someone broke into my apartment last night and tried to rape me," she said, her voice blunt and brittle.

"Oh, my God." He turned to her and his face fell.

"I'm fine," she said. "I fought him off, and he ran away."

"I'm sorry." He folded his arms, his blue eyes staring into hers. "Is there anything I can do?"

She began to speak but stopped. If she said anything, she would just take her anger and frustration out on him. It was pointless.

When he saw she wasn't going to answer, he drew closer. "Kate left yesterday," he said.

"She left? What do you mean?"

"I was going to ask you," he said. "Have you heard from her?"

"No," she said.

Hurt passed over his face. "If you do, tell her to call me." He glanced away, down the hall. "I guess it has to do with her ex-husband."

"Or maybe something you did," Holiday said. It felt cruel to say it, but this was the Kyle she remembered: always blaming circumstance, never allowing that his own actions might affect others.

"I told her to let go," he said. "But she's upset. It's . . . it's like what you and I had. It was hard for me to let you go, but I finally have. I realize now how important that is."

For perhaps the hundredth time she considered telling him about their unborn child, about the hurt and anguish she had endured, and about the loss that had yet to fully vanish. But it was too destructive. It was better he never know.

Jefferies clenched his hands into fists, seemingly on the verge of saying something that he couldn't quite voice.

Before he could say anything, Bill Epstein approached, stopping awkwardly as if frightened of coming too close. His string tie was gone, replaced by a tacky necktie depicting orange and green footballs on a field of hash marks.

"Dr. Jefferies, I need to speak to you," he said, blatantly ignoring Holiday.

Feeling angry and nonplused, Holiday left them and found a wall phone halfway down the hall. She called her home answering machine and checked for messages. There was one.

"Holiday? It's me, Kate. I just wanted you to know that I'm going to be out of town for a little while. Things—" She paused. "Things have gotten a little weird."

Holiday glanced back down the hall. Jefferies and Epstein were engaged in an animated conversation that quickly turned heated. Kyle brimmed with aggression, and Epstein shuffled his feet on the floor, seemingly cowed. Her breath caught in her throat when Kyle jabbed his finger repeatedly in Epstein's chest.

"Anyway, sugar, I need to ask a favor. Could you feed my babies for me? The fish once a day, the plants every other day. I won't be gone long, sugar. You hang in there. Oh, and could you turn on my TV? My babies like company. Thanks. I'm sorry to ask, but I just have to get away. Kyle is acting like a stressed-out bear, and I'm depressed to begin with. Call you soon, sugar."

Holiday hung up the phone just as Jefferies stalked off. He left Epstein muttering to himself under his breath; the technician gave a start when he saw Holiday had been watching.

She joined him, at the foyer near the window. "I'm sorry about the other day," he said.

"No offense taken. I can see you're under a lot of pressure."

Epstein laughed humorlessly. "Yeah, right. So when do you think you're going to be back in charge of the department?"

"Pretty soon, I hope. I'm laying low for a few days and waiting for all my clearances to be reinstated."

"I see," Epstein said. A fierce resolve suddenly appeared in his eyes. He pulled her to the window and leaned close.

"I just decided something. Something really important. I have to talk to you," he said, speaking rapidly.

"Go ahead," Holiday said, stepping away from him. Something was wrong that she hadn't noticed before. He was jittery, and breathing so hard, he was nearly panting. He seemed to be on the verge of some sort of nervous collapse.

"We can't talk here," he said, his voice even lower. "Tonight, at your house. You live in Gregory's building, right?"

She had come to know Bill Epstein, if only a little, and she could tell he had more than a petty workplace grievance on his mind. He knew something. "All right, Bill," she said. She scribbled her address and phone number on a scrap of paper.

"I'll come by around eight. Is that all right?" His mood had changed; now he seemed surly and antagonistic, as if she were the cause of whatever disturbed him. He walked off without another word. She heard the elevator bell chime. When she turned the corner, Epstein was gone.

17

AFTER WATERING KATE'S IMPRESSIVE ARRAY OF PLANTS, feeding her tropical fish, and checking to make sure all the appliances were turned off, Holiday stepped into the hall. Then she remembered the TV. "Company for my babies," Kate had said. Pausing a moment to entertain the idea that Kate may have been putting her on, Holiday stepped back inside and turned on CNN—something steady and sedate, she figured—and let herself out into the hall.

The corridor was silent as she returned to her own place. Holiday went immediately to Kate's apartment after work, because she dreaded being alone in her own. Michael Waters had changed her locks and given her a new set of keys at the security booth downstairs, but memories of violence filled the place. Her familiar things—furniture, possessions, rooms—were no longer comforting.

Bill Epstein was due any minute. Holiday spent several minutes going through her mail, finding the junk credit card offers and typical mass mailings every doctor receives. Before she was finished, she heard a knock at the door.

Epstein strode into the living room without so much as a greeting, settled on the sofa, and took a long sip from a can of soda that he had brought with him. Holiday shut the door and walked toward him tentatively, trying to gauge his state of mind. His haircut had degenerated into an unruly mass of curls. He wore his normal work clothes—jeans, a slightly tight dress shirt—but his expression was vacant, as if he had burned out inside and adopted a stoic, impassive numbness. He was still wearing his relatively conventional necktie.

"Where's the bola tie?" Holiday asked, sitting in the chair across from the sofa.

Epstein frowned and yanked at his collar. The tie popped off with the sound of releasing plastic, exposing itself as a clip-on. "Jefferies told me I have to wear regular ties from now on," he said. "Like it makes any difference what I wear."

"When I'm back in charge, you can dress however you like," Holiday said. It had grown dark outside. She reached out and turned on a lamp, illuminating the room and casting shadows.

"I'm not worried about that at the moment," Epstein said. He took another drink of soda and put it on the coffee table. Catching himself, he grabbed a piece of junk mail, placing it carefully under the can. "Don't want to leave rings," he muttered. "This is nice wood."

"Thanks," Holiday said. She would let him move at his own pace, and get to what he had come for in his own time. He seemed far too tightly wound for his own good.

"I lied to you the other day, when you came to the labs."

"Oh, really?" Holiday said. His statement was so matter-of-fact that it threw her off-balance.

"Yeah. When I told you that I didn't know anything about Gregory. That was a lie. Actually I visited him in jail the day before."

His mood was oscillating between sullen terseness and a childlike need to confess. She spoke in soothing tones. "The night before? Why didn't you say anything to me, Bill?"

"I don't know. I was messed up in the head about it."

He lapsed into silence, reaching out for his soda. Sitting back, he looked around the room with appraising approval. He behaved as if he were thinking about buying the place.

"Look, he told me about you and him," he said suddenly. "That was part of it. I didn't ask anything about it.

He brought it up. As far as I'm concerned, it's none of my business."

"I appreciate that." She wondered if Gregory had also told the police; he might have, to explain where he had been that morning. She wondered what Detective Harper had made of the information. Whatever the case, he didn't bring it up. Maybe he thought she and Gregory had worked together. That would have explained why she hadn't been contacted again—perhaps they were investigating her.

"He kept telling me he was innocent. Part of the reason I went there was because I wanted to find out why he did it. You know, what his motivation was. I figured that's also why you came to see me."

Holiday leaned back in her chair. "That was part of it. I wanted to find some answers."

"Yeah, right, so did I," Epstein said eagerly. "But Gregory kept telling me he was innocent. I mean, I know the guy. I've worked with him a long time, and I trust him completely. He has an attitude, granted, but he's so decent, it makes me sick sometimes."

She remained silent. From the ceiling came a loud metal creak as the building settled. She imagined for a moment that Epstein's tension was spreading to the walls and floors.

"When he told me he was innocent, I believed him. At least then I did. But when I went outside and got in my car, I was back in the real world. Where there's evidence against him."

"I know what you mean. I've felt the same thing," Holiday said. She wondered what Gregory had said to Epstein about her. Their night together now almost seemed like something that never happened.

Epstein took a deep breath. He looked as if he had come out on the far side of nervous exhaustion and was living on adrenaline. "Anyway that's not what I came here for." He picked up his empty soda can and scowled. "Do you have any coffee?"

"Sure," she said. "Come into the kitchen while I make it. You can keep talking."

In the kitchen one of the big bright bulbs in the ceiling had burned out. "I can replace that for you," Epstein said, looking up.

"Thanks, but I don't have any extra bulbs."

"You should keep them around. You never know." He watched her spoon out grounds into a filter and leaned against the refrigerator, all the while staring up at the hollow blackness of the spent bulb.

"The university, which means Jefferies, is cracking the whip on me to get complete documentation on the Takamoto incident. They're supplying data to local police and the federal government to put together a criminal case against Gregory. They'll probably file a civil suit against him, too, to distance themselves from him."

Holiday rinsed the coffeepot. "A civil suit might do more harm than good to the university's reputation," she said. "My guess is, they will just leave him to the criminal justice system."

"That's what I thought, too," Epstein said, contradicting himself. He began to pace. "So, listen. Finding out that the program had been changed was easy. Right after Takamoto's death, when the police were there, I called up the executable code that ran from the program. It was dumb luck, really. I probably never would have noticed anything, but the program as I saw it the night before took up an amount of megabyte space that ended with the first three digits of my home phone number: seven eight seven."

Holiday listened intently as she switched on the coffeemaker. She hadn't heard this before.

"When I called up the executable code after the murder, I saw that it was different. That meant the program had been changed."

"It was definitely changed from the night before?" Holiday asked.

"Right, since we put the whole thing to bed the night

before. Of course I had to go back to the source code to find out precisely what that change was."

Epstein was losing Holiday in technical talk. "I'm not a programmer," she said impatiently. "What are you talking about?"

"It's simple. Source code is what we programmers write, in a high-level programming language: in this case, C++." He paced more quickly, warming to the chance to describe his work. "Then we use a program called a compiler, which translates the source code into instructions the computer can act on instantly—those are called executable code. It's sort of like the computer's own language."

"And why did you have to look at both?" Holiday asked.

"I saw that the executable code had been changed, which meant that the computer was being told to do something new or something different. The problem is, executable code can only be read by the computer. It looks like a bunch of nonsense if you bring it up on the screen. You can go through it and figure it out, but it takes time."

"And you can read the source code?" Holiday got two coffee cups out of the cupboard.

"Of course. Gregory and I wrote it. And when I found the change, I saw that it was in the area of the program that told the robot how to operate the laser. I found that basically, instead of duplicating the surgeon's motion, it was being told to fire the laser at highest power and swipe back and forth—ten seconds after it was initially activated."

Holiday grimaced, remembering the ruined mess that Han Takamoto became within seconds of the laser's firing.

"At the time I used my network access privileges and found out that Gregory's password ID had been used that morning to change the program commands. That's how Gregory became the murder suspect."

They carried their coffee cups to their former positions in the living room. Holiday threw every switch that might possibly cast any light on where they sat. Something about the progress of this conversation made her want to cast away all the shadows.

"Bill, don't take this the wrong way, but you haven't told me much I don't already know. Is this what you came here for?"

Epstein blew on the scalding coffee and took a sip. "No, that's the point. You knew Gregory was implicated, but I'll bet you didn't know precisely how. And it's important you know."

His nervous distraction had vanished, replaced by eagerness. Holiday pulled her hair back from her face and nodded calmly, trying to get him to frame his ideas slowly and reasonably.

"So, look, here's the thing," Epstein said, his voice quavering. "I'm putting together a package of documentation for the criminal case, and I'm being really careful because I know that I'll be on the witness stand if there's a trial. If I'm going to send my friend up on murder, industrial espionage, and God knows what else, I want to make sure *I* don't have any doubts."

"Especially because, just for a while, Gregory convinced you he was innocent?" Holiday asked. She spoke carefully, not wanting to insinuate to Epstein that she harbored the same hope.

"Exactly," Epstein said. He stood up and walked to the window, cracking it open a few inches and looking back to Holiday.

"So I checked the user roster sheets for all computer log-ins over the past two weeks. The computer runs them automatically, then they come to me. Part of my job is that kind of network maintenance. And, sure enough, there it was: Gregory had logged into the system at six-thirty that morning."

"Six-thirty?" Holiday thought about the morning of the surgery. They rose early, Gregory left around six and, he said, he took a shower and logged onto his computer before checking his phone messages and learning that Shawn had been shot.

"Right," Epstein continued. "He told the police he was home then, but I think he left out the part about you. The other day he told me he had just left your place; either way he was alone in his apartment. So when I found the log-in time and password, I found that it was a remote log-in."

"What's that?"

"It means that Gregory entered the computer system through a modem from a place other than his machine at the labs. Which is consistent with his sabotaging the system from his home."

Holiday sighed. Was he telling her that he had found more evidence to convict Gregory? Then why this secrecy, this excitement, this paranoia?

"Wait, wait," he said, sensing her mood. "Hang on. You see, I found it was a remote log-in with his access code, all right. But it was a remote log-in from *Seattle*."

"At six-thirty in the morning?" Holiday said, her voice brittle. She tried to put together all the details, wondering if she properly understood the intricacies of the system. "But Gregory—"

"Gregory definitely was in Los Angeles at that time on the morning of the surgery. He called the hospital before he rushed in to see his cousin. It's impossible that he could have got up to Washington and come back in that span of time."

"Then he's innocent." By now Epstein had wandered over to the dining area, pacing small erratic circles as he spoke.

"Maybe," he said. He rubbed his hands together. "He could have loaned his password to someone in Seattle and used them as an accomplice. Then he would have an alibi."

"But what if he didn't do it?" Holiday shrugged out of her suit jacket, suddenly restless. Gregory had been wronged, she believed it now—and he had been mis-treated by her worst of all.

Epstein's face tightened. "Then he's the victim of a stolen password. I think that's the case, I really do. Be-cause if I were going to sabotage a system like tele-presence, *I'd* steal someone's password so that they couldn't directly trace it back to me."

Holiday stood up. "Then why are we here talking about this? Why in the world haven't you told the police?"

"Because of fucking Kyle Jefferies," Epstein said ven-omously. "I took it all to him this morning and explained it. He told me to sit on it for a couple of days until I'm completely sure."

"But you are sure, right?"

"Of course I am. I'm as sure as I can be. But he said this could lead to all kinds of legal complications. He didn't say what he meant, but he said he would fire me if I called the police on my own."

Holiday caught her own reflection in the window and saw someone she didn't recognize—for a second she saw herself as a teenager, gawky and open-faced. She turned away. "But why? Waiting could mean losing the chance to find out who really planted that subroutine."

"I know," Epstein said, almost shouting. "That's what I told him this afternoon, when you saw me arguing with him. I can't leave Gregory in jail when I could get him released. It's not right."

"Then that's it. I'll have to deal with this." She walked to the kitchen and picked up the phone. Epstein cried out for her to stop.

"Don't call right now," he said. "I don't have any of the documentation on me, and the police treated me like dog-shit when I tried to explain everything to them the day of the murder."

"Harper, right?" Holiday said, thinking of the detec-tive. He could make someone feel flustered and guilty by casting a doubtful glance.

"That's him," Epstein said, rubbing his forehead as if ruefully reliving the encounter.

"So we'll go to the labs right now," Holiday said.

Epstein drew a breath, finally nodding in assent. "In an hour. I want to stop at my place to let my dog out. I haven't been home yet."

"Come on, Bill. This is more important than that." Holiday picked up her purse, ready to call downstairs for a valet.

"That's easy for you to say," Epstein said. "You don't have a golden retriever ready to make a mess all over your living room."

He wasn't going to change his mind. His stubbornness was characteristic of the workaday Bill Epstein she had come to know.

"All right, then. In an hour. It'll be nine forty-five. We'll meet and call the police from the labs." Holiday held the front door open for him. He paused in the landing, turning on her with grim determination.

"You're going to have to go to bat for me on this one," he said. "Jefferies is going to try to get back at me."

"Bill," she said, pausing, "if things happened as you say, there's a chance he won't be working there much longer."

Epstein's features lit up for an instant, then he frowned and left. She closed the door behind him, knowing what she said was true. When it emerged that Kyle had suppressed evidence, he might face criminal charges. Two weeks ago she might have seen this as the kind of ammunition she needed to stop him, to fight back as he tried to maneuver her out of the department. But now, she knew, that killing blow—which she might have to strike to save Gregory—was something she didn't want.

Stop it. Kyle may have brought professional disaster upon himself, but there was no reason to think about fatal blows and death.

Save when mentioning Han Takamoto, whose killer, she realized, was still free.

* * *

Bill Epstein left Dr. Powers's apartment and walked quickly down the carpeted hallway to the elevators. He tried to focus on his breath, keeping it deep and calm. His anxiety attack, by his own measure, had lasted more than twenty-four hours.

The elevator light didn't come on when he pushed it. So he stood there and waited, tapping his foot, trying to clear his mind.

The elevator definitely wasn't coming. It had been almost five minutes. He glanced up at the security camera, and wondered if the maintenance crew knew about the breakdown. Shrugging, he walked to the end of the hall and opened the heavy door leading to the fire stairs. He had to get moving. It was going to be a big night.

9:02 P.M.

Michael Waters sat in his security booth with a heavy feeling of resignation. What else could go wrong? Through the front door of the place came the answer: Clay Simmons. And out of uniform. His baseball cap looked like he hadn't taken it off in six months. He had probably gone out to the parking lot to smoke a joint.

"Back already?" Waters asked sarcastically.

Simmons looked at his watch as if he had never seen it before. Stoned, Waters thought, definitely. "Am I late, Mike?"

Waters snorted. "Was that a break you took or a sabbatical?"

"Sorry, boss," Simmons said. "It won't happen again."

"Where's your jumpsuit, anyway? You know you have to wear your uniform at all times here." Waters gestured to his own blue suit.

"Sorry. It's in the wash," Simmons said quietly.

Waters turned to the bank of security monitors. "Well, you picked a good time to take a break," he said harshly.

"A couple minutes after you left, both the elevators went down."

"That ever happen before?" Simmons asked.

Waters shook his head. "Not since I've been here. Took me ten minutes to get the company on the phone, and they just had some trainee who didn't know what the hell to do."

"Who fixed it?" Simmons asked.

"I did," Waters said. "I knew management would squawk about getting someone in at time-and-a-half, so I went downstairs and had a look myself. The system just got switched off, I guess. I reset the timing and it went right back on."

Simmons whistled appreciatively. "Pretty good. I wouldn't know anything about dealing with that elevator system."

Of course you wouldn't, Waters thought. "Well, we were lucky," he said. "We didn't get any complaints, so I guess no one needed to use them in that fifteen minutes. We had to hold a couple of people in the lobby because—and this was a real bitch—the door to the stairs was locked, and I couldn't find the key."

"Here's the key," Simmons said. "I was using it yesterday, it must have got stuck in my pocket. I must have forgot and left the door locked." He smiled bashfully at Waters.

"You're kidding me."

"Sorry, Mike. I know I've been messing things up lately."

"You can say that again." Waters winced. "If you want to get ahead here, you've got to try harder. I know you're not stupid, Clay."

Simmons slapped his hands nervously against his thighs. "Say, Mike, did anyone try to go in the stairwell door from outside?"

"No, it was locked, too."

"Oh. Anyway, thanks for covering for me, Mike." Clay Simmons clapped his supervisor on the back and walked into the office area, away from the front desk and security monitors.

If Michael Waters had turned around in that instant, he would have seen Clay staring into his hands at the fresh scratches on his palms. But Waters didn't turn around. And Clay, after staring at his boss's inviting, unprotected back for a moment longer, went to the bathroom to wash away the traces of what he had just done.

18

BY NOW HOLIDAY WAS READY—NO, EAGER—TO SEE IF THE security glass surrounding the virtual reality lab could withstand a good solid kick. She was wearing walking boots with thick soles—if not thick enough to shatter the barrier, then perhaps sturdy enough to leave a nice, clearly defined footprint on the seat of that computer operator's pants.

She watched him walk into the room containing the night operators' stations. He had refused to let her in, even when she said she was here to meet Bill Epstein. She tried to remember his name. Jay? Ray? It might as well have been Manta Ray. She tried to contain her anger and focus on why she was here.

Bill was a half hour late. She never should have agreed to let him go home first. The hell with his apartment, she should have offered to pay for the cleaning. From the way he acted, she shouldn't have let him out of her sight.

There was no sense standing there. She took the elevator down to her office and tried to stay calm. This was the time she always liked best at hospitals, when visitors had been sent home for the day and only essential staff remained.

It was a time when the hectic battle against illness and disease was largely ceased until morning. To Holiday, this pause represented a concession of sorts to a higher power. Though she had grown up a New England Episcopalian, as a child religion had meant enduring interminable church services. When she began practicing medicine, for the first time she felt the presence of a spiritual force greater than science and human reason. Years ago she and Kyle had talked about this. While she experienced this awakening, his last traces of religious feeling were extinguished by the suffering he witnessed every day.

Holiday's office was dark and deserted. Pam's presence was everywhere, in her photos and the organized chaos of her desk. It made Holiday feel guilty to think that Pam might not be happy with her new post, that Holiday's troubles and lack of attention to workaday detail might have had an adverse effect. She resolved to make work life better for Pam, or at least more tolerable.

The desk lamp shone bright and harsh in the otherwise darkened office. Flipping through her Rolodex, she found Kyle Jefferies's home phone number. The Rolodex card had been distributed by his own office, she saw; under the area code and number were the triple-underlined words "Only for emergencies." Well, this qualified.

Kyle answered on the seventh ring. He sounded gruff and irritable. She knew that a frequent side effect of his driving energy were periods in which he simply crashed, sleeping until he absolutely had to emerge from his slumber. His acidic tone relaxed when he realized it was her.

"What is it? Have you heard from Kate?" His voice was still low and slurred; as always, he was very slow to wake up.

"This isn't about Kate," she said. "It's about Gregory."

There was silence on the other end. "I know what Epstein found out, Kyle. Gregory didn't sabotage the system, and I don't know what you were thinking when you tried to hide that fact."

"I'm not hiding anything." In his slurred voice she could hear him straining against the haze that still gripped him.

"You're hiding information that can get Gregory out of jail. I'd like to know why, but only after he's out. I'm at the hospital now. I want you to come here and meet me."

"Holiday, this can wait until morning. We don't have anything firm enough to—"

"Kyle, don't whine." She surprised herself with her anger. "The evidence is solid. Call the lab, tell them to let me in, and then get down here right away. I think you should be here to explain yourself when the police come."

He was silent again. "This isn't like you, Holiday. But if that's the way you want it . . ."

"That's the way I want it."

He hung up. She replaced the phone in its cradle, closed her Rolodex, and slowly made her way back to the lab.

This time she was let in immediately. The night operator waited by the door when she arrived, and held it open for her. A short, curly-haired man in chinos and a Columbia University sweatshirt, he apologetically explained that Jefferies had just called.

"Don't worry about it," she said. "I know you were just doing your job." He was visibly relieved. Kyle's return to power in the department, even temporarily, had brought back an obvious paranoia and fear among all the staff— even this man, whose job was merely to keep an eye on the machines at night and make sure the loaded programs were running properly.

Holiday waited for him to return to his back room, but he stayed with her. "I'm fine," she told him. "You can get back to work."

"I really should get back there," he said halfheartedly.

She realized what was going on: Kyle had ordered him to keep an eye on her until he arrived. Ignoring him, she sat down at a terminal and used her log-in ID and password to enter the computer network. Surprisingly, it still worked. No one had thought to eliminate her access completely.

"I don't think you should do that. Dr. Jefferies told me to have you sit tight until he gets here."

Holiday murmured a nonsensical agreement, examining the network menu, then punching up the submenu for VR and telepresence. The operator watched her, paralyzed with indecision.

"Has Bill Epstein been in tonight?"

"No, Dr. Powers. Should he be?"

"What's your name?" she asked, ignoring his question.

"Gary Landon," he said.

"I thought that was it. I'm sorry I forgot it."

"That's all right," he said, brightening a little. "We only met once, when I was coming on the night shift."

She accessed the menu for telepresence projects. "I remember," she said. "By the way, it's all right for you to leave me alone here. I'm not going to break anything."

"I know that," he replied, laughing softly.

She gave him an expectant stare. He reluctantly walked away, muttering about attending to projects in the back room. She was sorry to force him to choose between conflicting orders from two of his superiors, but as soon as he was gone, she focused on the computer.

There was nothing she could do with the machine. She was in the system, and could access the source code for the telepresence program; unfortunately it was written in an advanced technical language she couldn't even begin to understand. As for the records of Gregory's supposed off-site log-ins, they were beyond her reach, accessible only through network privileges that she didn't have.

Bill wasn't going to show up. Perhaps he had simply backed down, or maybe he had lied to her. The computers hummed, the room full of information that she couldn't access.

She stared at her reflection on the glass wall. She had reached a complete impasse in every way. The evidence supporting Gregory's innocence seemed insubstantial, the product of a conversation with a technician who didn't bother to back up his claims. In the reflection she sat with her shoulders hunched, her head dipped low.

Her reflection looked like photos she had seen of herself at various points in her life: when she was a girl, adrift amid affluence without meaning; when she was a medical student, overwhelmed and suffering; after Kyle had gone to California, blaming her for the demise of their relationship when he had been the one who abandoned her. Looking into that glass, she saw herself as all ages at once—the adolescent, the undergraduate, the woman in her late twenties—and felt the struggle and frailty that united them all.

She sat up straight, pulling her hair away from her face. *Don't give in.* Kyle would be there soon. She thought of her father coming home from work, boisterous and over-bearing with his "beautiful little girl." She understood that she had always felt this way: waiting for someone to arrive with their demands, ready to do what was expected of her—and that at night, alone, she would look back and see that it had all been an act, that she hadn't been herself.

Kyle was there, at the door, watching. In the glass now she was sitting straight; her tall frame seemed poised and assertive. This was who she was now—not the girl or the young woman. She drew herself into the present with a resolve that was at once strange and invigorating.

"Kyle," she said.

"Holiday, why don't we go to my office and talk." He wore slacks and a rumpled dress shirt. His hair was mussed, and a long tuft shot back from his forehead over his thinning pate. Under a tan raincoat he held a leather briefcase.

"Why bother? There's no one else here. This is the place that matters, not one of our offices. We just play politics there."

He looked at her strangely. "All right, if that's what you want. Suit yourself." He put down the coat and valise.

"Why did you cover up Epstein's data? What did you think you were going to gain?"

"Hold on a minute. You sound like there's some kind of conspiracy going on here. I only wanted Epstein to be absolutely sure before we passed the information on to the police. I didn't want anyone chasing their tails."

Holiday looked into his eyes; their steely blue with flecks of turquoise hadn't changed. He looked away awk-wardly, then sat down. "What's going on with you?" he asked. "Why is this so important?"

"It's important because you're keeping an innocent man in jail. I knew you could be heartless, but this is beyond even that."

Jefferies looked as if he had been slapped. His face, puffy with sleep, dropped slack. "You're right. I'm sorry."

He pulled the briefcase to his lap, twirled the combination lock, and opened it toward him. He took out a thick file and put it on the table next to them.

"Here's everything Epstein found. Maybe I made a bad call by not doing anything about it right away. That's probably true."

"It was more than bad judgment," Holiday said, opening the folder. "It was pure malice, and I don't understand it."

"Malice had nothing to do with it."

"What, then? The real killer is out there somewhere. It almost seems as though you don't want him to be caught."

His face reddened. "Are you threatening me?"

"No, I'm not," she answered, surprised. She leafed through the papers. Everything Epstein had claimed was there—the system logs, the times and dates. She knew these would satisfy the police.

"I'm here now, anyway," Jefferies said. "I'm helping."

She cut him off. "I'm going to get Detective Harper here right away. It's not important anymore why you did this."

He cast his eyes toward the ceiling. "All right, I made a mistake. But just because I wanted to hold on to this information a day or so doesn't implicate me in some kind of conspiracy."

Holiday tucked the folder under her arm possessively. "Are you asking me to cover for you, Kyle?"

"You don't have to put it that way." He kicked the table lightly.

"Then tell me why."

He looked away, muttering, "Because I thought something wasn't right about Hampton. I couldn't believe he was innocent."

"That doesn't make any sense," she said calmly.

"It doesn't have to. There's something about Hampton that I don't like, or trust—even though I know you and he had become friends. I wanted to be damn sure he didn't have anything to do with that *disaster* before I was the one who freed him."

"I don't like you bringing up my personal life, Kyle," she said. "It has nothing to do with this."

He said nothing. She remembered how, in Boston, Kyle always came to her apartment, keeping her from his. His two-room place was tiny and austere, the cheapest apartment he could find close to the hospital. It wasn't until she helped him balance his checking account one month that she found he sent much of his income to his parents for his father's chemotherapy. He never mentioned it to her, though he could have borrowed nearly any amount of cash from her family. She never offered to help, knowing what his response would be.

Holiday opened her purse. Inside was Detective Harper's card. Kyle sat down before the computer terminal and stared at the menu that Holiday had left on the screen. He raked his hands through his hair. "Are you going to divulge all the circumstances regarding this new information?" he asked.

Years of mutual knowledge and old intimacies were packed into his tone. She picked up the phone and took a deep breath. "I am."

Jefferies shrugged. "Then go ahead. Get him here."

Holiday dialed Harper's home phone number, which he had scrawled across the back of his card next to the word "nights." He was skeptical and brusque on the phone, but promised to be there within a half hour. Kyle stalked off to his office, promising to return.

Harper arrived in a worn leather jacket and blue slacks that might have once been fashionable. He looked every bit what he was: an off-duty cop, tired and irritated at being called away from home for a development on a case he didn't like or completely understand.

"Dr. Powers," he said, shaking her hand. His cologne was old-fashioned and smelled of clover. "I should tell you straight off that the department is working with the feds on the case. Which means we share our information and they keep theirs to themselves."

"That doesn't matter," Holiday said. She put on her suit jacket and buttoned it, wanting this exchange to be as formal as possible. "I have evidence that Gregory Hampton didn't murder Han Takamoto."

Harper ran a hand over his beard stubble and stared at the papers as she explained Epstein's discovery step by step, going twice over technological terminology that Harper didn't immediately grasp. He was intuitively intelligent, and quickly became impatient for her to reach the end of Epstein's conclusions. She finished by stating her involvement with Gregory, a revelation that Harper took in stride. He sat on the edge of a table, the file in his hand.

"So you can see—" she said.

"Wait. I'm thinking." He held out a hand to silence her, staring blankly ahead. Finally he appeared satisfied. "Hampton has an alibi. Of all the damned things."

Jefferies returned, swiping his security card through the electronic lock. He stiffened when he saw Harper. "Detective," he said.

"I remember you," Harper said, rising to shake his hand. "You were at the murder scene, right? I took a statement from you."

"That's right," Jefferies said. He wore a blue Pacific University lab coat over his wrinkled dress shirt.

"You're here late," Harper said, checking his watch theatrically. "Do you have anything to do with what Dr. Powers just told me?"

Glancing at Holiday, Jefferies said, "The person who discovered this information is working under me. I've been in possession of the evidence for almost twenty-four hours because I wanted it verified. Dr. Powers pointed out to me that the information was worth bringing to your attention right away, so I reversed my decision."

Harper pulled an apple from his jacket pocket, rubbing it on his slacks until he had buffed it to a waxy shine. He bit into it and spoke with his mouth full. "When did you plan to bring this to us, if Dr. Powers hadn't been so persuasive?"

"As soon as I was satisfied as to its veracity," Jefferies said dryly. "Perhaps even a day was too long."

Harper inspected the apple for imperfections. "Maybe so," he said ambiguously. He looked at Jefferies with a pained half smile. "Let me tell you what I told Dr. Powers. Don't take any out-of-town vacations until the investigation is closed. With all the media play this case has got, a lot of people are eager to see results. It looks like everyone just became a suspect all over again."

Kyle appeared ready to protest, but he stopped himself.

"Doctor," Harper said. His face was more haggard than she remembered; only his deep-set eyes shone like those of a younger man. "Where is the man who discovered this?"

Significantly Harper addressed the question to Holiday. "I don't know where he is, and I'm a little concerned," she said. "He was supposed to meet me here tonight."

"Do you have any idea what happened to him?"

"No. Bill was a little upset when I saw him earlier this evening. He had worked closely with Gregory." Holiday was unsure whether she wanted to say specifically that his distress had been caused by Jefferies's delay.

"Sure, sure," Harper interrupted. "When you see him, have him call me. He's going to have to give a fresh statement."

He stood up and put the folder under his arm. "I'm going to have to take this with me obviously."

"There are copies in my briefcase," Kyle offered.

"Can I have one?" Holiday asked quickly.

Jefferies glanced at Harper, as if for permission. The detective shrugged. "I don't care. Just don't show it around outside your department—especially to the media. This stuff is going to be evidence if the case goes to trial, and I'd hate to have it ruled inadmissible because someone fucked up."

Holiday reached out for a copy of the network lists. "Detective," she asked, folding the papers and putting them in her jacket pocket. "Does this mean Gregory's going to be released?"

"Ask the feds," Harper said, with more than a trace of bitterness. "But I don't think they can hold him any longer. They're going to be concentrating their attention on Seattle after they see this, I'd imagine. Whatever, as long as they get out of my office."

Harper zipped up his leather jacket and made for the door. Passing Jefferies, he lightly punched his shoulder. "Remember what I said about vacations, Doctor. You'll be getting a call from me."

Kyle glowered and walked out without a word. Holiday followed Harper to her car. It wasn't entirely rational, but she wanted the safety of being with a policeman.

"Say, Doctor, do you mind if I ask your professional opinion on something?" Harper asked as they passed under a row of floodlights. "I've got this ingrown toenail that's killing me. Too many years in cop shoes, you know what I mean?"

She glanced down at his worn leather wing tips. "Do you think the toe is infected?" she asked as they walked.

"I don't know." He fished in his jacket and found a half-smoked cigarette. "To tell you the truth, I haven't had that good a look at it."

They stopped while he lit the cigarette, his hand held over the flame against the slight breeze. "Call my office in the morning and I'll have my assistant refer you to an podiatrist," she said. "You should probably have it looked at. You might need outpatient surgery."

"Thanks, but I need to go to someone in my department's health plan. I was just wondering, you know. I don't like to go to the doctor. I thought there might be something I could do myself."

"Don't mess with it," she said quickly. He grinned a little, and they resumed walking. "Keep it clean. If it's infected, you'll just make it worse by trying to treat it yourself."

"I know, I know. You're right," Harper said, coughing as he exhaled a cloud of smoke. They arrived at Holiday's car. He leaned against a lamp, shaking his head.

Holiday put her key in the car door. "What's wrong?" she asked.

"Maybe you can tell me. None of this is making any sense to me." Harper threw down his cigarette and crushed it, lighting another. "All I see in this case are doctors and a couple of computer geeks. I don't see any of them being wrapped up in this murder."

"Why is that?" They were alone in the lot. She could hear a siren approach, headed for the hospital ER.

"Because they all have plenty of money," Harper said. "Hampton I understood—a little chip on his shoulder, unhappy with his job."

"Gregory isn't like that." She threw her purse inside her car. "He isn't the kind of person who would kill—for any reason."

"That's not what people were saying a few days ago." Harper exhaled smoke. "You should have told me before now that you were with him that morning."

"I know."

"Hampton's still in the county jail. You can be there when they release him." He ground out his second cigarette. "I would have eventually found out, you know. It wouldn't have looked good. I might have thought you two were working together."

"I wasn't thinking. I—"

"You felt betrayed. You didn't understand how he could do something like that to you." Harper rubbed his neck. "Well, it looks like he didn't—at least for now. But you, and him, and that jackass Jefferies are all looking pretty shabby. Do you understand that?"

"I haven't done anything wrong, Detective. If you think I would throw away my life and my career for money, or for whatever, then you're not as insightful as I thought."

"Makes sense to me," he said, walking toward a Ford sedan two parking rows away. "But then I don't know the whole story. Give me a call if you think of anything else you forgot, Dr. Powers." His voice faded with his footsteps as he moved out of the light, slowly making his way to his car.

19

AFTERNOON DOWNTOWN WAS RADICALLY DIFFERENT THAN IN West L.A. The heart of the city was all concrete, with a blazing sun muted by brown haze hanging low over the skyscrapers. A wave of desert heat had descended upon southern California, parching already sterile lawns and postponing the cleansing winter rains. It felt as though autumn had turned back into summer, ignoring the temperate winter in between.

Heat emanated from the sidewalks and streets, wearying the pedestrians, the vendors, and the street people. A steady stream of human traffic moved in and out of the dirty stone jail: police attorneys, sad-faced women visiting husbands and boyfriends. Holiday sat alone in her car, already sweating though she had been parked for only ten minutes. She played the radio low and stared out the window.

Gregory was inside signing a final series of forms. When she arrived to pick him up—finding him with several dangerous-looking prisoners also waiting for their release—he was relieved and happy. Then came his anger and resentment; his brow furrowed when he was told he had to wait. When she told him to calm down, he told her harshly to mind her own business. Waiting in the car had been her way of getting away from him.

Gregory left the building and squinted into the sun. He had lost weight. His features were drawn and tightened, though most of the bruises had faded from his nose and cheeks. As he drew nearer, she could see his jaw pulse with tension. He wore the same shirt, slacks, and tie, now wrinkled, that he had the morning Takamoto died.

He was silent as Holiday maneuvered through the maze

of one-way streets, winding her way back to the Santa
Monica Freeway.

"Back from my vacation," he said, staring coldly ahead.
"As you can see, I packed light."

Holiday kept her eyes on the road. Traffic degenerated
into a free-for-all near the on-ramp, and she was caught at
a red light with her car in the middle of an intersection.

"Not a bad time," he added with sarcasm. "Stayed out
of trouble, saw a couple of guys I knew."

The light turned green. Holiday drove slowly, allowing
the more manic drivers to swerve around her.

He laughed. "You know what they say. The county jail
is just another name for a nigger convention."

"Stop it, Gregory," Holiday said. Her eyes felt hot as
she steered into the five lanes of freeway traffic.

"Why?" he asked. She glanced at him; his handsome
features were contorted into a bitter mask. "Tell me that
isn't what everyone was thinking. That you can train 'em,
give 'em a good job, but they'll always blow it in the end."

"Stop it, Gregory," Holiday said, her voice breaking.
"That really isn't what I thought. It isn't what I thought at
all."

Traffic was heavy on the freeway, and she had to slow
to a crawl. The car was stifling hot, and she switched on
the air-conditioning. "So what *did* you think?" he asked.
"I didn't see or hear from you. You tell me—what was I
supposed to think?"

His voice was choked. She wanted to hold him, and
admit that she had doubted him. She wanted his forgive-
ness. Instead she said, "I didn't know what happened. I
had my face on the nightly news, my job put in jeopardy,
and everyone saying that it was you that caused it. I . . .
I didn't know what was true."

"Yeah, well . . ." His voice trailed off. "Thanks for
picking me up. So Epstein found a way to prove I didn't
do it."

She suddenly realized that she still hadn't heard from
Bill.

"I thought that weasel was after my job," Gregory said, chuckling. "For a while I even wondered if he might have set me up."

Traffic eased a little, and Holiday was able to accelerate into third gear. "He isn't a weasel," she said quietly. "He was worried about you. He was happy when he was able to clear your name."

"You're right. Bill's a good guy," Gregory said. "But my name is never going to be clear."

"What do you mean by that?" she asked calmly, wanting only a respite from his hostility.

"What I mean is that, released or not, everyone thinks of me as the black saboteur who builds computer systems just to trash them," he said. "I had a lot of time to think in there. I'm going to take my savings and get the hell away from everyone."

Holiday slapped the steering wheel so hard that for an instant she feared she had broken her hand. The car veered into the next lane, provoking a volley of blaring horns and squealing brakes. She turned to Gregory, who met her gaze with stubborn fierceness.

"God damn it, just shut up," she screamed. "You hurt me, all right? Is that want you wanted? You hurt me as much as you were hurt. Are you happy now?"

Gregory was, she realized, satisfied he had provoked her anger. "It's not about that," he said. "I don't even care anymore."

She yelled with an inarticulate burst of rage that resounded within the car. Her breath caught in her chest. "I'm taking you directly to the labs," she said. "I don't care what anyone says, you're getting in there. I want you to look at the logs and the data files for yourself to see if there's anything Bill Epstein didn't notice."

"You're not listening," Gregory said. "I don't care. If you take me there, I'm just going to clean out my desk, go home, and call the building manager to put my place up for sale."

Tears ran down her cheeks. In the rearview mirror she

looked terrible: ruddy, pinched, exhausted. She had known this was going to be difficult, but he was torturing her. He was an irrational stranger.

He seemed to sense her despair and was silent for a moment. She heard him swallow hard and tap his knuckles on the dashboard in a soft, slow rhythm. Their relationship, whatever it was or might have been, felt like a piece of fabric that had been torn apart.

"I was thinking about leaving, too," she said as they neared the exit for the university. "When you were in jail, it was more than I could take. But I stayed. Because if I run away, I might as well give up on my life. If you run away, then whoever framed you will get away with it."

They pulled off the freeway into the chaotic traffic near the university. People flooded the sidewalks and walked in the streets. She drove slowly, keeping a wary eye out for bicyclists.

"I'll look at the logs," Gregory said. "After that I don't know. I don't think there's anything here for me now."

"Just—" She stopped herself. "Just see what there is to see. I don't care what you think about me. Do it for yourself."

At the labs Holiday found that her security clearance had been reactivated. Somewhat surprised, she and Gregory entered. His presence caused a stir among the technicians, most of whom came forward to shake his hand and welcome him back. Gregory was cold and restrained.

Holiday spotted a familiar face. "Gary Landon," she said. "You were here last night."

"Bill Epstein hasn't come in, so I'm sticking around until the night jobs finish processing."

"Is Dr. Jefferies in today?" she asked.

Landon shook his head. "Jefferies called this morning to tell me to activate your security codes, but that was it. It's good to see you both back," he said, smiling tentatively at Gregory. "When did you get out? No one told us anything."

"I need you to set me up with a terminal," Gregory

said, ignoring him. "Has anyone taken over my office yet?"

"We were going to turn it into a shrine," Landon said with a grin. Gregory didn't respond. "No. The door's open. No one has been at your terminal except for Bill, and that was just for a few hours."

"Set me up with network privileges so that I can get on the system," Gregory snapped. Landon began to refuse, but Holiday interrupted.

"There's no one here to say no," she said. She realized how this must have looked; she and Gregory were both tense, appearing abruptly, making demands. "I'll take responsibility, Gary."

"Jefferies did activate your clearance," Landon said, obviously ready to be convinced. "Maybe I should call up Dr. Hermoza."

"The lady said she'd take the responsibility," Gregory said.

Landon, obviously tired of fighting, led them to Gregory's office, where he set up a new computer password and reinstated his former boss's network access. He left and shut the door quietly behind him.

Holiday immediately made for the ratty sofa in the corner, flicking away the bits of stuffing that spilled from its cushions. She hadn't slept the night before, having spent her time waiting at home for Harper to call, then leaving early to pick up Gregory at the jail. *Mission accomplished. I got him here.* "Wake me up if you find anything," she said, folding her jacket into a pillow. He didn't respond. His attention was fixed on the computer screen and the records that Holiday had given him.

Holiday felt the rough twill of the sofa on her bare arms. Sleep came easily, quickly. She woke once, briefly, to the sound of Gregory talking on the phone. His voice mixed with a dream that slipped away when she tried to remember it.

"Holiday." Gregory crouched before her, his face near

hers, his eyes gleaming with intensity. He kept a hand on her shoulder as she awoke.

"Wake up," he said. "I found something."

10:45 P.M., December 11, Tokyo

It was late, the end of a very long day for Moshiro Tamo. His ascent to the head of the Mitsuyama Corporation's board of directors had been swift. Within twenty-four hours after Han Takamoto's death he had consolidated his position by promising favors and calling in political debts. His greatest advantage was that, while the remainder of the board met in a state of numb disbelief, he had already calculated precisely what needed to be done.

There were others within the company who were glad Takamoto was gone, but he didn't consider them his allies. Tamo didn't even consider the small group he had marshaled as his power base to be his allies. As far as he was concerned, he had none. He had put together the factors that left Takamoto dead on the table. Of all those who wanted the old man's power, only Moshiro Tamo had seized it.

He leaned back in the plush leather chair that had once belonged to Han Takamoto. Already Takamoto's pictures and trinkets were gone from the walls and shelves. Within the year he would see to it that the old man's name was never mentioned again.

At the other end of the room was Dr. Mishima. Tamo had left him there to wait, nervously clutching a tumbler of single-malt scotch. Tamo poured himself another drink and took a long drag on his cigar.

"Doctor," he said. "It's unusual for anyone to visit me here so late at night. Much less someone who has no connection to me."

Dr. Mishima nervously stood. He was old, nearly as old as Takamoto had been. His hair and eyebrows had gone gray.

"Don't you have anything to say to me?" Tamo asked.

"You have disturbed my solitude. We should not even be seen together."

"I'm sorry," Mishima said. "I am very upset. The police came to my house last night. It is the second time they have spoken with me."

Tamo stared at the older man. Tamo knew his own strengths; his appearance was severe, his thin mouth and dull, piercing eyes so striking that weak men had difficulty maintaining silence around him. Mishima would be no different.

"I am upset," Mishima repeated. "They were very insistent. I think they know something."

"They know nothing," Tamo said calmly. "I have conducted my actions under the utmost secrecy. My only fear is that there may be a weak link in the chain I have created."

A moment of understanding played across the doctor's wrinkled features. "No, no," he said, shaking his head vigorously. "I told them nothing. I will never tell them anything."

"Of course you won't," Tamo said. "Because you do not know anything. I asked you to keep me aware of our departed friend's medical condition. I gave you a small allowance for doing so. What is wrong with that?"

The doctor stiffened. His eyes involuntarily moved to the door. "Nothing is wrong, of course," he said. He bowed his head. "But I did not know you would use the information in the way you did. I would not have dreamed that—"

"Old friend," Tamo said. "We have known each other for several years. You knew of my ambition. It was not a secret."

"Of course, but I—"

"Are you unhappy with the allowance you currently receive? Do you think it unfair? I can certainly arrange to have it raised."

Tamo's new office was soundproof and temperature

controlled. He luxuriated in the moment of complete silence, feeling the doctor's anxiety grow.

"I do not want more money," Mishima said.

Tamo smiled. "I insist," he said. "You will find a surprise in your next payment. It is the least I can do for your trouble. I am sure that the police will not bother you again."

Mishima's expression turned deeply sad. He was a man with morals, Tamo realized, and must have been sorry for what he had done. Surely he could not have known that reporting Takamoto's cholecystitis would lead to his patient's death. It took information from other operatives, closer to Takamoto, to bring it all together. And, of course, the foreigner.

"Leave me now, Doctor," Tamo said. "I have work to do before I can leave tonight."

The doctor nodded sadly and left, closing the door quietly behind him. Tamo sipped his scotch and looked out at the lights of Tokyo below him.

The doctor would have to die, that much was obvious. It was now time to see if his men had the capacity to kill. And if preliminary investigations into the foreign doctor's actions proved damning, he would have to die as well.

Tamo looked around the office, at the seat of his new power. There were other men like him in the world. He would have to be very vigilant. For the rest of his life.

20

WITH THE DECK DOORS OPEN, HOLIDAY'S APARTMENT FILLED with a cool morning breeze. She stepped through the empty spare bedroom to the square concrete deck. Leaning against the rail, she allowed the wind to muss her hair, which had grown longer than it had been in years. Back inside she poured another cup of fresh coffee and took a batch of unopened mail to the sofa.

Gregory's discoveries were all she could think about, so she had set aside a half hour to relax and think of nothing. Glancing at her watch, she saw that her time was nearly up.

He had tried to explain to her what he uncovered, but Holiday had no idea what it meant or what they could do about it. He would be there soon, back from visiting Shawn, and she almost dreaded seeing him again. He still could barely bring himself to look at her, much less talk to her with warmth or intimacy.

The kitchen phone rang, jarring her. She realized that she had been drifting gently to sleep. It seemed she couldn't get enough rest lately; no matter how much she slept, her eyes burned with fatigue and her mind wandered. Probably some kind of stress reaction, she thought—nothing a month in a sanitarium wouldn't cure.

She heard silence on the line and thought it was another anonymous threat. Instead she heard the distinctive rumbling cough of Phil Hermoza.

"Powers? Are you coming to the hospital today?"

"Maybe later, Phil. I have some things to take care of first."

Silence. She hadn't seen Phil since Takamoto's murder. Messages from him had piled up on her desk in the interim, and she knew he would be personally hurt that she hadn't called back, as well as professionally angry that she hadn't returned to work regularly. She knew she wasn't helping her case for reinstating her full privileges.

"Well, I'd really like to see you in here today." He was insistent, much as he had been years before when, during a period of stress-induced illness, Holiday missed a week of vital labs in medical school. It was as terrible now to disappoint him as it had been then.

"I'm sorry, Phil. There's been so much upheaval in the last couple of days. I spent yesterday getting Gregory out of jail."

"You took him to the labs without my knowledge or permission."

She pictured him in his typical phone-call posture— elbows on the table, the receiver cradled in his huge shoulder like a child's toy. "I thought we owed it to him not to treat him like an outsider, Phil."

"It's not a matter of what we owe him. Think about how it looks—he might have been in there fucking with evidence. It might blow the case if we're ever able to find out who sabotaged the system."

She hadn't thought of that, but he was right. They had to remember now that their acts might be analyzed by the police, by attorneys in a courtroom. But if what Gregory found was true, the outward appearance of their actions yesterday might be irrelevant.

"I can vouch for him, Phil, he was double-checking what Epstein found. Nothing more."

"Speaking of Epstein, he hasn't showed up the last two days. Have you heard from him?"

Holiday leaned back against the doorway. "I saw him two nights ago. He brought me the log-in information after Kyle—"

"After Jefferies sat on it, I know. I had a delightful talk with Detective Harper of the LAPD yesterday afternoon. He can't find Epstein, either, and he wants to talk to him in a bad way."

She heard a slam on Phil's end of the line. He had a

cordless office phone and had apparently closed his door for privacy.

"I don't where he is, Phil. Maybe we should report him missing."

"No need for that. The LAPD are already looking for him."

It made no sense, unless Epstein figured he had done his part by passing on the information and didn't want to be involved any further. But why would he disappear? She knew how much his job meant to him. "I have a bad feeling about Bill," she said.

"Yeah, well, I have so many bad feelings that I can't even tell them apart. To begin with, why did I have to hear from the police about all of this? Why didn't anyone notify me?"

"It all happened so quickly," she answered weakly.

His voice turned breathy with irritation. "Well, you should know that I recommended Kyle take a little personal time until this shit gets sorted out. Mostly I'm afraid I'll wring his neck if I see him."

Hermoza didn't sound like he was joking. She had an almost irresistible urge to slam the phone down.

"I don't know what I'm going to do with him," Phil said, calmer now. "I know you and he have had your differences, but I need you both. So I have to hold back on my first impulse, which is to fire him. And to tell you you're finished if you don't get in here today and start carrying your share of the load. I'm sending cases to the Bart that we should be doing, for Christ's sake. It's unacceptable."

When Phil resisted using profanity for so long, it meant he was truly disappointed. Now was the time to tell him what Gregory had found. They should call the police, explain everything, and return to their lives. But then Gregory might leave, and the truth would be unraveled by others. Whatever happened, she wanted to be there when the person who had done this to her life was discovered.

"I'm sorry, Phil. I know I'm trying your patience."

"What about Hampton?" he asked curtly. "We should get him back in here as soon as the dust clears. We've lost enough time on the simulators. I don't give a fuck what administration says, we need him—and we need the cash from the Bart project."

"I don't know if Gregory is coming back to the university."

"The hell with that. Of course he's coming back. I'll break his back over my knee if—" Phil paused, realizing that he was drifting too far into hyperbole, even by his standards. "What's his problem?" he continued, his voice suddenly calm and rational.

"He's angry that he didn't get any support when he was in jail."

"What did he fucking expect? A cake with a file in it?"

"No, he feels that I . . . we assumed he was guilty, and that we were ready to see him convicted of murder without trying to defend him."

"I can understand that," Hermoza said. "But for the love of Christ, what does he expect? We're colleagues, friends, but we're not the Knights of the Round Table. If there was evidence I had killed someone, would you defend me just because we've known each other for a long time?"

"I'd do what I could. I know that now."

"We all do what we can, but we're also living in the real world. Listen, have you checked your E-mail?"

"No, I haven't even thought of it," she said.

"Everyone in the department needs to check it every day. We've got to get you a home terminal so that you can log in." She heard his door open with a creak. Their conversation was public again. "I sent you a message saying your full privileges are restored as of next Monday. And that includes your position as head of advanced technologies."

She couldn't have predicted the effect this news would have on her; her heart thudded with giddy excitement. She had options now, a life she could return to. "Thank you, Phil. It means a lot to me that you made things happen so quickly."

"The main hassle was with malpractice insurance—the company couldn't understand telepresence and how the death wasn't your fault, so they classified it as gross negligence." Hermoza muttered softly, and she heard his secretary reply. "So get in here and justify my support, Powers. Are you going to talk to Hampton soon?"

"I might talk to him today, I don't know." She lied instinctively, still hiding her relationship with Gregory.

"Well, kiss his ass for me. We've got to get him back or you're not going to have much of a department to run. Give him the royal administrative butter-up. Tell him we'll raise his salary up to ten percent. And that we'll stock his favorite brand of cupcakes in the cafeteria. Whatever it takes."

"I'll try, Phil."

As they said good-bye, Holiday thought she was probably the worst person in the world to convince Gregory to stay. He had only agreed to come over that morning reluctantly. Only the tragedy kept them together now. Once it was resolved, she knew that he would vanish from her life, like all the other unfulfilled opportunities and broken promises.

It was almost nine. Gregory was running late, but he said he was stopping off at his apartment to take care of something important. Which meant that he might come with answers. To kill time, she called Boston and left a message for her parents. Then, one eye on the clock, she opened a carton of books and put them on a shelf one by one. She felt resolved to stay, to dig in her heels and get on with her life—whether Gregory would be a part of it or not.

He finally arrived near ten, a folder in his hand and deep circles under his eyes. He helped himself to coffee and sat on the sofa.

"You haven't unpacked much since I was here the last time." He yawned and looked around at the cartons strewn throughout the room, running a hand through his short curly hair.

"I was taking out some things before you came. I figured it's about time." She brushed her hair from her face, wearing it down that morning because—she admitted to herself—she thought it made her more attractive. She was dressed casually, in jeans and a man's shirt.

Gregory opened the folder. "You're not going to believe what I have," he said, as calmly as if he were unfolding a take-out menu.

She sat down next to him. On a piece of legal paper in ballpoint pen were scrawled a series of numbers and Internet addresses. "Look, before I tell you about all this, I want to say something to you."

Holiday folded her hands in her lap. If he had risen and left at that moment, she wouldn't have tried to stop him.

"I want to say that I had no right to talk to you like I did yesterday. I don't know what I expected, but I realized last night that I wouldn't have done anything differently than you did."

She stared at the floor as he wrung his hands; he took a long, deep breath, struggling with himself. "I don't blame you. A lot of things got confused because of that night we spent together. It's not right for me to use that against you like I did. I have a lot of anger, but that's not your fault."

He might be staying, she realized. She wanted fiercely for that to happen, and also feared it. She kissed his forehead. "My feelings for you haven't changed," she whispered. "Maybe I tried to convince myself they had, but it didn't work."

He stared into her eyes for a long moment, his head shaking almost imperceptibly, his mouth moving without sound. He took her hand and held it for a moment, his expression impenetrable.

She knew nothing could happen between them until they found out the truth—about Takamoto, about the anonymous attackers, about themselves. "Tell me what's in the file."

"Someone stole my password, and I don't know who. It's possible I never will. It could have happened here, or it could have happened in San Francisco, Chicago, or Seattle, for all I know."

"Why?" she asked, settling back on the couch.

"I was in all those places in the last six months. It's possible someone was waiting for me to log in to the Internet so that they could intercept my password. It isn't easy, but it can be done if you have the right network privileges—and you know the precise whereabouts of the person you're going to rob. You have to be at the same network node to effectively steal a password."

"What does that mean?"

"The same in-house network. You'd have to be in the same place, with total access to the same computer system, and you would have to know the precise moment I logged onto the machine."

"Then Bill Epstein could have been involved."

He shook his head. "I thought about it, but my gut feeling is that he wouldn't betray me like that. The only way to know for sure is to go to the person who performed the sabotage, though, and he, they, whoever it is—isn't in L.A."

"Lincoln, Nebraska, right? At the university computer center." She looked at the list on the page before her. There were telephone codes and interchanges she didn't recognize.

"That's what I thought last night, that's why I woke you up," Gregory answered, sighing. "But it isn't that simple."

"Bill found out the remote log-in was from Seattle," Holiday said, trying to piece together the thin strands of what he had told her the night before. "And you called the network manager there, who checked the logs and found that log-in was remote from Denver."

"Right, and I called that address, and their logs said *that* remote log-in originated from Lincoln."

"And that was the end of the line, right? The person who put in the subroutine did it from the University of Nebraska."

"I *thought* it was the end of the line when the network manager there told me the log-in on his records was on-site," Gregory said. "But it didn't make sense. I've never been there, and I don't know anyone in Nebraska. But I got a call from the computer lab manager there last night, because he misread the network records. The log-in to the University of Nebraska was also a remote, and this time it didn't even come from America."

"Wouldn't that be harder to detect?" she asked, realizing the odd numbers on the pad were international communications exchanges. Gregory had apparently been running up quite a phone bill.

"Not at all," Gregory said, pulling a pen from his pocket and marking the various numbers as he spoke. "Computer networks don't distinguish between countries. A message is a message, it doesn't matter where it comes from. It turns out Seattle, Denver, Lincoln, and even London were just transitory stations that the information passed though on the way to our computers at the university."

"Like layovers on an international flight."

"Pretty much, only they stop for only a fraction of a second. The only information the user supplies is the ultimate destination of the data. How it gets there is up to the machines. It's like taking a flight to a faraway place—the airline decides where your stopovers will be."

Anger had crept back into his voice, and she moved away from him a fraction. A month ago he would have explained these concepts with pleasure and wonder; now he interpreted them with impatience.

"What's on your mind?" Gregory asked, snapping his fingers in the air as if waking her from a trance. "You're fading out on me."

"It's all right. Go ahead."

With a curious glance that softened his features and made him seem suddenly boyish, he put the pad on the sofa between them. "Well, this is the end," he said. "Whoever the bastard is that sabotaged my system and set me up for murder—they did it from Sweden."

Holiday felt her mouth drop open with shock. Gregory still stared at his file, oblivious.

"The University of Stockholm Medical School computer center, to be precise." He spoke with obvious relish, each syllable a pearl representing solutions, a face yet unseen, an outlet for his hostility.

"I don't know what to think," she said softly. She tried to remember—had Bo been unduly interested in telepresence? That was ridiculous; he hadn't even been to Sweden in more than five years, if he was to be believed.

"It means I'm going on a trip—to give someone a very unpleasant surprise," he said, standing up. He looked around the room. "Where do you keep your phone book?"

"In the kitchen," Holiday said automatically. When Gregory stalked into the kitchen and began rustling among a pile of papers and books on the counter, she leaped from the sofa. "Why do you want it?"

He found the yellow pages under a ragged *Better Homes and Gardens Traditional Family Cookbook,* given to Holiday as a birthday gift years ago when she had first moved out on her own. Gregory opened the phone book flat on the counter. "I'm looking for whatever airline can get me on the next flight to Stockholm."

"What are you talking about?" Holiday said. "You don't know anything about the person who did this. They might be dangerous."

Gregory looked up soberly. "I'll take my chances. Anyway, it took a pretty skilled computer engineer to pull it off, and computer engineers aren't the most dangerous people in the world."

"Don't laugh this off," Holiday said. "We'll take every-thing you found to the police and get on with our lives."

He shook his head, pulling out a pen and underlining a number in the book. "Look at what the police have done for me so far," he said. "Do you think their first priority is getting me justice?"

When he picked up the phone receiver, Holiday jammed down the hang-up switch. Gregory reached out to remove her hand.

"Stop," she said. "I have to tell you about some things that happened while you were in jail."

Standing there in the kitchen, she began telling him about the man who attacked her in her living room. His rage disappeared, and with concern he hung up the phone and reached out for her. She made him stay silent, though he seethed and softly cursed when she told him about Kyle Jefferies's delay in bringing the police the data that had freed him.

"Let me finish," she said angrily. "I'm trying to think everything through myself, and you're exhausting me. Gregory, for God's sake, you have to let go, just for a little while."

"The hell with that," he said. "Did he know about you and me?"

"I think so. He gave me that impression."

"That's funny. You weren't exactly likely to go public about your one-night stand with a black criminal."

The only thing she would remember about what hap-pened next was Gregory's expression; it shifted rapidly from numb shock through flashing rage to pained sadness. When the discolored patch appeared on his cheek, she realized she had slapped him. No words passed between them for a moment, and when his hand fell from rubbing the spot she had struck, he was rigid and calm.

"Go on," he said.

"I was surprised when you told me about Stockholm, because my friend Bo Swenson is from there. I knew his son a long time ago." She was shaking now—afraid of her physical violence, which had come so easily, and of the pleasure she felt from finally making him stop trying to hurt her. The second feeling chilled her more.

"I met Swenson at a Christmas party a couple of years ago," Gregory said. "What are you thinking?"

"I guess it means we should give him a call. He might be able to tell us something."

"That's out of the question," Gregory said flatly. "For all we know, he might have had something to do with it."

"That's ridiculous," she said defensively.

"Think about it," he said. "Jefferies hides the evidence, you almost get raped or killed, and this guy you just made friends with is from the country where all this shit came from. Maybe Jefferies and Swenson were working together."

"That's impossible," Holiday said. "Bo Swenson doesn't even know Kyle. And anyway, he wouldn't do something like . . . it's insane, it really is." She wanted desperately to call Harper, to have that sharp, unforgiving mind tell her what he thought.

"Maybe," Gregory said. "But there's something going on here, and I think you're part of it."

"What? Are you so paranoid now that you—"

"Don't be silly." He grinned. "I trust you, Holiday. No matter how much of an ass I am, I do trust you. What I meant was maybe someone's interested in hurting you, not me."

They both jumped when the phone rang. Holiday picked up, and an obsequious telemarketer launched into a pitch about a package cruise to the Caribbean. She hung up, leaving him in midsentence.

"And I guess that's part of the conspiracy?" she asked. "They'll lure me to Barbados and bore me to death pitching time-sharing seminars?"

Gregory looked puzzled. "Never mind," Holiday said. "If someone is after me, then it's my problem—and I want to go to the police and let them handle it."

"Holiday," Gregory said. "We're both involved in this.

As far as we know, maybe Jefferies wanted us *both* taken care of. You know he wouldn't mind that happening."

They were chasing shadows. But a nagging notion remained. In the horrific hours after Han Takamoto's death, she *had* thought about Kyle, about the grim satisfaction she saw in his face when the police descended and her life unraveled.

"It's too risky," she said. "Kyle would never jeopardize his career. His work is the most important thing in the world to him, along with the power it gives him."

"Maybe you just answered my question. And don't forget—whoever planned this, it's worked so far. It's possible we might not find a thing in Stockholm, maybe just a timed program that could have been put in place by anyone in the world. But how could we live with ourselves if we didn't at least go there?"

He reached out to put his arms around her before she could react. Feeling his strength, his tenderness, she buried her face in his chest.

"Come with me," he whispered. "If we don't get any answers, at least we tried. It's the only way we can know for sure, the only way we can start fresh and try to be together—if that's what you want."

Holiday pulled away from him. "Don't use that against me," she said. "Don't you dare tell me I have to do this for us be together."

"You're right, I'm sorry," he said. She let him take her hand, enervated by the tumultuous emotions he evoked in her. She stared into an inner abyss, where a silent voice told her anything could happen. Nothing was as it seemed.

And Gregory, vowing his trustworthiness—wasn't that what he said before? She took a long, deep breath, finding within herself only one weakness, one undeniable factor that might cloud her thinking. She was falling in love with him.

Santa Lucia's Day

MAPHEX DOCUMENT DECODER RUNNING

FROM: 00382T@MC.COM
TO: MT GROUP
121296

NOTE PROTOCOL REGARDING ELECTRONIC MESSAGES:
ACCOUNT NUMBER CHANGING EVERY TWO HOURS FOR
ACCESS TO RESTRICTED INFORMATION. USE NUMBER-
GENERATOR PROGRAM TWO TO FIND CODES FOR FURTHER
MESSAGES.

CONGRATULATIONS ON QUICK MOVEMENT, FOCUS,
DEDICATION AND LOYALTY ON THE PART OF NEARLY
EVERY MEMBER OF THE GROUP. WE WILL ALL REAP
REWARDS EQUALLY.

OUR FUTURES WILL BE DETERMINED BY OUR ABILITY TO
MAINTAIN SECRECY THROUGHOUT THE FUTURE. OUR
COMPLICITY WILL BE LIFELONG. ANY WEAKNESS IN THE
GROUP ENDANGERS THE HONOR AND LIVES OF OUR
MEMBERS AND FAMILIES.

THIS STAGE OF EVENTS MUST BE CONCLUDED. CLOSURE
PLANS HAVE BEEN IMPLEMENTED. CONTACTS MADE
THROUGH NORTH AMERICAN BRANCH OF OUR OPERATION,
BECAUSE OF MISCALCULATION, MUST BE CORRECTED.
DISCLOSURE OF ACTIVITIES WILL BE MADE UPON
COMPLETION.

AMERICAN BRANCH HAS ASSURED SUCCESS. BE ADVISED
THAT SUCH ERRORS IN THE FUTURE WILL BE GROUNDS FOR
TERMINATION. NOT ALL OF US WILL HAVE THE
OPPORTUNITY TO CORRECT OUR MISTAKES.

MAPHEX DOCUMENT DECODER QUIT
FILE DELETED
DISK SCAN RUN—00382T@MC.COM NOT FOUND
SIGN OFF

21

THE CUSTOMS LINE AT THE ARLANDA AIRPORT IN STOCKHOLM was immensely long and moved agonizingly slowly. Legendary Scandinavian thoroughness led the officers to treat each bag like a potential threat before reluctantly allowing it to pass into the country.

"Jag vill skicka efter en lakare," she said quietly to Gregory, looking down at the guidebook she had bought on the way to Los Angeles International Airport after they phoned an order for tickets to SAS Airlines. She had read the better part of it during the interminable flight and layover in New York, in between fitful naps.

Gregory looked away from the head of the line. "What are you talking about?"

"It means, 'Please call a doctor,' in Swedish."

"I don't think we'll be needing that one with you here," he said. "How about, 'I'm a stupid American who can't speak your language'?"

Gregory spoke loudly enough to be heard by the other passengers around him, but no one turned to look. Holiday sensed reserve from the people here, and thought of a short story by Hemingway she had read as an undergraduate. It was about late-night desolation and loneliness, and haunted people who wanted cold reassurance.

"A clean, well-lighted place," she said.

Gregory surprised her by recognizing the title. Apparently he hadn't spent all his life in front of a computer screen. "I see what you mean. I think I know what he was talking about now."

They finally reached the customs officials and had to declare their destination and intentions. The process took several minutes but was eased by the officials' fluent English; Holiday and Gregory lapsed into the wordless apprehension they shared during the long overnight flight. They tacitly understood that to speak of their plans would tear the thin gossamer web of intention that had brought them there.

Holiday had lied to Phil Hermoza, saying she needed the rest of the week off to visit her mother in Boston. She hated lying to him. And when the wide-body plane lifted off from Los Angeles, she remembered too late Harper's admonition that she shouldn't leave town until the investigation was over.

The customs agent handed her suitcase over the long inspection counter and turned his attention to the next in line. Holiday stopped in the concourse and looked outside. The weak Scandinavian winter sun shone low and slanted over the spotless buildings outside; snow had been plowed to either side of the street, and flurries swirled in a light wind. Gregory joined her at the window.

"I can put up with a little winter," he said. "In a few hours we'll know everything. I have a feeling."

Holiday wondered whether that knowledge was now what she even wanted. "Let's go," she said. "There's no point waiting."

Los Angeles

This was the man who showed up at Dr. Powers's apartment the other day. Clay Simmons knew it as surely as he felt the bruises from the kicks she gave him a few nights ago. He probably deserved the punishment—he got out of line and a little overexcited—but having to see her leave with that old man was more than he could take.

Clay got Swenson's address from her datebook. It was a shame, really, how vulnerable people were. Locks, alarms, guards—you can spend a fortune to stay safe, but it's worthless if someone is really determined to hurt you.

At this time of the morning Swenson's home alarm, if he even had one, would probably be deactivated. It was a quiet, sedate neighborhood, with plenty of hedges and bushes, so it had been easy to creep alongside the house and find a hiding place in the backyard with a view inside. Swenson was inside brewing coffee, watching it run from the filter basket into the pot. Clay thought the guy should have better things to do than stand around and watch the java drip. He wondered if Swenson had touched Dr. Powers, and it made him hate.

Swenson leaned back against his sink with a sad expression. What the hell did he have to worry about? Swenson got to hobnob with a beautiful woman. Swenson had money and a good job.

Well, there were other things in the world to *really* be sad about. Things Swenson was about to discover in vivid, painful detail.

"Dr. Swenson, I understand you're a friend of Dr. Powers, all right? But she's out of town for a few days and she told me to keep her whereabouts to myself. You'll have to wait until she gets back."

This Pam Lincoln was the kind of woman Bo would have loved to have on his staff. Bright, loyal, in command of the situation. She was also driving him crazy. "Miss Lincoln, I—"

"*Ms.* Lincoln, Doctor. No offense intended or taken, but that's how I prefer to be addressed." Her voice was steely.

"Of course. I'm so sorry, Ms. Lincoln. I'm afraid I show my age at the most inappropriate times."

"No one's too old to learn new tricks, Doctor. You're a perfect gentleman, I'm just helping you out so that the next time, when you're talking to someone easily offended by this kind of thing, you won't make the same mistake."

He could hear her typing in the background. He was losing her attention. "Ms. Lincoln, please," he said. "I must know where Holiday has gone." He hoped she had gone home, to Boston.

"Dr. Swenson, I can tell you're concerned."

"I'm extremely concerned. I've known Holiday for many years. I can't go into it, but I'm concerned for her safety. You have to understand, Ms. Lincoln. This is not a frivolous request."

There was a long silence. Boston. It *had* to be Boston.

"Stockholm, Sweden," Pam said with a sigh. "I wasn't supposed to say. So now you tell me: what kind of trouble do you think she's in?"

Bo stood motionless for a moment, his head spinning. He heard a noise outside, like the clatter of someone rattling a chain. He looked out but saw nothing.

"Dr. Swenson, did you hear me?"

"Of course, Ms. Lincoln," he said, trying to calm his heart. "She's in no trouble. I was mistaken."

"I'd like to believe that," Pam said warily. "But from the sound of your voice I'm not so sure."

"You have to believe me." What *was* that noise? He hung up the phone and brutally rubbed his fists into his eyes, trying to bring himself back into focus. What did she know? Why had she . . .

Another noise. Quietly, not even sure why he felt such stealth was necessary, he stepped to the window and peered out. There was nothing there, but he could see only a fraction of the yard.

He had four patients to see that afternoon. On the verge of panic now, wondering when she had left and whether she was in Sweden yet, Swenson undid the back door chain. The old wooden frame creaked as he opened the door and stepped outside into the sun.

"Hello," he said, somehow instinctively sure that there was someone out there. "Can I help you?"

The gate was open. He always made sure it was closed. He moved down the back steps, feeling tension vibrate in his legs as he walked.

A hand reached out and touched his shoulder. As he turned, his body felt old and slow. He reached up to defend himself, choking on a tight, constricted breath.

"So sorry, Dr. Swenson."

It was Jorge, the Latino man from the gardening crew that came to his house once every two weeks. The young Salvadoran man, dark and leathery from years of sun, was the gardener who spoke the best English. Jorge always delivered the bill and oversaw pruning the orange tree. Swenson had once given him free medical advice on his newborn son.

"Good Lord, Jorge, you scared me," Swenson said, feeling ridiculous.

The young man stammered, obviously terrified that he had offended his well-off customer and could lose steady, regular business. "Dr. Swenson, I apologize," Jorge said, shaking Bo's hand. "We didn't know you were at home. Please accept my apology."

Swenson pulled away from Jorge's anxious grip. "Of course. It was a natural misunderstanding." They walked together around the side of the house, through the gate to the driveway. Bo waved at the other two members of the crew.

"Any special instructions, Dr. Swenson?" Jorge asked.

Bo felt numbness in his arm. He had to relax—if he were at the hospital, he could get some oxygen. "No, not at all, Jorge. Just the usual."

Jorge yelled to his partners to pull their truck into the driveway. Swenson went inside when they began to unload the lawn mower and the electric hedge trimmers, donning acoustic headphones to save their ears from the din they would create.

"Please lock up the gate when you're done, Jorge. I'll be gone for the day." He went back inside the house and locked the door behind him. Outside, the gardeners started work, their engines loud even in the kitchen.

Bo paced the kitchen, muttering to himself. He would have to do more than cancel the afternoon's appointments—he would have to cancel the entire week's. And he would need his credit cards, plane tickets, cold-weather clothes.

In the living room he hunted through his rolltop desk

for his passport. He returned to the kitchen and picked up the phone.

"What city?"

"Los Angeles, please. I need the number for—"

Something wasn't right. Before the gardeners arrived, he had been looking in his closet for his appointment book. He was positive he left the double folding doors ajar after finding the book—because he would have to pick out a jacket to wear to the hospital—but when he was in the living room a moment ago, both doors were shut.

"Sir? Do you need a listing in Los Angeles?"

Swenson hung up and walked toward the living room; his ears were beginning to ring from the noise outside. Through the doorway he saw the closet was now open.

In that instant he tried to recall where he had hidden his handgun. Then a sharp pain exploded through his neck and shoulders. He first thought that he was having a heart attack, but then realized the pain didn't originate inside his body. Before he fell to the floor, Swenson understood that he had been attacked from behind.

The lawn mowers outside roared with a grinding metallic noise. Swenson felt far away and dislocated from what was going on; with mild surprise he felt himself lifted to his feet from behind. An instant later he was slammed into the waist-high kitchen counter, his breath escaping him with a great whoop.

Swenson grabbed a dull steak knife from the counter and turned; he couldn't catch his breath. The blade was immediately knocked from his hand, rebounding against the wall and falling harmlessly to the floor. He faced his attacker, a snarling man in a sweatshirt with a baseball cap pulled low over his eyes.

"I know you!" he yelled. "You're the—"

The man slapped Swenson before he could finish his sentence, and a wide arc of spittle and blood flew from his mouth and landed on his attacker's sweatshirt. Bo tried to speak but was knocked to the ground by a blow to the head that he was partially able to dodge, lessening its impact.

Play dead, he thought. He lay on the floor, trying to take shallow breaths, hoping the younger man would go away. The lawn mowers and trimmers still ran outside.

"Get up!" Simmons screamed. One of the louder machines became silent for a moment, then started up again. "Get up, or I'll stab you in the back."

Swenson looked up between crossed fingers and saw his assailant standing over him clutching the thick, sharp bread knife that had been drying in the dish strainer. He raised himself to his knees and was grabbed by his shirt collar with violent force.

"I'm going to kill you because you fucked the doctor," Simmons said, standing over Swenson with the knife raised in the air.

"What the hell are you talking about?" Bo asked, trying to look unafraid. The man was completely crazy, and twenty years his junior. Swenson knew he was going to die.

"You know what I'm talking about! They hire me to do their dirty work, but you're the dirty one." Swenson avoided the man's eyes, unable to bear the malice and insanity there. For an instant he saw a shadow passing by the window outside—one of the gardeners, going about his noisy business. *I'm a middle-aged man, I can't fight him.*

Swenson grabbed his chest and gasped. "Oh, my God, not now," he muttered through clenched teeth.

"What are you doing? What's the matter with you?" Simmons wailed, suddenly fearful. He waved the knife in the air, confused.

The dirty dishes on the counter fell to the floor and shattered as Swenson reeled. His breath came in short, constricted bursts, and he raised his hand to his throat, clawing as his knees buckled. Simmons watched helplessly as the older man slid down the counter.

"Help me," Swenson gasped.

"What am I supposed to do?" Simmons screamed, still brandishing the knife.

Swenson turned, a dirty frying pan from the stovetop in his hand. He swung the thick black metal skillet in a tight motion, smashing into Simmons's face, flattening his nose and breaking the skin in a wide gash across his forehead.

The bread knife dropped to the floor as Simmons reeled back, his hands to his face, wailing with hurt betrayal. Swenson stepped into the next blow, striking across his temple, driving the hard metal into the skull with a sickening thud of collapsing bone. Clay Simmons fell to the floor, facedown, completely still.

Outside, the motors still ran. He had gone too far; the man was dead. Swenson fetched a mop and a garbage bag from the pantry, then stood for a long moment staring at the telephone, wondering where to begin.

22

HOLIDAY LEANED BACK IN THE TAXI'S CRAMPED BACKSEAT, lulled by the car's motion through the snowy streets of Stockholm. Light snow kissed the windshield as they moved along the K1 highway south from the airport, along the waterways covered by shifting ice that split the city into islands.

The afternoon sun had set save for a faint trace of light along the horizon. Car headlights and streetlamps split the dimness in the approaching urban center like strange beacons; for an instant she entertained the illusion that the lights gave off snow. But that was wrong. The snow was all around. In the distance the Royal Palace loomed with its solidity, an anachronism in the gloom.

Gregory sat silent beside her, staring at the stone and brick buildings they were passing, the modern steel and glass and the bridges connecting the city, passing by the window in a cityscape spotted with dense groves of evergreens. His hands clenched together in his lap, he watched Stockholm with only faint interest. Holiday could feel from him a sullen, melancholy determination.

The white-haired cabdriver glanced back in his mirror through thick glasses, turning away when Holiday locked eyes with him. She took off her gloves and untied her scarf. Her spine was still stiff from the long flight, and she felt dehydrated. With clinical detachment she realized she might be coming down with a virus or influenza.

"What will we do when we get to the university?" she asked, turning to face Gregory. "They might not even let us in the door."

"I've heard this is an open society," he answered, staring ahead. The snow shifted from flurries to downy flakes.

"We'll just walk in. I doubt anyone here is going to be uncivilized enough to kick us out."

The driver glanced in the mirror again. She shifted in the seat, glimpsing shimmering darkness on a frozen waterway at the end of a passing street, a black nonreflecting sheet of nothingness that caught her eye and was gone. It had grown darker outside. She wondered how people could live in such darkness half the year.

"This place is depressing," she said, unzipping her coat. The anemic heater in the cab had finally warmed up.

"You can still go back," Gregory said, then caught himself. He reached out and gently brushed a coil of hair away from her forehead.

"What would I do then?" She tried to keep her voice neutral. "Wait for you to come home? Count on you to fix my life for me?"

Her voice trailed off. She knew she stayed for many reasons, the least flattering among them because she wanted her own name, her own reputation, restored. With sudden certainty she realized she had been trying to make this voyage Gregory's burden. It was wrong.

Outside she saw, as the car drove by, a group of people gathered under spotlights in a densely wooded park, putting up red ribbons and decorations for Christmas. It made her feel like an intruder.

"I'm staying with you because I need answers, too," she said quietly. Her admission felt like an oath to face the hidden powers she knew existed from the moment she first heard of the Stockholm connection. Until this moment she could have lived with never knowing who killed Takamoto if it meant a return to stability. Now her future was bound permanently with this blind rush into the unknown.

"More than anything," Gregory said softly, "I just want all this to stop. I want my life to be normal again."

She heard a vulnerability in his voice and took his hand. "I like the sound of that."

Holiday shivered. She reached out to turn the lever on

the already shut window, trying to seal them from the windy cold outside. She knew they had just lied to each other; "normal" would have been staying home, rebuilding their lives. They had left that behind.

"Whoever killed Takamoto might kill again," she said in the instant the thought reached her mind.

The driver looked at them in the mirror. Gregory shook his head. "They killed Takamoto with machines, from far away. That's different from pulling a trigger. This is like the Wizard of Oz—I think there's a little coward behind the monster."

She was about to reply when their cab pulled over to a corner near a stone gate at the university. Gregory fumbled in his jacket for the wad of bills they had exchanged at the airport, and fanned them in front of the bemused driver, who delicately plucked two from the roll and drove away with a curt grunt of thanks.

"Friendly guy," Holiday said, watching the cab pull away.

"I can live with it," Gregory said, stretching his back. "At least you know where you stand."

Beyond the gate was a wide street lined on either side with plain brick and stone buildings. The foot traffic intensified on the streets beyond the gate—young men and women carrying backpacks and books, their breath condensing into pale clouds. Holiday had expected the students to be clean-cut, to conform to her vision of Scandinavians. But they were like students anywhere, with their scraggly beards, wrinkled clothes, and burned-out look of fatigue.

Holiday touched a young woman's shoulder. The girl, buttoned into a fur-lined parka, regarded them with suspicion. With clipped phrases from her guidebook Holiday obtained directions to the *Sjukhuset*, the hospital. Then the girl was gone, disappearing into a thick fog pluming from a ventilation grill at their feet.

Holiday buttoned her coat to her neck. The girl's directions led them to the heart of the university. The buildings were older and built of exposed brick, a core of stolid solemnity nestled within the modern architecture at the campus periphery. A chattering group of undergraduates emerged from a classroom building, so reserved they kept their eyes averted from the strangers in their midst.

A spontaneous sense of absurdity came over her. She hadn't told anyone where she was—except for Pam, and only because of a last-second apprehension. Her mother and father, Philip—she hadn't talked to any of them in weeks. She didn't know if Philip was still maintaining his drug rehabilitation, or if her parents were healthy. This cool, dark place felt like a place where everything ended rather than began.

Before them stood the main hospital, a dark glass structure rising ten stories over an empty square of frigid benches and empty kiosks. It was a building designed with a sense of importance and function, its sheer faces and tight corners seemingly embodying the assurances of medical science.

"Are you all right?" Gregory asked.

"I . . . I just had a strange feeling."

He looked into her eyes. For the first time since she picked him up at jail, she fully sensed that part of him that made her feel secure and safe. She wasn't alone.

"Holiday, don't worry. If anything goes wrong, we'll leave. We can get back to the airport in thirty-five minutes and be on the next flight out. I promise."

"I know," she said. He visibly relaxed, as though recognizing something in her that calmed him.

Five minutes after stepping into the building Holiday felt that absolutely nothing constructive was going to happen. The icily polite receptionist summoned her dismayed superior from an office adjoining the gleaming foyer. In clipped English the woman, her glasses dangling from a gold chain, told Holiday and Gregory to wait.

This was the entrance for administration and faculty; no traffic moved through the automatic doors save for men and women in suits and overcoats, who moved almost silently through the lobby.

Gregory stiffened when a tall, handsome blond man in a black suit and thick prescription glasses emerged from a hallway and, with a gesture of recognition, moved toward them slowly and deliberately. His heels tapped hollowly against the polished lobby floor. Holiday thought he looked as though he had been waiting for their arrival, though she knew that was impossible.

"My name is Dr. Carl Strindberg," he said in English, his voice a rich baritone. He had the air of a man just interrupted from something, and vaguely irritated with the distraction. "I normally am not in charge of greeting visitors, but since you arrived unannounced and speak only English, I was enlisted."

"We came to Stockholm on a whim, or we would have contacted you in advance," Gregory said, extending his hand. "We're in Scandinavia for a couple of weeks, for pleasure."

"I see. That is fine," Strindberg said, obviously uninterested. "Anna told me that you are doctors?"

"I am," Holiday said. "I'm a general surgeon at Pacific University in Los Angeles."

Strindberg looked interested. "A very good program. Which department are you in?"

"Noninvasive surgeries and advanced technology."

She had, of course, made international news when Takamoto was killed. Strindberg must have heard about the murder, seen the images. The question was whether he remembered her face.

Strindberg looked at her searchingly for a moment. "Excellent," he said. "I am in pediatrics, but I have many colleagues who would greatly enjoy speaking with you about your work."

"We wanted to drop in unofficially," Gregory said. "I work at the university with Dr. Powers, in surgical computer technology."

"And what is your field of practice, Dr. Hampton?"
Strindberg asked. His voice dropped in volume.

"I'm not a doctor, I'm a computer engineer."

"Ah. So you are a wizard. A magician." Strindberg
folded his arms across his chest and smiled.

"You could say that."

"I must admit that I am ignorant of computers, for the
most part. Perhaps we can organize a seminar while
you're here." Strindberg leaned forward with an ironic
smile. "Maybe we shouldn't let you leave until we have
extracted as much information from you as we can."

Holiday looked outside; it was completely dark. "In
fact we came here primarily for Mr. Hampton's benefit,"
she said. "He heard that your computer research department was very impressive."

Gregory was caught off guard by her directness.
"That's right," he said quickly. "I'd like to see the main
computer room."

Strindberg nodded, tight-lipped. "That should not be
any trouble. But I don't think we can organize a formal
tour."

"I wouldn't think of it," Gregory said.

Holiday stayed a few paces behind as Strindberg led
Gregory into a small office to obtain plastic visitors'
passes. In the staff elevator she remained silent, fighting
off a wave of exhausted dizziness. She felt the first signs of
sickness, a dislocation of herself from her surroundings,
and it frightened her. It was important to stay alert.

"I don't see a lot of black people here," Gregory said
when they stepped out of the elevator on the subbase-
ment level.

Strindberg laughed eagerly. "There are not many Ne-
gro Scandinavians," he said, amused. "But Sweden has
historically been very tolerant. We gave asylum to American black objectors to the Vietnam War, Mr. Hampton."

"I didn't know that."

Strindberg's eyes shone with satisfaction. "Many people do not. But then they would have to admit we are not such a repressed, icy people, wouldn't they?"

Passing through a security door, they reached a series of narrow corridors branching out into office space. Workers sat in rows at small cubicles before personal computers. Holiday realized this was the apparatus of state-sponsored medical care; what she saw was a bureaucratic processing center, directing information traffic.

Strindberg spoke to a thin, pale woman at a lone desk near an unmarked door, gesturing at Holiday and Gregory. The woman rose and used a key card to open the door.

"I don't have everyday access to this area, but it's not forbidden to me," Strindberg said to Gregory. Holiday sensed that Strindberg had taken a liking to him. As they walked down a long, featureless corridor, Strindberg spoke over his shoulder.

"You may think us Swedes cold and impersonal," he said. "Americans in particular believe this."

"I don't know," Gregory said neutrally, peering into open doorways as they walked. "People often misunderstand one another."

Though they were underground, Holiday sensed the ice and cold above them like an animate presence. Even the lights down here seemed inadequate to dispel the dark blanket of winter.

"Very true," Strindberg said. "You see, Mr. Hampton, Swedes do not make superficial friendships. There is no 'have a nice day' here, but when we make friends, we are friends for life."

They reached a temperature-controlled room housing a series of bulky, loudly humming mainframe computers. Strindberg closed the door behind them, making sure the insulated frame was sealed.

" 'Friends for life.' I like the sound of that," Gregory said, staring at the row of computers as if transfixed.

"Good. So perhaps we will meet again." Strindberg shook both their hands and made to leave.

"That's it? Is there anyone here?" The room was empty.

"I will fetch the supervisor for you. His name is Neils Guliksen." Strindberg produced a business card from within his suit jacket, handed it to Gregory, and left.

The room was windowless and full of the low hum of the computers. The dry air and fluorescent light made Holiday's eyes burn.

Gregory, however, was energized. "This is an impressive setup," he said. "It's actually comparable to what we have in L.A."

"It sounds like you've bought into your own story," she said.

He leaned over a terminal and stared at its rows of flashing numbers, the screen casting a pallid light across his forehead. "I haven't forgotten why we're here, if that's what you mean."

A thin, balding man in corduroy pants and wrinkled dress shirt abruptly opened the door and joined them.

"I am Neils Guliksen," he said in heavily accented English, staring into a terminal screen several paces from his visitors. "I was told you came here to visit my department."

"Are you the director?" Gregory asked.

"Of this computer center, as well as technological applications for the entire hospital," Guliksen said, his accent lessening.

Gregory cocked his head with uncertainty, as if he saw something in Guliksen that escaped Holiday. "Excellent," he said, introducing her and himself.

Guliksen chewed his lip, still looking away. "And you are here because—" He turned to Holiday, as though he hoped she would finish his thought for him.

"We hoped to have a brief look around your facility, at your processing capabilities and methodologies." Holiday smiled disarmingly, she thought, but received only a cold, suspicious stare.

"I am very busy. I am sorry to disappoint you, but there

is no time." Guliksen half turned, moving toward the door.

"Come on, my friend. We came all this way," Gregory said. He took a step toward Guliksen and accidentally kicked a chair. The lanky Swede's eyes opened in alarm; Holiday thought he had just caught himself from violently recoiling.

"A few minutes. That is all I can spare."

Guliksen led them through an open room lined with cubicles inhabited by programmers. His manner increasingly desultory, he pointed out the central processor that ran the internal office network. Gregory posed detailed questions about the network layout, processing times, and total staff numbers.

"That is it," Guliksen said when he led them back to the room housing the mainframe computers. His "tour" had been little more than a walk through the office space. He now evidently expected them to leave.

Gregory sat on a wooden table, careful not to disturb any of the equipment. "You have some good ideas on billing and notification," he said. "When I'm home, I'll pass them on to those departments."

Guliksen picked up a stack of printouts, glancing toward the door. "You do not deal with those matters?"

"I used to, but my department is more specialized. I'm working on virtual reality systems for surgical simulators and off-site telepresence procedures. Do you know what I'm talking about?"

The heating system gave a belch as some gear had slipped, then was silent. Guliksen put down his printouts and looked into Gregory's eyes as though searching for something. Holiday saw that Guliksen had given himself away, even if he didn't realize it yet.

A young woman stepped into the room and sat down at a terminal, flashing through menus and jotting notes on a pad.

"Do you have someplace private where we can talk?" Gregory asked.

Guliksen glanced at Holiday. "I'm afraid those programs are not my specialty." Guliksen tried to step past Gregory but found his path blocked.

"I'm interested in what's going on here," Gregory said, speaking quietly. "We both know we have things to talk about."

The young woman looked up from her work. Guliksen sighed and spoke to his employee in Swedish. Something had broken within him, some pressure had been released. His shoulders slumped, his pallid face devoid of resistance.

"I suppose there would be no harm," Guliksen said.

Guliksen motioned Holiday and Gregory to a pair of metal chairs in his office and sat behind his beaten desk. The room was small, with computer promotional posters on the walls and spiral-bound technical manuals overloading a creaky case. A photo of an aged couple was propped on a credenza, but there was no sign of a wife or children. He put his elbows on his desk, and Holiday glimpsed his deep loneliness.

"You notice the offices are crowded even though it is time to go home for the day," Guliksen said, looking at his watch. "In the winter I let them take two hours off at noon to enjoy the sun. Then they work an extra hour at night. It's a small gesture toward their happiness."

Holiday and Gregory took off their coats and pushed their duffel bags to the corner of the room. Guliksen watched intently, with the air of a man looking for small victories amid defeat. "So what is it that I can do for you?"

He sounds like a man headed for the electric chair.

"Mr. Guliksen, do you know who I am?" she asked.

He rubbed his nose wearily. "Should I? Are you a famous doctor? I am a technician, I do not keep up on medical studies."

"She's famous for her part in a murder," Gregory said. "A man died after a computer system was sabotaged through an off-site log-in."

"An off-site log-in. I do not see your point." Guliksen exhaled loudly, a small rattle catching in his lungs. *A smoker,* Holiday thought.

Guliksen ran a hand through his dark, sparse hair and stared at a poster on the wall depicting a windowsill looking out on a lush valley.

"Let us be . . . candid?" he said, looking at Holiday. "Are you with the police? The government?"

"No," she answered. "Mr. Hampton designed the system that was sabotaged. I was the surgeon performing the procedure."

Guliksen licked his lips, a gesture Holiday found oddly revolting. "Then I do not see why I have to speak with you. You should leave."

"You're not getting rid of us," Gregory said. "We're not the police, but we could have them here in minutes."

Guliksen's eyes widened with the fear of the hunted. Holiday saw it was a familiar feeling to him—to be threatened, bullied, coerced.

"We can see you're upset," Holiday said. "We came here for answers, not to harm you."

Guliksen glanced at his closed office door. "You came here from America looking for your answers," Guliksen said with amusement.

Holiday traced a progression in her mind, from Takamoto's lifeless body, to the unknowable intricacies of the world information network, to here in this basement beneath the frozen earth. Neils Guliksen, she sensed, wasn't the end of this chain. If anything, he was a node in a system, like the computers that housed the remote sabotage for an instant before speeding it to its destination.

Guliksen broke the silence. "A colleague asked me to create a theoretical model. It was a puzzle, a challenge: how to enter a secured computer system, make minor modifications, and exit without being noticed. It sounded like espionage, but I found it interesting."

Holiday was motionless and rapt. Gregory stiffened beside her.

"He provided me with general information on the functions of a particular network. I couldn't have written the system in its entirety—my colleague works more in virtual reality than I do. It was a very elegant creation, but poorly protected."

Guliksen glanced at Gregory. "I designed a subroutine glitch, a little hiccup that would go unnoticed. It would cause, at most, a minor and momentary malfunction."

"A hiccup?" Gregory asked with astonishment.

"My idea was to make the surgical laser pause for an instant, then resume normal function. Then the operation could proceed normally. Maybe then I would call and tell you what I did, anonymously of course, and you would make your security stronger."

There was a deep, ingrained self-delusion in Guliksen's tone. He kept his words academic and anecdotal. Holiday felt him slipping away, his rationalizations solidifying like the sheets of ice outside.

"The laser paused for a moment," she said evenly. "But then it fired out of control. There was a specific, murderous intent in your remote interference."

"I know that." Guliksen's accent resurfaced, like a shield between his words and their meaning. A timid knock at the door silenced him, but he stayed seated. He opened a file cabinet in his desk and produced a bottle of vodka and plastic cups.

"I will not ask you to drink with me," he said, half filling a cup. "You are not guests in the conventional sense." His eyes filmed over as he took a long, greedy drink.

Gregory turned to Holiday, blinking as though he had witnessed something incomprehensible. She had feared that his anger and rage would surface; instead he had turned passive with astonishment.

"You see, I could not make my harmless adjustments without obtaining a password to your system," Guliksen said, staring into his cup. "That is not an easy thing to get."

"How did you get mine?" Gregory asked.

"The person who introduced this idea to me obtained the password. He must have been very well connected."

Holiday realized Guliksen was toying with them, playing out his last measure of control. "So imagine *my* situation," he said. "I was approached to solve a puzzle, a minor thing. I would have been too much a coward even to think of it if I hadn't been forced to."

"Who approached you?" Holiday asked.

"He put it all in place, and I never once questioned his motivations. Of course I had little choice." Guliksen seemed drunker by the moment. He had probably started drinking even before they'd arrived.

"When he gave me the password, it was too late for me to back out. He is a big man, like you, Mr. Hampton." Guliksen extended the plastic cup toward Gregory, toasting him.

Gregory delicately leaned forward in his chair, as though trying not to startle Guliksen. "This has bothered you since it happened," he said. "Why did you let yourself be forced to do it?"

"Because he would have killed me," Guliksen said, his eyes wide, amused at the memory of his own fear. "He is insane."

"And he made the program go the step farther, he made it actually kill the patient?" Holiday asked.

"That was me. But I was made to do it. It was after work, in the evening. He comes to me and says, 'We do it now, while it is early in Los Angeles. We must do it now.' " His voice lowered to a whisper. "He struck me."

Holiday felt a sudden sense of embarrassment for Guliksen; he was reliving his debasement, practically begging for absolution.

"He told me the operation was to be on an animal; how could I know he was lying?" Guliksen spoke in the meandering tones of a man talking to himself.

"You didn't believe that," Gregory said.

"I made myself believe it. Until I saw the television. I

have been waiting for someone to come. At least you are not the police."

"Don't pretend you don't understand," Gregory said, his voice thick and hoarse. "This wasn't harmless hacking. You're an accessory to murder."

"Even if you didn't—" Guliksen began. "You must both hate me." He looked to Gregory, then Holiday, his features contorted with regret. She could barely look at him.

"This other man—where is he now?" Holiday spoke slowly. She sensed Guliksen was on the verge of turning incoherent.

"Give us his address," Gregory said, pushing a pencil across the desk. It skittered to the floor.

Guliksen poured another drink, suddenly gruff. "He is not here anymore. He is a doctor, transferred out of Stockholm."

"Tell me," Gregory shouted. His voiced rebounded in the low-ceilinged room. Holiday heard footsteps outside.

"It no longer matters," Guliksen slurred.

A knock at the door: weak at first, then stronger. Guliksen stood as if to open it, but Gregory rose in the same instant, slapping Guliksen's face open-handed. The harsh impact knocked the Swede back against his desk, where he recovered himself enough to sit. Someone outside tried the doorknob, but it was locked.

Like a man in a trance, Guliksen raised his voice and spoke to whoever was outside.

"Who was it?" Gregory asked. "Who made you do it?"

"It is always this way, isn't it?" Guliksen glared, rubbing his jaw. "The man with the biggest fist always gets what he wants."

"The hell with that," Gregory said. "You've caused more pain than you could ever imagine."

Guliksen paused, his expression clear. "You are right. It was Lars Swenson. He is now in Umea, working at the university hospital. And I hope the snow swallows him up and takes him to hell."

Gregory turned to Holiday with an agonized expression of recognition. She wanted to reach out to him for comfort, but she had none to give.

"Lars?" she said, looking at Guliksen. He looked dead. He soon would be, she realized.

"Lars Swenson," he said, his voice distorted by the handkerchief he produced from his pocket to cough into. He seemed irritated to have to repeat himself. "You look like you know him."

She felt as though all time had somehow come to exist at once: Kyle had reappeared with his acrimony and his bureaucratic weapons; now Lars, in the snows, a murderer. Until then she thought she was following the trail of those who almost destroyed her life. Now it was as if they had been behind her all along, waiting.

"You said Lars worked on virtual reality projects." Her voice sounded like someone else's, hollow, betrayed.

"When he wasn't playing with expensive equipment for his own purposes. I would be glad to see him gone if only for that."

"Show me."

Holiday stood in darkness, a void that felt alive with electricity. Before her floated several rectangles bearing symbols and icons.

Pushing a button on her handpiece propelled her into the void, the motion so intense that she nearly fell. Before her floated a cartoonish representation of a hand, and when she flexed or pointed, the sketched appendage duplicated her motions.

She reached out into the surreal space and grabbed one of the bars. It glowed with a greenish tint and, outside her headphones, she heard the computer hard drive whir, retrieving the program.

Suddenly she was in a grassy meadow, gentle hills all around her flowing gently toward the horizon. Strange, slapstick noises filled her ears, and she turned.

First were the orange ostriches, bounding with realistic

motion toward her, then passing her by. When they
reached the hills, they stopped; unable to learn how to
climb, they hopped in place.

Next were the ducks, improbably floating on the sheer
textureless grass at her feet, turning up to leer at her as
they passed.

Holiday nearly screamed out, but instead reached out
with her virtual hand and stopped the program. The ostriches, the ducks: they had been created at MIT in the
early nineties, graphic representations of motions created
to mirror those of real robots. She had been in charge of
the project.

Lars had stolen them from her computer somehow.
He'd been doing this for years.

Now she saw, behind the other icons, a floating bar
bigger than the others, more colorful. She pressed the
button, gliding through the virtual space, and grasped the
object. Again the machinery hummed as it retrieved data
to process into the headpiece and earphones.

The world in front of Holiday blacked out, then turned
to static. The program was crude, unpolished, as though
its author never intended it to be seen by anyone else.

A photograph filled her field of vision. Then it blurred
and changed shape. Lars had scanned an ordinary picture
into the computer and lent it three dimensions with stereoscopic technology. It felt as though she could move into
it, lose herself in it, but when she tried, she was stopped as
though by an invisible wall.

It depicted a blond, beautiful woman dressed in white
robes, the crown of her head adorned with candles. Her
mouth was open in song. It was Anita Swenson, young
and alive. In the foreground stood a small blond boy, en-
raptured with his mother.

Then the picture dissolved and Holiday saw herself,
years younger, standing on Newbury Street in Boston.
Her image smiled with innocence but seemed slightly uncomfortable with having her picture taken. Her expression was that of young love.

Next was a blackened field. Rotating silently was a three-dimensional transparent image of the human hand and forearm. It had been modified to represent Lars's self-inflicted injuries, the damage to the antecubial fossa, the ruin left when surgery debrided damaged tissue around the brachial artery and nerves.

The hand dissolved, replaced by a photograph of Han Takamoto, composed and posed like an official portrait. He was whisked away, and Holiday witnessed again the ruin of the old man's body, destroyed on the operating table.

Now there was a flow chart, floating in newly blackened space. Each box contained characters written in Japanese, and she couldn't read them. At the top, though, the heading was written in English as well: "Mitsuyama."

The rest was a jumble, a mixture of source images moving too quickly. She thought she understood one, but another appeared before she could be sure: first an aerial view, as though pirated from a weather satellite, of a long train rail running through milky, frigid whiteness below; incoherent static, then a town viewed from the sky, as though her view was that of God looking down on the snowbound community ensconced amid frozen nothingness; a long series of halls—an architectural simulation—that she began to recognize as a hospital; then a schematic drawing of a large, boxy shape, surrounded by long, thin tendrils.

The images dissolved, replaced by a man's face. The three-dimensional image was better than the photos, as though the source image was produced stereoscopically. Holiday strained beneath the visor, shocked by the lined features, the wild, thin hair, the blue eyes focused forward but unseeing—staring into a view known only to himself. She gasped when she realized it was Lars.

Holiday removed the visor and put down the headpiece. She felt that if she took a breath, she might not be able to let it out again.

"What happened? What did you see?"

She turned to Gregory, who stood with Guliksen. The Swede looked away. He had seen these things, too, she knew.

"We have to leave," she said. "We have to go to Umea."

23

IN THE HOUR BEFORE THE TRAIN PULLED OUT OF THE STATION IN Stockholm, Holiday suspected someone was staring oddly at her on at least three separate occasions. She saw herself in a mirror, pale and disheveled, her eyes glassy and her lips chapped dry. The nascent glimmer of influenza she had felt earlier in the day had turned into reality.

Which didn't mean that no one was looking for them. Holiday felt as if she had pulled one of the Fates' strings, opening a gateway. Guliksen wouldn't have called the police, he was too frightened, but he could have notified someone, even Lars, about her and Gregory.

Now the train coursed north on its tracks with a smooth, hypnotic rhythm. They had left Stockholm at seven the previous night, and the entire voyage would take twelve hours. It was the middle of the night and the cabin lights were dimmed, but most of the passengers were awake. Still she couldn't shake the sensation that someone was watching.

Across the aisle four men and a woman talked and laughed in loud voices, passing liquor flasks among themselves. Occasionally one of the group would steal a curious glance at Holiday and Gregory.

"It's a real party in here," Gregory said. He sat facing forward with his hands in his lap, his head rocking gently with the train's motion.

Holiday stared at his profile, his straight nose and small ears, his hair cut close at the temples and the hint of beard stubble on his cheeks. It was as though they had made a pact of silence once they boarded the train, once they moved inexorably away from the city into the plains of snow and ice. She still hadn't told him what she saw in Lars's virtual reality file, the sequence of events and images that included the very tracks upon which their train now rode.

A woman in the nearest group of passengers erupted with laughter, spilling her flask on the floor. The men elbowed one another in their rush to help clean up the mess.

"At least someone is having a good time," Gregory said. He shut his eyes and leaned back.

Outside the window was a frightful nothingness, as if night had drawn a shade over the world. As they moved north, the houses and lights dotting the landscape grew sparser, the brief stops at towns fewer. By the moon Holiday could see a cold white blanket of snow reflecting the pattern of an intensifying snowfall, and brief flickering lights in the far distance that disappeared as if they had never been there. She and Gregory were no longer in a world of human comforts and safety—they had entered the vast uncaring domain of nature, a land of extremes in which science and medicine are absent.

A blond man in a worn suit reeled down the aisle and took the empty seat next to Holiday. He was lean and slight, with a mane of mussed hair jutting from his head in chaotic tufts. His eyes were bleary. With an air of weary resignation he spoke to her in Swedish.

Gregory had fallen asleep, his arms folded and his lips pressed tightly together. Holiday looked at the man and shrugged. "I'm sorry, but I don't speak Swedish."

He smiled as if she had made a subtle joke. "You're an American, aren't you?" he asked. He pointed toward the front of the car. "I made a bet with my friends up there that you were. Not for money, just a drink. Would you like some schnapps?"

He extended a flask clumsily toward Holiday's face, and her stomach lurched at the sweet medicinal odor of liquor.

"No, thank you."

The man smiled and took a drink. "Is this your husband?"

Glancing over the man's shoulder at the plains outside, for an instant Holiday felt as though the train weren't moving at all. It seemed they were traversing the same mile of land over and over.

"Yes, he's my husband," she lied.

"That's very good," the man said, taking another sip of schnapps. Loud laughter erupted from the front of the car, and he peered over the seats with a grin. "My friends are having a good time. Would you like to join us?"

"No, thanks," Holiday said. She noticed a few spider-web veins around his nose. She still felt watched, observed, but it hadn't been him.

He coughed and looked out the window, reserved now, as though he thought he may have offended her. "So sorry to have bothered you. My name is Anders." He extended his hand.

Holiday introduced herself. His hand was moist and clammy.

"Dr. Holiday Powers?" Anders repeated. "My friends and I are doctors as well."

Holiday looked over the seats at his group. They were all flushed and obviously drunk. "Do Swedish doctors always drink so much?" She winced inwardly at the slight edge of New England prudery in her voice.

Anders leaned away. "A drink now and then, especially on a long train ride, is nothing to worry about, Doctor. Americans have an attitude that is . . . pure . . . what is the word?"

"Puritanical?"

"Yes, that's right." Anders's eyes gleamed with recognition. "Here we do not share that view. We will be hard at work two days after we reach Umea, and we will be ready for our patients and our surgeries. But this time belongs to us, do you see?"

"Of course," Holiday said. "I didn't mean to sound judgmental." She felt Gregory stir beside her, grumbling in his sleep. "We're also going to Umea," she added, wondering whether she should tell even this harmless stranger their destination.

"You have strange tastes in tourism," Anders said, the corners of his mouth twitching with irony. "My friends and I are going because we were rotated by the King's Committee from temperate Malmö to Umea. And in the middle of winter! Do you believe it? I keep saying, 'I must have done something bad to deserve this, I just can't remember what it was.' "

Anders was becoming progressively drunker. The last vestiges of his Swedish reserve were gone, and Holiday could see that he was a carefree, outgoing young man. And harmless.

"So you and your husband are going to Umea," he said, slurring slightly. "Whatever in the world for?"

Holiday laughed, caught up in his good humor. "We're interested in the university medical facilities. It's a working trip for us."

"Dr. Powers," Anders said, looking out the train window, momentarily entranced by the nothingness. "In the summer months, when the flowers are blooming, it is a nice town. But this time of year it is all snow and wind. And no sunlight, less even than Stockholm."

"We're not staying long, just visiting the university hospital." For a moment she allowed herself to pretend that something awaited her at the end of the long frozen rail besides dreadful uncertainty.

"The hospital," Anders said as if the word contained infinite mysteries. Then, forgetting himself in his drunkenness, he stared for a long, uncomfortable moment at Holiday's chest through her sweater. He caught himself and cleared his throat, trying to get his bearings.

"Is the hospital close to the train station?" she asked, ignoring his mortification.

Anders brushed his hair away from his eyes. "I don't know, I have never been there. Probably everything is close to the train station. This is not Paris, you know."

Gregory kicked at the seat in front of him, grumbling

loudly and rubbing his eyes. Holiday took his hand as he slowly woke.

"From what I have been told, you can't miss the university. It is a small college town," Anders continued, oblivious of Gregory. "There are ninety thousand people there, you know, but from what I hear, it's a quiet place."

The light in the car dimmed a fraction, perhaps a concession to the late hour. The passengers had abandoned the normal cycles of living, opting for drink and conversation. Holiday wished that it could all stay this way forever, that they could hurl into nothingness forever, that there was no Lars, no killing, no Umea rising from a boundless sheet of ice.

Anders rubbed his eyes, looking around him as though he saw the train for the first time. "Of course the town will also be busy with the celebration."

"What celebration?" Gregory asked in a thick voice, stretching his arms. Though he had slept only a few minutes, his eyes were blurry and surrounded by dark rings.

"Of course," Anders said, slapping his forehead theatrically. "You do not have Santa Lucia Day in America. There will be processions and celebrations for the children."

Holiday remembered now—Lars in Boston, his hair grown long and unruly, the Christmas season approaching. He called his mother on the thirteenth of December and spent the entire afternoon talking to her. Holiday remembered he ignored her when she stopped by his dormitory room, his face glowing as he spoke into the phone.

And she remembered Lars's images stored in Stockholm. First among them was his mother in her flowing robes and crimson sash, her eyes in otherworldly rapture as her song honored the girl martyr dead for centuries. And Anita's only son stood at her feet, adoring her.

A fragmentary idea played through Holiday's exhausted mind, of the martyr dying for faith centuries ago, of Lars's mother dead by her own hand on Santa Lucia Day—a sacrifice to Bo Swenson's ambition on the day

Lars remembered for beauty, safety, and the warm happiness of family. And this was the day of the year when Lars had tried to join his mother in oblivion.

"You are awake, sir. Very good." Anders shook Gregory's hand and introduced himself. Holiday fought against fatigue to piece together her thoughts. The images were a trail, a progression . . . first Anita Swenson, then Holiday herself, then Lars's deformed hand. *What came next?*

"You American doctors can look for jobs wherever you like, am I correct?" Anders said to Holiday.

"I'm sorry. What?"

"Anders told me how he gets rotated around the country without his permission," Gregory said, yawning. "Are you feeling all right?"

"I'm fine. I just haven't had enough sleep."

"I should join my friends. It was rude of me to take up your time." Anders twirled his flask from side to side. It was nearly empty. "I will live at the university doctors' quarters. If it pleases you, come find me. We will have dinner together."

"Thanks a lot. We appreciate it," Gregory said, watching the young doctor rise and lurch toward the front of the car. His friends' voices had lowered to a restless murmur.

Gregory looked out the window, shaking his head. "It's snowing harder than ever," he said. "I wouldn't mind seeing a town or something, just to make sure we're still on the right planet."

"Wouldn't it be something if we just kept going and never stopped?" she asked.

He looked at her oddly. "I guess I know what you mean."

Holiday felt a burning in her eyes and a queasy pain pass through her abdomen. She was exhausted. Her body's regulating systems were off balance and wouldn't improve until she could rest.

"We need to talk," Gregory said. "Are you up to it? You look tired."

She looked over her shoulder to the seat behind them, where a middle-aged man was asleep with a newspaper in his lap and a small bottle of liquor clutched in his hand. He snored heartily.

"These people drink a lot, don't they?"

"Yeah, I haven't seen so much drinking since my fraternity at Stanford took a weekend trip to Lake Tahoe."

"You were a fraternity guy?" She laughed involuntarily. "I didn't know that."

He looked at the ceiling, mildly embarrassed. "I guess I'm not the typical fraternity type. It was just a way of meeting people."

The train lurched and then righted itself; behind them glass clinked as the cabin shuddered. She paused before speaking. "I want to know everything about you, Gregory," she said hesitantly. "I don't ever want to feel like I can't trust you. Not again."

His eyes widened with surprise, and she remembered their first night together, their fumbling conversation in her kitchen.

"And I'll tell you everything you ever want to know when this is all over. I'll never hide anything from you, Holiday."

She stared at the flawless white plain outside. The snow formed squalls in the moaning wind, then settled into great drifts. "I know I'm demanding, Gregory," she said. "Everyone in my life has expected so much from me, or else they wouldn't tell me what they really wanted. Maybe it's asking too much, but I need you to be perfect for me."

Gregory took her hand, kissing it. "I need to know everything about Lars Swenson," he said, pressing the back of her hand to his cheek.

Holiday told him about Lars, about his year spent in America, about his mother's death and his own attempted suicide. When she told Gregory that Lars was Bo Swenson's son, he stared at her blankly.

"Were you and he lovers?" Gregory asked.

"Lars was my first," she said quietly. "And we got together a few times after he returned to Sweden."

Gregory hid his emotions behind a stoic expression, only his throbbing temples betraying his dismay. She knew this was precisely the kind of knowledge that drives an inflexible stake through a man's heart. "Do you still love him?" he asked.

She paused. "I loved him very much, and part of me always will," she said. "But it was in the past. He and I aren't the same people anymore."

"Do you think your relationship with him has anything to do with Takamoto's murder?" he asked.

"I . . . I can't see why." To avoid looking at him, she stared out the window; the shining moon hung suspended in inky sky.

"I don't want this to come out the wrong way," Gregory said, gently releasing her hand, "but the murder could have been a way of getting back at you for something. Maybe my involvement was an accident."

"I haven't talked to him in years, Gregory," she said. She felt heat around her eyes and temples. "And he walked out on me. I can't see why he would want to hurt me."

"Obviously he's insane, Holiday. I'm just trying to figure out what he was trying to accomplish."

"I can't think straight," she said. "I think I'm getting sick."

Gregory put his hand on her forehead. "You feel hot," he said, alarmed. "I'll go get you something."

"No, don't. All I have to do is make it to—" Her mind faltered. "To Umea. Then I can rest."

She was silent when a pale, drunk fortyish man reeled down the aisle calling out in a slurred voice to the passengers in the car. The man wore a Red Cross Medical Corps pin affixed to his lapel, and noisily made his way out of the car to the next.

"I think we're being watched," she said.

"You have a fever," Gregory said. "We never should

have done all that walking in the cold, not coming straight from L.A."

"I'm a doctor, remember? It's just a minor bug." Holiday stood and leaned against the seat, dizzier than she thought she would be. "We'll find Lars and . . . get him some help. Then we can go home."

Holiday was leaning into the aisle; a woman bumped her, heading for a small die-hard group still drinking and staring at rail maps.

"He needs help, all right," Gregory said. "Preferably while he's locked away and can't hurt anyone else."

Holiday sighed, too tired for the argument she knew they could have. "I know, but he should see a familiar face before he has to face the consequences of what he's done."

"That's your opinion," Gregory said.

"And for a good reason," she said, her voice rising. "I knew him years ago, Gregory. He's not an evil man."

Gregory stared at her inquisitorially. "I have to find a rest room," she said suddenly, needing to get away from his gaze. "I need to splash some cold water on my face."

"Why don't you let me come with you?"

"No, I think I can handle it." She felt herself smiling. "But you have to promise me," she said, leaning over him, "that there'll be no violence when we find Lars. There's been enough damage."

Gregory covered his mouth with his hand. "I shouldn't have slapped Guliksen, but I'm not out for some kind of John Wayne revenge," he said. "I don't know Lars, but it's obvious he meant something to you once. So don't worry."

"Thank you," she said, standing straight again. "Lars is sick. And also he—" She began to tell Gregory about Lars's mother, about Santa Lucia Day and the haunting visions he had stored in his computer, but stopped. "Santa Lucia Day has powerful associations for Lars. That's why I think he might be delicate when we find him."

"Delicate," Gregory said, shaking his head. His stubbornness was becoming familiar to her, like other negative traits in people she loved. Her mother's ignorance of Holiday's goals and accomplishments, her youngest brother's sad need for drugs and chemical oblivion. Her father's unwitting refusal to understand her as a person.

Gregory's eyes flashed, as though he knew what she was thinking. "I'm sorry," he said quietly. "But you heard Guliksen—Lars is violent, maybe homicidal. He's not the man you knew all those years ago."

"You don't understand," she said, slapping the seat. She felt a little out of control. "You have your anger, Gregory, your righteousness. But what do I have? I have to make some sense of my life, my past."

She was talking too loud and knew she was attracting attention. Gregory glanced at the other passengers, speaking in a gentler voice. "All right, I promise," he said. "We'll get Lars help, then put it behind us."

"That's . . . that's all I want." She leaned over to kiss his forehead and nearly lost her balance.

She left him quickly, walking to the end of the car and releasing a switch in the door, which opened with a faint hydraulic hiss. Still there was the sensation of being watched, now from somewhere in front of her. Two cars back she found a rest room. In the aisle nearest sat a man in a dark suit, engrossed in a paperback. Next to him sat a stern woman in some sort of uniform, who regarded Holiday querulously. Holiday stepped into the cramped rest room and locked the door behind her.

A light flickered on. In the mirror she looked sick, with dark rings around her eyes and her hair hanging limp and stringy on her shoulders. Her head felt light. Running cold water on her face, shivering, she drank water from the tap. *Of all the times to come down with the flu.*

Emerging from the small bathroom, she looked around. This car was more sedate, filled mostly with sleepers. She tried to remember all the towns they had passed through—Soderhamn, Iggesund, Sundsvall—names without meaning, places she would never see.

She needed to eat, and the dining car was in the rear of the train. She walked back through the car, touching the seat backs for balance as the train shuddered. In the enclosed, closet-sized space between cars she paused, catching her breath before punching the button to open the next door. She had lost track of how many cars she had passed through.

The door opened to the next car, still not the dining cabin. The sky outside the window was still a snowy void. Holiday imagined how the train looked from the frozen plain outside—the long row of lights moving steadily along the tracks, Holiday within walking backward through the cars as though trying to return to where she began. She stepped through a jumble of outstretched legs as a group of drunken men in ski sweaters politely allowed her to pass.

The dining cabin was locked and dark. She turned and nearly stumbled over more legs in the aisle, trying to recall how many cars lay between her and Gregory. Another button at the far door gave her entry to the dark limbo between cars, and the door closed behind her as the train swayed through a graded curve.

Reaching for the button that would open the door, Holiday realized she wasn't alone. In an instant outstretched hands grabbed her and covered her mouth, pulling her close. She was weak, tired, and couldn't fight. She had a terrible sense that now she was lost, that she would never reach the end of the tracks.

"Holiday, please don't yell out. It will only make trouble for us."

Her eyes focused in the dimness as the hands released her. Then she saw who was there.

"Bo! What are—" A surge of panic passed through her and she lurched for the door. Swenson moved quickly, blocking the way.

He wore a long lined overcoat and his hair was disheveled. A small valise lay at his feet. "I boarded the train just after you in Stockholm; it was luck that I saw you there."

He stepped toward her, and Holiday shrank away from him. "You've been watching me." Backing into the corner, she felt her heart pulsing in her ears. "Do you know why I'm going to Umea? It's because of Lars."

"Please, listen to me," he said, glancing furtively into the cabin ahead. "I did not think anything so terrible had happened, but I knew it was true when your assistant told me you had gone to Sweden."

Holiday pressed her back against the wall. She felt searing betrayal that Pam hadn't kept her secret. Detective Harper might have called, the police could be waiting for them at Umea.

Then she realized what Bo had said.

Swenson stared at her, his cheeks sallow and his brow wrinkled. She saw he had a deep bruise under one eye. "One month ago Lars began calling me regularly, asking me questions."

He raised a hand to silence her before she could interrupt. "Whether I had access to travel schedules of certain individuals at Pacific University, whether I could obtain timetables and research schedules—all for your surgical technology unit."

"What did you tell him?" She scanned her memory, trying to remember if she told Bo anything that Lars could have used.

"At first I was tempted to help. I would have done anything to bring him closer to me." He paused, searching Holiday's eyes as though his absolution might lie there.

"I told him nothing; it was beyond my power to find out these things. And the department was in flux, about to be passed over to your authority."

"Didn't this strike you as strange?"

"Of course. His questions were too specific, and it was clear he already knew much about your department and the hospital."

"What kind of things?"

"He refused to speak about you in any way." Bo ran a hand through his hair, his eyes catching the light. "He was very interested in Mr. Hampton."

Holiday took a sharp breath. "Gregory is with me," she whispered.

"Of course. I saw him in Stockholm, at the train station."

She moved away from the corner, trying to pace, but there was no room. A short metallic shriek came from below, somewhere in the great steel workings of the train. "You never told me," she said simply.

"When the Japanese man was killed, I immediately thought that Lars had known it would happen. He refused my calls, and I heard from a colleague in Stockholm that he was due to be transferred north."

"You hoped the situation would resolve itself, that Lars would never be implicated," Holiday said.

He closed his eyes. "I don't understand my son. But he is all I have now. The Japanese man was dead, nothing could bring him back. I thought eventually I could reach Lars, that I could help him."

The stereoscopic image returned to Holiday: the angelic mother, alit with flaming candles and a blood-red sash, the boy in rapture. What came next? Takamoto . . . the baroque design of Mitsuyama's management, the tracks they now rode on. Lars had left a trail.

"It's now Santa Lucia Day," Holiday said.

Bo stared at her blankly. "I heard about Hampton's release from jail. I knew the investigation would continue."

"And until then you were willing to let Gregory rot in jail to save Lars?"

The door opened with a shrill clatter. An elderly woman in a long blue dress and bifocals, startled, stared suspiciously at Bo and Holiday. Bo reached out and opened the far door, muttering solicitously in Swedish. The woman gave a curt nod and passed through.

Holiday blinked. The images had a pattern, a progression. The tracks, then Umea from above. Then the hospital.

Bo spoke in a low voice. "I would not have allowed Hampton to suffer wrongly."

"How can I believe you?"

"Because you know me, Holiday. That's not what I am."

She needed to look away from him, away from those eyes. "Don't, Bo . . . just don't."

Bo was silent. It was hard to think of more than one thing at once, and the air was becoming stifling. She remembered a shape in Lars's image bank, a square with long tendrils emerging from its body.

"There is one more thing," Bo said. "I came to warn you."

Bo stepped into the narrow sliver of light afforded by the door's window. In addition to the bruise under his eye, he had a deep purple laceration under his ear. His lips were cut and swollen.

She reached out to touch his face. "What happened to you?"

He grimaced, turning away as though embarrassed. "A man broke into my house and tried to kill me. I suspect there was a connection to Lars. Perhaps someone thinks I was involved."

The train suddenly rocked from side to side with startling violence. Holiday gripped the wall, moving toward the door.

Bo moved close; she smelled his expensive cologne mixed with perspiration. "We are in this together."

She pushed him aside, opened the door, and walked quickly through the next cabin as the train swayed and groaned. At the next door she pushed the release button and was quickly in the next car. Several rows away she saw the back of Gregory's head. She found her seat without turning to see if Bo had followed.

"What's the matter?" Gregory asked, sitting up quickly.

Holiday tried to speak but was silenced by the abrasive noise of the train's wheels grinding against the track below. In that moment Swenson appeared, sliding into the row behind them.

Bo reached over the seat and extended his thin hand to Gregory, whose mouth hung open for an instant with shock.

"Mr. Hampton," Bo said in a gracious baritone, his ease and manners returned.

Gregory shook Bo's hand reflexively. He turned to Holiday, gripping his seat armrest as the train shuddered again. "Is there something you want to tell me?"

"He knew," Holiday said simply, leaning back and closing her eyes. For a moment she felt the warm hand of oblivion within her, and an overpowering need for rest and sleep.

"How much did he know?" Gregory asked.

"That Lars was involved in the killing, Mr. Hampton," Bo said. Holiday's mind flooded with images: the Mitsuyama hierarchy, the view of Takamoto's corpse. There was a connection.

Bo's voice rose with entreaty. "You must believe me, it was only a suspicion. But it appears that I was correct."

The train keened again, louder this time, and slowed before regaining speed. Passengers rose to look out the windows, commenting to one another in low voices.

"They put me in jail for what your son did." Gregory's voice was affectless, a grim razor tone.

"I'm sorry," Swenson said. "I have also suffered. A man attacked me at my house just before I left Los Angeles. He would have killed me."

"What happened to him?" Gregory asked.

Bo paused. "Joining you before you reached Lars was more important than explaining to the police why I have a dead man in my house."

Holiday gasped and turned to look at Bo. He seemed

small, frail, and impossibly alone. "We have all borne the cost of my son's actions."

Gregory stood and leaned over the seat back. "You were attacked by someone connected to your son?"

"I have to assume so," Bo said. "I think Lars was part of something greater than himself."

Gregory looked around the cabin. "I thought the same thing."

"Of course he's right," Holiday said. "Someone had to have provided him with your stolen password, Gregory. It couldn't have been Guliksen—he was told only enough to play his part."

In that instant the train filled with a discordant roar of metal on metal. The cabin jerked and pitched forward. Gregory was thrown against the seat behind him, nearly tumbling over. Holiday closed her eyes, and her ears were filled with confused shouts and screams of outrage. Then she was thrown into the seat back in front of her, striking it with such a powerful concussion that she bounced back into her own seat. She registered a warm, seeping pain moving from her chest down into her legs.

For a moment there was only silence, until moans of pain and surprise could be heard from everywhere in the car. The cabin was plunged into complete darkness, and the train's engines protested with an earsplitting whine, then fell completely silent.

Holiday felt little. Her body was numb save for a warmth that suddenly turned into a severe chill. She hunched in the darkness, calling for Gregory until she felt his arms around her. Outside the window, in the moonlight, the snow fell harder now, a dense wave of ivory flakes descending like a shroud.

"We've stopped. It's over," Gregory said, smoothing Holiday's hair and holding her close. She huddled against him, trembling with a sudden thrill of adrenaline.

A crackling voice came over the intercom. Holiday thought something was wrong with her until she realized it was speaking Swedish.

"Where's Swenson?" Gregory asked, turning in the dark and feeling the empty seat behind them.

Holiday's eyes adjusted, and the low moonlight shining through the window illumined the long box of the car with gray, fuzzy contours. Bo rose from the floor, his hand on his head.

She watched him sway and nearly lose his balance. "Are you hurt?"

"My head," Swenson said, his voice tremulous.

Passengers began to call out for their companions. A few groans grew louder. "We've got to help those people," Holiday said.

"Hold on," Gregory said, pulling her close.

"We're going to be here for a while," Swenson said, stepping into the aisle and falling into the seat across from Holiday. "On the intercom they said our emergency stop was due to the storm. The tracks are damaged, and the path ahead is closed. We're twenty miles from Umea, and an evacuation crew is on the way."

Holiday looked out the window. Now that the train was motionless, the windows quickly covered with snow. Before the view disappeared, she had a final view of the plain outside, extending into the night like an endless blanket of deadly whiteness.

24

THE WIND HOWLED LIKE A FORLORN VOICE, BATTERING THE IDLE train with angry gusts that sent the cars gently swaying; it felt as though the train had partially slipped the rails. Inside, the passengers were silent with shock. Holiday tended to an old woman with a broken arm in the front of the car, creating a makeshift splint out of two serving trays and a silk scarf. The other passengers seemed to be stable. She joined Gregory, who was crouched by a window, staring outside.

"This storm has really picked up," he said to Holiday. Bo joined them after checking reflex responses in a young man injured by falling luggage. Bo's own eyes were red and glassy, but his head injury was relatively minor. "There's no way they can fix those tracks in that snow."

"At least the heat is working," Bo said, rubbing his forehead. "We would freeze otherwise."

The cabin door opened and a man entered wearing a Swedish railways jacket. He was thick-waisted and ruddy, his mouth obscured by a generous mustache. His appearance set off a clamor among the passengers, whom he silenced by blowing a steel whistle.

Bo listened carefully as the man spoke. "He apologizes for the emergency stop and says that medical assistance will arrive soon."

An angry voice yelled from the front of the car; Holiday saw it was Anders. The conductor retreated into the next cabin to repeat his speech.

"We won't arrive in Umea until late afternoon," Bo said. "It's nearly seven A.M., and they will have to bring the injured and elderly to safety before anyone else."

"We can't wait," Holiday said. "It'll be too late."

"Too late for what?" Swenson asked. "Lars will still be

there. He obviously can't take a train out of Umea, unless he goes farther north."

"It's Santa Lucia Day," Holiday said. "You have to know what that means to him."

Since the crash her mind had been stuck on the final image in Lars's file, the boxy shape with its long flowing tendrils. It followed the Mitsuyama chart, the hospital corridor. But what was it? Her slight fever felt like gauze in her mind, softening and blurring her thoughts.

The other passengers had settled into their seats, sleeping or drinking, content to watch the snow fall. Anders and his fellow doctors, including a petite, ashen-haired woman who regarded Holiday with a cold, lingering stare, moved to the back of the car. Anders had obtained a first-aid package and stopped to dispense painkillers to those suffering bruises and abrasions.

"We have to check on passengers in the other cars," Anders said to Holiday. The whites of his eyes were ringed with red; the hangover had set in. "Would you please join us? We could use extra hands."

Bo nodded. "Of course."

Holiday stepped between Bo and the Swedes. "We don't have time."

"What are you saying?" Bo picked up his valise, looking past her. "We have nothing but time."

"You're trying to avoid Lars again." Holiday moved close to Swenson and spoke quietly. She fought off pangs of conscience—she had never imagined not treating a patient in need. "You can't abandon him, not this time. You might never see him again."

Swenson's shoulders slumped with weary impatience as he listened. "You mean he might kill himself? Perhaps he will be doing the world a service."

"You don't mean that," she said. "I can't forgive you for not telling me what you knew. But you were there for me when I was falling apart. Why can't you do the same for your son?"

Swenson stiffened as though Holiday had struck him;

he began to turn away from her angrily, but stopped. He waved his hand to the doctors and told them to go without them.

Anders and his colleagues left the car, the young woman glancing back at Holiday with open disdain. It was one of the hardest decisions Holiday had ever made.

Gregory lightly brushed her shoulder. He was dressed for the outside in his hat and coat, with only his eyes exposed. She began to put on her own coat and gloves.

"You can't go out there," Swenson said. "It's too damned cold. We're twenty miles from town. It's insane."

Gregory struggled with the steel latch that opened the cabin door to the outside. The other passengers stayed in their seats, their curiosity dampened by shock.

"I . . . I don't have a warm enough coat," Bo said faintly.

Gregory shrugged. "Steal one of those doctors'."

Holiday and Gregory stepped through the door. She saw Bo sprint through the cabin toward the nest of papers and coats the Swedish doctors left behind.

Outside, Holiday instantly felt a cold more intense than she had ever experienced, a flesh-freezing chill and wind that rendered her immobile for a moment. The storm's sound was a hoarse yell.

"There's nothing out here," she shouted. A chill passed through her, and she pulled her collar tight around her neck. Every part of her body cried out in outrage, demanding she find someplace warm.

Gregory folded his arms tightly against his chest. In the brief moments between wind squalls, when the sheets of snow temporarily turned to flakes, they saw the same unbroken white plain in the darkness. It seemed so infinite and dreadful from the train; now it was different, a vast reality at once deadly and mundane.

"We can only stand these temperatures for about fifteen minutes or so before we get frostbite," Holiday said. Another wind gust swept choking snow into her face. She raised a hand to her nose and eyes, gasping.

"Umea is almost due north," Bo yelled, his shoes crunching through the snow behind them. He wore a silver parka, too tight in the shoulders, and a thick woolen hat, his hands gloveless. From his pocket he produced a small metallic compass. "The tracks head straight there."

"You're a regular Boy Scout," Gregory said, walking away from the train and peering into the distance.

"At least I'm trying to be constructive," Bo yelled. "I hope you're sane enough to admit we cannot walk twenty miles in this storm."

Gregory disappeared into the snow, shielding his eyes.

Bo shivered next to Holiday, his hands in his pockets. "Mr. Hampton has no place here," he said. "If he has come seeking revenge for the days he spent in jail, I don't want him with us."

"We've both come for answers."

Bo turned away from the wind. "You really only knew Lars for a year. He was always difficult, always delicate."

"You left him alone with his mother, you were barely a father even when you were with him," Holiday shouted.

Bo's eyes widened. "He told you this?"

She tried to spot Gregory, but he had vanished in the storm. "You know how Lars felt, Bo. I don't know whether he was right."

A figure emerged from the snow; behind it, Holiday saw a flickering light. She set off toward Gregory.

"What do you know about a father's disappointment in his son?" Bo called out from behind her.

Holiday had no answer. Years ago she had looked into Lars's soul and found that his father loomed in his life like a terrible arbiter, the force that haunted him, always beyond his control. The frail man behind her had once possessed the power of a giant.

Out of the snowy nimbus Holiday saw Gregory emerge. She rubbed her jaw with wet gloves, trying to calm her chattering teeth. Then she saw the headlights, from at least a dozen vehicles.

"Rescue crews," Gregory cried out when he reached her.

The motor sound was at first indistinguishable from the wind. Then the rescue vehicles neared, turning the dead land to a turmoil of pitched snow, revving motors, and shouts. The trucks, with oversized ribbed tires, rode in a pyramid formation, each with an enclosed flat bed wide enough to hold at least a dozen people. The din grew unbearably loud; Holiday held her hands over her ears and felt animal panic, as though she were a deer trapped in headlights.

Then the pack passed. A single vehicle broke formation; as the pack moved into the distance, cars stopped next to the individual cars ahead. The snow quickly enveloped the other trucks, and only the one sent to rescue their car could be seen. The driver put the engine in idle and stepped out in a heavy orange snowsuit and goggles, carrying a plastic first-aid kit. He walked directly toward them.

Gregory stepped behind Bo. "Tell him there are a couple of severely injured people inside who need immediate attention."

The rescue worker walked stiffly and mechanically, his boots tossing clumps of snow from his feet. "But no one is injured critically."

"Exactly," Gregory hissed. "So nobody will die without this truck."

Holiday looked out across the plain as Bo spoke to the driver. The snow eased for a moment and she saw shifting hills of snow, rocks spotting the immaculate fields with ruptures of jagged black.

The rescue worker listened to Bo for a moment, then hurriedly forced open the train door. Through a window Holiday could see him in the cabin, discarding his cap and goggles.

Gregory scrambled through the snow, leaping into the truck and revving the engine. Holiday grabbed Bo's arm. "Come on."

Bo's hair was covered with a thick mat of snow; moisture dripped from his eyelids. He looked at the truck wearily. "All right," he said, glancing back at the train. "We had better hurry."

The truck was spartan and difficult to drive. Gregory cursed and struggled with the gearshift, the transmission moaning and grinding as he eased in a semicircle away from the train.

"We have to hope they came straight from Umea," Gregory said, grunting as he turned the enormous steering wheel. "And that the snow doesn't completely cover their tracks before we make it."

"They must have come from Umea," Bo said from the backseat. "There's no other sizable town for a hundred miles."

Within a minute the train was gone behind them. Holiday looked back; no headlights appeared in the darkness. Gregory attained a cruising speed, and they plunged deeper into the lightless morning.

The windshield wipers cleared away enough snow to allow a distorted vision of the ground and the thick tracks left by the rescue team. Holiday stared at the tracks, buffeted as the wheels hit rocks and clumps of ice, mesmerized at the unchanging landscape outside.

Bo listened to the CB radio's low pulse of conversation. "They said nothing about a missing truck. Perhaps our young rescue worker believes it was borrowed by one of his colleagues."

"Let's hope so," Gregory said, staring out the windshield.

Holiday lay back against the seat. Lars's images played against the screen of her closed eyelids. The satellite images had shown the tracks from above, the transportation to Umea. Then the town itself. The progression led to the hospital, where they were going. It was as though he left a deliberate trail for her, leading to the final shape, the abstract box with its arms. If she could only figure out what it was.

Holiday jerked forward in her seat. "How long have we been—"

"Almost an hour," Gregory said. It was completely dark outside. "It's eight in the morning. I thought I'd let you get some rest."

Holiday turned to the backseat; Bo sat with his arms folded. A brief smile flickered across the corners of his mouth when their eyes met.

"How are you holding up?" she asked.

Bo glanced at Gregory. "I visited Umea when I was a student. It was many years ago, and I spent most of my time in operating rooms. But if we can get to the hospital, I could find the doctors' quarters."

They had reached the outer fringes of Umea. Gregory found an unlit access road and steered toward it, still following the tracks left by the emergency team.

Bo leaned forward. "I was sent here for two weeks for hernia surgeries. They had quite a waiting list they were trying to pare down."

"Tell her about it when we get home," Gregory said, staring ahead.

"I'll do that, Mr. Hampton," Bo answered, his voice meticulously polite. "You are right. We are here for a reason."

The snow grew heavier, and to the right Holiday saw a long brick building lined with open garage bay doors. Here the tracks stopped, but after a turn onto a two-lane road they suddenly reached civilization. The town was eerily quiet, the small homes lit inside like oases of warmth. No one else was out in the storm save for an occasional jeep or truck that passed silently, its wheels gently rolling over the packed snow.

"I know the university is near the center of town. Keep going that way," Bo offered. Gregory's hands tightened on the wheel.

Umea was a small town, without the waterways and islands that livened Stockholm. They passed public squares and stone churches that might be magnificent in the daylight, but for now the place felt like an encampment carved into the unforgiving face of winter.

The snowstorm made it impossible to see more than twenty feet ahead, but it also enabled Gregory to drive the stolen truck through the center of town. Holiday pointed, followed signs, felt herself brimming with instinct and vague memory from the aerial views in Lars's file. She had always been able to do this: go to a strange place, wander intuitively, and somehow find what she was looking for. Within a half hour they drove into the university medical complex. It was a compound of featureless, utilitarian buildings behind a brightly lit brick archway and glass doors.

"Don't go near that emergency entrance," she said, pointing to a lit red cross. "They'll think we're part of the rescue team."

She cleared her throat, the act of speaking suddenly an exertion. Her eyes burned and her vision blurred. Whenever her adrenaline flagged, she felt the flu progressing, waiting for her to let down her guard.

Gregory slowed the truck near a long row of parked cars. People in heavy winter coats walked through the entrance two hundred yards away. As everywhere, hospital life went on no matter the circumstances.

The parking lot was under several inches of snow. Under a bright lamp a plow made a desultory pass across a vacant lane of cement, pushing a great mass of snow into a waiting pile. As soon as the strip was cleared, the snow covered it again.

Outside, the snow fell with such force that Holiday heard its muffled impact upon the ground. Holiday peered up into the darkness, trying to get a sense of the medical complex's dimensions; as far as she could see, the main building was joined by other structures on all sides, extending back along a gentle hillside.

They walked into the bright, spotless lobby, unnoticed

332 HOWARD OLGIN, M.D.

by the front desk staff and a group of doctors conferring over coffee within a glass enclosure.

Bo shook snow from his hair and looked around. "I remember this place," he said. "The doctors' quarters and dining area are in this direction." He pointed toward a set of doors and, his expression calm, walked to the reception desk and spoke to a heavyset woman seated behind a bank of phones. He talked to her in a droll, deep voice. The woman erupted with hearty laughter.

"At least he's finally making himself useful," Gregory said, looking around the lobby.

Though it lacked the outward wealth and funding shared by Pacific University and the Bart—the paint was institutional drab, the walls bare of the self-promotion seen in most American facilities—the Umea hospital looked modern and progressive. A bank of computers lined the office behind the glass, and the staff had the calm, efficient air of professionals with resources at their disposal.

Bo returned. "I have Lars's room number. His rotation does not start until this evening, so he may be in his quarters."

Holiday followed Gregory and Bo through double doors into a long corridor lined with individual consultation rooms. After an elevated enclosed walkway between buildings they were in a residential wing, lined with closed doors and unoccupied.

"Lars lives in Room Three twenty-three, that way," Bo said.

Bo suddenly seemed tense, distracted, as though he had heard something strange. Holiday stared at him, confused, until she heard what had caught his ear. Far down the long corridor, echoing quietly down the length of the white hall, came a chorus of feminine voices.

"Santa Lucia Day," Holiday whispered. The voices rose toward a crescendo, a high, lilting sound of eerie beauty.

Bo walked ahead, entranced. Holiday followed, the

voices losing their ethereal wonder as she grew closer, leaving only the hollow, limited tones of a small group of women straining into the final verse of a carol.

Bo was already in the room when Holiday stopped at the doorway. It was a cafeteria, with long benches pushed aside to one wall. A table had been left in place, filled with coffee, pastries, and bottles of beer. A huddle of male and female doctors and staff stood transfixed before a group of women dressed in white robes, arranged in a circle around a partially hidden figure.

Holiday strained to find Bo. The women stepped away as the song ended, their voices fading. There, tall and serene, wearing a burning candelabra atop her blond hair and a red sash around her waist binding her flowing white robes, was a beautiful woman, the last to stop singing. Holiday strained to see her face but couldn't.

The crowd stared with the intrusion of the gaunt, wet-haired man who stepped into the circle of singers. Bo stood alone behind the woman, his hands at his sides, staring at the back of her head with frightening intensity. Finally the woman turned.

She was indeed lovely, Holiday saw, with a stark Scandinavian face and a proud, almost haughty expression. Startled to see Bo behind her, she regarded him with a bland, uncertain smile. Bo stepped away, shaking his head.

Holiday moved through the room to take Bo's hand. She scanned the faces, half expecting to find Lars's thick hair and ravaged face. He wasn't there.

"For a moment I thought that—" Bo said in a trembling voice.

In his pallid skin and haunted eyes, the wrinkles dripping moisture from his thin hair, Holiday saw something she knew. Loss, betrayal, a nameless hurt that surfaced without warning.

"I know," she said. "You have to concentrate on the living, Bo. On your son."

Her words shocked him out of his trance. "Of course,"

he said, turning away from the young woman. She met Holiday's eyes with puzzlement, lingering for a moment.

"Lars isn't here," Holiday said to Bo. "We should check his room."

Gregory waited in the doorway, awkward and out of place. Bo led them into the sterile residential wing, walking ahead alone, his head stooped and his steps almost too fast to keep up with.

"What was going on in there?" Gregory whispered.

"Bo . . . thought he saw a ghost from his past," Holiday said.

"Lars?" Gregory asked. There was no time to tell him; Bo turned a corner and vanished. When they caught up with him, he was standing before Room 323.

The corridors were like tendrils, the walkways like arms. The main hospital building was a great concrete box. Holiday stopped walking; this was the terminus, the final image in Lars's progression. She tried to remember Umea viewed from the air, if she had seen the hospital below.

Bo rapped his knuckles against the wooden door. No answer.

He turned to Gregory. "Mr. Hampton, do you know how to pick a lock?"

Holiday prepared for Gregory to react badly, but his manner toward Bo had softened a degree since the older man strode into the circle of singers. Gregory merely shook his head. "I wasn't in jail long enough."

"No matter," Bo said, turning his attention to the door. "These locks were always a joke."

Bo leaned against the door with his shoulder, beads of perspiration and melted snow falling from his forehead. The wooden doorframe groaned with a splintering noise.

Holiday looked up and down the hall. There was still nobody there; the doctors were probably either at the Santa Lucia gathering or readying the ER to treat injuries from the train. The door gave way with a crack and opened, the knob clattering against the floor.

The room was brutally austere, especially for a career physician. A single bed sat unmade in a corner under a long curtained window, beside a chair and a small dresser. Bo switched on the light, spellbound in the private sphere of his estranged son's life.

An open door led to a shower and toilet, out of sight upon first entering the room. Holiday's pulse quickened; for an instant she saw a shadow behind the shower door. Then the form was gone, a phantasm.

"Not exactly a high roller, is he?" Gregory said, looking around the room. There was little there: a stack of medical texts, a pile of folders burgeoning with notes, dirty clothing haphazardly strewn across the floor and chair. An ashtray filled with cigarette butts perched on the desk amid several vodka bottles and dirty glasses.

This wasn't the Lars Holiday remembered, so fastidious that he ironed his slacks a second time at midday so that they wouldn't wrinkle. In his small room in Boston he'd tacked colorful prints on the walls, and the room was always full of eclectic library books he checked out for stimulation during his few off hours. This was the room of a hollow man, full of stagnation and the haphazard resignation of bad living. She saw with revulsion an abandoned plate of food on the floor in the corner, covered with a fine film of green mold.

"Our man isn't here," Gregory said, tossing aside a stack of dirty laundry and sitting in the vinyl chair. "Any ideas?"

Bo sat on Lars's bed staring at the nightstand, where an old-fashioned rotary phone occupied a cramped space with another ashtray and bottle. Behind the debris was a faded framed photograph of a young, smiling blond woman.

The room had begun to feel close and hot, and Holiday felt a trickle of sweat run down her back. She wished she had a thermometer to see how high her fever was running.

"Swenson, come on," Gregory said. "You know this town, right?"

"Stop," Bo said. He reached out for the photograph and, after staring at it for a moment, turned it facedown on the nightstand. He looked up at Gregory apologetically. "Please stop talking for a minute."

Holiday opened the curtains. Low light appeared in the morning horizon. It wasn't right—the hospital wasn't the form she remembered. It was too fragmented. Lars's final image was that of a sturdy block surrounded by arms. But why did the arms have to be wings of a building?

"I don't mean to be insensitive," Gregory said gently. "But this is no time for you to lose it. If this day is so important to Lars, then—"

She was going about this all wrong. *Think.* A central structure, the lines like long spider's arms, *but mostly in a straight line, long parallel lines. Each like the tracks seen from the sky.*

"Mr. Hampton, I—"

"Stop, both of you." They turned to her, surprised. "I know where he is. I've seen it before."

25

THE SNOW EASED FOR A MOMENT, THE STORM'S ENERGY FADING. Then, as though angry at being taken lightly, it began to rage harder, the snow falling in great heavy clumps from the dusky sky. Holiday felt her body protest anew when she stepped out of the taxi. She was racked with shivers, her throat a universe of roughness and pain. She didn't care. The pictures had come together, she had seen the images coalesce in her mind's eye.

Across the airfield she saw an unmarked twin-engine jet moving across the runway, bound for a lone hangar in the empty field. Two other planes bearing SAS symbols across their fuselages were parked near the gates, grounded by the storm. The terminal was lit inside but looked deserted through the windows. He wouldn't be there, not when his fate lay by the hangar.

There was no barrier between her, the runway, and the hangar on the opposite side—only snow, knee-deep until she would reach the relatively clear runway. She could make it.

Gregory and Bo called her name angrily behind her. "Holiday, stop, for God's sake. You're delirious," Gregory said. "Let's go inside and see if any planes got out in the storm today."

She held out a hand to silence him. "Look, by the plane."

The craft hadn't pulled into the hangar for shelter; instead it parked out of the wind, by the open hangar doors. No smoke emerged from the engines.

Through the veil of snow two figures in thick winter coats stood several paces apart, immersed in conversation.

Gregory caught up with her. "Does it look like Lars?" he asked.

Bo squinted into the snow, pulling his valise to his chest.

It was time to follow the trail to the end. She waded furiously through the snow, cold wetness soaking her pants to her thighs, until she reached the plowed tarmac leading to the runway.

In moments Gregory was beside her. "Slow down," he said, peering at the two figures. A gust of wind blew a sheet of snow across the field, making the plane invisible for a moment.

Holiday walked like an automaton, fighting off weakness and focusing on the steady rhythm of their steps. Pulling her hat down to her eyes, she glanced back at the terminal, now farther away than the hangar. Bo, several paces behind them, turned his face away from the wind. His mouth was moving, as though he were talking to himself.

The figures finally saw Holiday and Gregory. She kept walking. One was shorter, his face obscured by a ski mask and goggles. He held a small package. The other was tall and obviously muscular under his parka. His left hand was hidden in his pocket, the arm's curvature strange and unnatural.

"It's Lars." The men stepped apart when she began to jog, her boots slipping on the runway's fresh powder.

She ran to the larger man, too quickly for him to react. When she was but feet away, she saw his gleaming blue eyes open with surprise between his scarf and his hat. He stepped away and she followed.

"Lars, it's me," she said, her voice trailing away in the wind.

He was still, his damaged hand stuffed into his jacket pocket. From behind Holiday came rapid footsteps crunching in the snow. She turned with fear, but it was only Bo. Gregory stood several paces away, nervously watching.

Bo walked to his son without speaking, his arms outstretched. Lars swatted at his father with explosive aggression, striking the older man and nearly knocking him to the ground.

"Lars," Bo cried out, his feet sliding as he cringed away. "Stop it. We've come for you."

Lars stared at his father for a moment, then moved toward Holiday as if he were merely an apparition. Even through his winter gear she could see him tremble.

"Holiday," he said, and in that instant his identity was beyond question. His voice, deep and sonorous, had grown husky and was tinged with desperation. "I never imagined I would see you again."

"Did you tell these people you were going to be here?" the other man said from several paces away. There was a quality to his voice that Holiday knew but couldn't place.

"Of course not," Lars said. "I am not a fool."

The man shoved his hands in his red ski-jacket pocket and moved closer. Holiday glanced at the plane; someone else was in the cockpit.

"I think maybe you are," the man said mockingly. He rocked on his heels with a spasm of frustration. "What is wrong with you, Swenson? Do you have a need to destroy everything, including yourself?"

"They don't know," Lars said. "Let them leave. We can finish the transaction and be done with each other."

Bo watched helplessly, as though Lars's slap had robbed him of his last reserve of sprit.

"We know everything, Lars," Holiday said. "We talked to Guliksen. I saw the images you stored, and I'm beginning to understand."

The man took another step forward, peering at Holiday through his goggles. "She knows, Swenson, you see? You're a liar. We stipulated that you would do the job alone. First you contacted Guliksen, now you brought Powers and Hampton into it."

Holiday peered into the man's goggles. *He knows who we are.*

Lars shook his head spasmodically. "I needed help. The password you gave me wasn't enough. I didn't have the ability to make the laser fire—I could only if I knew how to implant the command."

"Exactly. And Moshiro Tamo found out," the man said. Holiday felt frozen to the tarmac. If only she could have a quiet moment alone, she could have remembered who he was.

"Guliksen is gone by now, Swenson. We reached him this morning. That was a complication Tamo didn't like, and he blamed me for it. I have to make amends with him."

The man pulled his hand from his coat. Holiday saw Lars's eyes widen with panic. He lunged toward her and drove her to the ground, and the world exploded with ice and noise. She heard a chaos of voices and a pair of explosions. Lars lay cold and heavy atop her.

She relaxed in the snow, unable to feel her body. *Maybe I'm dying.*

She opened her eyes. Gregory knelt over her. "Get the hell off her," he yelled, roughly pushing Lars to the snow. She stood, dizzy, her leg numb and icy under her torn pants leg. At her feet blood flowed in the snow. The anonymous man lay facedown, unmoving.

A shining gun lay discarded near the body. Lars leaped to his feet and grabbed the weapon, reaching the airplane in seconds on a dead run. He pulled open the craft's door and stepped inside.

Moments later the pilot emerged, a slight Asian man in a blue uniform and military-style tie. He held his hands above his head, grimacing in the pelting snow. Lars followed with the gun, throwing aside his hat to reveal his face and long flaxen hair. Holiday gasped; this was the man she saw in the virtual reality world, his skin sallow and loose, his eyes sunken and staring furtively. The Lars she knew was gone.

He looked at her. "Lars, what are you—" she began.

"Not now," Lars yelled. He motioned to Gregory. "Make sure that he's really dead," he said.

"Do it yourself, fucker," Gregory said, his breath billowing in the cold. "I'm the one who saved you. I almost got killed."

Lars nodded respectfully. "Thank you. I am in your debt."

"I only did it because Holiday was standing next to you. The guy practically shot himself." Gregory knelt beside the body. "He obviously wasn't a professional, or he wouldn't have fumbled with the gun like that."

Holiday helped Gregory turn over the body. He swiftly unzipped the man's jacket; a rush of steam plumed from his gunshot wound. Holiday checked his pulse, then removed his goggles and cap.

"Mike Hyata," she said, staring into the dead man's eyes. "The bullet went right into his heart. He must have died instantly."

"It's too bad. I liked him," Lars said. He nodded toward a small parcel that Hyata had dropped while struggling with Gregory. "Bring that here, Holiday. It belongs to me."

Holiday hesitated until Lars pointed the gun at her.

Lars held out his hand for the package and turned to his father. Bo stooped over his own valise, clutching it protectively. "What's in your bag, Father? Something for me?"

"Photographs from when you were young. I brought them to show you." Bo straightened himself, wincing. Holiday saw a minute line of crimson on his head that had seeped from his wound and frozen.

Lars's angry, ugly laughter resounded in the still air. "My God, Father. I have been trying to forget everything about you."

"But you called me, until you found I wouldn't help you. And you met with this man on Santa Lucia Day. You haven't forgotten." He stepped toward Hyata's body. "Who is he?"

"A business acquaintance who overreacted, that is all."
Lars's tone was oddly brisk.

"He's with Mitsuyama," Gregory said. The voice startled Lars, and he jerked back and pointed the gun at
Gregory.

"You don't want to do it," Gregory said calmly. "This
isn't a computer program. I'm flesh and blood."

"Who in the world *are* you?" Lars said in a petulant
whine.

"Why was Mike here, Lars?" Holiday asked. He turned
to her and his contorted features relaxed. For an instant
she saw the face she remembered, the open-eyed intensity
with which he approached the world. She remembered
the inner friction that had once driven him and had
turned him into the wrecked man she saw now.

"He was here to pay me," Lars said evenly. "For killing
Takamoto."

"He was angry with you because you promised more
than you delivered." She wanted to keep him talking.
Someone inside the terminal may have looked outside
and seen Hyata's body on the tarmac. But the snow still
fell hard. At that distance they may have seen nothing.

"I recruited Neils." Lars raised the gun to the sky. "He
had programming skills that I needed. And they had him
killed. Can you believe it?"

"And that package is the payoff?"

Lars shoved the parcel in his pocket. "It's a passkey to
a bank account. They were willing to spend a lot to be rid
of Takamoto. An entire faction within Mitsuyama con-
spired against him. Hyata was just a tool."

She understood. Hyata, on one of his international recruitment trips, met Lars. He saw that Lars was desperate, that his surgical career was over, and that he was
experienced in surgical technologies. Knowing in advance
about Takamoto's telepresence gambit, Hyata was able to
pull together the factors to kill the old man. The people
who would then control Mitsuyama would owe him an
eternal debt.

"Congratulations, Lars," she said, bitterness in her voice. "You're a genuine assassin."

"You have to understand," Lars said gently, almost pleading. "They recruited me. They offered the opportunity."

"To become a killer?"

"At first as a doctor, but what kind of a doctor can I be with my injury?" He turned his arm, the hand still in his pocket, toward her. "What they offered was a chance to get away, to live again."

Holiday felt a surge of pity for him. Takamoto died, and Holiday and Gregory suffered, because Lars was lost within himself.

Lars seemed to sense her sadness for him, and turned away. "Stand up, Father," he said. Bo sat on the tarmac, half-covered with snow, staring blankly at the nearby fields. "What's the matter with you?"

Bo stayed on the ground. He looked at his son and tittered bitterly. "I think that this is your way of getting back at me. After all this time, after all we have both lost."

"No!" Lars yelled. He pointed the gun at Bo. "This has nothing to do with you. You took Mother from me, you abandoned us. I do not care about you anymore. You cannot affect me."

"What was supposed to happen now?" Holiday asked, trying to keep Lars's attention to her.

His expression softened. "Perhaps I can find treatment, with sufficient money."

Lars pulled his free arm out of the parka. The hand was curled inward like a claw, the skin gray and lifeless, the forearm emaciated. She had seen the damage in the three-dimensional imager, but the external reality was worse than she thought. The limb was useless, deformed. It was a surgeon's nightmare.

Lars lowered his voice to a whisper. "They told me there had been experiments done in Japan. They could *cure* me, Holiday."

"What surgery could reverse damage so extensive?" Holiday said, staring at the hand. "It's simply not possible."

"They have *money*, Holiday, and resources," he pleaded.

She could say nothing. Such surgery was decades away, if it was ever developed. They had made false promises to him, lies he accepted though his medical knowledge should have told him otherwise.

"Things have gone badly here, but perhaps I can still find the surgeon they spoke of," Lars said.

He turned to the pilot, who seemed terrified that Lars remembered his presence. "What was your destination?" Lars asked.

"Stockholm," the pilot said in a strained voice. "But this storm will keep us in Umea."

Lars looked at Holiday, shaking his head. "Hyata told me we could go to Paris in this plane, then board a larger jet to Japan. He lied."

The pilot's knees shook when Lars forced the gun under his nose. "Were you going to help him kill me? Would you dump my body in the ice, where it wouldn't be found?"

The pilot shut his eyes. "I was told nothing. I am only a pilot."

"Hyata brought the gun to shoot me. Where? Inside the hangar? From behind, when I wasn't looking?" Lars waved the gun wildly. Holiday raised her arm, bracing herself for the shot.

"Leave him alone, Lars." Bo extended his arms to his son. "Come with me, boy. Let's get out of this cold."

Lars reared back with laughter, turning to Holiday. "Do you hear this? He calls me 'boy' when I am thirty-five years old."

"Listen to your father, Lars. Come with us." Holiday stared into his eyes. He was on the precipice of a deeper, more violent madness. She knew this was her final chance to bring him back.

Lars paused for a moment, about to speak, when Gregory lunged forward from behind, grabbing at Lars's gun hand.

Holiday watched each moment unfold with excruciating vividness. Lars roared with indignation and pulled away. Gregory clawed for the gun but slipped. Lars pointed the gun at Gregory, then stopped. Instead he lashed out, smashing the metal pistol into Gregory's temple.

Gregory fell to the ground, the snow around his head quickly stained deep red. Holiday rushed to him and found him still breathing.

She heard Lars talking to his Father. "I will not harm the pilot, Father. But I will force him to take me away from here."

"This man is injured, Lars. We have to get him to a hospital."

Lars shuffled his feet like a boy. "You are a doctor, you do something. Who is this man to you, anyway?"

"He was jailed for Takamoto's killing," Holiday said, feeling Gregory's skull and finding no breakage. He was unconscious, though, and had obviously suffered a concussion. "You've hurt him twice, Lars, and he's a good man."

Lars bent slightly, observing Holiday's examination. "I didn't kill him, did I?" he asked calmly.

"He's alive, but I can't do anything for him out here. This cold will only make his condition worse."

Glancing back toward the terminal, Lars squinted into the snow. "I think we have attracted attention," he said. Three figures had emerged from the main terminal.

"I must go, Father," Lars said, and leveled the gun at Bo. "This is my final opportunity to repay you for making Mother suffer."

Bo dropped his arms to his sides. "I have paid, Lars, more than you can imagine. Go ahead. I cannot fight you anymore."

Holiday stared at the dull metal of the gun's barrel,

tensed for the bullet's concussion, expecting to see Bo fall
to the snow. But Lars's hand began to shake.

"Father," he said in a choked voice. "I wish you were
not here to see me like this."

"I . . . would give anything to change what has happened to you." Bo's face was streaked with tears; his
mouth trembled and he held out his arms. Holiday
couldn't tell if he waited to embrace his son or the gun's
fire.

Lars dropped the gun to his side. "Good-bye, Father."

He took the pilot's arm gingerly with his deformed
hand and motioned toward the plane. The men from the
terminal had stopped several hundred yards away, seemingly unsure whether to approach.

The pilot, expressionless, stepped inside the plane. Lars
turned to Holiday. "Come with me," he said.

Holiday shook her head. He was a stranger, his heart
and mind foreign to her now. She knew it was beyond her
to save whatever remained of the man she knew. "No,"
she whispered.

Lars sighed impatiently and pointed the gun at Gregory. "I will shoot this man if you don't come. I'll set you
free when we land, I only want to talk. It's been too
long."

Lars stepped toward Gregory and pointed the gun
down at his motionless skull. Holiday nodded in rapid,
unthinking assent. She felt a strange sense of release, a
certainty that Lars would destroy her.

"Take care of Gregory," she said, turning to Bo.

"Don't do this, Lars," Bo yelled. "Put a stop to this,
boy."

Holiday saw that Bo was gone from Lars's mind, as if
Lars had pulled the trigger and left his father dead on the
cold tarmac. She hesitantly climbed the set of retractable
steps leading into the plane.

It held only eight seats arranged around a low circular
table. The atmosphere was plush, with velvet cushions, a
squat stocked bar, and thick shades fastened above the

windows. It was a charter, not a corporate plane—the Mitsuyama logo was nowhere in sight—but it was obviously a luxury craft. She fell into a seat and opened the shade, watching snow swirl in currents of agitated wind.

Lars stepped through the door, calm and preoccupied. Bo called out, "The storm is too intense! Your plane will crash if—"

Lars slammed the door shut, sealing it with a hand crank. Leaning into the cockpit, he pointed the gun at the pilot. "Fly south," he said. "I'll give you instructions along the way."

Holiday peered past Lars; the pilot began flipping switches on the instrument panel. The engines responded with a rising whine, still warm from its earlier landing. "We can't fly in this storm," the pilot said in a cautious tone.

"Of course we can. You are an excellent pilot, I am sure."

The plane jerked forward, and Holiday slid, her knee striking the table in front of her. She heard the pilot talking to himself in Japanese.

Lars turned to face the cabin, his maimed hand behind his back. "This is good. We will have a little time together." He shoved the gun into his pocket. "You will be safe. I pledge my life."

The plane narrowly missed Bo and Gregory as it eased across a short expanse of tarmac to the runway. Holiday saw Bo bent over Gregory's prone form. The three men moving toward the hangar broke into a cautious jog in the snow, waving frantically at the pilot. She exhaled with disappointment when she saw their SAS uniforms—they weren't police and they were unarmed, helpless to stop the takeoff.

When the plane was in position, Lars turned to the cockpit. "Now," he yelled.

"There may be ice on the wings," the pilot cried. "We will crash."

Lars considered for a moment, then took the gun from

his pocket. "You are a nice man, but if you do not take off, I will shoot you. Put yourself in my place. It doesn't matter to me now."

The plane bucked forward and quickly gained speed. Holiday tightened her seat belt, feeling a feverish rush of fear. The heat inside the cabin made her weary, her fever more intense, but her mind was strangely clear. Lars lurched to a seat across from her and buckled himself in as the ground outside began to blur.

"We will have good luck," Lars said, opening another shade and peering out the window. The plane rose from the ground and quickly hit the ground again with a sharp impact; Holiday felt the plane sliding. A second time the plane lifted. Though it started to fall again, this time it stayed in the air.

Lars smiled, lodged the gun between his knees, and reached up to brush his disheveled hair away from his eyes. His deformed hand remained in his parka. "I must look a mess," he said, smiling boyishly.

"You look fine," Holiday said. She allowed herself a glance out the window; below her the white plains extended toward dark hills, the compact mass of Umea lay blanketed in snow. Even now Lars's sequence of images held true.

The pilot banked into a long, lazy turn, still ascending, into a loop that would bring them into a southward heading.

"You're just being kind," Lars said, ignoring the vista outside. "You are still very beautiful."

These gentle tones, this warm, shy manner, were those of her first love. She'd expected to find Lars raving mad, lost in his fantasies like those he stored in Stockholm, but in truth there was a sort of pathetic logic about what he had done. But he was weak, and he had let the past consume him. In this way he had taught her something.

"The police will be waiting for you wherever you land, Lars. It isn't too late to turn back."

Lars leaned back and smiled. "You haven't changed.

Always with the advice." As though worried he might have offended her, he hastily added, "But of course it was always very good advice."

Holiday noticed the plane was slow to gain altitude, though the engine labored and plumes of exhaust followed them through the sky.

"We cannot go back," Lars said, oblivious to their stalled ascent. "I assume there is a parachute somewhere. Perhaps I will jump out somewhere along the way." He cast an idle glance about the cabin.

"Stop it, Lars. There's something wrong with the plane," Holiday said, feeling her pulse rise. "What's happening?" she called in a loud voice to the pilot. There was no response.

"We are in the air, everything is fine," Lars said tersely, looking out the window. They were still in a lazy arc above Umea, and Holiday could see the airfield below, its terminal building like a discarded matchbox on a clean white floor. Extending from it she saw the runway and access roads like tendrils from a squat, square body. Beyond the town she saw a black gash in the earth, some kind of massive hole.

Lars leaned toward Holiday. "There are things I must tell you," he said, whispering like a conspirator. "When I left you the last time, it was because of my mother. She killed herself that day. On Santa Lucia Day."

The plane pitched to the side, banking precariously.

"I know," she said gently. "Your father told me. Why did you leave without saying anything to me?"

Ignoring the question, Lars snorted. "Father told you. He even takes that from me."

She sensed him lapsing into an irrational state. *Was he always like this? Has he changed so much, or was I blind when we were young?*

Lars's eyes shone with an almost supernatural glint. "It was my mother's death that started my . . . my difficulties. I was not like this when we were together. Perhaps it started from the very moment I heard she took her life, and that is why I left. To protect you."

"You never called me, Lars. You vanished."

"I thought of nothing but my own death." Lars shook his head, his eyes closed tight. "When I was a child, I said I wanted to be a doctor. Mother told me that was wonderful. She said that it was a day we would all remember. But Father laughed. He told people at the hospital about his son, how the boy who couldn't tie his own shoes wanted to hold a scalpel."

"But you're not that child anymore, Lars."

"Remember when you were sick, Holiday? When you were worried from your studies?" Lars stared into nothingness. "I made you feel better. I was strong for you."

He opened his eyes. "I have done terrible things," he said with a sudden, jolting air of clarity. He stared at Holiday incredulously. "I thought they could cure my hand."

Before Holiday could respond, the plane dropped, emptying a stack of cushions from a storage compartment and sending the bar cart tumbling to the floor. Holiday gasped when she looked out the window; the ground rushed closer at a horrible speed, the buildings on the edge of Umea too near. Lars rose from his seat, cursing, and stumbled toward the cockpit as the pilot righted the plane.

"What's wrong with you?" Lars implored. "Why can't you fly?"

"It's all wrong," the pilot blurted in a high voice. "It's the ice, the snow. I can't keep us in the air."

Holiday watched Lars pull the gun from his pocket and point it at the pilot. *It's over.*

"Get us higher!" Lars demanded.

Outside the window the buildings shrank and the far hills fell away. The pilot engaged another loop, the engines straining, and Holiday realized they were turning back toward Umea. The craft felt almost out of control, shuddering constantly in the winds.

"Don't turn back," Lars said, holding open the cockpit door for balance. "I will kill you if you turn back."

"I have to take us back," the pilot screamed. "I don't even know if I can make it back to the airstrip."

The plane fell again, sending Lars tumbling to the floor and jarring the gun from his hand. Holiday looked out the window. In the distance the airfield runway was a line cut in the expanse of snow. She saw again the wide black rift in the earth, a fissure perhaps a mile southeast of the airport. From its regular, man-made shape, she knew it was a rock quarry. The artificial canyon emerged directly below their erratic path.

The plane gained speed as it lost altitude. Lars pulled himself to his knees, remembering the fallen gun. He looked at Holiday, his features turned feral with rage. Crawling, he found the gun and pointed it at the pilot.

When he fired, the plane shot upward tilted on its side. Holiday heard the cockpit windshield shatter and was thrown into a wall, feeling the impact move with sickly warmth down her body. She heard a glassy clatter from the front of the cabin and turned to see the bar upend, dislodge its contents of liquor bottles throughout the cabin, then crash into the airplane door. As if the metal were made of tissue, the door ripped open and a rush of air filled the cabin.

Holiday was able to grab onto a seat back to keep herself from tumbling through the open portal as the plane gained an even level. Lars saved himself by grasping a table leg to halt his violent slide across the floor. Beneath him, pinned by his chest, gleamed the shining gun.

Holiday leaned over the seat to look out the window. They were far too low, pitching and heaving toward the runway at an angle that looked dangerous if not impossible. Lars stood, feeling along the wall until he found a handhold at the near side of the open door. He braced himself and pointed the gun toward the cockpit, vainly trying to hold his arm steady with his disabled hand.

Without thinking, in a moment without logic or cau-

tion—these, she realized later, might have caused her to
pause—Holiday picked up a vodka bottle at her feet and
dove toward Lars. She swung the bottle in a low, tight,
arc, smashing it against Lars's head with all her strength.
In a shower of exploding glass Lars dropped the gun and
staggered.

He turned to face her, his mouth open in surprise, his
fury gone. His knees buckled, and Holiday lurched
toward him, only steps away, when the plane dropped
again. She felt only the briefest glancing touch of his fingers as he silently fell through the open door.

Holiday's momentum carried her forward; the plane
tilted on its side, revealing the ground below with nause-
ating clarity. As she grabbed vainly for something to stop
her fall, she saw the tiny figure of Lars spiraling into the
quarry, vanishing as darkness enveloped him.

She felt the cold wind on her face, the snow pelting her
like tiny missiles. She grasped for the doorframe and
caught a ridge lining the inside wall. Her fingers burned
with searing pain as an invisible hand tried to pull her out,
into the sky, down to Lars. In the instant she understood
she had no more strength to grip, the plane reeled to its
other side, flinging her into the seats.

Acting on instinct, Holiday fastened herself into a seat,
resisting the impulse to climb past the open door to see if
the pilot was still alive and conscious. Turning to the window, she saw the ground was far closer than she had
imagined. Wind and snow swept into the open door,
mingling with debris falling out as the plane dropped
toward the ground. She closed her eyes and put her head
down, bracing herself. In the final moment she knew they
had missed the runway.

Holiday's last memory then was of an impact so severe
that her teeth clapped together, her bones shook, and her
ears filled with the horrible abrasive noise of scraping
metal. She saw whiteness and felt a cold chill overtake her
as her vision left. Then there was nothing.

26

HOLIDAY REACHED OUT AND FELT COLD METAL AGAINST HER fingertips. She ran her hand along the surface until her arm could stretch no farther. Trying to repeat the movement with her other arm, she felt the pain.

Her eyes opened to bright lights suspended above her head, then white walls and a window with shades open to darkness. Trying to move, she felt the pain again, coming from everywhere at once, and stopped struggling. Looking around, she found she was alone.

Then the details began to emerge: the tubes leading from her nose, the thick, unyielding plaster casts immobilizing her left leg and arm, the IV tube inserted into the crook of her right arm. At the foot of the steel-rimmed bed—for this was a bed she lay in, she realized—a thick chart hung from a metal hook.

A woman dressed in white gingerly stepped through the door carrying a plastic tray full of pill vials and a thick notepad. Holiday opened her mouth to speak and felt a new kind of pain—her throat was unspeakably parched, so dry that her words came out as an anemic hiss.

"Where?" she whispered.

The woman turned, her workaday expression brightening. She left the tray on a nearby stand and approached the bed; without thinking, Holiday recoiled.

"You are an English speaker?" The woman had a soft, melodious voice, and Holiday cherished the sound. Now able to see her better, Holiday saw that the nurse was young, with thick arms and an angular face anchored by a long, straight nose.

"Yes," Holiday answered. Her tongue stuck on the word. "Water, please."

Though Holiday was unable to sit up to drink it properly, the water in the paper cup tasted better than she could have imagined. She felt the cool liquid soothe her throat and work into her body.

"You were hurt in a plane crash," the nurse said in a thick accent, taking the cup away. "Do you remember?"

Holiday stared blankly into the nurse's blue eyes.

"Do not worry," the nurse said, and Holiday abandoned trying to recall what had brought her there. The nurse patted the bed. "I will bring your friends."

Trying to place the woman's accent, trying to imagine what friends she might be speaking of, Holiday felt a rush of memory. It was a tangible, physical sensation that at once made her dizzy and sent a slash of pain through her forehead.

Bo Swenson, dressed in a brown suit and still carrying his valise, entered the room, avoiding her eyes. He sat in a chair by the bed. His eyes were vacant, his gray hair brushed away from his forehead in unkempt swirls.

"You're going to be all right," he said.

"The plane." She found it difficult to form sentences through the fog of her mind, which fired in haphazard, unreliable bursts. "How long?"

"Don't try to sit up. Here, I'll move closer." Bo's chair scraped against the floor. "You were unconscious for eighteen hours."

Outside it was dark. When the plane crashed, the horizon was tinged with faint gray light. "Gregory?" she asked, suddenly remembering him lying in the snow, bleeding.

"He's fine," Bo said, smiling faintly. "I asked him to wait outside while I spoke to you first. You know, he's far more agreeable since he was hit on the head."

Holiday tried to sit up, pain shooting through her lower back. Bo pushed gently against her chest, easing her back onto the bed.

"Please, I didn't mean to be flippant," he said. "Mr. Hampton didn't receive any permanent damage from his head wound. I stabilized him until an ambulance arrived.

In fact we've developed a kind of respect for each other over the past day."

He was speaking too quickly for Holiday to keep up; she squinted into the lights, confused.

"And the pilot?" she asked. Her memory continued to return in fragments. "That poor man."

"He made it too," Bo said reassuringly. "He had a number of broken bones, but his condition has stabilized."

"Thank God," Holiday whispered.

"Here, you need to drink more water." Bo extended the cup, and Holiday drank greedily. He smiled at her. "Mr. Hampton is a good man. He loves you. I hope you and he are happy together."

Through the window she saw lights playing in the darkness. After a moment she realized they were headlights, that Umea was alive again after the storm.

"I'm sorry about Lars," she said, looking away from the window.

Bo bent forward, his elbows on his knees. "As am I," he said. She tried to sense the depth of his sadness but failed. By then he was speaking again.

"Perhaps Lars is dead because of my own failings, Holiday. I will have what is left of my life to try to decide if that is true. I wanted to say farewell to you properly before I left, and to tell you that when I watched that airplane crash into the snow yesterday, I felt as though a piece of my own life was being taken away from me."

Bo stiffened, pinching the corners of his eyes with trembling hands. Her vision blurred, for an instant she thought it was Lars sitting next to her.

"The police have probably found the dead man in my house," he continued. "For that reason I gave an assumed name to the authorities here, but it won't be long until they find I was lying. I have to leave."

"Leave? Where?" Holiday sensed he was saying something important, but she wished he would slow down. As she comprehended one word, he had already spoken the next.

"Because of my partial knowledge of Lars's actions, I don't know what might happen to me in court. I've exaggerated my own injuries for the last day to avoid talking to the police. In any case, I have thought for a long time about this. My practice is failing, my life in Los Angeles has been shallow and empty for longer than I want to admit."

She began to understand. "You're . . . you're not returning to America with us?"

Bo shook his head, almost imperceptibly. "No."

"Then you're staying in Sweden?"

"My country has even less to offer me," he said. He pulled the valise to his chest. "I am going away. First to southern Europe, then perhaps Asia. Africa. Before I left Los Angeles, I emptied my bank accounts and brought the cash with me."

He hefted the valise to his lap. "I told Lars it contained photographs. That was a lie." Bo looked away from her. "I lied to my son because I wanted him to get into that airplane and leave, and I didn't want him to take my money. I never wanted to see him again."

"And now you never will," she said without malice, speaking before she considered the impact of her words.

"No, I won't. Yesterday represents but one of the many events that have damned me."

Bo stood, straightening his suit; Holiday felt an urge to offer him absolution for everything, to tell him that Lars in his final moments was so damaged within that he didn't at all resemble the talented young man he once was. She wanted to tell Bo that he was blameless, but the words wouldn't come.

"I am sorry that I did not act when I suspected Lars might damage the computer project," Bo said. "I hope you will think well of me in the future. And of Lars."

He turned and left the room; Holiday struggled to move, but it was impossible. The cast on her leg ran from her ankle to her hip, and every muscle screamed in betrayal at her attempt to rise. An instant after Bo was gone, Gregory appeared. He had a bandage around his head and was dressed in an ill-fitting hospital gown. But he was healthy, and beautiful.

Gregory buried his head in her neck, holding her, whispering to her. "I heard about the crash, and I was so sorry I couldn't do anything to keep you from getting on that plane. I would have died to save you."

He continued whispering for a full minute, his words lapsing into nonsense. Holiday held him tight with her unbroken arm, the room swimming in a miasma of blurry vision and fatigue.

Her eyes grew heavy. "I need to sleep. Would you stay with me?"

Gregory's eyes were rimmed with tears. He seemed ashamed of his outburst of emotion, smiling regretfully and wiping his face with the back of his hand.

"Don't be embarrassed," she said. "I love you."

"I talked to my aunt Beverly," he said. "Shawn is still in the hospital, but he has some movement in his arms. There's still hope."

"I'm so glad."

"And I'm supposed to tell you the police want to talk to you. I gave them a statement, but they have questions for you," he said, looking toward the door. "Are you up to it?"

"After I sleep," she said. "But could you do me one favor first?"

Gregory resisted at first, but finally relented. Gingerly, threatening to stop each time she winced in pain, he helped her to a sitting position and slid her from the bed to a wheelchair he brought from the corner. Sliding past a short table full of Swedish magazines, he pushed her to the window.

Holiday felt Gregory's strong hand on her shoulders. "I love you, too," he whispered, almost too quietly to hear. She reached up and took his hand.

"Why do you want to look out there?" he asked.

Looking down five stories, she saw the small, huddled figure of a man in a long overcoat and gloves, carrying a small leather valise, emerging from the hospital's front entrance. He paused for a moment outside, as if hearing someone call his name. Then, without looking back, he walked through the parking lot into the darkness. A light snow had begun to fall, the thick, downy flakes trailing him as he began his journey.

Epilogue

"PHIL, I HAVE TO GO," KYLE JEFFERIES SAID. HIS DOORBELL rang again. "I'll see you in the morning."

He was still in shock when he went to the door. But when he opened it, Kate was there. She was dressed in jeans and a linen shirt, her short hair combed away from her face. She was beautiful.

"Sugar," she said, smiling warily.

The few days since she left had been among the worst he could remember. Whatever else happened, he knew he had to have her. Bitterness, envy, jealousy—they had eaten at him like a cancer, and for too long. He needed Kate to save him.

Without a word she went past him into his house. He shut the door gently, wishing he could keep her with him forever.

She sat in his easy chair, sinking into it with a tired sigh. He nervously brushed a strand of thin hair from his forehead. He wasn't a handsome man, he never had been.

"I guess I owe you an explanation," she said.

"You don't owe me anything." He kneeled at her feet, resting his hand on her knee. She let him.

"I just drove from Oregon," she said. "My sister-in-law lives there. I sat out on a lake and watched the birds for three days."

"I'm sorry for the way I acted," he said. "I was distant, I was rude to you. It will never happen again."

"Oh, Kyle," she said, running a hand through his hair. "It probably *will* happen again. But it's all right. Let's just see what happens."

"Then you're back? You're staying?" he said.

She stopped massaging his scalp and lightly slapped the top of his head. "Don't be silly," she said. "I think we're

working on something good, sugar. Just behave yourself
and everything will work out."

A wave of elation passed through him. There was hope.
But first he had to tell her. "Have you seen a newspaper?" he asked. She shook her head. "Holiday and
Gregory Hampton discovered something about the telepresence sabotage after Hampton was cleared of the
charges. Instead of calling in the police, they went to Sweden to play Cowboys and Indians."

"Jesus, sugar, why?" She looked into his eyes with un-
nerving trust and openness. She didn't know Kyle had
suppressed the evidence that cleared Gregory, that he had
been jealous, hurtful, stupid.

"I don't know," he said. "But the man who killed
Takamoto is dead. Apparently it had to do with a power
struggle within the Mitsuyama Corporation."

"How weird," Kate said.

"There's one more thing. Holiday was injured in an
accident."

Kate's eyes widened. "An accident?" she said, her face
turning pale. "Can we call her? Is there any way to reach
her?"

"No, but I just got off the phone with Phil Hermoza.
She's fine, and so is Hampton. As soon as she's ready to
travel, they'll be back in L.A."

Kate had a faraway look as she listened; finally she
relaxed. "So she's all right. Kyle, promise me you'll be
friends when she gets back. She's such a sweet girl. I want
her and me to stay friends."

An obstruction-of-justice charge probably wouldn't be
filed against him. He had been petty and vindictive, wanting to hurt Hampton after Kate spoke of finding him in
Holiday's apartment early in the morning.

Holiday had let go of what they once shared, and he
thought he had as well. But jealousy had warped him. Full
of fear that Kate would reject him, he began to resent
Holiday for no longer loving him. It sounded unspeakably
foolish now.

He had tried to hurt Hampton, an innocent man, because Holiday might have loved him. Now it seemed the case was solved, so the authorities would likely turn their attention elsewhere. In any case he was a survivor, and he would survive this.

Unless Kate rejected him, unless she found out what else he had done. She would surely leave him again, this time forever. He didn't know if he could survive that, not now.

"I promise, Kate."

Buried in that morning's *Los Angeles Times* Metro section was a story about a body found in a Beverly Hills doctor's home. Bo Swenson was missing, there were signs of a struggle—and the battered corpse of Clay Simmons, a handyman with a record of rape and robbery, lay in the kitchen. By tomorrow the story would be all over town. The media wouldn't be able to resist.

And Bill Epstein had been found dead twenty-four hours before. He was last seen at Holiday's high-rise, where Simmons worked, the night before she and Hampton left for Sweden. Kyle hoped beyond reason that Simmons hadn't killed him.

Jealousy. Kyle had met Simmons weeks before, when he was visiting Kate on one of their first dates. So many coincidences—speaking to Clay in the lobby, finding that he also grew up in a poor farm town, knowing (after peeking in her employment file) that Holiday was moving into the building in a couple of weeks. Without that file, without speaking to the sociopathic Simmons, none of this would have happened.

Jefferies paid Simmons to keep an eye on Holiday, and to make a few intimidating phone calls. Holiday had been fragile in the past. Kyle had hoped she might break and go home, enabling Kyle to regain his full power and position at Pacific University Hospital. It had been that easy to do something completely wrong, to allow himself to act on the most venal impulses within his soul. But after Takamoto's murder, when Holiday fell to the floor as if stricken, he realized that he had betrayed everything he ever thought he stood for.

Simmons was sick, sicker than Kyle could have imagined. First came the attack on Venice Beach. When he heard someone had broken into Holiday's apartment and nearly raped her, he knew that he had unleashed a monster. He wondered if there was any evidence to link him to Clay Simmons. He simply couldn't remember.

"Wake up, sugar," Kate said. She gave him a light, playful slap on his cheek. "I'm back five minutes and you're already lost in space. You're going to change your ways, remember?"

At least Simmons was dead. Kyle would no longer have to deal with the man's madness, his midnight calls, and the years of blackmail that he knew were to follow. Kyle Jefferies realized he might emerge unscathed. *I might get away with it.*

"I'm sorry," he said, turning to Kate with a rueful smile. "What did you say?"